Ace Books by Michael P. Kube-McDowell

THE TRIGON DISUNITY
EMPRISE
ENIGMA
EMPERY

ALTERNITIES
THE QUIET POOLS
EXILE

MICHAEL P. KUBE-McDOWELL

EXILE

ACE BOOKS, NEW YORK

EXILE

An Ace Book
Published by The Berkley Publishing Group
200 Madison Avenue, New York, New York 10016

For
Gwendolyn Zak
and
Beth Fleisher,
For all the reasons they know,

and
for friends lost and left behind,
but warmly remembered.
Wherever Time has taken you,
May Fortune hold you gently in her hands.

ACKNOWLEDGMENTS

The author wishes to thank Kathy Mar, for the late-night blue-skying at Studio Bohemia; Gwen Zak, for support and assistance at every turn; Matt, for the hugs and for understanding; Dr. Barry Childs-Helton and Dr. Sally Childs-Helton, for fielding my questions on folklore and idiophones, and for letting me sit in with the band; Clem Zak; Paul Reiz at Kinko's; Liu Binyan, Ruan Ming, and Xu Gang, for *"Tell the World"*; James Edward Oberg, for *New Earths;* my agent, Russ Galen; and my editor, Susan Allison. Thanks also to the Sanyo CM-1440, for offering mercy to my eyes, and the Toshiba T1000SE, for liberating me from my desk; to Kitaro, Kodo, Glen Velez, the sacred harp singers of Chicago and The Imperial Bells of China, for helping take me to Ana; and to Greg, Sandy, Myra, Mike, Mew, Iain, and other friends (real and virtual), for their sufferance and comfort during the long months of my own exile.

CONTENTS

1   The Arch of the Thirteen Bells   1

2   Eki: The First Bell   20

3   Kad: The Second Bell   32

4   The Whispering of Air   47

5   Apos: The Third Bell   63

6   Puli: The Fourth Bell   77

7   The Trembling of Ana   93

8   Ubela: The Fifth Bell   107

9   Botad: The Sixth Bell   122

10 The Burning of Oran   135

11 Ojawit: The Seventh Bell   151

12 Jineha: The Eighth Bell   165

13 The Rising of Kawa   180

14 Ixozacu: The Ninth Bell   194

15 Xehaniv: The Tenth Bell   209

16 The Judgment of Kedar Nan   225

17 Ana-imoda: The Eleventh Bell   240

18 Kawa-rami: The Twelfth Bell   256

19 Anadan-Kawadon: The Thirteenth Bell   270

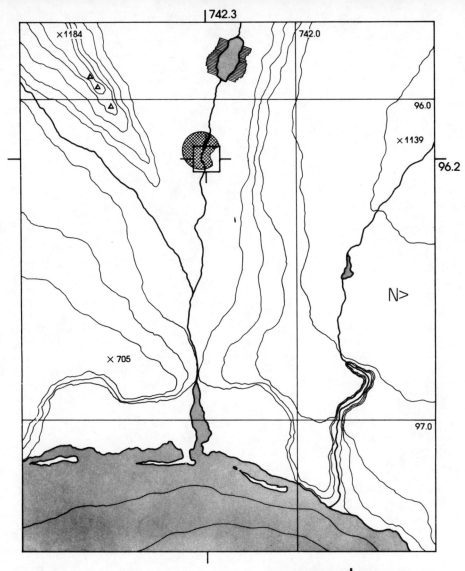

742.3

742.0

×1184

96.0

×1139

96.2

N>

×705

97.0

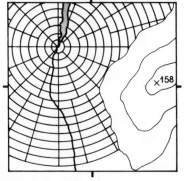

CONCORDAT GENERAL SURVEY
LINK: ACTIVE

TAURIN (GSN 4859302)
CONTRACT REPORT
CONTRACTOR: HAMMADI REGISTRY
    ARANIA (LYNX SECTOR)
REPORT DATE: AR 3156.34.1766
A.E.S. VERIFICATION: NONE

△ REF ANOMALY REPORT

×158

1

The Arch
of the Thirteen Bells

On the day that I met the traitor, my name was Meer Fastet—
Meer, son of Fas, unblessed. I was a young man of the outer rings
of Ana, and my world on that day was limited to the long houses,
the work circles, and the streets.

On the day that I met the traitor, his name was Kedar Nanchen—
Kedar, son of Nan, honored by a woman. He was a man of the
central city, his world the world of the high bank, the honor school,
and the hierarchy.

Kedar was not yet a traitor. That would come later, after we
became friends, after the world changed.

When I left Fas's home for the long house at fifteen and took
the mark of my line in the temple at Cor-Agama, I had been ready
to build houses in the dusty-dry outer rings of the Fifth Hundred,
houses for the women we hoped would favor us. It was the most
common sweat share for men—whether newly marked or newly
turned out by women who had once honored them—who did not
belong anywhere or to anyone.

But instead, I was made a toolman.

Not one in twenty in my long house would have asked for the
toolman's cart, had the choice been theirs. The toolman works
alone, they told me, and works too hard. Never an end to stuck
gates and flood vents, cracking roof beams, burned sun cells,

faltering nats—and with the ground ever restless beneath us, the city crumbles faster than we can build it.

Give me the weaving houses, the crop barns, the share shops, they said, where the work is the same every day and a man can find camaraderie with his own kind. If I must do sun work, let me be a gateman, a greenhand, a builder—let me be someone with a place in the making of something from nothing, a little touch of the woman's magic.

Right and right and right. The call list was never shorter than ten days full for the carts in my circle. A toolman started under brown, dusty dawn, finished in the ocher dusk, and was alone for the hours between. One day's calls could scatter you to every corner of your cluster, and other clusters beyond if you were skilled and your specialty in demand.

And forever and everywhere I had to drag the single-axle cart behind me, up and down the ramps, along spoke and ring. New toolmen were heard to complain that by the end of calls the cart felt more like a slab of stone than anything on wheels.

But all of those complaints were secret joys for me. I thought myself a healer to Ana, correcting a flaw, treating a wound, banishing a blemish on her face. The solitude of the toolman was a blessing for someone who had never ranked first in any group of boys or men, who had never fully escaped the humiliations handed out by those who did hold that rank.

My routine was built from novelty, and the problems that awaited me as often required me to apply my mind as my tools. And the first hundred days in front of my cart—*my* cart, by custom as private and proprietary a space as any woman's house—built the muscles in my slender limbs into wires of spidersilk, until I was no longer ashamed to wear the mark of the Genet, whose aspect is hidden strength.

So though the cart was chosen for me, I would not have chosen differently. It was a sweat share, but one I could keep for a lifetime, even after a woman honored me and took me into her house. I saw myself in Gowon, who seemed content as senior in our circle, as the older husband of Iola and spark of two of her five children.

What was more, I learned by watching Gowon and Qili that no one saw the city like a toolman of reputation did, and that one could advance to some measure of privilege on the opportunities of initiative. Even in my second year in the craft, I brought back from my explorations news and gossip enough to lift my status in the long house, and there were always many ready to run the roads with me, knowing that I measured the women with care wherever I was sent.

Gowon and Qili surely enjoyed even greater advantage. And they were old, Gowon nearly forty, and would need replacing when they shortly died.

I remembered that thought with some guilt, though, the first day that Gowon was confined.

That morning our aedile, Gadi—a dour and humorless man who I much enjoyed twitting—faced us with a fistful of purple sugar-paper call slips in his hand. I knew that the color marked the calls as urgent, though I had never been handed such myself.

"Gowon is too sick to leave his bed," Gadi said. "We will cover his calls, today and as long as we need to." The 'we' was pure overspeak; Gadi never lifted a tool himself.

Four slips went to thick-waisted Qili, who frowned as he studied them, then wandered off shaking his head and muttering softly. I thought with a smile that Qili would drop an extra measure or two running those calls on top of his own. I had no great love for Qili, who always seemed to be short of breath or patience.

Two slips went to Donkor, two more to Gil, Gadi's handful thinning quickly. I waited without expectations. I still had much to learn—I would not have been allowed to touch a ring gateway, a temple fount, or any mechanism of real complexity or importance. I did not think that Gadi would trust me yet with anything urgent enough to find a place on Gowon's list.

But at the end, there *was* a purple slip for me. I looked at it, still surprised, and understood that the urgency was not in the what, a bit of wallwork from the sound of it, the nearest thing to routine a toolman might see. The urgency, I saw, was in the where, a house on 5-out, in the heart of Ana.

"This is eight clusters away," I said to Gadi. "Don't these people have their own craftsmen?"

"No," said Gadi. "Not inside the sixtieth. Even the green rings are tended from outside."

"Aren't there toolmen closer, then? I'll be half the morning on the spoke roads." There was a full call list already tacked to my cart, as always, and all I could see at that moment was tomorrow's free day vanishing.

"Gowon goes to the center city all the time," Gadi said. "His work is known. And the purple slips are promises—my promises, for this circle. One of us has to make the call."

"And my legs looked most idle to you."

"Gowon chose," Gadi said, turning away.

"Oh," I said, looking down at the slip again. Learning that Gowon had chosen me changed everything. I owed him a double-handful of favors, and the guilt about my death-thoughts had not vanished. "Take this one first?" I called after Gadi.

"You should already be on your way."

That was when I realized that the others were gone, their cart stalls empty. "I am," I said, back-pedaling toward my cart. "I'm crossing Clarus Ring, waving to the field hands. They've never seen a toolman move faster. They are impressed, and salute me as I pass. You're having a dream that I'm still standing here."

"You're having a dream that I believe you."

"It's a good one. One of my favorites." I caught one of the dragpoles with my foot and tipped the cart up, grabbing the handles on either side as they swept up to waist height. "Gadi, will Gowon be back?"

"I'm not a physician," was all he would say.

Gowon did come back, after missing six days—but not for long. By the festival of Apos, he was dead, his body turned inside out by the bursting tumors of the sun mange. He was Received with honor, his spirit returned to Ana, his substance broken to nurture the nap of new bast plants in the vat fields of Agama Cluster.

I made a point to be there at his Reception, and to thank him silently for all of his gifts, and most of all for his last: the call on 5-out, in Banteng Cluster, nearly in the shadow of the arch.

Out in the three hundreds, the houses and ringwalls block the view of the arch more often than not. You must go to the rooftops or the elevated spoke roads to get a clear view of the flattened half-circle rising—how far, a score of rooftops?—over the bend in the river Kawa where it passes through the womb of Ana.

And even then, the thirteen bells which hang beneath it are usually lost in the shimmering heat haze that rises from the streets. From the rooftop of Fas's house, I saw as many as the five largest bells, but rarely, and never Eki and Kad or any of the smaller pairs.

But every child learns early that the arch is a compass, the changing shape it presents setting your place in the city at a glance. My brother Eral taught me how to read it, as Fas taught him, and I was never lost for longer than it took to climb a wall or a ramp and look toward the center of Ana.

The secret is a simple one. South of the river, only four spoke roads run all the way from the outer boundary ring to the plaza. From the half-east spoke road, you see the arch side-on, its shape that of Ana-imoda's breast as she lies in recline. From the half-west spoke, you see the arch end-on, its shape that of Kawa-rami's staff. From the west or the south spokes the shape of the arch is that of the great flower bell, Anadan-Kawadon, the vessel of life in which Ana receives Kawa's gift.

The perfection of it seemed a marvel to me when Eral explained it. It touched and embodied all the mysteries, of life from barrenness, of substance in Ana and spark in Kawa—of the gift and blessing given us through *imoda* and *rami,* that we might become like the apocryphals who made us, immortal.

I think I cried when the understanding broke on me. At that age, I looked forward to taking the mark of the Genet and advancing its standing, and did not see clearly that, without the blessing of Anadan-Kawadon, all lines would perish and even the strongest would be brought down. The test is hard and the time is short, and taking one's mark is only the beginning of the run, not the end.

The other secret of the arch I knew then was a small one. I learned it with Der, whose mother's housewall touched Fas's at the north corner, and who so became a friend of mine.

Together, partners in a dare, we had run out the half-west spoke road to the edge of the city, past the last completed ring and the unfinished work of the wall builders, past even where the surveyors' theodolites had marked how the city should grow.

We ran across the emptiness that would become the Fifth Hundred, out to the low moundwall and borrow trench which marked the boundary ring. There we climbed bravely to the top and looked out across the barrenness, squinted at the distant red-brown scarps that blocked the view south, knowing that we stood on the line that divided the blessed from the unblessed, the living from the lifeless, the city from the world.

And, of course, we crossed that line, first scanning all around to be sure we were alone, and then scrambling down the outer face of the mound to stand Outside for a breathless moment. We pretended that the taboos of the boundary meant nothing to us, but the thumping of my heart and the happy haste with which we turned back had the same cause—boyish recklessness surrendering to deeper fear. Even so, on the way home we vowed that the next day we would complete our conquest of the city by running all the way to the plaza and wading into Kawa where the arch spanned it.

Sore-legged though we both were, Der and I started off for the heart of the city as planned, using the arch as our beacon. But for the longest time, it seemed to grow no larger, and we to get no closer. And when at last the arch did begin to grow, it refused to stop growing at any reasonable dimension, until it seemed to stand more above us than before us, until I swore it was too tall and slender not to be teetering on its foundations and tipping toward us.

Der must have felt something of the same, for we never got closer to the plaza and the river than the eighteenth ring. We turned back reassuring each other that it was too far, too late, there were too many people, and that after all we had seen all thirteen bells and actually heard the high-voiced least pair ringing in the breeze that blows through the arch.

The truth, never spoken between us, was that with each step we felt the power that surrounded the arch growing stronger, and we were not as ready to defy it as we had thought.

Towing my cart behind me on my way to Gowon's call, I retraced Der's and my pilgrimage on the half-east spoke road. My remembrance smile was self-mocking, for I felt nothing but the sun this time. But the arch was no less glorious, the metal afire with hot reflections, the bells like carved stone favors hanging in a doorway. I stopped on the high road to admire it, until another craftsman cursed me for blocking his way.

The arch did not vanish when I went down onto the ring road to look for the house; I could find its curve at any moment with a mere turn of the head, even over the high roofs. The high roofs— I had been so focused on the arch that I did not notice until then that every house in that cluster was fully expanded, with a fan of three sleeping rooms in back and a two-story shell in front. Every house. I was amazed.

There were three-mods all over my home cluster, of course— every crown mother had one, and some younger mothers as well. But doubles were vulnerable to tremors. You could not block-build two stories high without a brace wall. And who wanted to stand on or under such an architecture when the blessing bells were ringing? I still remember Nipa and her daughter Femi, buried in their house by the last grand tremor.

But the doubles on five had no brace walls. They were the same plan as houses everywhere in Ana, though they showed few cracks and no seams in their smooth, fine-grained house and lot walls. What few patches there were stood out harsh and vivid against the older matrix. I knew what I was seeing, but still marveled. They had been built by suites of nats, not circles of men.

The house to which I had been called was a long way around to the west on five, almost all the way to Kawa and the Five-Ring Bridge across him. By the time I found it, I felt even more lost. This was not Ana as I knew her.

I was accustomed to houses as individual as faces, made up with bright-colored shape art and murals of the apocryphals. But not one in three of these structures bore as much as a woman's line mark. The color range was no wider than from dirt-blond to a reddish beige, with a few patches of near-white where the nats had picked up a vein of calcite or white clay in the building. What better medium for an artist than this glass-smooth matrix? But the houses were bare-faced, subdued.

At first I wondered if it was the walls themselves, that they would not hold the brush strokes, sloughing the paint off like dirt. Perhaps the exceptions were the dead.

But there were other oddities as well. The yards of many plots were growing wild, the branching greenery reaching so high above the walls which contained it that the house nearly vanished behind the curtain. How could a woman in such a house sit at her window or come to her roof at dusk to watch the runners and be seen by them in turn? Why would so many close themselves off so from the life of the streets and the cluster?

An answer was in front of my eyes, but I was slow to see it. How could I be expected to? When my vision was not blocked by olarith and blackwhistle, it was blocked by preconception. Every woman hoped that her next child would move her to a new house closer to Kawa and the arch, that another woman's death would answer her own wish. It was unthinkable that so many of these houses would be empty when so many wanted them.

But there it was, the proof before my disbelieving eyes—house after house with no blessing bell hanging in its doorway arch. Empty houses, with no woman to call them home. Not all, but all too many, one in two, two in a row, three. No wonder the plots were overgrown—no wonder the walls were bare.

I was sure I had divined the answer, even though the answer seemed a greater mystery than the mysteries it solved. So when I reached my call and it proved to be like so many, with no woman's line mark and no blessing bell, there was no reason to hail greeting, or wait an invitation. I vaulted the streetwall, ducked under the blackwhistle, and boldly walked through the doorway and into the dimness—to find a front room full and furnished, walls hung with weavery, a cage of books suspended from the ceiling near where the ladder to the upper room pierced it—a house well and fully inhabited by *someone.*

Hastily, lest my trespass be noticed and give offense, I retreated to the street and my cart. From there I hailed the house in my best mannered-stranger form, but no answer came. So I waited, sitting in the shade of my cart, bewildered beyond words, afraid to leave and more afraid to enter, cursing Gowon and Gadi for sending me here unprepared, chalking endless games of cross-ki in the fine street dust.

It was not until Kedar Nanchen arrived, an hour past mid-day, that it came to me that this house belonged to a man.

Kedar Nanchen had a long stride but a light one, and was nearly on me when I first noticed him. He wore a disk-brimmed sun hat, like the greenhands favor, but he was no sweat laborer. His hat was deep red, not white and stained, and finer hand work than I knew. The face beneath it was hard to see, shadowed in the day glare, and harder to judge.

The rest of him was hidden under a long-sleeved manteau, the sort young women wear when they must go out in the full sun, the sort old men and fat men and frail men wear to conceal their flaws. In Agama Cluster, at least, for a young man to wear a manteau was to invite ridicule from men and rude dismissal from any women worth desiring. But I did not know what it meant here, for this man was clearly not old, and I suspected neither fat nor frail as well.

"You are Gowon?" he asked as I scrambled up from under my cart. "I am Kedar Nanchen. Finished already, are you? Wonderful. Let's have a look."

I corrected his presumptions as gently as I could, but still he frowned at me. "A waste of your time, to wait when the work still waited for you. Did no one tell you the house would be empty?"

"A woman's space is not to be violated without her invitation—"

"True. But I am not a woman. And so long as you are not a thief, all I had to fear from your violation was a timely repair." He shook his head. "Never mind. What is your name?"

I told him, and Kedar said, "Then bring your tools and come inside, Meer Fas, and I will show you what needs your attention."

He vaulted the streetwall lightly and started up the path, but I did not move. He looked back at me wonderingly.

"This house—you have all this to yourself?" I asked. I think I must have sounded angry, though what I felt was mostly astonishment.

"Yes," he said, and waited.

"With no woman's blessing? With no children?"

"The woman who honors me keeps a house elsewhere, with our son. My other children are with *their* mothers, as should be."

I gaped rudely, then compounded the offense. "Who *are* you, that the trustee of allocation allows this?"

"A man of modest attainments," Kedar said, and a smile broke across his face. "Ask anyone who knows me."

I think he meant it, in some way I didn't grasp. Perhaps from his perspective it was even true. From mine it was nearly a lie. The privilege Kedar enjoyed dwarfed those Gowon or even Gadi enjoyed—a house of his own! Kedar lived in a world within Ana that I had not known existed, much less understood.

Later I learned the labels for his special status, the answer to my question—prefect of the honor school, and youngest sitting member of the Councilors' Circle. Of course such a man required space of his own, a place to meet with students, the privacy to think, to plan. How easy it became to think of such aberrations as right and proper. The most understanding judge of indiscretion is the man who wants or has enjoyed the same license for himself.

Still, if Kedar had told me that day who he was, I think we would never have become friends. I would not have allowed it, would have turned away from him just as Der and I had turned away from the arch, and for the same reason. But he made himself my equal, and that changed everything, gave legitimacy to my curiosity, my very presence.

Once inside, Kedar shed his manteau and sun hat, stripping to his duskies, the high-waisted calf-length linen shorts favored by runners, revealing a body sleek and toned. He pointed me toward the center mod, which was rigged out as a storehouse—hung with dozens of cages filled with more books and a queer assortment of artifacts arrayed according to no obvious plan.

He did not need to point out the problem. The sculpted matrix of the small back wall, from the upper right corner to the edge of the vent grille, was disintegrating, leaving behind a rough and coarsely pitted surface. On the floor at the foot of the wall, whitish chips of matrix the size of thumbnails littered a finer dust. I knew what I was seeing: the nats had wilded.

"More since this morning," Kedar said.

"Your beetles are dead?" I asked. The scuttling housecleaning animates are not nats, but nats inside them render the litter to power the beetles. When the beetle nats wilded—and they were usually among the first to go, the toolmen's lore had it—the beetles never again left their nests.

"Long since. If there are a dozen working beetles anywhere in the First Hundred, I'd be surprised. I can think of only one house where I have seen them."

I had never seen them. No house I'd ever been in, not my mother's or any of her neighbors', had even had a nest.

Kedar gestured. "Can you do anything for this?"

No one could. Gowon said that the nats had been wilding as long as anyone could remember, and no one had found a way to stop them. There were tricks that worked sometimes to slow or quarantine the wilding—but not to stop it.

But I could not say that. I had to try. Anyone clever enough to rid a house of wilded nats and restore a healthy suite would have become as famous as a toolman could ever be. And besides, it was my first chance to play with a living suite. Out beyond the First Hundred, all of the buildings in Ana are dead as rocks.

So I tested the suite in every way I knew. I gouged a line across the wall with an awl and watched it heal itself in the wake of the cutting point. I streaked it with a thumbful of joint stain and watched the oily black smear fade and vanish. I opened a crack with a wedge and hammer and watched it close and disappear. I marked off a square with trigger pins and turned it blood-red, then life-green, then sun-blue. I took a disk with a hollow punch and waited while the flaw filled—a dozen breaths was all it took, and no scab or scar showed afterwards.

And then I did it all again, while Kedar retreated up the ladder to his upper room—on the ceiling, the side walls, in the shell room, the side mods, marveling at the magic of the builders and bemoaning the loss of the secret. Except for the diseased patch in the center mod, the house was still more alive than dead. I found spots in the galley where the painters would not respond, and a few scattered scuffs, all in expected places, marked for me places where the cleaners were exhausted.

I was playing with the house like a child with a wonderful toy, making it perform its tricks for me. Guilt eventually put an end to that, but not to my curiosity. So when I interrupted Kedar at his work, it was with a question, not an answer for his.

"How old is this house?" I asked him. "How long has it been alive?"

His eyes seemed to light with approval, and he rose from where he sat cross-legged on the floor. "That's difficult to know. Would you like to see the memorial?"

It would not get me any closer to completing my day's obligations, but I said yes.

We went outside—Kedar did not reclaim his manteau, though the sun was still high—and to the small open space between the back wall of the lot and the back of the house. The house memorial was in the usual place, where the three sleeping mods fanned out and created two V's of windowless wall between them, like the spaces between the fingers of a hand.

But I had never seen a memorial so crowded or chaotic. All four walls were filled with the names of the mothers who had lived here and the children they had borne. There were few dates and no plan—the earliest glyphs seemed to be those at eye level, but later ones had been pinned both above and below, and it was impossible to tell at a glance exactly what the order had been. On the second wall—near where, inside, the nats were wilding— some of the inscriptions were incomplete, erased by a white blotch a hand-span across.

There was no consistency to the memorials, which in itself seemed to say something about the span of time they represented. Some were austere—a line of unadorned names, mother first, children after. But others tried to tell an entire family's story in signs—apocryphal marks, births in the house, crown children, deaths.

"Have you counted them?" I asked, my voice a whisper.

"I couldn't not," Kedar said. "Two hundred and fifty-eight mothers. One thousand four hundred and seventy-seven children."

I shivered in the hot sun at the thought of a house that had so many ghosts. "Can Ana be so old? And this house?"

He opened his hands to take in the roster of names before us. "Surely it must be that old, and older."

"Does no one know the number?"

He shook his head. "Only Ana, and Kawa."

"And the apocryphals, who made us in the first days."

Turning his right wrist up, he looked down at the mark of his line tattooed there. I could not read his expression. But my gaze followed his, and I saw what I had failed to see until then: Kedar's mark was the same as mine, the large-eyed, long-tailed blaze of the Genet. I turned my wrist up and held it out for him to see, and he nodded acknowledgment.

"Your name is here, I think," he said.

I laughed. "So are the names of all my friends, no doubt. Not many can have been left out."

But I began looking all the same, and soon found it in the clutter low on the first wall. Beside the serif lettering was the crown sigil which meant a fourth living child—the attainment which earns a woman the honorific, *imoda* and the right to pass the blessing in her temple.

Wonderingly, I crouched and touched the sigil. "*I* was *my* mother's crown child," I said.

"That must give you pride, to have brought that honor to her," said Kedar. "I was my mother's first—"

"So you brought her her first house—"

He nodded. "But she died in labor with her fourth, barely half a year after I took the mark. My brother and sister were still unmarked. They were spirited away by the dan, so they would not be culled. But even if they live, in the houses of line kin, they are lost to me." He turned to me and smiled hollowly. "I touch the world for all of them. Cherish your family, Meer."

I have never told this story before, not in its fullness. But I have thought about it often, and always it has seemed to me to be riddled by auspicious coincidence.

But chance, I have come to see, is never truly random. Chance is not chaos. Understood in its full depth, chance becomes the halo of the choices of others, which sometimes bring calamity and sometimes bring opportunity.

And life becomes a concatenation of chances which sum to an impossibility when looking forward, but sum to an inevitability when looking backward. I did this, you did that, he did this, and here we are—and if we had chosen differently and arrived somewhere else, looking back we would still see what passed as perfect and inevitable. Think on your own life if you doubt me. Chance gives shape to destiny.

On the day that I met the traitor, I bathed in the halo of the choices of Kedar, of Gowon, of myself, but, finally, most providentially, of Ana.

Ana is the life-giver. For so long as she passes the blessing to us, the flaw in our essence is healed, the apocryphals' creation made complete. I am of the line of the Genet, wear the mark of the Genet, but I owe my life to Ana and live in her world, for without Ana the life-giver and Kawa her consort, the people would have perished in one short lifetime. The apocryphals are banished, unable to reach us except in dreams. It is Ana who sustains us, by sharing with us her own fertile power, and the quickening spark of her consort.

When Ana stirs and calls softly for the touch of Kawa, and the lesser bells ring under the arch, then that becomes a propitious day to join. The men stop their work when Ana trembles with longing, listening for the echo of her call: the house women coming to their doorways and ringing their blessing bells, the clean bright sound rippling out across the rings and roofs like a wave of promise. I have seen staffs rise to the sound alone, in anticipation of the night. The honored men smile to themselves, knowing that they will share their blessed's bed, and the young men hope and make plans, saying, "Tonight we run the roads."

But when Ana shudders and cries out in a grand tremor, and the great bell Anadan-Kawadon is heard out to the ends of the spoke roads, then it is time to lay down the tools and leave the houses, for she is calling the marked to the temple to renew the blessing. Whether it is Ana's need or ours which brings the grand tremor is beyond me to say, but when we meet her in the festival places it is said that she, as well as we, takes succor from the blessing ceremony.

It seemed that neither had been needy, though, for we had passed nearly three times through the festival calendar without hearing Anadan-Kawadon rung by Ana rather than by the *rami*. The last grand tremor, the one that toppled Nipa's home, had come while I was still a child, and I was left behind in the house with my sister Netis while my mother went to Cor-Agama alone. From the roof, we could hear the singing—not the words, but the passion in the voices—and I was filled with a heart-emptying envy at being excluded.

And then when Fas returned glowing, almost floating with joy, I sulked inconsolably for days. Even taking my mark had not fully erased my grievance, for no festival since had been the equal of my expectations, had filled me with what I saw in her eyes that day. Ana had not touched me, or I had not let her. I clung to my apocryphal, and shut out Ana's power.

So foolish, was I.

I was standing by my cart, looking diligently but with little hope in the guides for help with Kedar's problem, when the knee-buckling first shudder came. I staggered backwards, and the ringwall took my legs out from under me. As my stocks jittered in their racks, I found myself on my back in Kedar's plot, staring up into the swaying branches of the blackwhistle and a hurtfully bright sky. The ground vibrated beneath me and the choir of the thirteen bells, the voice of Anadan-Kawadon the soloist, rang in my ears.

Jumping up, I looked toward the arch. I could see it swaying, the bells swinging wildly beneath it. But the tremor had already passed, was already only a memory in my senses.

I heard footsteps, and Kedar went by me, vaulting the ringwall and crossing the street. He seemed like a child, self-absorbed and energetic, as he climbed to the top of the fencewall separating two facing houses. Then he turned, standing atop the wall like a conqueror, and I saw the happy glow in his eyes. "What are you waiting for?" he called back to me.

"I don't know what to do."

"It's a blessing call."

"Should I go home? I should go to Cor-Agama—"

"Why? Come with us."

I wondered at the plural, but questioned only the propriety. "I can take the blessing here, at the plaza?"

"Why should Ana care?" he asked.

I had no argument for that, so I hurried to follow, before *he* could find one and change his mind. When I reached the top of the fencewall and looked toward the arch, I knew why he had spoken as he did. All around me, ahead, behind, were the people of the first cluster, hundreds of them, thousands perhaps, out of hiding and walking the fence-tops toward the plaza, taking the high shortcut across the rings in their pilgrimage to the great temple at the base of the arch.

And I was to join them under the gleaming saddle-dome, and take the blessing from the fount built by Ana herself. Following Kedar, I realized that, at long last, just as I had when Der and I had come to the heart of the city for adventure, I could feel the power here.

But this time, I did not turn from it.

I will not try to tell you everything I saw and felt and learned that afternoon. It matters more to me than to you or this story, and there is much of it that I still cannot put into words.

But you must see the picture. The plaza is set off from the first ring of houses by a narrow mosaic band, gold and crimson blocks set off by royal-blue borders. Had the colors been any less vivid, I might not have noticed them, for the celebrants were already singing when Kedar and I reached that point—singing one of the wordless shape-songs with such an energy that it filled me with eagerness.

The *imoda* and *rami* say that to stand in the center and lead a shape-song is to be lifted up by the power, and in that moment I believed it. My feet were light, and grew lighter with every step.

There were hundreds of others crossing the plaza with us, closing on the temple from all directions, some running, many finding their voice and joining in as they walked. The white pavement we trod underfoot was emblazoned with the marks of the apocryphal animals—all two thousand of them, even the lines which are gone, each mark as large as an arm-span, spaced across the expanse of the plaza. At any other time I would have stopped to look at them, to look for mine. But the drumming had started, and I could barely keep pace with Kedar.

I followed Kedar's back through the massed bodies to a place not far from the central dais, where the *imoda* stood in her white robe beneath the mouth of the blessing chalice of Ana. Her arms were spread wide and raised above her shoulders, her eyes closed, her head tipped back as she sang. At the opposite side of the dais her *rami* stood beneath the fount of Kawa, waiting for the sign.

Though I sang as loudly as I could, I still could hardly hear myself. The drums, voiced in fours like the shape-song, set a pulse-beat like longing, like the walk-up to ecstasy. I could not see the drummers, or count their number. They seemed close by, seemed to surround me. I watched the *imoda,* her arms edging higher, hands seemingly reaching for the ceiling high above.

Then, over the voices of thousands, over the throb of the drumming, came the breathtaking sound of Anadan-Kawadon, ringing in full voice once more. But this time the only tremor was that which ran through the bodies of the celebrants as the song broke apart into a wild and wordless roar.

From the fountain of Kawa shot a jet of water which arched across to the blessing chalice, quickly filling it and sending a cascade of water spilling out over the lip. The *imoda* received the blessing with eyes closed and arms still uplifted, the first shock staggering her, the streaming water sculpting her robe to her body as she glowed, enraptured.

Someone started a chant-song, bright and happy, as the *imoda* called her *rami* forward to share the blessing with him in a drenching embrace.

Then from the edge of the dais came the runners with their water-satchels, and each took the blessing in turn, man from woman, woman from man. The throng parted to let the runners pass out of the temple, heading out in pairs for the spoke roads and the satellite temples where the *imoda* and *rami* of smaller gatherings awaited them.

On any other day, I would have been among those waiting in Cor-Agama for the runners from the plaza. But Ana had chosen this day, and Kedar had brought me to *this* place.

My skin tingled. I stood on tiptoe like an impatient child. The crowd broke and reshuffled in a practiced and unhurried way, and many began to funnel toward the saddle-dome's four anchor points, where ancillaries standing on small rostra offered themselves and the blessing to the procession of celebrants. But Kedar and the other men around me were moving toward the central dais, where the *imoda* herself stood.

Dark-haired and radiant-faced, she was older than my mother, round and well-pillowed where Fas was angular and thin. She swayed unsteadily, eyes closed and face upturned, as the celebrants passed both in front of her and behind her, taking the blessing with a caressing touch or a kiss on wet fabric. Some were content to catch a trickle from her hem in a cupped palm, or skim a few drops from the undercurve of her breast, and walk away sucking the water from their hand. Kedar received the blessing from her belly with both hands and then rubbed it into his own groin.

When it was my turn, standing close to her trembling, swaying body, I was paralyzed, agonizing over the right way, the greatest need. Finally I stepped forward, lightly touched her hips with my hands, and took the blessing with a kiss in the hollow between her breasts, from her heart. When I retreated, I was trembling, too, and my cheeks were wet with skin-warm blessing water from her robe and sudden tears.

Carried along by the exodus, I stumbled outside, and was blinded by the brightness. A woman I could barely see startled me with an enthusiastic hug around my neck, then melted away into the glare. Her scent lingered teasingly in my nostrils.

Kedar had disappeared among the thousands milling on the plaza, but I did not try to find him. I was disoriented within and without, my focus lost. Somehow I found my way to the stair-stepped bank of Kawa, where the plaza falls away to the edge of the river. I sat there for a long time, unmolested, watching the rushing water.

The blessing seemed to fill me. My chest ached as though bruised. My throat was thick with thoughts striving to spill out, but I did not trust the thoughts or my voice. My limbs were charged and restless, as though I were about to run the rings. But I could have been a stone man, a decoration on the bank of Kawa.

This was where Der and I had meant to come. I felt like I had completed a journey, one I had started years before without realizing the purpose or the dimensions. I felt like I had come home. But I knew that I was *not* home. I was a visitor, given a taste at another's table. The emotions that crossed in me were colored more by anger than gratitude, by envy than by pleasure. I had found what I had been missing or denying, and learned it did not belong to me.

I stayed there on the stair-bank until the plaza was empty and the shadows across it long. When I finally stood, I could not have said if it was to walk forward into Kawa and let it carry me away, or to turn and leave. When I started up the stairs and back toward Kedar's house, I wondered if it was merely the habit of living that had chosen my direction.

Then my footsteps took me across the sign of my apocryphal, tattooed into the skin of the plaza. Chance again, you will say, and I will not argue. Chance becomes purpose in the hands of some men. Kneeling in the middle of the great mark of the Genet, I laid my hand to its heart, whispered thanks for the gift of his attribute, and then carried on with lighter steps.

• • •

The twilight city was coming alive as I neared where I had left my cart. Women were coming to their rooftops, and the ring roads were alive. Laughter spilled from the windows of Kedar's house, his and a woman's, and I knew, hearing it, why he had disappeared at the temple.

I closed up my tools quietly, prepared to steal away and accept the price of my dereliction. I had lost the morning to ignorance and the afternoon to indolence. I had failed in this call and neglected my others. Gadi would invent new words reviling me in front of the circle.

But Kedar appeared in his doorway before I was through, and motioned to me. "I want you to finish the work," he said when I joined him.

"There's no point in my staying. I haven't the skill."

"Not tonight," he said, handing me the purple call slip. It was signed, as though I had already completed the repair. "Tonight, you carry a blessing for a woman of Agama. If she waited for you," he added with a smile. "You were a long time at the plaza. Talk to Gowon on your liberty day, and see what he can teach you. Then come and tell me that you're ready, and I'll ask for you again."

"Tomorrow is my liberty," I said. "But there'll be no liberty days for a festival or more, after that tremor."

"Take your free day," he said. "Ana will wait. And come back."

"Gadi won't allow it."

"Remember that Gadi has his own masters," Kedar said. "Some of whom can be reasonable. Talk to Gowon tomorrow, and I will look for you on the day after. Now hurry, before your chosen replaces you."

"I will talk to Gowon," I said slowly. "But I have no reason to hurry this evening."

Kedar cocked his head curiously. "Is there one who's caught your eye?"

"Baral," I said. "Baral Tabiata. But she refuses me."

Kedar smiled broadly. "Go back and let it be known that you took the blessing from the *imoda* of the temple of the arch. This Baral will look at you differently."

Because Kedar knew things that I did not, I listened. And later that night, I learned in Baral's arms that he was right. So before my liberty was over, I let it be known to Kuai and Meli as well, and gained still more proof.

And the blessing of Ana was as powerful in the passing as it had been in the receiving, for Baral and Meli both took the spark of the Genet from me in those couplings. Only Meli would ever acknowledge it, and invite me to join her in her new house with her first child, my son.

But already, the world was changing.

Eki: The First Bell

"Meer?" said the woman hopefully.

In the bright light from the slatted window, her dark hair gleamed. Shifting in the bed so that her cheek rested on her lover's shoulder and her breasts pressed warm against his chest, she waited for acknowledgment. When none came, she bravely added, "Must I go back to the hostel?"

The danera's name was Sachi—bliss—and she pleased Meer Faschen well. She came to him and filled the small bed in the single mod of his workhouse with heat and eagerness, and did not ask too often if Meer might want her to leave the hostel and live with him there.

It would be counterfeit honor, since she had no blessing bell to hang, and never would. But it was still the brightest prospect for her to escape a danera's mattress, and he let her cling to it—so long as she did not ask too directly, and compel him to be honest.

"I have hearings to complete, a theft judgment to prepare," he said, his tone softening the words. "Petitioners will be coming."

"I could stay here," she said. "I'd be quiet. And when twilight comes we could go up to the roof to corner-sing. The mother next over, Elidi, was nice to me. I saw her collecting her share from the cartmen, and she smiled and said hello."

"I want to go running tonight," said Meer.

"You could go running, and I could stay here," Sachi said, drawing a line down his sternum with a fingertip. "And I'd turn my head from everyone else, but when you came by I'd catch your eye and invite you up to join me. And you could climb to the roof and have me there under the stars, so I could show your neighbors how much pleasure you give me."

"Temptress. Elidi would never speak to *me* again," said Meer.

"Maybe she would invite you in, if she knew how fine you are," Sachi said mischievously. "Do you think she's worth wanting?"

Meer gently extricated himself from the embrace and the bed. "Elidi is mother to one of Oran's children, and *imoda*. I think I will not go out of my way to offend her." He smiled. "And she is not half as pleasing to look at as you."

She sat up and finger-combed her hair. "It's just that I hate walking back in the day, and everyone knowing," Sachi said, frowning. "And Hirudu has been cruel to me in front of the others. She spends her days thinking of new ways to be hateful."

"What does she say?"

"That I'm ugly, and empty, and I will never have a house— that my breasts are wasted on me, because they will always be dry." She smiled bravely. "Those are old now, so I can say them— they do not hurt so much. But she won't leave me be until she cuts me. So I have to fight with her or hide from her, and neither suits me."

Her pale blue manteau hung from a peg by the door, and Meer caught it down and handed it to her, as much a message as a courtesy. "Hirudu is young?"

"Marked two years, if that."

Meer nodded. "And some of her friends have already left the hostel, no doubt. She cuts you because she's afraid she'll become you. Time will teach her to be more charitable."

"I would like to hasten the teaching," she said, standing and dropping the manteau gracefully over her body, conscious as always of her audience. "Or curse her to what she fears."

"Curses rebound to the source," Meer said. "Wish triplets on her instead. That will hasten the teaching, I'll warrant."

She smiled and stood on toe to kiss him. "Wicked man. And will you give me triplets when the blessing rebounds as well?"

"Be careful what you wish for, Sachi. And blessings are Ana's to give."

Drawing back, she looked away and said, "Or not, in her wisdom." Her voice was tight. "Have you time to walk with me to the hostel?"

Meer grinned. "So Hirudu can see the kind of man who favors you?"

Sachi flushed guiltily. "It would do her vision no harm."

"I can tell you now that she will only find fault with me as well," he said. "But give me a moment to wash, and I'll go with you."

Still nude, Meer pushed back the curtain and passed out into the shell, with Sachi following behind. He was drawn up short by the unexpected sight of a young man standing just inside the entry arch. The stranger was a head shorter than Meer, but lean and hard, with unreadable eyes. Sweat clumped his long-stranded hair into sodden braids. It looked like he had been waiting for them; certainly he would have heard their every word.

"Meer, son of Fas," said the stranger.

"Yes," Meer said, staring, searching for a name for the wrongness he felt. "Sachi, if you—"

"Another day," Sachi said brightly, her voice masking any disappointment. "Your next petitioner is here." She kissed his cheek and brushed past the stranger with a nod and a smile.

With Sachi gone, Meer was suddenly conscious of his fragrant nudity. "A moment, so I may—" he began, gesturing toward the hygiene partition.

"I bring you a message from Kedar Nan."

A chill raised the skin on Meer's limbs, and he fought to keep his expression calm. "A message from a ghost?" he said, circling toward the washbasin. "Kedar Nan must be dead nearly fifteen years."

"Kedar said that you would not want to believe it," the messenger said.

Meer had turned away and rinsed his hands in the basin, and now reached for a scrub cloth. "An easy prophecy."

"He said to ask you, 'What is the name of the world?'"

A sudden dizziness blurred Meer's vision, and he groped for the edge of the basin with his hands. "You are from outside?"

"Yes."

"From Edera?"

"Yes."

"What crime did you commit?"

"I am no criminal," the man said, bristling pridefully. "And I am not here to answer your questions."

Meer stared at the messenger's reflection in the mirror. Until that moment, Edera had only been a name to Meer—a name wrapped in common contempt and ritual hate, a name for the squalid dying ground of the diseased and the barren. Edera was the exiles' colony, said to consist of no more than a few mud walls and fragile cloth tents where Kawa empties into a lifeless sea.

There was no commerce between the communities, and no thought given to the exiles except to give insult, such as when young men urinate into Kawa and joke that they are refilling the dipping pails of Edera. Cut off from the resources of the exarch and the blessing of Ana, the lives of Edera's few inhabitants could only be wretched and brief. If any thrived, it was whispered, they did so by suckling dry teats to milk and feasting on the flesh of the fallen, or by merging with a dark apocryphal.

Meer's visitor was a curiosity, but not a horror. He had offered no threat; the only threat was in his presence. Still, Meer's skin crawled, and he wanted nothing else but to be rid of the visitor. "Leave the message, then, and go."

"I carry the message in memory."

"Then *tell* it to me, and go," Meer snapped, whirling to face the intruder.

The messenger closed his eyes for a moment, then began to speak. It was a trance-memory, word-perfect in as many repetitions as might be needed, the messenger's voice even carrying a hint of mimicry of Kedar's rhythms.

"Meer, I am glad my message finds you well. I am in Edera, and I am dying. I do not regret these years, but I want to come home. I wish for my spirit to be returned to Ana, and my body Received with honor, so that all know my debt is paid. If the law has not changed, death ends the sentence of exile. But as you well know, my only son preceded me into death. So I ask that you, Meer, son of Fas and my brother in the Genet, do what would have been his right, and come to Edera to take my body home. I ask this as a test of honor." The messenger opened his eyes. "That is Kedar's message. Do you need to hear it again?"

"No," said Meer, his voice a hoarse whisper. He slumped heavily on the edge of the basin and crossed his hands in front of his groin. "No."

It was jarring to think of Kedar Nan dying, more jarring yet to think of him still alive. Most jarring of all was to have the traitor whose name shall be silence intrude on Meer's comfortable place and his quiet life after all this time. Already he had begun to amass objections. Edera had no status, no official recognition. No free Anan of Meer's acquaintance had ever visited the exiles' world. None even bragged of such a journey. There was no reason to think that any would receive permission to make one. The way was unknown and unsafe, the land along Kawa empty and unblessed—

But it was asked as a test of honor. And there was a debt sufficient to sustain the obligation, pointed to but unnamed in Kedar's message.

Meer looked up and was surprised to find the messenger still standing there expectantly. "What?" Meer demanded. "Do you expect me to come with you now?"

"No. Guiding you is not part of my promise. Kedar asked me to wait for your reply."

"Will he live to hear it? Will he be alive when you return?"

"I don't know," said the young man. "What is your reply? Will you come for him?"

"I don't *know*," Meer said, his ambivalence reaching his voice as tight anger. He rose up from the basin and gestured sharply with his hands. "How can I? You came here unmolested, by whatever tricks. Why can't you bring him back?"

The messenger's look of impatience hardened to one of disgust. "Do you think we *want* to give him up to you, to this place? I only brought you his message because it's what *he* wants, and because I love him," he said. "So give me an answer. I can't wait for your courage to heal. What message do I take back?"

Meer stared. "You may say—" He looked down and away, his chest rising and falling with sharp, painful breaths. "You may say," Meer said, his voice softening, "that the name of the world is Taurin."

"Is that an answer?"

Meer looked up and fixed the messenger with a hard gaze. "Enough of one. And all the answer I have for you now."

Meer Faschen, third intercessor for Banteng Cluster, in the First Hundred, did not go running that night. Dazed by his encounter with the messenger, he stumbled through his afternoon hearings in a distracted and inattentive state. And in the twilight hour, he walked the spoke road home to Huyana, moving like a tall, white ghost among the workmen's carts and the lean-limbed youths setting out for courting.

Ordinarily, the workhouse on 33-out was Meer's quiet refuge from unwanted demands and obligations. Though it boasted only two rooms and was plagued by powdering walls which shed fine dust into the air when the ground shook, inside the green-cloaked fencewalls he could enjoy as much privacy as he chose. The front window caught the brilliant sunrises, and over the years Meer had made the small yard a garden of Ana's most brightly colorful plants.

He would pass two, three, five days in a row there, tending the garden, receiving a light schedule of petitioners, sleeping alone by choice in bedding often fragrant with Sachi's scent. And Huyana did not seem to object overmuch to his absences.

But in an instant of transformation, by the power of simple words—*I bring you a message from Kedar Nan*—the workhouse no longer felt safe. What other visitors might come out of the wasteland in the night? Meer did not wish to be there to receive them, and there was only one place in Ana that felt more secure.

The wisdom of the streets said that a woman required a house, but a man needed only a place to sleep. Whatever truth there might be in that, the fact was that the workhouse was not truly home. Home was where a man went to be loved, not to be alone.

By that measure, Meer's home was the well-kept three-mod on 60-in where his daughters were growing toward the mark with alarming speed. Huyana schooled her children with wit and patience, honored Meer still at intervals with earnest joy, and, these days, rarely took a younger man to her bed. A reasonable man could not expect more of a twelve-year pairing.

Huyana and the girls, Tori and Eir, were on the roof when he arrived, finishing a meal of fruit-boats and sugar bread. Tori, the younger, scrambled excitedly down the side ladder when she saw him. She threw herself at him for a sticky-fingered hug, then launched into an animated discourse on the reasons Siri was no longer her hand-kin.

Eir's greeting was much more subdued. She waggled her fingers shyly at him as he crossed the yard, but her attention was on the street behind him. His arms full of Tori, Meer slowly climbed the ladder to the roof, wondering how it was that the women knew what they wanted, how they chose from the parade of suitors. If only men could read that book, too—

Over her protests, Meer let Tori slide down his leg to stand on her own. As she reclaimed her platter, he settled cross-legged beside Huyana.

"Honored husband," she said with a small smile.

Taking her hand in his, he pressed it to his cheek and kissed the cupped palm. "Blessed wife."

"Have you eaten? There's a little more below."

"No," he said, watching Eir, who sat apart from the rest of the family, close to the edge, as though by turning her back on them she made them vanish.

Eir's body had begun to change, and it seemed as though her mind were changing with it. A cycle ago, she had been as loud and sassy as Tori, with hardly a thought to the mysteries or her marking. Now she perched on the roof as though it were her own, as if she might decide to come down to the yard if one of the runners passing the ringwall pleased her eye. She was pulling away from Tori, pushing away from Huyana, pretending to be a woman, preparing to leave home.

"Another cycle, no more," said Huyana with the prescience of familiarity.

"Can they sense it coming?"

"Of course," Huyana said. "Which is why it's such a trial for them, hated or welcomed be the change."

He looked at her in surprise. "Some hate it?"

"Did you never wish that you were still a child?"

Lips drawn tight, he looked away again. "The river flows the wrong way for such wishes."

"For them, too." She reached out and clasped his hand. "You are so very quiet tonight."

"Let me be quiet, for now," he said, twining his fingers in hers.

Before long, Huyana sent the girls below to clean up after the meal, and she and Meer stretched out on their backs on the roof to watch the violet sky change to a spackled black bowl that turned slowly overhead. Meer stared up into it and tried to measure its height with his eyes. Would it seem any lower from the top of the arch? he wondered. Would it look any different from Edera?

There was singing from a few houses down, muted but pleasant—a sweet-voiced woman practicing the difficult center-call of the Jineha chant for the coming festival. For a time another voice joined in, helpfully offering the male counter in a shaky baritone.

An elder neighbor from the next ring, making his way along the top of the fencewall in the dark, stopped briefly to ask Huyana if her share had been short lately and whether Meer thought there was a thief in the cluster.

"All that's been stolen from me this year is time, Ciro," Huyana answered with patient cheerfulness.

"It'd be the children, I'm thinking," the man said. "Or those lazy cartmen. And I can't be there to make sure they give an honest count. But if I find out who's stealing, there'll be some work for our intercessor and the executioner both. Meer, you tell Kamil to expect a petition from me."

Meer looked at Huyana in puzzlement. "I will."

"And Huyana, you be sure to open the gate to your reservoir before you forget yourself. They'll finally be flooding our ring tonight, Tosia tells me, and her son is a gateman."

"I will, Ciro."

Ciro wandered away atop the wall, shaking his head and muttering to himself.

"Nothing's been stolen," Huyana whispered. "His blessed fell from her ladder three days ago and can barely remember her name. We've all been helping out, putting up her share, cooking for her until it comes back. But he takes everything she says as sacred and storms out to defend her. I don't know which of them is sadder."

The air chilled quickly, chasing some of their nearer neighbors down from the roofs. Later, the announcement tone from the city voice, sounding from all the open windows, called the rest inside to hear the evening report. Huyana started down herself, but Meer reached out and touched her arm. "Stay here with me. Eir can tell us if there's any news that matters."

From below, they could hear the familiar timbre and words of the city voice as the daily bulletins began. "Blessings to the people of Ana from the exarch Oran-rami Anadon, Elect of the Councilors' Circle, and all the trustees of Ana's gracious joy—"

"Will you tell me what news *you* have that's weighing so heavily?" Huyana asked. "Has Chane lost standing at the honor school? I can think of no other calamity that would strike you so deeply."

"No, Chane is doing well. I saw him yesterday," Meer said, sitting up. "He seems happy. He was with new friends, and seemed to belong there."

She waited for him, and in the silence they could hear the news continuing: " . . . On this day, Ana welcomes with joy fifty-one new children—among them nine bell-children. So on this day, Ana rejoices with her nine new blessed, women and mothers: Siti Vedistera, of the mark of the Amur. Aja Etera, of the mark of the Sun Bear . . ."

Meer was still looking off into the deepening darkness when he spoke again, his voice pitched so low that Huyana could barely understand him. "I received an—an appeal today from Kedar Nan," he said.

"Who is Kedar Nan?"

The question was asked with open innocence, and Meer tried to conceal the relief he felt. He had said the name as a test, wondering if it were still spoken over the walls, if Huyana had somehow learned the history her youth and his resolve had hidden from her. Mercifully, it seemed she had not.

"An exile," he said, turning to her. "He sent a messenger, asking me to see that he is returned to Ana and Received when he dies."

A worried looked crossed her features. "This messenger—another exile?"

"I did not know him. He said he was from Edera. I did not ask for proof."

"Meer, can they enter the city so easily? I thought the boundary was patrolled by the sentries."

"The boundary is too long to be well watched, I am afraid," Meer said. "But the messenger concerns me least. Kedar Nan's appeal was worded as a test of honor against my mark."

"Why you? Did you hear his trial?"

Meer nodded, looking past her. "I did."

Frowning, she said, "I can't claim to know the law. But I know you, and I know that you must have been fair in your hearing and your judgment."

"There were many—complications."

"But does he have a right to ask such a thing?"

"Even those sent to the killing yards are given reunion. A judgment of exile is against the man, not the body. Ana cleanses her own substance."

"Then let him come to a gate, and you can tell the sentries to drag his body in when he falls."

Meer shook his head. "He asked me to bring him from Edera. It was clear he expects to die there."

"Then let him stay there. Are you truly giving thought to this?"

"I am torn."

"Will you hear my advice?"

"I came here to hear it, Huyana."

"Then my advice is this: Husband, breathe deeply, so your sense can revive. Kedar Nan wants revenge, not reunion. This is no test of honor—it's a trap wrapped in honor."

"I do not think so."

"No? If he can hire a man to bring you a message, he can hire another to carry his body to the east gate."

"Kedar cannot rely on the other exiles," Meer said. "He does not trust them." It was a supposition that took the shape of conviction when he spoke it.

"Then you can't trust them, either," Huyana said, edging closer. "Listen, Meer, listen. You have no obligation to this criminal. It's not your place to assure his return to Ana. Leave that to his fellow criminals, or any who still claim him as kin. Leave it to those who watch the boundary, or the syndic of arbiters. But think no thought of going to Edera. You are not responsible for the fates of those who come before you accused. You have sent how many into exile—"

"Five," Meer said. "Kedar was the first."

"—and how many more to execution?"

"I do not count them," Meer said. "I do not welcome those hearings. I much prefer the everyday petitions and disputes."

"But there have been many more than one."

"Yes."

"Do you propose to accept an obligation on behalf of each of them? Is that the role of an arbiter?"

"No," Meer said slowly. "My obligation was to hear their charge fairly."

"And did you hear Kedar Nan's charge fairly?"

He thought a long time. "I did everything that was expected of me."

"Then he is no different than the others because he was the first. Promise me, Meer—on pain of leaving my house and bed—that you will leave this in someone else's hands."

Meer reached out and clasped her hand. "Does this frighten you that much?"

"More than it does you, it seems. I don't want you touching that kind of evil, and it touching Eir and Tori."

Squeezing her hand firmly, he said, "I will give you that promise. This will not touch this house."

Huyana allowed the amendment, or it escaped her notice. Reassured, she hugged him, then excused herself to see that the children had completed their tasks. "Will you join me in my bed tonight?" she asked, pausing on the ladder.

He smiled. "I will."

But the smile was forced, and in daylight would never have passed for sincere. *How can I accept your advice, Huyana, without telling you the whole story? But if I told you, you would never see me the same again—* Even answering her innocent questions, Meer was pricked bloody by conscience.

Stretching out on his back once more, he pillowed his head on folded hands and stared up at the sky dome. The stars were at full brilliance now, and he linked the white points with imagination to build hexagons and spirals, tilted houses and wandering rivers. Some said that the apocryphals looked down from the night sky, but he could not see them. Faith improved the clarity of a man's vision, or so it was often claimed. Sometime later, his eyelids closed of their own accord, and he began to doze.

Meer was awakened by the sound of water gurgling in the streets. The familiar musty wet-dust smell rose up and enveloped him as the leading edge of the flow swept past the house and continued down the ring toward the outgate on the lower Kawa.

Descending from the roof, he went to the ringwall and watched the street become a shallow river. He checked to see that the sticky fill trap for Huyana's cistern was open, and heard the traps for surrounding houses trip open with a chatter. Small sucking vortices at the edge of the shallowly flooded street marked the inlets. Air hissed from the yard vent as the cistern filled.

"I remember asking my mother, 'Where does the water come from?' " Huyana said softly, from behind him.

He turned away from the ringwall and invited her into an embrace. She moved close and snuggled against him, her bare arms cool. "What did your mother say?" he asked.

"She said that at night, the houses drink from Kawa, like babies from a breast."

"The same thing Fas told me," he said. "Did you believe her?"

"Of course. And she was right, in essence if not detail."

"I wouldn't believe Fas until she allowed me to stay up and see it for myself."

"You were a suspicious child."

"I had an older brother," he said archly. "You learn not to be too trusting."

She laughed lightly. "Is all in order? Are you ready to join me inside?"

"Yes," he said.

"Good," she said. "I need warming. And I was beginning to miss you."

Her touch and nearness were soothing, but could not banish his tortured reflections. Huyana surely knew that his attention was divided, but she granted him a kindness and did not mention Kedar Nan again as they cuddled quietly in her bed.

Huyana's kindness could not spare Meer from wrestling with the question of conscience, but it saved him, at least, from further lies—or from confessing that, promise or not, he still had not decided what to do.

3

Kad: The Second Bell

Meer had hoped to find dan Amra alone, but it was a faint hope, and a vain one, even in the early hours of the day.

With their houses empty of children, the dan were each other's company, and the life of the city was their work. The elder wisdom of Ana flowed from the dan, and the real news of the city flowed through their circles. If there was any obligation which went with their otherwise privileged status, it was that the dan would not hide themselves away.

So Meer was not surprised that Amra was not in her house. But he found her in the corner grass court nearby, sitting in a shaded chair and flanked on either side by younger dan he did not know. Dan Amra's fall of waist-length hair, shot through with gray, was knotted at the right and spilled unbraided down that shoulder. Her hands were busy twisting flaxcord into a healing fetish. A young girl hovered behind Amra's chair, watching every loop and twist intently.

"Meer Faschen," said dan Amra, looking up from her knotwork and conversation as Meer drew near. Her small, oval face wore all the labor her body had endured through the years, but her children had not stolen the life from her eyes. "You see, I remember, even though you never come to see me."

He nodded acknowledgment. "I've brought you something," he said, crouching on the ground before her. He offered up his closed left hand, opening his fingers to reveal a mottled dark green sphere resting on his palm. "You see, I remember, too."

Smiling gently, Amra captured the stone between her fingertips and raised it before her face, turning it back and forth as she examined it.

"Malachite," she said. "A lovely gift, even if the polish reflects another's sweat. Someday Ana will be this green and beautiful." She pocketed the marble and resumed her work on the fetish. "Was this the only reason you stopped to see me?"

"Perhaps he's found the young barren so pleasing he wants to taste an older vintage of the same drink," said the dan to Amra's right. She laughed at her own rudeness.

Amra's smile was tolerant at best. "Perhaps, Naia, though somehow I doubt it. It doesn't take very many like Sachi to fill a man's empty time."

"It takes a great many men to fill a danera's empty places, though," said Naia, and laughed again.

Meer glared in Naia's direction, but bit back a rebuke out of respect—grudging and strained, in this instance—for her station. "Amra, I hope you'll forgive me my absence from your company. And I hope you know from the petitioners I send to you that I think well of your counsel."

The third dan, at Amra's left, then joined in. "*I* wouldn't be offended. I'd lose respect for any arbiter who was forever turning to me for advice."

"I've known such," said dan Amra. "But I would lose respect more quickly if he was forever making poor judgments."

Eyebrow cocked, Meer asked, "Have you heard complaints?"

"Oh, not a great many," she said. "Though I may not hear them all. But Patrin insists that you didn't hear him fairly, that you favored Stal because you hoped she would favor you."

"Patrin is a jealous man with a shrunken heart," Meer said.

"Quite so—"

"And a festival month without his mark should give him time enough alone to realize it. Stal may favor who she pleases."

"Even her arbiter?"

"Even him—should she have such a radical change of heart."

Dan Amra nodded to herself, the answer apparently satisfactory. "There are few men who don't want her. But more are turned away disappointed than not. Why Patrin is her favorite—that puzzles me. I will never understand why we women are drawn to so many bad pairings." She looked up and smiled at Meer.

"Was there something you wanted from *me*?"

"Your private counsel, dan Amra. A bit of your time."

"Only a bit? A bolder man would want a whole morning, at least," Naia said, chortling.

"Naia, you've become tiresome," said dan Amra with a sidewise glower.

The look chased the amusement from the other woman's face. Showing a quick frown, Naia hugged herself and looked away, as though disinterested.

Turning in her chair, Amra held up the fetish and looked back to the young girl, still quietly waiting behind her. "Do you think that you can finish it?"

"I—it needs a sealing knot?"

"A focus weaving, first, here at the top, in your mother's sign."

"I can do that," said the girl.

Amra handed the fetish back over her shoulder to the girl. "Show it to me when you're done." She held her empty hand up to Meer, who caught hold of it and helped her up. "Walk me to my house," Amra said. "We'll talk there."

Meer offered a hand to help Amra over the ringwall of her home. "Is Naia always so harsh-tongued?"

Loosing a weary sigh, Amra paused, perched atop the masonry. "She was the youngest of six, and she paired with a man who tended the vat fields at the great lake—away for days at a time and as talkative as a standing staff when he wasn't."

"Simple thoughts and not much patience."

"Just so. Her children were terrors—the oldest tested her early and won, and the rest followed his lead. In her whole life, I don't think Naia was ever *listened* to." Amra shrugged and slipped down off the wall. "Now everyone in earshot *must* listen, and she can hardly say a word that isn't wrapped in old bitterness."

"Being rude is her retribution."

Amra nodded. "It's a poor triumph when you make a stranger your victim because you can't reach those who made a victim of you. But enough," she said, and touched his hand. "Come inside, and you can do the talking and I the listening."

The upper room of Amra's house belonged to the proxy dolls of her children. There were eight in all, one for each child borne and nurtured to independence. Some were as tall and substantial as a five-year-old, some skillfully enough rendered in cloth, stone, wood, and clay to fool the eye in a sideways glance.

A house once and always filled with children . . .

A few of the proxies were simpler, mere stylized trophies and totems in human form. One was so crude—a stick-figure in clay, unclothed and no taller than a newborn, with no facial features save for two deep pits for eyes—that Meer found it disturbing, and had to wonder what story shadowed it. Remembering how hard he had worked to imbue his proxy with his own spirit, how much it had meant to him to leave something of himself in Fas's house, the mouthless clay child spoke to Meer of great pain.

But simple or subtle, all of Amra's proxies had an honored place. Meer had seen dan homes where proxies were consigned to lining the foot of a wall or filling an otherwise empty bed. Amra's dolls were posed as though caught in a frozen moment of life: peering out the window at the street, standing shyly in a corner, sleeping in a chair, lying in a circle around the scattered stone marbles of a game of knock.

"Do they bother you?" asked Amra, watching his face.

"No," Meer said. "It's just—so many."

"I lost one at birth and two before their marks," Amra said. "I took the spark eleven times."

Meer's expression was respectful. "You were generously blessed."

"The last one nearly cost me my own life. I closed my bed to my chosen until Ana reclaimed her blessing and made me dan. Do you think that was selfish of me?"

"If prizing your own life is selfish."

"But *is* it?"

"Not by my measure."

"Nor by mine—but I confess to being prejudiced in the matter. This is a gentler life," she said. "But look at me, talking still. What did you want to share with me?"

"I've heard from Kedar Nan."

Her gaze narrowed into a suspicious challenge. "Do you test me?"

"No, dan Amra," he said softly. "I do not test you."

"Because I won't be tricked. This name you spoke is an empty sound. It dies before it reaches my ears. It touches not a single memory."

"I will say his name for both of us. And you need not admit to your memories to listen to me. I've heard from Kedar Nan. He's in Edera, and dying."

"Well," she said. "Well and well." She displaced one of the sleeping daughter-dolls, cradling the figure in her arms as she settled back in the chair. "This is Pava, my youngest. Her own hands, this work, and I taught her every stitch. She made her proxy soft, so that I might still cuddle her."

"Lovely."

"But not half as lovely as Pava herself. She could make Stal envious. Have you seen her?"

"No."

"A pity." She shrugged. "Well, then, tell me more of your fiction, and amuse me with your inventive mind."

Despite her studied casualness, Amra listened attentively as Meer told her of his visitor and his message. A dozen years senior to Huyana, she doubtless remembered first-hand, as he had expected she would, Kedar Nan's last days in Ana—and those memories would add the dimension which had been lacking in Huyana's advice.

When he was finished, Amra nodded slowly, then set Pava gently on the floor beside her. "I have questions."

"Ask them."

"Does the *arbiter* believe an obligation exists?"

"Not in the law."

"Somewhere else?"

"In the mind of Kedar Nan."

"Nowhere else?"

Meer hesitated. "He was guilty of the offenses."

"Then why is there an issue? 'No' is the answer the arbiter wants to give, and his blessed confirms him in it. Why should he keep asking for assurance? Is doubt speaking? Guilt?"

"He wants to be able to sleep in peace."

"Ah," she said, raising an eyebrow. "But what does he fear— the nightmares, or being wakened from them?"

"If one exile could reach him with a message, another could reach him with a knife."

"So a new fear, then, and not an old guilt."

"I—he has a right to his peace."

She nodded thoughtfully. "Does this arbiter know if his visitor was stopped and caught?"

"No," he said. "It could be dangerous to ask, since he made no report himself."

"Perhaps it's not too late to do so."

Unconsciously, he had retreated from her barrage of questions. Now his shoulders touched the front wall, halting his flight. "I want to be left alone."

"I do not find that among your choices," she said, dropping the pretense with him. "The three I see are these: You can do as asked. You can ignore the challenge, and hope it ends there and your nights remain undisturbed. Or you can report your visitor, and hope to make this someone else's problem."

Meer started shaking his head even before she finished. "I *can't* report it. The bucket has stood too long—no one wants to burrow in it. There's too much to explain. *I* would be suspect. 'Why did he come to you? Has he contacted you before? Who else is part of your conspiracy?' " Meer waved his hands violently. "No."

"Then there are only two choices: go to Edera, or learn to sleep lightly."

Meer sighed. "I like those choices no better."

Standing, Amra quietly replaced Pava in her chair, then crossed to where Meer was standing. "You knew him?"

He nodded. "Yes."

"I only know *of* him," she said. "Let me ask you this, since you knew him. Does he deserve what he seeks? If that truly is what he seeks."

"Ana made him deserving, by seeing to his punishment."

Clucking, she said, "That's a ritual answer, and I want honest thoughts. The man, Meer. Is the man worthy?"

He blinked, and drew a slow, deep breath that was nearly a sigh. "Yes. He is. Or he was. I don't know what he's become."

"Hundreds died following him."

"Yes," Meer said. "Hundreds at least."

"And you still think him worthy."

He met her steady gaze squarely. "Yes. In the time that I knew him, he was most worthy."

"Then haven't you answered your own question?" asked Amra. "If the exiles *will* not return him, and you *do* not, it won't be done. He'll be separated forever from Ana, and you will always know that his last chance ended with you. Only you can say how peaceful your sleep will be then."

She paused, but when he said nothing, she went on. "You need not go yourself, of course. Hire it done. Use your influence to prevail on a sentry captain or an ambitious scout. Make it a public obligation. Take it to the temple. You may pass this burden, Meer. But I don't think you dare ignore it. You asked for my counsel, and this is it: You must do *something* for Kedar Nan."

Kell Cluster was large enough to need two hives for the work of the hierarchy, and settled enough to sacrifice a hostel to the cause. With fewer unblessed women and unattached men than the younger and more vigorous clusters out toward the city's edge, space once needed for housing the newly marked could be turned over to the hierarchy.

Meer moved under the awning spanning the hive's central breezeway, shrugged past three men holding a hushed discussion, and slipped the hood of his sun vest off his head. The smaller hive had only sixteen offices, with Allocation using the hostel's common room as a storehouse. But that was still enough to collect a crowd of petitioners and complainants. The rooms marked for Maintenance and the four divisions of Allocation were the most busy, and the timbre of the voices inside the most angry and impatient.

But in the back of the hive, away from the street, Meer found the office of the trustee of records quiet and nearly deserted. He flashed the shield of the syndic of arbiters before the clerk. "I need to locate several people who may live in Kell Cluster," he said.

"Of course," said the clerk. He flipped open the lid of his records box and addressed his next words to it. "Coron, in Kell. Citizen address."

"Ready," said the box.

"Are they all of age?" the clerk asked Meer.

"Yes," said Meer. He had remembered seven children Kedar Nan had sparked, in six women, before crossing the boundary of Ana into exile. Even the youngest of them would be an adult now.

"The first name is—"

The list might have been longer, but time had crippled Meer's recall. Meer had only met two of the women who had favored Kedar, and four of his offspring. The others were only shadows in poorly-remembered conversations.

Meer supplied the clerk with what names he could remember. Each time, the clerk repeated the name into the box. Each time, the box replied a few moments later, "Not assigned share in Kell Cluster."

"That was the last," Meer said finally.

"I'm sorry I couldn't help you."

"Perhaps you still can. Can you ask for earlier records? I'm sure that these people did live here once."

The clerk frowned. "Why would the trustee keep a library from years ago? What use would it be, knowing what *was*? It's hard enough keeping up with the *is*." He gestured at a multi-colored stack of forms. "If I fall as much as a day behind in the changes, someone with three children will get a share for two and vice versa, a toolman will show up to fix something already fixed and not show up where he's needed, and those people at the other end will be in here, burning my ears and threatening my appointment."

"I understand," Meer said.

"How would it be done?" the clerk went on, closing the lid and tapping the cover. "I'd need one of these for every day, to keep things as they were that day. I'd need an extra room, just to store them in. Besides, who would ever use them? Your need may be legitimate, but how many other good purposes are there? Keeping all that history would only encourage memorialism."

"Yes," Meer said, biting back his irritation. "I should have realized."

"What kind of case is this, anyway, that you don't have a messenger doing your sun work?"

"A case I hope to keep out of the hands of the captain of executioners," Meer said. "A case I hope can be settled without me, if I can bring the right people together."

The clerk accepted that. "Mind, though, that this is why the syndic sends sentries on inquiries, to save you the time and me the foolish questions."

"Of course," Meer said. "But why involve the syndic when the issue is purely private? I'm sure you understand. An arbiter can do small favors now and again, if there's no harm to the general good."

"Yes," the clerk said thoughtfully. "Yes. I wish that I could help you."

"Can you at least tell me if any of them are dead?"

"I post a deletion the same as a transfer," the clerk said. "And when I do, that person is gone from the share list. These people, they could all be dead, or all be somewhere else in Ana, and I wouldn't know the difference. I have enough to worry about without keeping track of the dead or departed."

"Yes," Meer said. "Permit me one more foolish question. Can you search the rolls of all the clusters, not just Kell? What about Jiris Cluster, the next west?"

The clerk shook his head sorrowfully. "If there was a way—but I haven't the access. For Jiris, you'll have to ask in Jiris. For all of Ana, you'll have to ask the trustee himself."

That was the solution Meer had been hoping to avoid. The trustee of records sat in the Councilors' Circle, and, it was said, was a confidant of the exarch. Inquiries under his nose would not go unnoticed. "Then I suppose I must go to Jiris."

"I could arrange a sentry to handle this quietly. The syndic of public safety and I understand each other."

"No," said Meer. "Thank you."

"You'll remember that I tried to help you, at least?"

"I will."

Meer learned no more from the hive in Jiris Cluster, or in Altha, one circle out from Kell. So, reluctantly, he returned to Kell, and went to the one house he could not forget—that of Rida Valtera, Kedar's last blessed, and the mother of his son Lenn.

The house belonged to another woman now, a short jet-haired woman whose slender body was grossly distended by the near-term child she was carrying. A new canopy of blue coarseweave covered over the yard between the side wall and the house, and in its shade an infant no more than a year old rested sleepily in a sand-sack.

"Your second?" Meer asked, touching the woman's belly.

"Yes."

"May you have many blessings," he said, and showed her his shield. "I want to ask you about this house, and those who lived here before you."

"I know nothing of them."

"There was a woman named Rida. You might know if she died, or was moved. And she had several children. I am most interested in the children."

The woman shook her head. "Before me, a woman named Stoya lived here, though I never knew her. She died from a beating, and her sister took the children. All this is from gossip. I knew none of them."

So the house had changed hands twice—perhaps more than twice. "I want to see the memorial."

She retreated a step from the ringwall. "We keep no memorials here."

He climbed over the wall and advanced on her. "Do not treat me like a fool."

"I am no memorialist," she insisted. "If I had found a memorialist's work when I took this house, I'd have destroyed it. I'm faithful to the law. And I want no ghosts here. But I found nothing. This house is mine and my children's."

Her belligerence masked fear, but it did not seem that fear was the mother of her words. "I am glad to hear that you are faithful to the law," he said finally. "Tell me this—who of your neighbors has lived here the longest? Who is the eldest of the dan?"

She pointed. "Dan Ula," she said. "Two rings to the center, and three houses round east."

Meer took to the top of the walls and reached her home quickly. When he hailed, dan Ula invited him inside, though she did not interrupt her bustling at the galley when he joined her. This time, he did not offer his shield. The dan's long memories were a threat he cared not to face.

"Dan Ula, I am looking for the children of Rida Valtera."

She paused and studied him curiously. "It does not do for a man to chase after scattered seed."

"True. But I was not Rida's honored."

"If this were the business of the hierarchy, you would not need to ask me."

"I was a friend."

She turned and looked at him. "What kind of friend? The skies have turned many times since that household scattered."

"A careless friend."

"A cowardly one, more like. That house knew great pain. Those who stood with Rida were not rewarded for their loyalty."

"No," said Meer. "They were not. You may think what you wish, dan Ula. But please tell me what you can of Rida's children."

She dipped a cupful of water from the standing basin and sipped at it before answering. "There were five, by three she favored. A daughter by Jian. That one went to the hostels and never came back. She may have given herself up—taken the name and house and children of a dead woman of her line."

"May have? You don't know?"

"These things are not done loudly," she said. "Rida's son by Wu was haunted by his mother's dishonor. He shunned her, but was never at peace. He chased death for years and finally found it, in the last of many fights he started."

She drew another cupful of water, but did not offer him any—a purposeful slight, in all likelihood. "The other three were all kin by spark as well as by birth—two daughters and a son. Do you know of Lenn's fate?"

"Yes," said Meer.

"I thought that you would. The daughters were both quite young, and went with Rida. I could not guess where they might be now."

"For all your words, you've not told me anything I can use to find any of them."

"I did not promise you that I would," she said. "But tell me this—do you look for Rida as well?"

The question caught Meer unawares. "Does she live? Do you know where she is?"

"I know where she was. The exarchy found ways to punish her as well. She had a fine house, and they took it back from her. She was sent all the way out to the Fourth Hundred, to Hebei Cluster, where the water always tastes of dust and the houses are as shaky as Ula balancing on one leg. And how many of the fine young men there do you think stopped at her wall to offer—at her age, and with the wear of five on her and no title to show for it? Mothers and lovers of traitors have few friends in the temples."

Meer would not be baited into saying more. "Hebei Cluster," he said. "Thank you, dan Ula."

As dusk gathered overhead, Meer walked slowly through the streets of Hebei Cluster, staring at hooded faces, dusty faces, brashly young and vital faces as the faster traffic flowed around him. The creak of hand-bikes and carts, the slap of sandals and rush of fabric, the loud laughter and soft words fused into a single voice speaking a language he did not understand. He looked on them as through a glass wall, held apart from them by the thoughts and memories he carried and which they neither knew nor would understand.

Where were the others who had stood with Kedar Nan in the plaza that night? There must have been ten thousand. But Ana had turned, renewed, and the young faces he saw around him knew nothing of those young faces then.

Where were the survivors of the shattered star? Surely one among them was not afraid of the memories. But who were they, and where were they? Meer had made no effort to keep contact with the handful he knew or had met. In truth, he had made every effort to escape their eyes and their judgment, even after fear had securely seized their tongues.

Even slow steps carried him toward his destination. As the sky darkened and the pale yellow solights were beginning to glow from windows and doorways along the ring, Meer found himself before the house of Rida Valtera.

The yard was dust-choked and brown, the strangled branches of two plum-yew bushes the only sign that it had ever been greened. Curtains were drawn over the windows and doorway, a further snub to the neighborhood and defiance of convention. But Rida's blessing bell still hung in the doorway, and on the outside wall beside the doorway hung the three strikers given her by her favored mates. And hung highest, the sharpest rebuke of all for any who knew its meaning, was the long red-handled carved-bone striker which had been Kedar's offering the first night Rida invited him in.

She had not turned away from the memories, even if holding to them had embittered her.

Meer stood at the ringwall, frozen by a painful ambivalence. If only there was some other choice—

But too many years had passed. Kedar's daughters had disappeared into their own lives. Were *they* shunned as well, or had they been able to escape shame? Would they even know their parentage? Kedar's youngest daughter had been barely a year old. Even if he found them, would they admit to their lineage? If they denied Kedar, could he blame them?

Meer stood at the ringwall for a long time, until the street was washed in night's shadow, and he became a ghost within it. Then at last he backed away, shaking his head as he did and whispering, "No. I can't add this to your burden." This time, as he retreated down the ring road and headed back toward the heart of the city, his footsteps were quick and nervous, and echoed in his ears like the sound of someone fleeing.

Through nearly thirty-three festival years, Oran Anadon, exarch of Ana, senior of the Councilors' Circle, had inhabited the keystone house on the high north bank of Kawa. Resting midway between the arch and the first ring road bridge upstream from the arch, the house shared the same crescent greenpark with the honor school, the workhouses of the prefects of Invention and Public Information, and the meeting house of the councilors.

Collectively, the institutions contained in the park were known as the high bank, though city maps bore the more formal title Arbor of Steadfast Prosperity. Meer Faschen was not of the high bank or the hierarchy which revolved around it, though his son would someday be able to say he belonged there. Nor did Meer, as a mere arbiter, enjoy the right of access to the exarch.

But he knew where to find Oran, and Kedar Nan's name opened doors.

The keystone house was a hollow square built up from eight shells: four doubles at the corners, and four singles to connect them. Meer was taken to the center courtyard, which was tented over with a spidersilk canopy striped in striking royal blue. He was studying the play of the light filtering through the fabric when Oran Anadon joined him there.

"So you've heard from Kedar Nan," Oran said without preamble. "I'd thought his flame blown out long ago."

Meer spun around and took a step forward. "I came to you directly, Oran-rami, because only someone with full knowledge of his history can understand. And because I knew you would be concerned that his messenger so boldly walked our streets."

"The boundary of Ana is a filter, not a barrier," said Oran. "But so long as any who return from outside find no home here, the boundary need be no more than that. When did this visitor come to you?"

Meer's hesitation consumed only a fraction of a second, but it seemed to him a thundering silence. "Last night," he said, deciding that the messenger had not been caught. "As the last of my hearings was ending—a danera from the hostel, having trouble with a young unblessed. She saw the man, too, but only for a moment. I sent her away, to protect her."

The lie passed. "And the message?"

Meer repeated it as best he could remember it. Amusement lit Oran's lined face and jet eyes as he listened. "So Kedar Nan craves reunion with Ana. By all means, bring the old bastard home," he said, laughing. "It's long past time for him to be mulch in our fields."

"Yes," Meer said with a hard swallow. "I imagine the captain of scouts will know who to send—"

"Were you not listening?" asked Oran. "I'm sending you."

Meer stared, trying to fight down the pain that wanted to settle in his expression. "Me, Oran-rami? I am no scout. I know nothing about the outside, or where the exiles hide—one hears things, but they hardly pass for knowledge—"

"It will not be a difficult journey," said Oran. "You can take a scout's sunboat—"

"I've never stepped aboard one, much less piloted one."

"The captain of scouts selects for loyalty, not intelligence. An hour's instruction will suffice for someone of your ability. I myself learned to pilot a sunboat in a few minutes," said Oran. "You worry needlessly. Lower Kawa is placid most of the year. You'll be back with his corpse in three days, four at most. It's little more than an errand."

"An errand? I'll have to take my own food—I have no clothes proper for such a place—"

"The captain of scouts can advise and provide," said Oran. "The scouts go as far as *ten* days upriver with some regularity, and only lose the occasional thick-headed fool."

"Surely some younger man more familiar with the boats, or with Edera, could accomplish this more easily?"

Oran smiled, his eyes glittering coldly. "For the same reason you came to me, I look to you to do this. Where will we find someone who understands the import? We speak of the man whose name is silence. What explanations would you offer to halt gossip among the scouts and all who they touch? I wish for Kedar's return to Ana to be as invisible as his exile. Is your wish any different?"

Flushing, Meer looked down at the ground. "No."

"Very well, then."

Meer lifted his gaze. "But even if the journey's not difficult, as you say—surely it's not too much to ask that I have a guide—"

"The river is all the guide you need."

"Then a sentry to guard my back in a dangerous place. Surely a trustworthy sentry could be found. Perhaps among those who guard you here."

"I should hope that they *are* trustworthy," Oran said, implacable. "But the answer is no. You have safe passage, from Kedar Nan. You are his invited. And you will carry *my* safe passage, for the return. You represent the exarch of Ana. The exiles will not dare to harm you, and risk our wrath."

Meer swallowed, stiffened. "I see that you are determined that I should go, and go alone."

"Yes," said Oran. "I am. I rather relish the image of Kedar Nan humbled in death, his last words a plea for redemption to a man of Ana—and not any man, but the man who condemned him. For you to walk into Edera alone and unafraid, and take away Kedar

Nan's corpse—the message that will send to them, the symbolism of that act, is too precious to squander."

"What if I fail?"

"I see that," said Oran, "as a matter of little consequence. No one in Ana cares if Kedar Nan returns. I warrant few more care if Meer Faschen does. The person most invested in your success is yourself. And that, I think, is how it should be." Oran's voice turned metal-cold. "Kedar Nan should have been executed like his son, not exiled. He should have been made to watch his son die, then joined him. I forgave the error, but not the debt for the forgiveness. That debt is now due."

4

The Whispering of Air

Even with Gowon's advice, I was never able to cure the walls of Kedar's storehouse room. But since it was only a finishing nat which had wilded, the structure remained sound. I know, because I returned to it many times.

At first, I came back with call slip in hand. Kedar said he needed more storage for his growing collection, his journals and hand-bounds. This was no small thing, and it was not my place to offer to one what could not be offered to all, not when there were other houses and more basic needs waiting on my call. Allocation is the duty of the hierarchy, not of such as I was.

But I looked past my conscience, and made Kedar hanging cages as tall as himself and twice as wide as those the craft circles make as share goods. It took two days to build the cages, and most of a third to hang them and fill them.

Kedar spent much of that time with me, sitting and watching my hands, sharing the work when he could, asking after Meli, listening to my gossip from the long house. He seemed to be interested in everything, which I supposed was how a man acquired so many books and things and curious ideas.

Together with the smaller cages moved up from below, the six new hangings shrank the uproom by a third. No one man's possessions ought to have been able to fill them, but when Kedar and I had finished moving his collection to its new home, there were more pockets full than empty.

"Why do you have so many?" I asked him. "Is there so much to know?"

He answered me with what I thought was a riddle. "What is the name of the world?"

"Ana," I said.

"So I thought, too, once," he said, plucking a hand-bound from the stack I was holding. "But the name of the world is Taurin."

He riffled the hand-bound's leaves delicately, stopping when he found the passage he was seeking. " 'Taurin resists us. Twice now one of the prochlorophyll pools upstream has been found brown in sun death; we shall have to look after them more regularly. The lichen grass refuses to grow untended on the plains surrounding Ana, and so dust fills the air with every breeze that rolls down the valley. The cancers still come, despite everything the chemists can do. Taurin is a hard mother to her children.' "

"Whose words are those?"

Kedar looked up at me. "His name was Tonit, and he carried the mark of the Lutra."

I searched my memory. "The Lutra? Does that line survive?"

"No. This is a copy of a copy of a copy," he said, returning the book to me. "There is a great deal to know, and even more still to discover. If you wish to read the rest sometime—"

I looked around me. "Once begun, where would I stop? There's a lifetime of reading in this room."

"Many lifetimes," Kedar said, and let it drop.

But I did not forget Tonit, who had thought the world was named Taurin. As I packed away my tools, I thought about the lost apocryphals, and wondered who had been the last of Tonit's line. And when it was time to leave, I took the short detour to the plaza, and stood surrounded by the signs of the two thousand, wondering how many of them had gone out of the world since the first days, and who would stand in my footsteps and wonder after me and mine.

That was not the end of Kedar's needs and ideas. Not long after, he called for me again, to ask how I thought he might get a light for the uproom, which he had taken to calling the archives.

"I need the night hours for my work," Kedar said. "And there are students who want to come use my collection, if only it were possible to do so in the evenings, when they are free."

Like the cages, this was not a simple thing he wanted. Every common house in Ana has but a single lamp, in the center of the downroom ceiling. In the early mornings and late evenings, it lights the core of the house, the food and hygiene partitions, and spills some of its rays into the mods.

But the lamps throw little light up through the ladder well of a double. Not that it matters—all the lamps go dark not long after twilight. Before dawn, they all come on again, as the receiver of the Voice plays the waking theme.

When I was a child in Fas's house, it seemed as though the city were sending us to our beds, then calling us to our work. When I trained as a toolman, I was told that the lamps followed the necessities of conservation. It did not occur to me then that the lights went out across the city because order pleased the prefect of moral culture, not because the draw cell might be drained. I did not know then that a lamp with no link to the receiver of the Voice would burn sundown to sunrise if allowed.

But I do not doubt that Kedar knew, and did not care for the curfew imposed by his fellow prefect. "If we had another lamp, in the uproom," said Kedar, "and another draw cell which was not obliged to pump water, or speak for the Voice, or chill the coldbox, or feed any of the other demands of a household, perhaps they could give us light through the whole night."

And that was a reasonable thought.

Except this was at a time when new shells in the Fifth Hundred, some even occupied, were still waiting for their power kits, because every share good from the hot chemists was in short supply. But I cheerfully conspired with Kedar, suggesting he report his power kit defective, and promising that if he could procure a replacement, I would install it in the manner he wanted, and give him a lamp for his archives.

Through what connection I do not know, the next time he called me, a power kit was waiting. Kedar joined me on the roof while I burned the holes for the collector and cables, offered a third hand while I boxed the storage cell and hung the lamp.

And while we worked, he plied me with questions until I was weary of them and nearly so of him—what did I know of the inner workings of the storecell? Of the receiver? Could I explain how the collector captured light, and how the storecell contained it? Had I heard of houses which had lamps in every room, or a coldbox which could make water hard?

"You ask questions about things which don't matter," I told him.

"Until the questions are asked, it is not possible to know what matters," he said, standing in the middle of the room and looking up at the new lamp, bright in mid-day. "This will help so much. You don't realize."

"I know what matters," I said. "Stone in the staff and a squeal in the night. Ringing bells and round bellies."

He laughed lightly. "You are a poet of the simple pleasures."

"Is there any better pleasure in these than in a woman's whisper?" I asked, encompassing the library with a sweep of my hand.

"Pleasure?" His mouth pinched closed as he thought. "No, you are quite right, the simple pleasures are the purest. Asking questions is not the road to happiness. Pleasure and truth are not often matchmates."

"Then why walk that road?"

"Because there are more kinds of emptiness than the kind that pleasure fills," he said. "The emptiness in a body when the spirit is gone. The emptiness in a house when a child is away. The emptiness in a mind when a memory is beyond reclaiming. The emptiness of a journey without a destination."

I knew he spoke of Ana, not of himself, and pretended I understood, but I will not pretend it to you, for the truth was I did not. But before I left, I asked a favor of Kedar, not knowing the size of what I asked. And I went home with Tonit's journal, which I read that night, wanting to know what road Kedar was walking, and so took my first small steps on it myself.

As the days fled, Meli grew round with the child who would become Chane. Being the youngest in my house, I had never witnessed my own mother's transformation, and I marveled as the blessing unfolded. The spark had come from Kawa, through me—the substance came from Meli, through Ana. My pride in the first was surpassed by my wonder at the last.

Nor was I the only one to take interest in Meli's progress. When the quickening arrived, Fas and Meli's mother Ji both appeared for the ritual and pronouncement. I surprised Meli with a warding stick, to protect her and the child through the final quarter. The stick was jeweled with two pebble-sized fragments of ruby spinelle, which I cadged from a miner in barter.

In acquiring those bits of jewel, I descended for the first time to what some around me seemed to do casually—using my share task for advantage. The Voice denounces barter as a corruption of the share system, but it seems that only the greedy or the dishonest are ever punished for it. Food and crafts trade freely over lot walls, toys and pretties in the streets, totems and magicks through the dan. Rare is the man or woman who fails to master at least one of the six common arts.

Fas placed great value in my doing so. She told my brother and me that there's a magic in making things which is a fragment of the magic in Ana's blessing, and that that fragment is as necessary to men as the blessing is to women. This was why, she said, the fields and the sewing houses and the weaving barns, the building of Ana's own body in brick and stone, are reserved to men. There was wisdom in that, I think.

She told us, too, that gifts can soften a woman's eyes on us, which I have found a useful thing to know. And she reminded us that someday we would be grateful for the skill to make an artful gift for a woman we had given our spark. These were all good reasons, and both Eral and I invested many hours in our chosen arts.

But women pursue the same skills, if for different reasons. The common arts make beautiful what is plain, or make useful what is useless. Nothing worn or broken is ever discarded, except by those who have never learned to see the value which remains in them. There are waste wagons, to be sure, but they fill slowly, and are misnamed, for those wagons are brought back to the trustee of material supply for harvesting. Only those who want for nothing can afford to be careless with small treasures.

So nearly everyone, man and woman, learns to make something which might be bartered—to find and polish stone, to make toys and throws from rags, to weave basketwork from the yield of one's own lot, to brighten walls and faces with color, to take a simple share-garment and turn it into festival garb.

That, or they learn not to want what others make.

There was not much I had ever wanted before Meli favored me, except a woman. For Meli, though, I wanted everything.

But trading on your share work is a more serious matter than bartering in the common arts. Abuse of public trust is one of the named crimes which can put a man in the hands of the captain of executions. Even so, it remains a sore temptation, especially for those working in the share barns or on the wagons, where theft and misdirection are both easily achieved.

I did not do much for the gems for Meli's ward—merely parted with a small etching tool of little use to me but valuable to the miner who craved it for his stonework. I reported the tool lost, and in time I received another. But still, I crossed a line.

And Meli flourished.

But I was unable to mark Baral's progress in the same way. She withdrew from me as though the blessing of the grand tremor had been only my imagining, refusing my visits and curiosity. Finally she found a way to move to another hostel, at the north edge of the cluster, to wait out her middle quarters. I was not welcome at the quickening ritual, nor told later what house she had been given.

I would have made Baral a ward and a fine striker as well, but it was clear by then that she would refuse them.

Fas said once that I would find some women viewed a man as a necessary evil, a child as an annoying obligation—the house and the share that came with it mattered to them more than either.

Later I learned that there are ways to refuse the blessing, and many women who risk them. The dan traffic in bits of copper drawn into wire—precious like all metal, of course, but powerful, being an element of the bell bronze. It is said that a bit of copper placed in a woman's body by a dan who understands the magic will draw off the spark, and they will not conceive.

I have learned that some few go even further. There are women who disfigure their faces so they will not be called on, even if they become danera, open to all. There are even women who take their marks as men and live the life of a man, even to becoming the favored of another woman.

But all I knew then was this: Baral wanted the blessing I gave her far more than she wanted me.

If I had known how quickly the world was to change, I would have locked its form in my memory. If I had known how much I was to forget, I would have begun to tell this story sooner.

Somewhere in the time it took Meli to grow our child, I closed out my own childhood. It was, I thought, a transformation as profound as that I saw in Meli. But my transformation was invisible to nearly everyone but me. And when it was noticed, it was misunderstood, and ridiculed.

It began in my circle. Through Gowon's death, I had lost my mentor. Through Gadi's ill humor and resentment, I had acquired an enemy. Gadi was ever fair in assignments, fearing my connections, but what he said against me when I was not there cost me standing. And when Gowon died, I did not move up in the stalls—the reason given that I had fallen behind the others because Gowon had been too sick to teach me.

But I also lost standing because I was being pulled down other roads. There is little enough unclaimed time for a man working a sweat share, and I divided what there was between Meli and Kedar. Meli's share was the evening (and the night, for as many quarters as she and her sparking allowed it). I brought to her now the gossip that I collected on my calls, favoring her company above all others.

If it had only been Meli who took me away from them, they would have accepted it. But I gave Kedar the balance, the odd free day and the occasional evening call to his house. And I heard cutting talk about that, much of which I blamed on Gadi. Some said I had two lovers, but couldn't decide whether I liked taking or giving the spark best. Some said I had become Kedar's hand-servant, or his child.

None of that was true. Instead, I saw myself becoming his friend. And the harsher those I had once called friends were, the more clear to me that became.

I was changing, and I did not know who was most to blame. I was no longer amused by the old entertainments, and the circle was not amused by my new ones. I had lost most of my interest in running the streets, and all of my interest in playing scout to their conqueror, giving away my finds.

Instead, I wanted to talk about my readings, and ask the older men what they had seen of time. My curiosity about how things worked took a poor second place to new curiosities about why and who and when.

Consider—once, Meli and I spent my liberty day constructing rosters of our lines, taking names from memory and memorial, harrying the dan with questions.

Meli was Boroche, whose aspect is tenacity, a vigorous line. I remember that her list nearly doubled mine, and not only for a sharper memory. And I remember that I was silently ashamed. Absurd, yes? But I was caught in a curiosity I could not resist, to know the names of my mother's mother's mother, and all of the children whose blood I shared.

And consider—one evening, hearing the birthings called, I began to wonder again on the vanished apocryphals. I vowed to build a list, and over the next many days added every mark I saw or heard spoken of—the Dhole, the Amur, the Gaur, the

Oribi, and all the rest. I had always been aware of the women, whose marks color their walls and their clothing, but less so of the men, whose marks only color their own wrists. The list grew, but not quickly. I had tallied barely a hundred before additions became rare.

All this was still in my mind at the next festival run, which was captured by a man of the Thamin, a line unfamiliar to me. I thought on how the festival runs served us, how many women's minds were changed by the cachet of victory, how many lines had suffered because their men were too slow-footed to earn such advantage. I had been rejected by women who held themselves or their marks higher. If the Genet had triumphed, how would I have used the advantage? I did not know, because the Genet had never triumphed since my marking.

Watching the celebrants, I next wondered how many Thamin there were to enjoy being favored under the sixth bell, and made a promise to myself to tally the births four quarters hence. The tally seemed such a fine idea I could not wait, and asked the temple prefect at Cor-Agama what marks had been favored under Ubela, under Puli, under Apos, back through a year of festivals, back as far as he knew. And so my simple list became a census.

There was no one in the circle I could speak with of these things. To mention them would only have brought more blood words. And these were the least offensive of my thoughts, the ones I could share with Meli. The others—do you know the discomfort of a secret kept not because you are ashamed, but because you know the person you keep it from will, in their ignorance, judge you harshly?

Meli would have thought me corrupted by Kedar's example. I would rather say that I was enlightened by it.

Unspoken thoughts—I learned from Kedar that conformity was not an unalloyed good. Sometimes it could or even should be sacrificed to good cause. Hence rules were artifacts of convenience. Hence traditions could be challenged. This was an awakening, an awakening as profound as the recognition of change which came from reading Tonit's journal.

His Ana was hard at work on the Second Hundred, and struggling with a shortage of food—it seemed he was a greenhand, for he knew many details of the problems. The temples did not seem as honored in his time, for he never once spoke of them, though he recorded three tremors which, by his description, must surely have made Anadan-Kawadon sing. His Ana bustled at night, and slept

in the day. He wrote often of death. His language alone testified to
change, as there were many words I did not know—some which I
could guess at, and others I could not.

In glimpses and fragments, Tonit introduced me to an Ana
both recognizable as and distinct from Ana as I knew her. And
that was both unsettling and exciting. The fixity of things offers
great security. But when fixity dissolves, we are left to stagger
between hope and fear. So long as the bread comes each day,
how many would risk going hungry for the chance of something
better? How many had sold their curiosity for security?

These felt like dangerous ideas, and so I hid myself from my
circle, and even from Meli. Doing so was miserable, embittering.
I had once been free with my words, freer than almost anyone,
freer than wisdom would dictate—but I could no longer be. It
must have seemed to my circle that I went silent on them.

But I could not stay silent.

You knew Kedar, so perhaps you understand. I would despair
of explaining him to one who had never met him. How he never
spoke all that he thought, and yet did not seem a secretive man.
How he always left room for dissent, but so often took away your
reason. How his passions sometimes saddened him, but somehow
never made him impatient. How he embraced uncertainty as a
challenge, and the unknown as an opportunity.

In all of Ana, the only place I felt safe not only thinking
dangerous thoughts, but speaking them, was in Kedar's company.
Even had I owned every hand-bound and journal I went there to
borrow, even had his students closed me out as a stranger, even
had Kedar been as cold and closed as Gadi, I would have still
been drawn back to the archive house.

And I was neither the first nor the only one.

Any evening, I could expect to find young men from the honor
school in the yard and the archives. There were heavy shades over
the archive room's windows, and the students stayed late into the
night, working under the lamp I had installed.

The first time I discovered them there, they were turning the
white floor of the uproom into a great map of Ana. The ladder hole
was at the city's center, and I stood there on the high rungs like
some monstrous entity rising from Kawa as they crawled around
me clutching scratch slates in their hands and marking pins in
their teeth.

"What is it?" I asked. "What are you doing?"

"Building a clock," one said, sitting up on his heels. "Where do you live?"

"Agama," I said.

He looked across the map. "We need more samples from Agama. Does your mother's house have a memorial?"

"Yes."

"Can you write?"

"Of course."

"Will you write down the generations from her memorial and bring the transcription with you when you come back?"

"What do you want with it?"

He looked at me with puzzlement and said, before turning back to his work, "The memorials are the only clock that's been running since the founding."

And then I understood why the questions Kedar had asked that day on the roof *did* matter. He was searching for a clock in Ana's bones with which to calibrate the clock in Ana's flesh. The students could not correlate histories, for there were no histories to correlate—our metaphor is the circle, not the line.

How ambitious they were. I admired them. And I brought them back transcriptions from seventeen houses scattered through Agama's rings. I do not know how much I helped them. But when the committee on origins made their report, I felt as though I was part of their work, and I trusted what they told me more for having brought to them part of what they needed.

There were other committees which gathered on other nights— a committee on explorations, questing after the boundaries of the world—a committee on spirituality, debating the lineage of green growth and whether plants could be said to be alive—a committee on technologies, obsessed with a foolish quest to build a boat of the air.

They had too few hands and too many tasks, but they were also on fire, too earnestly foolish to be daunted. Kedar's students had already completed a census of the lines of the apocryphals—and I felt pride to have shared the same curiosity. But my effort was a feeble one beside theirs. I paged through their census of surviving lines—five hundred twenty-three, in those days—torn between grief for the lost members of the two thousand and amazement at the invisible dimensions of Ana.

Kedar did not make much of introductions, so I often saw the same face several times before learning the owner's name. I thought perhaps that was because an introduction would require

him to explain me, and he preferred not to. Even so, the students
did not seem to know what to make of me, and I wondered if they
talked about me when I was gone. But I clung to the pretense that
we were equals, and that I belonged.

Whether I belonged or not, Kedar quietly made me feel welcome. And when there was time, he offered me more.

"How goes Meli's sparking?" he asked one time as we looked
through the archives together. I remember I was there in mid-day,
a liberty day, for Meli had driven me off as an annoyance. "Does
she still receive you?"

The truth was she did not—plagued by disgorgement in her
first quarters, she now seemed condemned to spend her last
quarters bloated, aching, and perpetually weary. She accepted
my closeness and my caresses on her back and swelling belly,
but no more than that, the pleasure not being worth the discomfort.
And having fallen out of my old habits, I had nowhere else to go.
But I told him little of this.

"Do you want to run with me?" he asked, and I confess I
wondered what he wanted of me. We were not lovers, though
such pairings are said to increase the vigor of a line. I thought
perhaps I was about to learn the reason for his long kindness.

But my legs and lungs missed the joy of the twilight air and
the freedom of the streets, and I knew that a hard run would burn
away the restlessness that had grasp of me. So we went running
together, Kedar and I, through the pale-walled flood rings of Alte,
onto the ring road and across the Five-Ring Bridge, and into the
neighborhoods of the north city. He led, wordlessly but with
apparent purpose, and I followed, the hard breath in my chest
driving out most misgiving.

I had misjudged him, though. He left me in Bathek, in the
company of a woman of the Gaviid, dark-haired, droop-breasted,
sultry-mouthed, exquisite. I confess I was surprised when she
called us to her wall, and more surprised when it was Kedar who
went on alone. I wondered after if Kedar knew her, or had known
her, and where he had spent his night, half suspecting that he had
turned and gone back to the archive house, his purpose met.

Had I let Kedar hear my unhappiness? He would never say, for
he did not do things to be thanked for them. But I thanked the
woman of the Gaviid, with joy and vigor.

Forgive me if irrelevant thoughts catch and distract me. Recent
days have stirred many old memories.

I kept edging closer to the life of the archive house, but I did not share fully in it until I was finally admitted to the discussion salons. That first happened not long after Kedar and I first ran together, and it was the night the committee on origins offered its report.

Even now, I am not sure why I was invited—because I had proven myself to them somehow, or because I had shown interest in the subject, or because that night it was Rida who was hosting, or because Kedar wanted me there. Or perhaps it was merely an accident of familiarity—no, they would not have been that careless.

For the salons had been going on for some time, invisible to me. They predated the committees, the archive house—in truth, were the genesis of both. It was explained to me that the salons began as informal gatherings where students argued questions not considered germane to their formal studies. They became private salons when certain instructors took exception to the challenge. And they moved off the high bank completely when banned by Kedar's predecessor—whose late conversion to canonical strictness was not enough to preserve his position.

It amuses me still to think that the councilors then turned to Kedar to restore order.

And order he gave them, on the high bank. But elsewhere, the salons not only survived the ban, but flourished, meeting in secret in private spaces, keeping a carefully irregular schedule, the strongest of the groups transcending mere talk. They became a shadow school, the school of the unknown and the unthinkable, proud outlaws.

I heard things said in salons that I'd never heard before, and have never heard since. But none has stayed with me more clearly than the first time.

The room was too crowded by half, for no one had wanted to miss the report from the committee, and the salon's usual numbers were swollen by the presence of liaisons from several other salons, a surprising scattering of women, including Rida, and me. I found a patch of floor in an out-of-the way corner and rendered myself invisible, a spectator, as Rothe and Lenn presented their conclusions.

In thousands of nights of labor, they had woven together the fabric of Ana's lineage, and they laid it out before us, rent and tattered, but whole. This cluster could not be younger than so many generations, this cluster could not be *older* than so many.

This event, recorded here and here, ties the two together. Inside this line, all houses are built on this plan. Outside this line, all houses lack this quality.

The weave was uneven and fragile, but the pattern of the hanging was clear. It fell to Rothe to name the pattern aloud.

"Ana spreads across Taurin like the ripples from a pebble dropped in water," he told us. "But who dropped the pebble, and what was its shape, and how long ago did it fall?

"The first two questions are still beyond answering. But for the last, we finally have an answer.

"We are in the fifth age of the great plan. So the hierarchy and the prefect of information tell us, and that suffices for most. But for those who prefer their truth with a sharper edge, attend—by our tabulation, we are in the two thousand and eighty-fifth year since the pebble fell. This Ana herself tells us."

Rothe made the pronouncement with a grand solemnity, but, even so, the rest of the salon did not seem as surprised as I at his words. There was no outcry, no sharply taken breaths—only thoughtful nods and affirmative murmurs. Perhaps I ought not to have been surprised either, for Kedar had forewarned me, the day we met. How old is Ana? Only Ana knows—

But in the sweat shares, we were reminded often of the thousand-year plan, as goal and goad. It was the one arrow of purpose which cut across the turn of the festival cycle. Five hundred rings, one thousand years, one million blessed.

The count of years Rothe had given was far too large to credit. We were in the fifth age, building the Fifth Hundred. What we all knew could not be so wrong. Ana could not be two millennia old.

Still, only a single voice cut through the murmurs to say to Rothe, "I challenge the center."

I thought for a moment it was my voice, for the words were in my mind. But it was a tow-haired youth sitting in the first rank across the room. He was a stranger to me, a liaison from another salon.

"What do you question, Lasche?" Lenn asked, turning toward him. "Method or conclusion?"

"I question the meaning," he said, standing. "Have we so lately learned to count? Are we to place greater trust in your hindsight tally than in the tally of our fathers in an unbroken line, who needed no mathematics more subtle than the wit to add one to the sum each time Eki rang? Surely you don't argue that was beyond them."

"If the unbroken line were here for us to question, I would give its testimony great weight," Lenn said. "But we have only the word of their children, our mothers, twenty or fifty or a hundred generations removed. We know only what we were taught. We do not know that we were taught the truth, or that those who taught us were taught the truth themselves. Deceit and error both are invisible to the trusting."

"Have you presented this to the trustee of records? What says he? Surely he would be more concerned to know the *truth* than anyone."

"The trustee of records rejects revisionism," Kedar said. "He will not consider the evidence you have heard tonight."

"There," said Lasche. "What more proof do you need? The error is clearly yours, Rothe—if we can discount deceit."

Rida stepped forward then, placing herself between them. Her best virtues were all hidden to the eye, and so she was not the sort who stirred men to envy of Kedar. But I liked her, and I always listened when she spoke.

"Lasche, Lenn takes too dark a view of his discovery. And you make too tenacious a defense of your preconceptions. Ask yourself—does a child remember its own beginning?" She looked around the circle. "How many of you can remember if you cried at night, the shape and taste of your mother's breast, the names you gave your favorite toys, what frightened you and broke your heart? Could any of you have said on your own account who sparked you? There are no memories before there are words to shape them.

"Ana is such a child, and her memories as suspect as the products of a child's imagination. Perhaps the thousand-year plan fixes an event other than the founding—perhaps the last change in the festival calendar. A partial truth deceives as well as a lie."

"Why, the exarch himself speaks of the thousand-year plan," Lasche said. "Do you call the exarch a liar?"

"No," Rida said. "But he is not beyond being deceived by ignorance."

"I *do* call him a liar," said Rothe, breaking his silence to reclaim the center. "The words of the exarch are lies. Look at what's before us—the 'truth' halves our history—"

"To hide what?" Lasche made the question a sneer.

"At least you consider it a question worth asking," Rothe said, and looked at Kedar. "I will not pretend to certainty. But I fear the lies are meant to hide that we are dying. To conceal that our 'progress' is from strength toward weakness."

"Nonsense," Lasche said, but many others nodded and called out their approval. I was too astonished to make any response.

Deaf to the approval, Rothe answered the one objector. "Who cannot see how much has been lost? Do any of you deny that the old things are the best? That we hardly understand our tools well enough to keep them in repair, much less to make new ones? The chemists tend their vats in ignorance of the recipe.

"And all this goes unexamined, while we willingly aid in our own amnesia. We raise memorials to metaphors and metaphysicals, while we burn our mothers' bones for reunion and scatter the possessions of the dead. We hold hands and turn the slow circle with our backs to the world, clinging to a promise of transformation, never daring to look over our shoulders."

I will never forget his face, the passion and the pain in his eyes. "I will not accept that any longer," Rothe said. "I will know the truth, even if it burns me. I reject the lies and the liars—better no answer than a false one. I deny my mark, my line, and the spark of Kawa as delusions. Life comes only from life. I am the child of my mother and my own will. And I want to know what came before the beginning."

That was the beginning of the origin heresy, and I was glad to have been a witness. But I wish I had not been witness, later, to how the truth did burn him, and many others too.

Meli gave birth to Chane under Jineha, and Baral to a daughter, I was told, on the festival of Ixozacu. To her surprise and delight, Meli was given a house in the Third Hundred, in Liu Cluster, half around by the spoke road. And when I joined her there I found myself leaving behind not only Agama but the toolman's cart as well—I was apprenticed instead to the repairman of one of the cleaning barns. It was no softer work and the gearing of the thrashers no place to be careless, but it took me indoors, out of the sun, and even offered occasional moments of idleness.

How much of that was due to Kedar's favors, I do not know and did not ask. But in moving closer to him, I was drawn more deeply into his life. I became a regular at the salons, and even grew brave enough to speak my mind in that company. Kedar and I became a familiar sight together in the streets, for we ran even when neither of us was of a mind to heed or seek a soft-voiced invitation. We ran the roads for the blood-clarity and the vigor of our limbs, and for each other's company.

I knew more happiness in Chane's first year than in all the days before it.

And only once did I weaken and take myself back to Agama and past Baral's house, hoping to see her with her child, to find my daughter crawling in the yard, nursing in Baral's arms, crying, burbling, smiling. But Baral was closed away inside in the twilight time, content, apparently, with the child she had.

A dan who had known them both told me, years later, that my daughter favored Fas. But by then, the proof of my eyes had escaped me, for my daughter was the first of six innocents who would not survive their first festival year in Baral's indifferent care.

5

Apos: The Third Bell

Sachi woke with a start to find herself alone in Meer's narrow bed, and the padding cool beside her. Gathering the thin blanket about her bare shoulders, she moved to the doorway to peer out into the downroom. On the facing wall, the glowing white eye of the receiver of the Voice stared blankly back at her.

"Meer?" she called tentatively. No reply came, but she drew the blanket more tightly around her to fight off the chill that did.

A few soft but hurried steps took her to the doorways of the other mods, but did not produce Meer. She fought down alarm—what could have happened to him without her being awakened?

But the visitation by the exile was not far from her mind. Meer had been away for days, and loath to stay in the workhouse when he finally reappeared. He would not say much about that encounter beyond extracting a vow of silence from her, but she did not need his help to invent fears.

The visitor belonged to the world, not the city. What bargain had it made with the apocryphals to survive there, and what powers had it gained in the exchange? The visitor had entered Ana at the height of the day, boldly walking the streets as though invisible. Who was to say it could not numb her senses with a touch and spirit Meer away with a thought?

With shaky courage, she forced herself to call his name more loudly.

"Here," came the subdued answer.

Chiding her racing heart, Sachi followed his voice outside into the yard. She found Meer stretched out on his back on the ground, gazing up into the black branches of a spiny cypress, and came to crouch near him, tented in her blanket.

"You can't sleep?"

He did not look at her. "I found myself wondering what it would be like to sleep outside."

"And what did you find out?"

"That it's no easier to close my eyes out here than in there tonight," he said, and reached for her hand. "And that the ground is harder than my bed."

"And lonelier. Come back in. I'm awake now, too—"

"Not yet," he said. "I was trying to pretend Ana was gone, to imagine myself in a world of nothing—no roads, no houses, no green growth, no people, nothing but the coarse skin of Taurin under me and the sky overhead."

The darkness masked the puzzlement on her face, but not in her voice. "What is Taurin?"

He was slow to answer. "A name for the part of the world which is not Ana."

She shuddered as another chill coursed through her. "A world of nothing is beyond imagining."

Meer shook his head. "That's all that was here, in the beginning. Where this house stands now, and all its neighbors, and the spoke roads, the green rings, the water runs, the plaza—the day before the first of us appeared, this land was as barren as any land outside the boundary."

"Do you have to talk of such things?"

"Yes," he said. "I think tonight I do. But I can talk as easily to myself. Go back to bed if you do not wish to hear."

She said nothing, but did not move to leave. Soon, his grip tightened on her hand.

"Sachi, I don't want to start this journey."

"I don't want you to," she said. "I don't understand what's happening. You disappear as though you don't care about me, and then this afternoon you *had* to be with me—so you can tell me you're going away again. You want me to keep secrets for you, but you tell me it's dangerous for me to know why I have to be careful. What am I to think? What am I supposed to do?"

"I'm sorry," he said. "I know I have been unfair. But I could not bear to leave without at least one friend knowing where I've gone."

"Doesn't Huyana know?"

He shook his head. "I hope to be back before she misses me. With luck, these last ten days will have made her weary enough of me to assure it."

"You haven't told her?"

"I have told no one else what I have told you."

Sachi was silent for a long moment. "Thank you," she said at last. "That means something. But today's been so hurried—can't you give us another day? Because you know I *will* miss you."

"I've delayed as long as I dare," Meer said. "Oran sent me a reminder this morning, expressing his impatience—may his skin swell with pustules in his sleep."

"You have not learned the lesson," she said.

"What do you mean?"

"When you have no choice, there is no purpose in complaints," Sachi said. "You do what you must do, with as much good spirit as you can pretend."

He turned toward her and propped his head up on one elbow. "Is that what happens with me under the blankets? Is that what it means to be danera?"

"No," she said. "Just something we learn being."

To her surprise, he smiled. " 'The wisdom of the dan, the allure of the danera.' I never have thought it divided up quite that neatly."

"Simple answers satisfy small minds," she said, and kissed his forehead. "Come back to me, Meer."

"I have been promised that this trip is more distasteful than dangerous. So Oran insists, in any event." He struggled to a sitting position. "I'll come back."

"Shall I come with you to the dock tomorrow?"

"No," he said. "Someone from the exarch will be there, if not the exarch himself. I don't want them to know that you know."

"You sound more afraid of Oran than of the exiles."

"Of course," he said. "If that weren't so, I wouldn't be going."

"You said Kedar was a friend."

"He was. But that only flavors the decision—it did not settle it."

She regarded him curiously, in a way that made him uncomfortable. "I'm cold," she said at last. "I want to go inside. Will you come, so we can warm each other?"

"There's one more thing I have to ask—"

"What?"

"If Oran is wrong, if I don't return—will you tell Chane?"

She frowned. "It didn't take you long to taint the promise of your return," she said. "Will the little I can tell him do him any good?"

"Enough for him to tell the difference between an accident and an abandonment."

"How long do I wait?"

The question confounded him. "I don't know. Until you're sure."

They went inside together and settled into a familiar and comfortable lie, Sachi cradled back to front in his embracing arms, the blanket anchored by his feet and drawn snugly around them. She rubbed her softness against him, warming them both and hoping to coax a response from him. But his caresses were desultory at best, and she did not press the issue.

"What are you thinking about now?" she asked.

"Remembering," he murmured into her hair.

"Remembering what?"

"Little things," he said. "He asked me what dreams I dreamed, but never told me his."

"Then he was a voyeur."

"No," he said. "You don't understand. He needed us, but he gave us more than he took from us. It's just that some things went unfinished." He fell silent, but she waited, sensing he had more to say. When it came, it was said with pain. "He told me life should be ecstasy, but he never told me how to make it so."

"Meer, he died in Edera," she said with little sympathy. "He had no answer himself."

The scouts' dock below the bridge-dam at the eighteenth ring was much smaller than the busy dock above the dam, where Meer had reported for instruction—evidence that the bulk of the scouts' work was upstream, not down. Just two of the tan-canopied flat-bottomed scout boats were moored stern-in along the single short quay. And there was no supply and repair barn, only a small storage shell backing up the one-man shelter.

With measured steps, Meer stumped down the steep ramp leading to Kawa. The close-fitting scout clothing he'd been given was stiff and suffocating. It promised to chafe until softened by sunsweat, and then to cling to his raw skin. But no one wore a manteau on the river; he had been forbidden even to bring his own clothes along.

The shelter was empty, and the quay deserted except for a man in maintenance togs fussing with the rear collector of one of the boats. As Meer neared, the man came down from his step-stool and turned toward him, revealing the mark of the syndic of public safety on the sleeve of his blouse.

"Order of assignment?"

Meer dug into his shoulder pocket and produced the document. Giving it a cursory glance, the man brushed past Meer and went to the sentry post. When the document returned to Meer's hands, the mark of the syndic was stamped on the reverse.

"Take this one," the sentry said, nodding at the near boat. Then he climbed back up the step-stool by the far boat and resumed his work, ignoring Meer.

"Is it all loaded?"

"It is, with a standard ten-day kit."

Meer looked up the ramp to the top of the bank, but saw no one. Tentatively, he clambered aboard, ducking under the canopy of canvas and cell glass and edging his way, hunched over, to the lockers in the bow. Only when he had a float belt securely strapped across his chest could he start trying not to notice that everything beneath his feet was moving.

Crouching, Meer looked up the ramp again, and again failed to find what he was seeking. "Hey," he called.

"Something wrong?"

"Has anyone been here this morning? Looking for me, I mean."

"Everyone's here who's going to be here," the sentry said, his face hidden from Meer by the canopy.

"No one's going with me," Meer said. "I was expecting some-one, that's all."

"I don't think you should be," the custodian said. "I was told it would be a quiet morning."

Meer stared. A quiet morning, of course—with one of Oran's trusted the only person to see him off.

"Right," Meer said, his mouth tight. "Get the lines for me, then—so you can get back to the high bank and report."

When the sentry started to move, Meer turned away and slipped into the low-slung center seat. While he waited, he busied himself by checking the gauges on both motors—the collector for the day motor, the canisters for the boost burner. When he heard the free ends of the ropes thump one after another onto the stern deck, he pushed both throttles forward angrily, and the little boat eased away from the quay.

"Don't be sharp with the gate captain," the sentry called after him. If he said anything more, it was lost in the staccato popping of the burner and the thrashing of the props.

One boat-length out from the dock, the current caught the bow and swung it downstream. A few moments later, the boat hit the turbulent outflow from the base of the dam and began to chop and roll, fighting its undulations.

His morning meal lurching and careening inside his belly, Meer throttled back on the boost throttle until the burner fell silent, and the boat settled comfortably into the flow of the river. His balance challenged by the insubstantiality below him, he had vomited twice during his training session above the dam, and did not wish to begin with a repeat of that embarrassment. It was a near thing, but studied concentration carried him past the critical moments without disaster.

By then, the river and the boat's whirring motor had carried him through the great bend, between the plaza and the high bank. Meer had planned to look up into the mouth of Anadan-Kawadon as he passed under the arch, to satisfy a curiosity about the contours of the great bell's striker. But he had been distracted, and with the canopy covering all but the pointed prow of the boat, he would have had to crawl out onto the lockers to have a good view—an act which would probably have undone his hard-won victory.

When I come back, he promised himself. I'll have another chance coming back.

He noted that, clear of the bend, the water was smooth and placid, and so he edged the day throttle higher. It would not do to burn fuel all the way down to Edera—he had been warned to conserve it for the return against the current—but now that he was finally on his way, there was no reason to take any slower pace than his stomach and the collectors could manage.

With languid grace, the city slid by on either side of Kawa, ring after ring of homes and finished streets, garden-fields and greenponds. Much of the time, what Meer could see of it was limited to the succession of water outlets from the channel roads, the walls of the riverfront lots, and the footbridges which shadowed the boat at intervals.

The sameness of it all defied his attempts to measure his progress. Meaningful landmarks were few. The first was when the last completed ring on the highland plain north of Kawa fell away behind him. The last bridge announced the boundary of the Fifth Hundred. Not long after, he passed the last ring on the south bank, a yellowish haze of dust marking where a work circle was raising a house a few dozen lots away from the river.

From that point on, the plains were table flat, and Meer's boat the tallest object in the landscape bounded by the rock walls of the distant scarps. He expected it would be so all the way to Edera. But the river gate at the boundary surprised him.

Childhood memories told him that the inland boundary was little more than a line on an architect's map, an old and eroded moundwall arcing across barren land, more symbol than substance. But the apparition which loomed up ahead of him was a far more emphatic territorial declaration.

At the river gate, a bridge spanned the river between two elevated mounds of earth, with watch stations on either bank and a snipers' hut above. As he drew nearer, Meer saw that a barrier net hung below the bridge, low and substantial enough to block a boat from passing. Not only did the gate command the river approach to Ana, but the high lookouts gave the garrison an excellent view for a long distance across the plains.

He counted a dozen sentries, and expected there were others he could not see. There was no mistaking that his arrival had drawn the sentries' attention. With spotters on the bridge shouting direction, a scout boat with a pilot and two stickmen put out from the foot of the south watch station and headed upstream to intercept him. Its night motor barking shrilly, the gatemen's boat circled behind Meer's and drew alongside, bumping gunwales. As it did, one of the stickmen leaped nimbly onto the deck behind Meer.

Meer started to turn in his seat, but the sentry's thumb-stick cracked down on Meer's shoulder with enough force to send a jolt of pain all the way down his arm. But even at that, it was a measured blow, a warning—the same stroke, with more force, would have shattered a collarbone.

"Face front. Steer toward the dock," the stickman ordered.

Meer complied, seething silently as the pain in his shoulder dulled to a throb.

A few boat-lengths from the dock, the stickman ordered him to still the motor, and the boat coasted to a soft collision with the banked-dirt quay. The sentry boat sandwiched it there while strong hands seized the canopy posts and then the tie lines.

"Out," said the stickman. "Present yourself to the gate captain."

Meer climbed gracelessly onto the quay. Two men were waiting for him there: a child-faced sentry with the musculature of a lifter, and an older man, round-shouldered and jowly, holding a hinge-bound black ledger in his crossed arms.

"I am Meer Faschen," he said. Drawing himself up with as much dignity as he could muster, he held up the embossed metal disk he had been holding in his palm long enough to turn it hot. "My pass is from Oran-rami Anadon, on whose business I leave the city."

The gate captain squinted at the pass, then flipped the cover of his ledger back and glanced down at it. "What business is that?"

Meer repeated the answer Oran had dictated to him: "A man of Ana lies dead in Edera. I go to bring him home."

"Present your order of assignment."

The paper changed hands, and the gate captain studied the stamps and certifications. He made a notation in his ledger, then returned the document to Meer. With a gesture in the air, he waved away the waiting stickman.

"Are you carrying any proscribed materials?"

"No, none," said Meer.

The question was only a formality, to allow them to convict him of treason if any were found. But as the gate captain made a further notation, Meer suddenly wondered if his lies had been exposed, if he had angered Oran more than he knew. Perhaps the reason Oran's man had been at the dock that morning was not merely to eliminate one more witness, but to see that Meer took the boat which had been prepared for him, with an ampoule of nats, a cylinder of seeds concealed where Meer would never notice them—

"Stand aside for the inspection," the gate captain said.

His anxiousness turning into impatience, Meer looked on from the shadow of the watch station as the inspection proceeded. Meer had expected Oran's shield to speed his passage, but all it seemed to do was excuse his own person from scrutiny. In fact, he was driven to wonder if, as Oran's envoy, he was being treated to a demonstration of the gate captain's diligent thoroughness.

With all deliberate speed, the sentry had emptied the boat's lockers, inspecting the seals on each of the several bundles which made up the kit of supplies. The seals were all intact, for Meer had been instructed not to open any of the parcels before crossing the boundary. Then, having stripped the lockers of their contents, the sentry knelt in the middle of the clutter he had created, peering into the empty spaces and patting blindly in the far recesses. The gate captain stood by, dutifully recording the inventory.

Meanwhile, the prospect of any threat more serious than having his provisions handled by strangers seemed to have disappeared. The stickmen had vanished, the sentry boat was tied up empty farther down the dock, and the spotters on the bridge had long since disappeared inside one or another of the buildings.

None of it quite made sense to Meer, who was struggling to decipher the culture of the gate garrison. His brusque reception pointed toward an unexpected antipathy between the scouts and the sentries, as though the sentries suspected the scouts were in league with the exiles.

He wondered what would happen if he stepped forward and asked, "Is all this really necessary?" in as peevish a voice as his silent thoughts employed. Would they throw the parcels onto the dock and tear them open, littering the dock with canisters of ethanol, bundles of food, clothing, and cutlery, searching for the contraband they were now certain he was carrying?

"Subject acted in a suspicious manner," the notation would read in the ledger, "and was detained for interrogation—"

Or was boredom the culprit? There must be little for the gate garrison to do, day in and day out. How often was their routine interrupted by a scurrying shape on the plains or a boat on the river? Surely the exiles posed no real threat—not equal to such precautions and defenses. Did the garrison ever even see their real enemy?

Opportunities for officiousness must be rare, Meer thought, since everyone seems to be relishing this one so much.

Or perhaps it was simply professional jealousy, with the scouts viewed as lucky but undeserving adventurers, the way Meer had resented the freedom enjoyed by his elder siblings. *If that's what this is, I'll gladly give my pass to any one of you eager for a taste of excitement.*

But, mindful of the warning, he bit down on his tongue and his thoughts until the demands of bureaucracy were finally satisfied, and his boat was restored to him.

"Ana preserve the exarch," the gate captain said as Meer boarded. The captain signaled to the sentries on the bridge, and the barrier net began to rise with a squeal.

And the exarch preserve me, Meer thought, lifting his hand in salute. He pushed the day throttle forward, then raised his hand to his shoulder, fingering the hard outline of the pass sealed in the pocket there as the boat glided out to midstream.

Fat drops of water dripping from the barrier net beat a tattoo on the canopy as Meer passed under the bridge. When the sound stopped, he knew he was clear of the gate, and outside the city for the second time in his life. But this time, he would not be able to take two daring steps into the unknown and then retreat. He suddenly felt alone and insubstantial, the only living thing in a dead world, a mote of dust swept out of the city's streets and toward the sea.

Swallowing foul acid, Meer pushed the day throttle to its limit, and water gurgled under the bow. He made himself not look back at the gate. Four days, he promised himself. I will see it again in four days.

The first surprise awaited him not far down the river—but it was impossible for Meer to say how far. Time could still be gauged by the transit of the sun, but Meer had no way to measure how much river he had traversed when he discovered that the dead lands were not dead, after all.

It was not a discovery which required great powers of perception on his part—in fact, it was a revelation he could hardly have missed. The first intimation came as he was looking downstream, keeping the boat in the center of the river, and realized that he was seeing a color in the distance he had not expected or seen for some time: a rich, dark green.

The illusion persisted until the haze-smeared dab of pigment acquired violet highlights and resolved into a ragged fringe of shiny-leaved stalks and branches growing up out of the low banks on either side of Kawa. It was almost as though the male essence of Taurin had dropped his mask to reveal a scruffy beard. Denial giving way to puzzlement, Meer throttled back the day motor and let the river's stately current carry the boat toward and then into the curious oasis.

There were few of the larger forms, the waxwood and bitterroot, the blue needle and sugar stalk, but everything Meer saw was familiar, from plot or vat or green ring. Nevertheless, this was no greenhand's planting—this was chaos. There was a rough-and-tumble disorder, a raw wildness, in the growth which caused it to strike Meer's eyes and sensibilities as a blight, an infection.

But why was it here?

An answer was not hard to find. How many thousands of days had Kawa been flowing through Ana, flooding the rings and filling the cisterns, wetting throats and roots? Kawa faithfully brought his blessing to Ana—and, it seemed, carried a piece of Ana's creative magic away with him as a reward. This was Kawa's little garden.

But there was a harder question hidden behind the first: Why had the shores been barren for so many miles outside the gate, closer to the source of the blessing?

Meer threw both throttles forward and brought the boat around against the current, scanning for a place on either bank where he could safely go ashore. Finally he spotted a muddy-looking stretch just downstream of a shallow and nearly dry side channel, and ran the boat aground in the muck. The bow line was just long enough to tie around a securely rooted tanbush.

There were no workpaths or walkpaths through the jumble, but it thinned dramatically a short distance away from the water's edge. A few paces beyond that, the feeble fringe of the green growth fell away to the barren landscape he had expected and grown accustomed to.

Meer paused on the bank to survey the mix of forms—there was even a cluster of violet-leaved succulents, heavy with sun-browned berries—and then made his way to the hard ground. He started west, parallel to the river, walking at first, then trotting, looking for the boundary between the wild and the barren banks.

When he reached that spot, it became clear that the boundary was an artificial one. The riverbanks had been cleared, presumably by scouts—he could still see the marks of their cutting tools, a few footprints, and the holes left by spike anchors and roots. The ground was coated by a brittle crust of small white crystals, as though the growth had been poisoned by a killing agent.

He peered in the direction of the gate, squinting against the sun. It was invisible to him, which he supposed meant that he was invisible to its sentries as well. They had, it seemed, diligently cleared the banks as far as they could see, and perhaps a little farther—to destroy, he supposed, any sheltering cover that might allow someone to approach the gate unnoticed.

But there was another, darker cast to Meer's discoveries, and he found his thoughts lingering there. The world beyond the five hundredth ring was dead, everyone knew—except it was not. So perhaps the scouts scoured the river's edge to preserve the lie that Ana's blessings were reserved for the faithful and obedient, to make sure that no one ever stood on the boundary of Ana and looked out to see what they might think a better place to live. A lie? No, a simplification, true-in-substance. Surely some, seeing what Meer was seeing, would misunderstand.

Envisioning the scout detail laboring to denude this patch of ground, suddenly Meer found words for the pattern which had escaped him earlier in the day. *Those men at the gate were afraid—as afraid of the people inside as the exiles outside.* The size of the river gate and its garrison, the precautions taken on both sides of it, reflected the dimensions of their fear, not the dimensions of the threat.

Then one more thought pressed in on him with a certainty he could not defend, but could not defy: that no one knew the dimensions of the threat, because this was as far as the scouts came down the river. *This* was the real boundary of Ana. Here was the limit of her reach—of Oran's power.

It was an absurd proposition, an unsupportable leap of logic. Oran had said Meer could accomplish this journey alone, as much as promising an uncomplicated sally. So, clearly, there was no reason the scouts could not go all the way to Edera, all the way to the sea, anytime they wanted, as often as they wanted, in whatever numbers they wanted.

But did they? There were any number of reasons why they might not, starting with fear—and ending with a desire to protect the illusions spun by other truths that everyone knew, but were not so.

Fighting his disquiet, Meer made his way back to the boat. At the fringe of what he had started to think of as the green line, he paused to squat and relieve himself, an awkward business even with the drop-bottom on the scout's trousers.

We fuel this city with our bodies. We sweeten the air with our breath, soften the ground with our bowels . . .

Tonit. Why had he thought of Tonit now?

Because of Kedar. The house of his mind was open to all manner of unwelcome and uninvited guests. What did it matter if the banks of Kawa were green? Who could be surprised to find that Ana's gift is a vigorous one? Where was the mystery in denying the enemy a hiding place?

He sank to his ankles in mud freeing the boat, and ended up dangling his feet over the side and dipping his foot wraps in the swirling water as the boat drifted downstream.

The question was not why, but why not. He would not infect himself with fear. He would not look at what lay ahead with eyes of fear—Huyana's eyes, Sachi's eyes, the gate captain's eyes. Another day on the river, and he would claim Kedar's corpse and return. Oran would have his symbolic triumph, and Kedar his reunion.

And then I can once again have my peace.

The long hours of late afternoon carried Meer a long way down the river, past green-tufted islands of mud barely larger than his boat, past distant land islands of bare and broken rock which would have dwarfed the largest house in Ana. He listened to the heartbeats of the boat and the water beneath it, dozed in the heat, and avoided contemplation of yesterday or tomorrow. If he could not discipline his thoughts, he could displace them, by staying locked in the present, instant to instant, sense and sensation.

The path of the sun split the sky as the river split the valley. As the pink-haloed disk dipped toward where Ana lay hidden by distance and haze, Meer grounded the boat on the soft, sandy mud of the north shore for the night. The solid ground felt reassuringly substantial to his legs, and he loped a thousand steps into the desert and back to stretch and satisfy them.

When he returned to the boat, he spread a ground blanket near a patch of mint grass a shout's distance from the boat, and ate a meal that was tasteless on his tongue. By then the twilight chill was settling. When he washed and stored his utensils, he retrieved the bundled sleep sleeve from the locker and tore its wrapper open.

Meer had planned to pass the night ashore, and began with that intention. It was safer not to stay with the boat, he was told, for the boat was more easily found.

But the darkness which blanketed the river and the land which flanked it did not feel benign. He lay on his back looking up at the faint dusting of stars and found them cold and unfamiliar. He listened to the sounds of the air caressing drooping leaves and heard a body moving among them. He listened to the tick and groan of the fast-cooling rock and heard footsteps moving across it.

This is their time, he thought. The apocryphals owned the night; the exiles borrowed it for their purposes. Meer could feel both of them close by, and could not close his eyes. He clutched a squeeze lamp in his right hand, but dared not use it. The stars reminded him of another night, breaking the discipline of his thoughts, but he could not look away.

Pulling the sleep sleeve higher and tighter around him, he fought off crazy impulses—to wander off into the calling darkness—to walk into Kawa until he vanished, and then breathe its essence in. His body jangled, inventing sounds in his ear, and moving shadows in his eyes.

Finally he could stand the silence and suspense no more, and swept up the blanket and the sleeve in his arms as he hurried recklessly back toward the boat. He curled up in the stern, shielded from the disquieting stars by the boat's canopy, and tried once more to sleep. He did not ask for the Genet to come to him, fearing to hear his own desperation.

But even sleep did not come. Meer's limbs hated the awkward angles, his back and shoulders the seams and ribs, his skin the clammy cold, and his ears the gurgling slap of tiny wavelets against the hull. He was alone in a ghost landscape of the unknown and the unreal, and he could not lower his guard. Though fatigue left his body shivering and his eyes burning, Meer huddled awake all night in a corner of the scout boat, hugging his knees to his chest, afraid to sleep, more afraid to dream.

6

Puli: The Fourth Bell

Early in Meer's second day on the river, Kawa's personality changed as a second river, nearly as large and swifter-moving, joined with it.

The new river came tumbling down out of a red-walled valley which cut through the southern facade at an angle to the northeast, its mouth invisible from Ana. With the help of the morning light, Meer had spotted the gap in the facade, and as he started downriver he had taken note of its changing profile—the gap gradually widening at first, then receding, as though he were peering through a doorway and seeing farther and farther into the room behind it.

But though he wondered on what he was seeing, there was no real clue to its meaning until the south bank abruptly fell away, to be replaced by flowing water. The strong new current elbowed Meer's boat toward the north bank as it merged with the old. Taken by surprise, Meer brought the boat about and pushed the day throttle to the maximum, hoping the whining motor would hold the boat in equilibrium at the river juncture.

The new river clearly had great vigor, unlike the dry or feeble tributary channels Meer had seen to that point. In fact, it seemed more the equal of Kawa than a tributary. Did it have its own name and spirit? How far into the facade did it pierce? Was it possible there could be a city straddling *its* shores, concealed from Ana by the south facade?

Surely the scouts had come at least this far, and made this same discovery. And having discovered the new river, surely they had gone on to explore it. How could they not? If there *was* another river spirit and another city, the scouts knew of it, and therefore so did the syndic of public security, and Oran-rami Anadon. If there *was* another city, then perhaps the fear at the gate had foundation, and the exiled of Ana had friends.

It was impossible. Could such a secret stay a secret? If the syndic were willing to kill his own scouts to keep it so? Then Meer's own life must be forfeit, once his mission was completed.

No—it could not be. A second city of the blessed would overturn the structure of everything, unless the city was the child of Ana. Even Oran could not kill fast enough to silence the tongues once such knowledge entered the body of Ana.

But perhaps the apocryphals had once had their own city, before they created their lines in their aspect, before they were banished. Perhaps it was there still, empty and silent, patiently awaiting their return—

With a head shake, Meer chided himself for his fears and fancies. There was no reason to believe that the unseen was any different than the seen. But like a silver-blue road across the southern plain, the new river still tugged at Meer's curiosity. If only he had a more generous supply of fuel at hand for the boost motor, he would have been impelled to explore at least part of its length.

But there was no way to realize his wish. His boat had been provisioned in such a way as to limit Meer's options to one—going directly to Edera and returning. So with a resentful reluctance, Meer finally eased back the day throttle, swung the bow back toward the east, and let the combined rivers carry him toward his appointment, acutely aware that there was no prospect he would ever be given a chance to return.

His thoughts lingered behind him, however, for even with fears and fancies in check, the new river upset many settled issues.

It was obvious to all that Kawa flowed through the center of the great valley for the same reason that rain ran from the rooftops to the street, that berries roll to the bottom of a bowl. It had never occurred to Meer to wonder if there were some more organic connection between the river and the valley, any more than he wondered where the water of Kawa came from, or why the sea did not fill and flood the valley.

But now he wondered why Kawa would see fit to extend his blessing to a barren valley, why Ana—Taurin—would build a cradle she did not mean to fill. Was the south river simply awaiting their future, awaiting the completion of the Fifth Hundred and the settling of new cities?

There was so much more to Taurin than the children of the apocryphals could use, than the apocryphals themselves could use. How many times Ana's entire compass had he come so far? Several times, at least, and more emptiness lay ahead. Was it all necessary to the promise? There had to be some purpose to this creation. Had something gone wrong? Were they meant to scatter themselves across the face of Taurin?

We stand in a circle with our backs to the world . . .

Meer pushed away the memory. *Kawa the eternal provider, Ana the eternal creator—I am losing the vision. Will we inherit all that is when we are eternal like you?*

Past the juncture of the two rivers, the banks of Kawa began to change, as though fortifying themselves to contain Kawa's swollen flow, becoming rockier and ultimately dead barren as they gradually rose above the water. Before long both banks were steep-sloped walls of reddish rock as high as the canopy of the scout boat. Pinched on either side, the river ran deeper and darker under the hull.

The rock walls turned the river into a natural sluice, a trench-like channel eerily reminiscent of the ringwalls of Ana and the first hours of the journey, and restricted Meer's range of vision to the river itself. It had been comforting to be able to see long distances in any direction, despite the irregular screen of foliage. But the new contours denied him any glimpse of the plains or the facades to the north or the south. The top of the bank was now as far as he could see, and he glanced nervously from one side to the other, feeling very much like a target.

It was as though Edera had its own river gate, and Meer was plunging headlong into it.

There was no place to stop, and so he took his mid-day meal on the water, and voided his wastes over the stern like some fresh-marked boy on an Anan bridge. Before long the banks began to rise still higher, until half the river was in shadow and Meer was forced to steer to the sunlit side.

The sound of the boat bounced back to his ear from the enclosing wall, now a mottled pink and gray with a dusting of orange. A trickling tributary joined Kawa as a white-spray waterfall cascading down the bank. Here and there a green spike or two poked up from a cliff-foot mound of scree the river had not managed to sweep away, but that seemed a miracle in such a cold and forbidding place.

The once-smooth surface of the water was carved by countless pitching, dancing wavelets, as the rock walls deflected and distorted the currents. And the river was running faster, fast enough that Meer risked turning the boat around just to reassure himself that the combined motors could make headway against the current.

Knowing that he still had a choice made it easier to go on, though the skin on the back of his neck still prickled, and he gripped the wheel of the boat so tightly his fingers turned a bloodless white. Fighting a tremulous stomach, he peered hopefully downriver, looking for the end of the corridor of stone.

Instead, he found that Edera's river gate had its own sentries. And when he realized what they were, he vomited, so suddenly and without warning that he splattered his hands and arms, and the boat's wheel and throttles.

Disgusted by his own weakness, gasping from the breath-stealing pain that knifed through his chest, Meer fought for control. He lost, doubling over and spewing the balance of his meal on the deck between his feet.

When he straightened up and wiped his mouth weakly with his sleeve, the fist of pain was still hot in the center of his chest. He cried, because there was no other way to release it, and cursed Kedar Nan for bringing him there.

For the sentries of Edera were gruesome corpses, looming over the river from the rock walls between which the water tumbled. In daunting and uncountable numbers, they hung from the vertical sides of the canyon like impossibly agile climbers, wedged into crevasses, sitting on precarious ledges with knees drawn up to their chests, draped over outthrusts.

Arrayed in the sun, wearing stiff shrunken masks of yellow-brown skin, the corpses stared down accusingly, or looked longingly toward Ana, or hung their heads between folded arms, hiding black pit eyes. A few had missing or misshapen limbs, like the unfinished dirt-doodles of a child. Most were naked, though scraps and tatters of cloth hung from some limbs, fluttering in the wind like shabby flags.

The river itself seemed to have grown solemnly quiet in respect. With shaking hand, Meer stilled the motor, letting the boat drift through the granite house of the dead. Without the intervention of the temples and the reunion pantrophs, the task of rendering the bodies had fallen to parched air, battering rain, and the unshielded sun. Meer could only guess at how long it would take such forces to reduce a man or woman to dust.

Shame vied with guilt as he swallowed bitterness again and again. There could be no other answer—the faces looking out from the cliffs were the faces of the disappeared, the martyrs of Kedar's truth movement, who lived just long enough to see their dreams hurled from the sky and their trust betrayed. Swept away like dirt from the streets, then raised up from the waters, their husks waited here in vain for reunion.

He could not look away, though he dreaded the prospect that he might somehow recognize the shrunken, empty shell of someone he had known. That he had known some of these sorry wretches was beyond doubt, even if he could not say which. The earnest faces from the discussion salons and Kedar's archive—the hopeful people of the plaza—had he smiled at that one, called this one Friend—

Who had gathered the bodies and conceived this grotesque display? No one from Ana, who was still *of* Ana, surely. Such a horrendous task—only the consuming purpose that comes with blind anger could account for it. There was anger here still. The corpses' existence was a harsh reproach, their display a deliberate obscenity.

It could only have been done by survivors, Meer thought— whatever few escaped the fate of these many.

And if any of them *still* survived, he would find them waiting in Edera.

Such were the people Oran had sent him to belittle and humiliate. Oran had laughed at them, and then dispatched Meer to make sure they heard the laughter.

It could not have taken two hundred heartbeats to pass the corpses, reach the end, but it seemed far longer, for in all that time it seemed to Meer that his heart did not beat at all.

Finally the boat moved on beyond the last of the corpses, and drifted wide through a bend. Ahead was sunlight and open land, the rock massif giving way at last to a table-flat plain, the river widening to a lake.

Meer ran the boat recklessly ashore and abandoned it, making no effort to secure it. He ran away from the river on unsteady legs, ripping off and flinging away his scout's garb piece by piece as he went, the float belt first, his trousers last, until he was naked, without sign or taint of Oran's world. He ran on in an antic madman's gait until the ache in his lungs escaped as a wail, and he flung himself face-down on the blistering ground, to hammer it with fists and forearms until the fury in him was spent.

Then he slowly sat up, eyes dry but chest heaving, and began to scrub himself with handfuls of grit and sand. He did not end his ablution until his skin was raw and the agony in his flesh had washed away at least some of the agony in his spirit.

Empty, sapped by the heat and the horror, he curled into a ball and surrendered consciousness, escaping into a sleep too deep for dreams.

Meer could not say what sense woke him, but he woke with a gut-fear start of alarm. The moment his mind cleared, he knew the horrible error he had made. Taurin's star could kill the unprotected in an afternoon, cripple in even less time. And he had fallen asleep naked in the open sun.

Too quickly, he jumped to his feet. In doing so, he learned that his exposed skin—shoulder, back, and buttocks—was already painfully sun-scalded. Sudden dizziness almost dropped him back to his knees.

Why aren't I dead?

His mind turning with painful slowness, Meer scanned his surroundings. No Edera. No exiles. No apocryphal benefactor to have roused him with a touch. Nothing but the dark face of the rock massif, rising nearly straight up from the plain, a dark-grained and dark-fissured curtain across the valley—

Dark! Meer realized he was no longer in the sun. Creeping east to claim territory the west-moving orb had abandoned, the shadow of the massif had stretched out to embrace where he had lain. Likely as not, it was the drop in temperature as the edge of the shadow passed which had made him stir.

A fool's luck—

But he had hardly escaped his foolishness without penalty. He was teetering on the verge of a sun faint. The burn he wore was savage, and would only grow worse in the hours ahead.

Taking his direction from the massif, he started back toward the boat at a shaky trot, and discovered his right foot cut and bruised by unremembered abuses, which rendered his steps lame and his pace halting. As he retraced his way, he collected his discarded possessions one by one, though he did not attempt to don his clothes.

To his relief, the boat was where he had left it, though the marks in the bank showed it had slid back a foot-length toward the water. If the current had coaxed the boat away from the shore—

Meer left the thought unfinished. Dropping the float belt on the ground by the bow, he walked tentatively into the river, until he was immersed to his waist, clenching his teeth and shivering as the water's sandpaper caress reached his burn. Clinging to the stern of the boat with one hand, he rinsed his soiled garments until all the foulness had drifted away on the current. Then he bent his head, washed his face in a double-handful of water, and retreated to the shore.

There were no spare garments in his kit, so Meer spread the wet clothing over the gunwales and canopy struts, where the breeze could suck the moisture from them. He dug through the supplies hopefully, and was rewarded with a small vial of skin salve. It eased the scald above his hip enough that he could tolerate strapping the float belt against his bare skin. A half-canister of water slaked his thirst for the moment.

Only then did he realize that, sometime since he had risen from what should have been his dying place, he had made the decision to go on. Edera was close, had to be close now. The corpses of the river had shamed his fear from him, allowing duty to call him forward. But he could not, would not go on for Oran, acting in his name. He could only go on for himself, and for Kedar Nan.

Thus resolved, and with his boat and himself both curiously bedecked, Meer pushed off, turned the boat east, and continued on to find the colony of exiles.

Unconfined by rock walls or even substantial banks, Kawa spread itself ever wider ahead of Meer. Shortly after emerging from the cut through the massif, Kawa had lost all of its riverness. Now, dwarfing even the reservoir lake behind the Twenty-Ring bridge-dam, Kawa cried out for another name.

Meer had never seen a body of water so large. From the placid waters along the north shore, the south shore was an undistinguishable line in the distance. He realized he would need to come back hugging that far shore to know what might be there, if he reached the end of the river without finding Edera—

if there was an end, and if he would know when he had reached
it.

Hour on hour, he scanned the land for any sign of habitation,
but found none. His clothing dried and he gingerly dressed, and
still the shore wound on. Meer began to wonder if he had already
entered the sea, and Edera lay somewhere behind him, perhaps
high in the rock above the skeleton sentries. Nothing had been
as Meer expected, and so he expected Edera to surprise him as
well. He trusted no myth or assurance.

But when the north shore at last began to curl southward,
pinching off the vast river-lake that Kawa had become, and the
flat soft land began to pick up a slight rise, Meer's attention and
anticipation were both renewed. Not long after, they were both
rewarded by a glimpse of a few rude walls at the crest of a slight
hill well back from the shore.

Near the water's edge, a single ancient scout boat rested at a
cant, half-submerged, its canopy torn, its collectors and fittings
gone. There was no pier or quay, so Meer tied his boat to the
immovable relic and walked ashore from there, sinking to his
ankles in the muck as he struggled through the patchy roundgrass
which grew in the shallows.

Once ashore, he touched Oran's medallion through the fabric
of the shoulder pocket, but left it there as he waited, looking up
the long slope toward the buildings. But no one came to meet him
or to stop him. He could see no movement on the hill, hear no
sound from the scene before him. He wondered if the exiles had
seen him long before and fled.

Swallowing, he started across the hardpan jigsaw of cracked,
sun-baked mud. "Hello," he called as he drew nearer, then resorted
to a runner's formal cant. "Hello, the house. May you be blessed.
I am here for Kedar Nan."

But there was no answer. And it was a gross exaggeration to
call any of the structures ahead of him a house. The nearest to
him was no more than a shoulder-high caked-earth south-facing
wall with a tattered woven awning staked down to form a sun-
shelter. If the awning had been intact, it might have protected
as many as five, but wind-tears had shredded it into a mere
fringe.

There were two other shelter-walls of the same sort; near one,
Meer found a cracked food platter and a few bits of metal which
might have been utensils. Only one structure had a hard roof: a
small square building half-sunken in the ground, with a steep

dome pierced by two light holes. Inside was a deep cistern, dry, the fragments of a dip bucket lying in the bottom, and two larders, both empty, capped by the locker doors from the wrecked scout boat.

Meer emerged into the daylight and surveyed the sorry encampment. Edera was, if anything, shabbier and sadder than he had imagined. Every sign said that the colony was long dead, and surely any sensible scout would have believed those signs—the final tableau of a pathetic tragedy. Meer himself would have been willing to believe, short days ago. The site fit both myth and logic—as far as possible from Ana without giving up Kawa, the highest point east of the massif, commanding all spokes of the circle as the arch did in Ana.

It was real, but it was wrong. Neither Kedar's message nor his messenger could have come from here.

Cautiously, Meer hiked the last few steps to the top of the rise. He half suspected he would find another Edera on the other side, out of sight from the river-lake, hiding behind the deception of the ruin.

His suspicion was baseless; there was no other Edera. But what Meer did see from the summit staggered him. Spread out before him was a panorama of restless, white-capped water stretching from the foot of the slope below him to the horizon, and spanning the limits of his vision to the north and south. How much farther it extended, he could not guess, but he could believe he was seeing not even the tenth part of the whole.

It made sense, at long last, that Kawa was Ana's consort. For the first time in his life, Meer saw them as equals.

Kawa-sea had a sound of its own, and a sleeping power, and when Meer could finally shake off his awe, he laughed at himself for thinking the river-lake behind him was something grand. The river was nothing more than a thread of Kawa's blessing laid upon the land. The end of the river was there in his sight, just south of his eyrie, the color of the water turning from dusty blue to deep green-blue as it flowed into the sea, the change as clear a division as a line drawn across a page.

No wonder they built here.

Meer sat on his heels on the summit and let the sound and sight and power flow into him to fill his empty places. And when he rose at last to leave, he thought that the memory and understanding he carried away was worth all the misery of the journey. For this alone, he would gladly endure it all again.

• • •

Distracted from his wariness, his gaze lowered to the ground at his feet, Meer started back down the hill toward the river's edge and his boat. He had crossed most of the way through the ruin before he raised his eyes enough to notice what looked like a great festival flag at the shoreline, mottled red and snapping in the breeze. Hovering beneath it was a dark shape, hazy and squirming in the hot air.

For a long moment, he could make no sense of what he was seeing. Then, abruptly, the equation resolved. The dark shape was his boat. The flag was the sail of another.

His heart already racing, Meer broke into a breakneck, joint-jolting run down the slope of the hill. His burns screamed at him as his clothing scoured them.

In a hundred strides, the shadow of motion became the silhouette of someone aboard his boat, looking in the lockers, looking over the controls. The trespasser's own boat was bobbing in the shallow water alongside, riding high on what appeared to be a hull made of inflated bladders.

"Hey!" Meer called.

The silhouette looked up, then gathered up two oblong shapes from the lockers and tossed them end over end into its own boat. No possible response could have surprised Meer more. The stranger was calmly, brazenly stealing Meer's supplies.

"Stop that!" Meer shouted, but astonishment stole some of the authority from the demand.

Two more shapes, canisters of fuel or water, traced a short arc through the air and landed silently in the bladder boat. Meer's feet pounded the cracked ground, but he was still too far away to make a threat he could enforce, and still too incredulous to unleash his full anger.

In long seconds, Meer halved the distance to the shore, and the silhouette acquired a face and an age—male, past marking but still a boy. The young pilot gave Meer no more than a sideways glance as he burrowed into the lockers once more and came up with a food pack. Tucking it under his arm, the boy leaped to his own boat just as Meer reached the water.

Grim-faced, Meer plunged into the river without slowing, as though by will alone he could run across the surface and snatch the youth from his craft. But after a few splashing steps, the water dragging at his legs and the mud grabbing at his ankles stole

Meer's balance, and he fell forward full-length into the water. He came up drenched and raging.

"Damn your staff! Who are you? What right do you have to steal from me?"

The pilot had pushed off hard from Meer's boat, and his bladder boat was now three lengths farther from shore. "You're from Ana," the young pilot said—accusation, challenge, and self-warning.

"I want it back, all of it." Meer thrashed his way into deeper water. "Damn you, I need that fuel to go home."

Looking back as he hauled hand over hand on a rope to raise the sail, the young pilot seemed more amused than worried. "Won't be going home, then."

Meer stared. "You arrogant— You don't know who I am."

The sail caught the breeze and puffed out, and the boat started to glide across the water toward the outlet to the sea. "Don't care. Once you die, you're nothing but shit on the ground."

Swallowing hard, Meer realized he had lost the race. The bladder boat was swift and nimble. By the time Meer could wade to the scout boat, climb aboard, and cast off, the thief would have a daunting lead—even if he had not crippled Meer's boat by cutting lines and wires. He could not catch the youth; he had to pull him back somehow.

"Is that all you think of Kedar Nan, then?" Meer shouted at the retreating boat and the back of its pilot.

There was no answer.

"Is that what Kedar has become here—one more husk to nail to the rocks?"

Still, there was no answer. But under the pilot's hand, the bladder boat turned slowly into a circle that brought it past where Meer stood hip-deep in the river.

"Your breath fouls his name," the pilot said, his hard gaze a black dagger. "Speak it again and I won't leave your death to Taurin."

"I'll shoulder that risk," Meer said, feeling the edge swing to him for the first time. "My name is Meer, of the mark of the Genet. I've come for my brother Kedar Nan. If you know, tell me where I can find him."

The youth spat in the water. "Not if I had to die myself to keep it from you."

"You still don't understand, do you? Why does Edera send its dim-witted children to scout for it?" Meer shook his head. "I was *asked* to come. I was Kedar's friend."

"Liar. Kedar Nan has no friends in Ana." But there was a hint of doubt in the young pilot's face.

"Or in Edera, it seems—if this is the way you respect his wishes there. Weren't you told to watch for me? Isn't that why you came to the old camp, because I was expected?"

But that guess was a miss, for the doubt vanished. "I come here to help friends and sabotage enemies," the pilot said defiantly.

Meer nodded. "Then prove you know the difference. Come, where is Kedar Nan? Don't compound your stupidity with stubbornness."

"He's in Edera," said the boy, his expression turning smug. "If you've come for him at his request, you must know how to find it."

The bladder boat was drifting away, and Meer's moment slipping away with it. He started to reach for the medallion in his shoulder pocket, but shook his head and crossed his arms over his chest instead.

"I take it back," he said in a softer tone. "You are not stupid—just full enough of fear to appear that way. It seems it's the same with all of you. Even Kedar's messenger was so afraid of my coming to Edera that he only told me what Kedar wanted, not how it could be done."

He raised his voice, so it would carry across the water to the red boat. "How sad that Kedar had to end his days surrounded by such cowardice. The Kedar I knew did not believe in living in fear, or in wasting oneself in hatred. He must have been miserable here in your company.

"Go, boy," Meer called, his tone pitying. "You have your petty trophies. Go brag of your victory, how you left Kedar Nan's friend to become shit on the ground. If that's the highest you can reach, I won't begrudge you such a tiny pleasure. I will die better than you've lived."

The young pilot stared for a long moment, gnawing his lower lip, then turned the sail to the breeze. The bladder boat skipped lightly away, and Meer resignedly watched it go. After a long moment, he turned away toward the scout boat, intent on boarding her and taking inventory of the damage. If the controls were intact, there might be a chance he could follow, if not catch, the thief.

As he clambered over the side, a shadow passed across the boat. Meer whirled to discover the red-sailed boat cutting close across the stern, the pilot holding the food pack high over his head. With a grunt, he hurled the pack toward Meer. It landed on the taut center canvas of the canopy, bounced, and rolled off the edge. With a lunge that almost took him over the side, Meer caught it before it could drop to the water. Clutching it, he stared wonderingly at the youth.

The pilot pointed north. "Follow the coast, then over the ridge to the valley of Epa-Daun," he called back to Meer. "I will let *them* kill you for a liar."

Meer twisted around to peer into the distance. He could not see the north facade. The coast plain merged into the horizon. "How far? How long will it take?"

"Three days for a healthy man. Five for a soft one like you."

"Wait," Meer said, turning back. "Does Epa-Daun meet the sea as Kawa does?"

"Yes."

"Then I can stay on the water. Lead me there."

The pilot shook his head. "Only a fool would run the coast in a river boat."

"Take me there in yours, then."

The pilot shook his head again. "You are too feeble to fear, Meer of the Genet," he called. "But I do not trust you that much."

With that, the youth turned away, opened his sail full to the breeze, and skimmed away across the water, taking away the choice to turn back and leaving little behind in return.

The controls of the scout boat proved undamaged, but all of the fuel stores were gone. All that remained was the canister already connected to the delivery line, and already half empty. Meer conceded unhappily to himself that he could not dare waste any of it, and gave up all thought of pursuing the red boat, which was soon out of sight.

Sitting in the bow, Meer wrestled with the question of how much *he* could trust the young pilot. As hard as Meer had worked for the reversal, he wondered if he could believe it. Was Edera truly to the north, or was that misdirection? Could it be reached by land, or was that a deadly invitation? Was his boat truly unsafe for the sea, or was that an attempt to trick Meer into abandoning it?

Every word could have been a lie, and the return of the food pack a clever purchase of credibility.

He could not go back, not past the beginning of Kawa-lake, and he was unwilling to stay where he was, where sleep might mean death. He had to go on.

And to go on, he had to choose a direction, and a means. He had to guess how much he could believe.

In the end, he chose to believe the one thing the pilot might have thought Meer already knew, and therefore would not have dared lie about. He would head north, and count on finding Edera somewhere past the horizon.

But if he set off on foot, surely the pilot or his kin would sink or steal the scout boat before Meer could return. What's more, the pilot would be able to give Edera several days warning of Meer's approach.

And if Meer did ever return to Ana, a corpse would be coming with him—but only if Meer still had a boat in which to carry it. He could not possibly pack Kedar's body overland.

The pilot had come by sea. Meer would go by sea, and he would sleep on the water, where only by luck could they find him in the dark.

Though he navigated his way through the mouth of the river and onto the dark-hued sea without incident, the seed of fear planted by the young pilot threatened to grow wild as Meer turned north to follow the coast to Edera.

Even where the sea looked quiet, it was always restless, surging, twisting under the hull, pushing the bow high or drawing it down, rocking the boat on its beam. And closer to the shore, the sea curled over and broke in rolling, tumbling lines that turned the water white and filled the air with a roaring sound. Even well out from the turbulence, gusts of wind blowing strong toward the shore shredded the crests of the swells into a white fringe that blew across Meer like rain.

Those same gusts caught the sun canopy like a sail, threatening to lay the boat over and let the sea rush in over the side. When Meer realized the danger, he turned into the wind and, half-standing, slashed at the canvas span between the collectors with his food knife until nothing was left but dangling ribbons. He settled back into his seat shuddering and queasy at the prospect of discovering how deep the sea ran beneath him.

Soon after, the pitch of the motor's whine began to rise and fall in step with the rocking of the boat, and the boat's forward motion became almost immeasurably sluggish. The collectors, tipping away from the low-hanging sun as often as toward it, could not gather enough light to meet the throttle's demands, and the reserve had been exhausted.

Panicked, Meer stilled the motor. The boat lost headway, but, in doing so, seemed to harmonize with the rise and fall of the sea. He twisted in his seat and tried to measure how far he had come. The low summit of old Edera was still in sight, but well off toward the south.

He thought perhaps his precious remaining fuel could take him back to Kawa-lake—but at the sacrifice of both the fuel and his progress. There was not much left of the day. The wind seemed calmer, and the swells tolerable. The boat was well out away from the rolling white water. By mid-morning, the collectors would once again be catching the sun's full power, and he could continue on.

Meer decided to stay.

He ate lightly and watched the world turn around him, the sun disappear from the sky. So long as he did not fight the rise and fall of the water, he could endure it.

But the air was damp, and a puddle of water sloshed fore and aft under the slatted deck as the boat rode the waves. Wrapping himself in the ground blanket, Meer hunkered down in his seat, absent-mindedly touching his float belt every so often for reassurance.

Thinking about the red boat, he wondered how they had made it, and if the pilot had sailed on through the night, if he were already in Edera. He wondered about the realm beneath him, and how many corpses rested at the bottom of Kawa-lake or the sea— a thought which made him so uncomfortable that he quickly cast about for a more pleasant one to drive it from his memory.

Presently he settled on a reminiscence of the first time he had bedded Sachi, how beautiful she was in wanting him. It proved such a safe and detailed memory that his staff twitched hopefully, and, by and by, he loosened his trousers and indulged it with a faint echo of the pleasures of that mating.

He did not mean to doze, but the motion of the water lulled him, and the haze of warmth in his groin betrayed him.

When he woke, he was sprawled on the deck beside his chair, drenched and tangled in the blanket, with the boat pitching ominously in the darkness and the sound of the surf all around him. *Too close, too close,* he thought frantically, scrambling to his knees and stretching out a hand for the throttles.

Before he found them, the boat nosed sharply bow-down, and a sudden rush of water lifted Meer and carried him away from the deck. He cried out in fear and surprise, but his throat filled with sea as the roaring engulfed him and a wall of water hammered down from above.

Gasping for air, but denied it, he thrashed wildly as the smothering wave drove him under. But his legs were still imprisoned in the blanket, and his hands found nothing to grasp. His bowels and his mind emptied as his helplessness against the power of the sea filled him with a simple, certain dread that was more primal than thought.

This is how I die, it said. *This is the taste of extinction.*

7

The Trembling of Ana

These are events of which Ana has no memory, of which no one speaks or writes. These are events we have been driven by fear to pretend never happened, which witnesses will deny to each other and themselves everywhere but in the whispers of their minds. And time can silence even those whispers.

I do not know how many still remember, but I do not know how any could forget.

Except the dead, of course—but we are especially not to remember the dead. The memorials have been scrubbed and scoured and erased from every surface Oran can reach, even those hidden in some hearts. No bodies, no bones, no shadows of our ancestry. These are dangerous things, as dangerous to those who cling to them as they are to the lies they threaten to reveal.

The shadows must have been dangerous to the lies, or Oran would not have burned so many young bodies trying to drive them away.

But the light which dispels one shadow creates another. And the brighter the light, the deeper the shadows it creates—and the more that can hide therein.

I do not know how many still remember, but I do know that few are reckless enough to speak of what they keep inside. I am no different, no better, perhaps worse. Until now, I have said nothing

of what I saw, what I knew, what I did. I turned my face away
with the others, shunning those who dared to let their anger or
their anguish show.

But there are many kinds of fear—and it is the fear driven
by guilt, driven by shame, which cannot tolerate the sound of
the truth.

I sentenced men to be beaten for speaking their hearts, because
that was what was expected of me.

I sent one to his death for shouting his condemnation of Oran-
rami Anadon by the temple of the arch, though I knew his crime
was that he spoke the truth.

I did not ask or want to be made one of Oran's protectors. But
Meli turned her face from me for that, and set me out, never to
acknowledge me again. She did not know how little choice I had,
or that my compliance was all that secured my safety, and hers,
in the horrible days after the star fell. I could not talk of those
things, and she would not have heard me.

Silence has not been without its price.

But I have hidden in both shadows, of long memories and hard
ones, and I will step into the light and tell you all that I can
remember. I will tell it as I lived it, poor witness though I know
myself to be. There were many who knew more, and at least one
of them lived among you.

Measure what I tell you against Kedar's memory, or your own,
and judge me as you will.

But first, let me give a name to these events, so that they can
be spoken of clearly and loudly from now on.

Names must be chosen carefully, Fas told me, because the
naming of a thing shapes it. And the names we give these memories surely shape them in our minds: the drowning of hope, the
rape of the children, the grand salon, the nights of mystery. Each
name sets its particular focus.

In that brief moment before the records were expunged and
silence fell, the councilors chose a name which perhaps you have
heard, a name which sets a focus of blame: the Iju rebellion. It
was Iju, they said, a dark apocryphal, whose aspect is deception,
whose line was extinguished long ago, who came to Ana. It was
Iju who sought to upset the pact between Ana and her people,
Iju's influence which brought on so much madness. And it was
Ana who repelled Iju and protected her blessed.

The very name was a lie embodying a fiction—but a well-
chosen lie. To dispute it was suspect. To ask questions was

suspect. To offer any contrary word was suspect. The very act of challenging official truth gave those around you reason to discount your words. And to persist in protest when your error had been corrected was to prove you had been subverted.

The Iju rebellion. That lie lives in the shadows of many who remember, and it must be extinguished.

I will never forget the grand salon on the plaza, or how the universe came to speak to us, or the drowning of hope. But to let those moments name what happened is to choose the wrong focus. We must remember where it started, and that it is not yet finished. We must remember it as they thought of it, as the crusade for truth.

Confrontation was coming, even before the first of the eight nights. That was, I think, understood and accepted by all. Rida's salon met quietly but argued loudly, and the questions asked there refused to be contained by the walls of Rida's home.

Had they confined themselves to questions of air, which concerned no one but them, they could have carried on in safety until boredom or consensus extinguished debate. But they refused to respect any limits. It was not enough to build a new understanding within the culture of the salon. It was necessary for all of Ana to embrace it as well.

The honor school taught error, and error could not be tolerated. The temples preached myth, and myth must be challenged. The women of Ana enforced conformity, and conformity poisoned the mind to curiosity. The exarch, the syndics, the trustees, the prefects were bound by an outdated vision of the possible, and had to be enlightened.

Kedar's students wanted their new truths and ideas heard, acknowledged, embraced. In their idealism, they believed, had to believe, that everyone would share their passion, would *want* to know. This and this alone, it seemed, they never questioned. They did not acknowledge and embrace the old truths about the selfishness, stubbornness, vanity, and infamy which are also part of the heritage of the apocryphals.

I do not blame them for that. In truth, I think it was part of why I admired them. But it was still an error—and the reason why, at some point, confrontation with the powers of the high bank was inevitable. How long it would have taken, what else might have fomented a crisis, I do not know. But it happened because it had to happen. Only the cause was a matter of chance.

•   •   •

Is it true? Have I begun to say 'they' where before I said 'we'?

I assure you, it is not to separate myself from their actions or their fate. Honesty insists that I do not count myself with them, because even after a full turn through the festivals, I was still a visitor in their world.

However free my tongue became in the salon, however welcoming their smiles or accepting their nods might be, however many books I read from Kedar's archive, I could not have become one with them without living my life over—even living my birth over, so that I wore the mark of the Sun Bear, or the Boroche, or any mark of grander aspect.

I had been apprenticed to two circles, had already sparked three children—by this time Meli was growing round again, with Saika. As much as they knew, and as nimble as their minds were, the students had not yet entered my world, the world which kept me from being fully equal in theirs. Matters of reflection and inquiry were their duty, but could only be my pastime.

They had done more learning, I more living. And I felt myself the one disadvantaged. I envied them—I do not think they envied me.

I would gladly call myself one of them, if only it had been so.

But I was *with* them, if not of them. And I was with them when it started, though Kedar himself was not. I was there the night that Weilin was late to the salon and then burst in, rude with enthusiasm, calling to us, "Come outside—come and see! There is something happening in the sky!" He did not wait, but dashed back out to the yard.

I do not remember what the subject was when Weilin arrived, only that Jalos had the center and grew angry at the interruption. He grew angrier still when several of us—myself among them—rose to leave. But it was no slight to Jalos that the matter of greatest moment then was what had roused Weilin, quietest of the quiet, to such a display.

What do you know of the sky? Of Weilin? You must know something of each to grasp this.

Weilin's passion was the arcana of the apparitions of night: the stars, the wanderers, and the ephemera. He was called Weilin Red-Eyes, with affection, because of his habit of giving up his sleep for his studies.

His notebooks contained endless tables of numbers, sketches for exotic measuring tools he hoped to build—he came to me for help with one—and arguments couched in mathematics. Hardly any in Kedar's salon claimed to understand Weilin's inquiries in more than a general way, and even fewer, least of all me, could have made an argument for their importance.

Weilin's true peers were a few like minds scattered through the other salons—with whom he met, it was said, to speak of the incomprehensible in terms of the impenetrable. The teasing was not always kind, and I thought him marked well to listen to us when so few were willing or able to listen to him.

Until that day, I could count only one instance when Weilin had asked for time in the center. That came soon after the first report of the committee on origins, in whose findings he had taken uncommon interest.

In his spare, soft-spoken way, Weilin told us that he had found a measure of the year in the appearance of the figures of stars after sunset, which he hoped might provide a foundation for any historical calendar being created.

Perhaps you know that at the start of each night, the sky is different than the night before. Each star and figure of stars appears displaced along the arc of the night, moving higher in their ascendance, dropping lower in their decline. This displacement proceeds until each apparition is displaced from the night sky, and, common wisdom says, disappears forever.

This is what the honor school called the postulate of the fixed and infinite sky.

But, being a more persistent or observant witness than I, Weilin made a contrary discovery—that, with the passage of many more nights, the star-apparitions reappeared, still fixed in form and figure, on the same night arc where he first recorded them. The sky was, contrary to wisdom, fixed and *finite*—the arc of the night was in fact a *circle*—and Weilin had taken its measure at three hundred and eleven days.

The meaning of this was not clear then, and is no clearer now. Much was made in that salon of the fact that the circle of festivals—embracing thirteen bellfests, each numbering twenty-five days—yields a year fourteen days longer than Weilin's circle of night.

Kaixi insisted on calling the circle of night a natural year, and championed the faction which held the discrepancy meaningful, if not further proof of deception. Boli argued that this calendar of the sky had no bearing on the circle of festivals, having more to do with the apocryphals than the temples. There was no reason for them to be in harmony, or cause for suspicion if they were not.

It is my memory that the salon ended with no resolution, and with Weilin's first purpose, of giving the new calendar of origins a foundation in phenomenology, seemingly forgotten.

But even so, the notion of a natural year survived in our speech as a reality of unknown meaning. It was adopted by the committee on phenomena, which hoped it might correlate the timing of the great storms and grand tremors, whose unpredictability was an offense to some.

Most of all, Weilin changed the way I, and many others, considered the night sky. From that day, we lifted our eyes to order, not randomness. Today's bright apparition of the apocryphal Rana might be one with the last apparition of Pan. Stars were independent of their riders. Their aspects were their own, perfect and eternal, against which we measured the imperfection of the wanderers and ephemerals.

This was the order which was violated on the first night of mystery. For Weilin called us out to show us a *new* apparition— one which did not turn with the sky, but stayed fixed over the city. Not star, not wanderer, not ephemeral.

The new star was brighter than many, but not so bright as to insist on our attention. I cannot guess how many Anans looked up and saw it that first night. Or of that number, how many knew the ascendant apparitions well enough to mark that the star was new. Or of that number, how many watched long enough to realize that the figures of stars were slowly flowing past it like the river past a rock.

I would not think that there were many.

Because of Weilin, we few gathered in the yard of Rida's house were prepared to see the new star for the oddity it was.

But none of us, not even Weilin, was prepared to understand.

I risk allowing you to think us more prescient than we were. The truth was that Weilin's discovery was at most a minor curiosity, an amusing mystery. No one foresaw where it would lead. No one grasped how something so far beyond our reach could touch us.

But the novelty and the flush of discovery were enough to keep us from returning inside, where Jalos, Rida, and half our number had remained. Someone suggested runners go to share the news with the other salons which were meeting that night. The suggestion found favor, but no one offered to absent themselves from the gathering—so we took to the streets together, laughing and arguing as we went, a salon afoot.

We were better at questions than answers, though Weilin found the uncertainty far more intolerable than did any of his companions. I perceived that his excitement was at least half distress. Weilin refused to allow us to call the apparition a wanderer or an ephemeral. He exploded in anger, stunning us, when Boli suggested the new star was simply a form of wanderer not yet known, the wanderings of which happened to create an illusion of immobility.

Thereafter, we called the apparition a star, to preserve the peace. But the pleasure of the evening was slipping away, with no clean resolution at hand.

Of all our questions, only one was answerable: Would the new star still be there the next night, or was it a passing specter? It had the appearance of a star and the manner of a wanderer, Kaixi pointed out, risking Weilin's newfound temper. There was an appealing symmetry, he suggested, in the prospect it also had the temporality of an ephemeral.

"There is an appealing simplicity in ignorance," Weilin said, "but it does not yield true answers, either." He raised his arm and pointed at the glowing apparition hanging over the sleeping city. "It will still be there tomorrow."

I do not think he felt his certainty as keenly as his need to challenge Kaixi. But with no salon scheduled, we agreed to meet on the high bank at dusk, on the lawns behind the honor school, to settle the matter. Then we scattered into the night.

I was one of three who returned to Rida's house, to inform the salon of our plans. But only Jalos remained, and he was still nursing a grudge.

"This would not have been allowed to happen if Kedar had been here," we heard him chide Rida. "We can't have reason without order, or dialogue without manners."

Our appearance saved Jalos the fierce rebuke he probably deserved. "Kedar is still absent?" I asked. "Where is he tonight?"

Rida could not say, though I cannot say we were greatly concerned by that.

If any of us had truly been prescient, we would have known that my question was the question of the night—and the first hint that something was happening on the high bank as well as in the sky.

No mention of the new star reached my ear in a day of gossip and rumor, and I held my own tongue, lest Kaixi be proven right and I be labeled an idiot on the morning.

But if the new star had fallen beneath the notice of Ana at large, the same could not be said of the honor school. When I reached the high bank shortly before dusk, seventy or more students were wandering the back lawn or sitting in the open, away from the buildings and trees. The number grew quickly as the sky darkened—it seemed that all of the honor school had heard, and many had come out to see what was being spoken of.

Kedar, though, was nowhere in sight.

Someone had thought to bring out two theodolites and set them up in the middle of the open lawn. That was where I found Weilin and Kaixi, the former pacing nervously, the latter sprawled on his back in the grass, telling a story on himself and laughing.

The suspense lasted only as long as it took for the brighter apparitions to begin to appear. Then Weilin, who knew better than any of us where to look, thrust a finger toward the sky.

"There!" he said. "There! You see? It endures."

That began a comedy of pointing, squinting, shrugging, and nodding, as those whose eyes quickly found the new star tried to help or correct those whose could not. While that went on around us, Kaixi came and clapped Weilin on the shoulders.

"It endures, indeed," he said, good-naturedly. "I concede my simple foolishness. Now, if you would just tell us what it is we behold—"

As someone off in the darkness started a corner-song, Weilin shook his head wordlessly and went to the nearest theodolite. Kaixi trailed after, and a circle of curious onlookers, myself one, formed around them as they fussed over the instrument.

The angle proved too sharp for the usual manner of viewing, the new star being nearly straight above us in the sky. Eventually someone stepped forward to remove the instrument from its stand, so Weilin could raise it in his hands and peer through the tiny lens at the sky.

"What do you hope to see, Weilin?" someone asked. "Does an apparition change in the lens?"

"A star does not," called a voice I recognized as belonging to Dejian, one of Weilin's friends. "The yellow wanderer turns from a point to a disk. The white wanderers take on shadings of color, but show no disk."

"A scout's telescope or a sentry's glass would do you more good," offered another in the audience.

"If you have such an instrument, run and get it," Kaixi urged. "The syndic of public security keeps no lab here for us to rob."

There was laughter at that. Then someone realized Weilin had not answered, and asked, "Is there anything to see, Weilin?"

"Something," Weilin said, lowering the instrument to his chest. "Dejian?"

A student came forward out of the circle and took the theodolite from Weilin, turning it skyward again. Then he gave way to another, who grunted in surprise when he put his eye to the lens.

"What is it, Shen?"

"I—I cannot hold it steady enough to be sure."

At that complaint, I drafted a strong-looking student to help, and together we spiked the stand deep into the ground at an angle, so that Shen could reattach the instrument and peer through its lens without touching it. Others, watching us, did the same for the second instrument, and a line quickly formed to peer through it.

By then, the singing had stopped, and many had gone inside, including Kaixi. But the gathering retained the unfocused festive flavor of a party, except where Weilin, Dejian, and Jiwei were concerned. The trio monopolized one instrument for as long as those watching would tolerate their placing work above entertainment. When they finally yielded to the eagerness of those waiting for a turn, they went off into the night together, talking in low voices.

I do not know what others saw, but I would swear that when I looked through the lens, the new star jumped toward me, while the apparitions which surrounded it did not.

I would have gone to find Weilin, to ask if he had seen the same, but before I could, we were chased from the lawn by sentries. They materialized from the dark at the west edge of the lawn and swept the gathering with their hand lights, demanding to know who had authorized this activity.

No one had, of course—no one had even thought permission was needed. A few words of good-humored protest were called out, but the sentries were immune to humor, and warned us to end the disturbance. I could feel puzzlement and indignation around me, echoing my own, as we began to disperse.

Indignation turned to resentment when one sentry came forward to seize the theodolites from those who were carrying them inside. But that was the only direct confrontation. The rest of the sentries stood back and allowed us all to withdraw quietly to the long houses or the streets.

"We must have disturbed the exarch's sleep," I heard someone say with sarcasm as we scattered.

But the noise of our gathering could not have carried much farther than the walls of the instructors' long house, or the work-house of the prefect of public information. Had one of them made a complaint against us? Who had we alarmed? And where was Kedar? Rida had promised to tell him what we had planned. Perhaps it was only distaste over the intrusion of the sentries, but this time Kedar's absence troubled me.

I wanted to be part of whatever talk followed, inside the students' long house, but the sentries had made me feel like a trespasser on the high bank, and the night was no longer friendly. I slipped away without good-byes, taking the long way home, east round to the Five-Ring Bridge, so as not to have to pass the keystone house.

Once south of the river, I made another detour, to take me past the archive house and Rida's, but both were dark.

As late as it was when I reached Meli's house, sleep came hard. I did not know why, but I was worried for all of us.

It is a curiosity—there are entire years of my life which I can barely remember having lived. The wheel turns faster and faster as the tally mounts, until it begins to blur past the vision and leave blank spaces in the heart. But those few days so long ago have stayed with me as though they had been captured in a mirror and echoed on the wind—

The next day, there was still no talk among my workmates, even though I risked asking if any had heard rumors of a new apparition in the night. But in mid-afternoon, Boli came to see me at the cleaning barn, and called me out to the entry. His voice was excited, his eyes alert as he spoke.

"Kaixi sent me to tell you," he said. "Chai has announced a general salon on the question of the apparition. It will begin at lights-down in the first green ring, out by the half-east spoke road."

The place he described is south of the river and as far around the ring from the keystone house as geometry allows. Even so, the reason for the choice was not obvious to me. "Why not at Rida's?"

"Rida will not host."

"The archive house, then."

He shook his head. "There will be too many for one house." He looked past me into the barn. "If there are any here who you think are friends of truth, bring them."

He started away, and I called him back. "Have you seen Kedar?"

"No," Boli said.

"Has anyone?"

"Chai saw him on the high bank, in the fenced garden of the meeting house, standing with the instructor of electrics. But no one has spoken to him."

I took a step toward him. "Boli—what is happening?"

His voice dropped as he answered. "Too many rumors, and too little truth. But Kaixi thinks Kedar is in trouble. He wants to send a delegation to the keystone house, to insist the exarch recognize our right to meet, and to demand to speak to Kedar. Kaixi will put his proposal for a vote tonight, and he will need all of our support."

Boli's earnestness infected me as long as he was there with me. Yet after he left, I saw it differently. It still seemed a small matter, confined to a small part of the city, far away from the lives of those who worked hard days in the retting barn, from Meli and Chane and the new child coming, from the men running the streets and the women calling from their rooftops.

One apparition more or less in the sky, a student party ended by a disapproving official, a prefect of the honor school called to account for his discipline—how could these be matters of such ominous import? I did not want Kedar removed from his post, but that was the worst trouble I could imagine for him, and it would not change how I felt about him.

And the rest of the city would hardly notice at all.

Boli's manner pointed to what had happened after I left the high bank. Confined in their long houses, whispering before classes, huddling together over their meals, they must have fermented a brew of anticipation, speculation, and restiveness—a brew so strong that now nothing could dissuade them from stepping forward to insist on a role in unraveling the mysteries which were starting to compound.

I confess I thought that Kaixi had lost perspective. I even thought the students foolish, their intrigues imaginary. Finishing my afternoon's work, I started homeward thinking how reassuringly commonplace the day had been, away from the high bank.

Even the clouds which blew down the valley and poured rain onto the city could not change that perception, for rare as rain on the city proper was, it was still part of the pattern. Children were everywhere in the streets when it ended, splashing giddily through the riverlets. The rain cleared the dust from the walls and freshened the blanket of air over the city.

Everything was in place, everyone at peace. The night before, I had felt guilty as a criminal, though I could not name my crime. I had skulked home through the streets vaguely afraid of the powers I had long looked to to secure my safety.

That was not how I wanted to live. I wanted to live in the same world as Meli, to not be troubled by mysteries I could not solve, or be trouble to people I could not offend.

By the time I reached Meli's house, I had resolved not to attend the general salon. Her second quickening was not far off, and my gift, a cut-weaving in the mark of the Boroche, needed my attention. Perhaps she needed my attention as well. The prospect was more attractive than huddling in a green ring in the dark, feeding on fear.

But I swear to you that there is something in the fabric of existence which abhors complacency. And the shock we received that night was a rebuff to not only my own, but to the complacency of all Ana, which I had so recently found admirable.

The evening announcements had ended, and Meli and I were turning to the final tasks of the house. Meli had put Chane down in the off mod—an anticipation if not a promise that she and I would couple—and he was already asleep.

Then the voice of the city, which had just fallen silent, began to speak to us again. These are the exact words, as Kedar's salon remembered and recorded them:

"Children of the peoples of Arania, listen to the voice of Hoja den Krador, praking of the stetship Hammadi."

Meli's eyes were wild as she looked at me. "What is happening?" she whispered. "Who speaks to us with Ana's voice, but another's tongue?"

But it was not Ana's voice. It was louder, far louder, and curiously inflected, like the accents of Logda Cluster, but new to my ear. It echoed across the city like the ringing of the great bells of the arch, like the rumble of a grand tremor. And Ana shook, as I shook, unable to answer Meli.

For it *was* Ana's tongue. I knew the word *praking,* the name Arania. I saw them, in the moment they were spoken, as I had seen them written in the journal of a man named Tonit, who lived in the world when Ana was young.

"Your leaders have chosen to keep from you news of great joy," said the voice of Hoja den Krador. "They have refused us the right and the chance to embrace you, because they are afraid. And this brings us grief we cannot bear. For we have come to you from the infinities, as brothers and friends."

Staring at the receiver on the wall, Meli gravitated to my arms, and I wrapped her in as much protection as I could spare. But I was under assault as well, and faltering—and Hoja den Krador was not finished.

"We are what you were," he said. "We come from the place you left behind. We have followed you to learn from your adventure and grand experiment, and to teach you what you have forgotten of your heritage.

"This is not a time for fear, but a time for rejoicing.

"Your leaders know how to speak with us. We will be waiting to hear from you, through them. But now, come outside your houses and look up into the sky, so we may give you our greeting."

Meli was afraid, and did not want to leave her house, but I dragged her outside by the hand. The yards and streets were filling as our neighbors poured out of their homes, and there were sounds of shock and anguish on the air. I looked up to find the new star a hundred times brighter than it had been, its color dissolving from white to blue to green to a gold bright enough to paint our faces—all honor colors.

The greeting display lasted only a few repetitions, then faded to the familiar brightness of Weilin's apparition, leaving the streets milling with shocked and fearful people who could not stop staring up in wonder.

Chane was crying, and Meli pulled away and ran inside to tend him. In a little while, I followed, tearing myself away from the temptation to go along the ring road offering what I knew as reassurance, and inviting one and all to Chai's general salon on the question of the apparition.

I could not go—I could not leave Meli. But I found out later it did not matter. The salon did not meet that night. Not long after Chane was lulled back to sleep, the familiar voice of Ana delivered one final announcement.

"Citizens of Ana—there is no reason for alarm," he said. "The announcements you may have just heard are meaningless frauds. The captain of sentries is at this very moment close to apprehending those responsible for this deceitful intrusion into your peaceful evening. Once identified, they will be sternly punished. You can assist in our efforts by refusing to listen to rumor, and by staying in your homes until the morning call."

He repeated the message twice, which made me doubt it even more than I did on first hearing. But Meli took some comfort from it, which stilled my tongue.

Sometime later, delivery wagons rumbled through the ring roads with sentries aboard, chasing stragglers indoors. The sentries rattled their sticks threateningly on the tailgate and called, "Stay inside your homes. Order of the exarch. No one to be in the streets 'til morning call."

When the wagon had gone past Meli's house, I wanted to go to the roof, but Meli's arms demanded I stay with her and Chane.

I remember thinking, as I held her, that somehow we must bring Hoja den Krador to Rida's salon.

8

Ubela: The Fifth Bell

On bloody hands and quaking knees, with shallow, foaming water swirling around him and the roar of the breakers behind him, Meer Faschen dropped his head and vomited the bellyful he had swallowed. The expulsion triggered lung-tearing coughs that stabbed through his chest, bringing an agony that nearly collapsed him. When the fit finally passed, he gathered himself and continued his feeble crawl up the beach and out of the surf.

His eyes were burning, blurring what little vision the night would allow, leaving him to feel his way, fleeing the muffled sound of the sea. When the sand under his hands gave way to sharp rock and hardpan, his body's exultation of relief sapped the last of the strength in his limbs, and he went down.

Cheek pressed hard against the ground, an arm pinned beneath him, his chest heaving, Meer lay on the high beach, quivering and unable to crawl farther, for an unmeasurable time. His mind was clear but empty, incapable of will or wonder. He stared blindly into the night, unable to form a thought or even to sense his own body.

Sometime in the night, a deep shiver that seemed to roll up and down his back, twisting and snapping his spine, brought on another fit of coughing. Meer tried to sit up, but the most he could manage was to turn on his side, doubled up like a sleeping child. Numbed or damaged, his right arm refused to obey him; it was a

dead weight hanging from his shoulder. With difficulty, he turned
onto his back, and he heard his arm fall heavily against the rock
beside him, but he could not feel it.

He had no clear memory of how he had reached the shallows,
and no clue other than the tautly swollen float belt across his chest
to help explain his escape from the depths. He had no notion of
how badly hurt he might be, or if he would ever rise from where
he lay. But as he lay there, he vowed with a ferocity which left
him weeping and shaking that he would never venture onto the
sea again.

When his right arm burned itself back onto his body, Meer
managed to ease himself into a more upright position on a canted
slab of cold stone. He lay propped against the rock and watched
as the sky over the water brightened, revealing the black corpse
of the scout boat only a hundred paces or so out from the water's
edge.

It rested nearly on its side, half-submerged, the collectors torn
away, the canopy pylons twisted and bent. The smallest inbound
waves broke over it; the largest battered it, as though determined
to smash it or drive it under. Looking at it, Meer knew that if
anything of value was still aboard, he would not be the one to
salvage it.

A softly glowing spike of light appeared on the horizon, rising
straight up into the sky. Moments later the sun broke the horizon,
gloriously bright, its heat reaching Meer almost with the first rays.
As it climbed above the sea, the sun painted a broken red-gold
band on the water, and changed the colors of the world.

Sitting up stiffly, Meer looked down at himself, taking inventory for the first time. Both of his foot wraps were gone, and
there was a long tear and a blood-black stain below one knee.
The medallion was still in his shoulder pocket, but his other
pockets were empty, including the thigh pouch where he had
been keeping his folding blade and the vial of sun salve. The
thigh pouch gaped open, and Meer could not remember whether
he had pinched it shut after his meal on the water.

It did not matter: The blade and salve, like the rest of his
supplies, were gone. He had been given little enough because
of where he was going: no knitters, no cleansers, no fire tablets
or crisis suite—nothing at all from the stocks of the chemists.

When he tried to strip off his trousers to find the source of the
blood, he became aware that his left hand was throbbing. Bringing
it before his eyes, he saw that the skin had been torn off most

of the knuckles on the back of his hand, the meat puffy and full of sand. Worse, his little finger was jutting out at an unnatural angle. When he touched it, fire shot up his arm to his shoulder and his jaw.

Clenching his teeth, Meer wrapped his right hand carefully around his little finger and the one beside it, then firmly squeezed them together. There was a soft pop and a sudden explosion of pain that dimmed his vision and brought a moan to his throat. But when he opened his fist the two fingers were parallel, ready to be taped together.

When that was done, he stood and carefully stripped off his float belt and clothing. The blood on his trousers was from a purpling bruise and gouge below the knee—he must have hit the boat hard when he was thrown from it, or when both were being tumbled by the waves.

Leaving his blouse and trousers spread on the rock where he had rested overnight, Meer stumped his way down the beach, stopping when he was ankle-deep in water. Wincing at the sting, he washed his wounds and his face, then cupped a handful of water to drink. Immediately, he spat it out. It was poison-bitter and foully salty, the aftertaste leaving him more thirsty than before.

He squinted along the beach in both directions, hoping against hope to see a half-full water canister washed up on the sand or bobbing in the shallows, but found only disappointment. Kawa had been kind to him. But it seemed as though the sea resented his presence, and was determined not to help him in any way.

Raising his gaze, Meer looked toward the southern horizon and wondered how far he had managed to come. Enough to subtract a day from the walk he was facing?—a walk he would now have to complete without food, sun shelter, or water which didn't burn his mouth.

It hardly mattered. The decision was out of his hands. He would follow the sea north until he found Edera or fell dead in the sand. One way or the other, he would not disappoint expectations.

The sun beat down on Meer's unshaded head as he hiked along the packed wet sand just out of reach of the waves. In the first hours of the day, he used every trick he knew or could devise to keep himself from perspiring, since that would only hasten his need to drink the sickening sea water.

For a time, he walked in the sea fringe, the water swirling around his ankles and cooling him. When that was no longer enough, he doused his back with double-handfuls of sea water, but the sun soon burned that moisture away. The next escalation was to remove his shirt and soak it in the surf, and duck his head, eyes squeezed shut, to drench his hair.

By the time hair and blouse were both dried to stiffness, the sun was well up in the sky behind him, and the sea wind had begun to blow. Beads of sweat broke out on his face from the simple exertion of his stiff-legged strides. Fighting dizziness as he walked, he swept the droplets off his forehead and chin and sucked them hungrily from his palm.

Finally, in a moment of desperate inspiration, Meer stripped off his blouse and split it up both sides, until only the high-neck fan collar held the front and back together. Then he draped the garment over his shoulders as a cape, tied the sleeves around his neck, and pulled one layer forward to form a sun cowl. His float belt, shrunken to its usual dimensions, kept the other layer in place to protect his back.

The cowl helped cool his head, but soon he was forced to admit he was fighting a losing battle. There was no hope of defeating the sun, or denying his thirst. His choices were to drink from the sea or stop and wait for darkness, and even then he would have to yield before long. His body felt unbalanced, abused, teetering on collapse.

Praying that desperation would sweeten its taste, Meer plunged into the water up to his knees and caught a handful from the trailing edge of a dying wave. Lowering his head, he sucked the precious liquid from his cupped hands. It burned his parched throat, but his mouth seemed to have lost the capacity to perceive any taste beyond that, which mercy made it more drinkable than he had dared hope. Throwing back the cowl, he drank greedily until his shrunken stomach cried protest.

When he straightened and looked up, there was a red-sailed boat bobbing just offshore from where he stood, its pilot clinging to the sail boom and looking in across the breakers at him.

Without turning his back, Meer retreated to the beach. He realized that the boat must have come up the coast from the south, and been hidden from him by the cowl.

The pilot was shouting now, and gesturing with his free hand. But Meer could neither catch the words nor decipher the signs.

"Go away!" he shouted. The effort hurt his throat, and the last syllable was half-strangled by phlegm. Pulling his cowl up, Meer started down the beach, eyes straight ahead, making a studious effort to ignore the new arrival. He made himself count a thousand steps on the sand before stealing a glance out to sea.

The red-sailed boat was still there, keeping pace with him.

Meer rushed to the water's edge and angrily shook a fist in the air. "Haven't you done enough?" he shouted with all the fury his voice could muster. "Leave me be, thief! I curse your staff. I curse your mark. I curse your blessed's belly. May your line be barren as long as the sun burns."

To Meer's surprise, the pilot waved in acknowledgment and turned his boat toward the shore. It slid easily down the face of a breaking wave, then was driven smoothly toward where Meer stood by the wave that followed and the sea wind that filled its sail.

Meer jumped back, realizing as he watched that this was neither the boat nor the boy from the day before. The boat was wide-set, floating on two parallel cylinders which reminded Meer, in shape if not in dimension, of the water bags carried by temple runners. The pilot was a square-shouldered man with a streak of bright silver at the temples and a mouth-trimmed beard.

The boat grounded lightly a few paces from Meer. The moment it did, the pilot dropped the sail and leaped out to drag his vessel out of the water. When he turned toward Meer, he was smiling cheerfully.

"That was your wreck back there?" he asked, pointing to the south. "Credit to you, you've gotten farther than most of them do. Then, not many have the balls to steal a boat from the scouts. I can only think of one other since I've been sailing a food contract."

"I—" It came out as a croak, and Meer felt himself swaying.

The pilot turned and dug into a draw bag. "Here," he said, holding out a water canister toward Meer. "This'll cut the nasty stuff. Morada's fine for growing skimweed and sailing a bladder boat, but drinking her like you did'll make a man sick."

Warily, Meer took the canister and uncapped it, pouring out a sample into his palm. He sniffed at it suspiciously, lapped at it experimentally.

"Death be to that, just knock it back," the pilot said. "You've got a hard salt soup in your belly. You might lose it all, but that'll leave you ahead by my count, and I've got more. Put a finger down your throat if you've a mind to."

Meer lifted the canister to his lips, tipped it back, and let the sweet liquid tumble down his throat. The pilot waited patiently as Meer drank, then reclaimed the canister and replaced it in his boat.

"My name's Treg," he said, and waited.

"Meer," he said, swallowing to keep the contents of his stomach there. "You're from Edera?"

"No," Treg said. "From Epa-Daun. Edera is an Anan name, and we reject it—means 'end-place.' Or dying-place. You've already seen as much of Edera as ever existed."

Meer swallowed again. "At the mouth of the river?"

Treg nodded. "How did you like it?"

"How long has it been since anyone lived there?"

"No one has ever lived there," said Treg. "But things being as they are, we hate to disappoint anyone's expectations and give them a reason to keep looking. So we tried to make it everything the myth requires."

Suddenly, Meer turned aside and emptied his stomach on the sand. When he collected himself, Treg was turning the bow of his boat toward the sea.

"Knew it was coming," he said, unperturbed. "You'll feel better now, and the next time it'll stay down. Have some food along, too, for when you're not so tender-bellied. Ready to get going?"

"Going where?"

"To Epa-Daun."

"In that?" Meer pointed accusingly at the boat.

"You had a different idea?"

"I'm not going out there again," Meer said, gesturing toward the water.

Treg crossed his arms and cocked his head. "Well, let's see— in your condition, I'd say you're looking at three days, maybe a little more, before you run out of beach. Then you've got to climb over Kennabar—what you call the north facade—which must be a good eight hundred feet to the top, even there, and another day at least to cross.

"Now, that's assuming that none of the highlanders whose plots you wander into up top beats you to death before they figure out who you are, on account of the fact that no refugee ever comes into Epa-Daun that way.

"On the other hand, if we get on the water without much more fuss, I can promise you that we'll be in Epa-Daun by sunset— you can really run on the afternoon winds. You make the choice. I can leave you some water and a bit of food, if you're enjoying this so much you've just got to stick it out alone. So just give me the word—how long do you want to be out here? The rest of today, or maybe the rest of your life?"

Meer looked from Treg to the boat, then the sea, then back again. "I don't trust it."

"You don't have to," Treg said. "You only have to trust me. Besides—I get a bonus for bringing you in. If you walk in, I get nothing. You wouldn't want to cheat me, would you?"

Meer took a step forward, and his lips drew into a line. "Yesterday a boy in a boat like yours stole most of my supplies, and wished me to dying as many ways as he could. By Kawa's staff, why should I trust *you*?"

Treg sighed. "I know, I know. I was planning to talk to you about that. Lial—my son—took you for an Anan scout instead of a refugee. That's the word here, by the way—don't ever say exile. Lial's only just started to run the coast on the family contract. I'm glad to have him to spell me, but I'm afraid he's still nursing the same blind-in-anger hate for Ana so many of the Epa-born seem to come to."

Staring, Meer could barely speak. "Women take the blessing—here?"

Treg nodded. "Uh-huh. Turns out Ana and Kawa don't have the blessing business all to themselves. There's a lot that's going to surprise you, if Edera was what you were expecting. I wouldn't count on anything being quite what you thought."

Drawing a deep breath, Meer stared at the ground and released it slowly. "All right," he said. "Let's go."

Treg broke into a relaxed grin. "Good. I was hoping for a little help, because the hardest part's gonna be at the beginning. At night it's no problem, got the land wind behind me, but it's a bit of a trick getting off the beach with the sea wind and the surf both against me. Grab hold like this on the other side, and let's see what we're made of—"

To Meer's surprise, but initially to his pleasure, there was little conversation once they had coaxed the boat clear of the surf and Treg directed Meer to where he wanted him, forward and on the right.

Both had their reasons for silence. Meer was still leery of his benefactor, and did not want to invite questions which might demote him from refugee back to enemy—while Treg was apparently well occupied with the business of sailing. The boat was not as simple to sail as it had seemed, and Treg had to work hard with a paddle-like stern pole to keep it from being pushed shoreward and into the surf.

Despite his suspicious disposition, Meer could not let himself attend too closely to Treg's activities. Even eye contact might start a conversation he did not want. So he settled himself looking forward and toward the shore, where a glance back over his shoulder would still give him a glimpse of the pilot.

But he was surprised to find, in those glances, that Treg seemed to be taking little notice of him. The longer it went on, the more puzzled Meer became at Treg's studied lack of curiosity. Ashore, he had been almost overwhelming in his gregarious loquacity.

Was the pilot under orders? *Pick him up—say what you have to to get him aboard—and then say as little as possible—*

Or was it just that Treg was accustomed to being alone, and just as content to keep his own counsel? It *was* a solitary task he shouldered—much like Meer's days on the cart.

Or it could, Meer realized, be nothing more than consideration for the condition of his passenger—leaving him undisturbed to revive and restore his health and energy.

Meer's own curiosity consumed him, but he refused it control of his tongue. Silence could not harm him. The same could not be said of the truth.

It was Treg's bladder boat itself which finally drew Meer out.

From the start, the boat set an impressive pace, even with its double burden. It seemed to Meer that the boat was running faster than the wind, though how that could be he could not imagine.

He found himself studying the details of its construction, from the rope hinges to the bound stalks which comprised the tripod mast. The cleverness of the design was as evident as the improvisation of materials. It was no challenge to see the weak points and the imperfect solutions, but the twin-float design, being wider, was far more stable on the water than the scout had been.

But it was the material which covered the bladders that most interested Meer. Dry and exposed to the sun, it was pliant and slightly tacky—the skin of his fingertips lingered slightly as he brushed them across it. But when he slid his hand down the side into the boat's own shadow and touched the bladder where it was wet, the material felt both harder and surprisingly slippery.

While Meer was examining the boat, a low, narrow sea island had appeared ahead. It seemed to be made of nothing but sand, and yet was substantial enough to shield the beach from the breakers.

Now they were closing on it, and Meer could see that there was a broad expanse of calmer water between the beach and the bar. Treg steered for it, running a minor cascade of white surf as the boat's course crossed with the curls being edged offshore.

In the sheltered waters, Treg seemed less distracted by his duties, and Meer finally turned to him.

"Where do these boats come from?"

Treg scratched at his furred chin. "This one comes from Mari's family—but the real crafthand is her husband Dorec. Splitting the float, that was his idea, and doesn't she ride nicely? The funny side to it is that he can't take one out himself—not that he's afraid, but because his head can't take the sea. He means to someday build one big enough to be as solid underfoot as Kennabar."

A chuckle rumbled deep in the pilot's throat. "And if he ever does, I won't be surprised to see him point it east, wave us a good-bye, and go off to chase the horizon," he said, showing a grin. "He's had a passion for it since he was nine and putting nutshell boats on Kawa by the Forty-Ring Bridge."

Frowning, Meer rubbed the top of the bladder. "But how does he do it? There's nothing like this in Ana."

"Oh, the clad, that's Mari's doing. She cooks it down from some brew of hers—she's always changing the recipe, looking for something a little tougher so Dorec can build bigger. They haven't made two alike yet—I know, because I get to test them all. This one's only been on the water eight, nine days. I get them before the sea farmers, because if a boat goes out from under me, I can still walk home."

"Have you ever had to?"

"Only once," Treg said. "We've one other boat-maker, Loria—you saw her work, the one my son was piloting. Loria's boats are a little faster on a light wind, but too small for hauling skimweed or passengers. You've still got nothing under sail up in the city, I take it?" He shook his head. "I don't understand—it's fair foolish to drive your boats on the sun when the wind blows all night. But then, there's a lot of foolishness upriver."

That was a gambit Meer refused to answer. He turned away to face forward again, watching the sand island slip by and the sheer-faced north facade sharpen in focus as the boat moved up the coast.

"Your stomach settled enough to stand the taste of food?" Treg called to him. "Or would you rather be hungry than sick?"

Meer peeked back over his shoulder to find Treg prospecting in a draw bag. "I'd most rather be neither."

"No telling without trying," Treg said, and passed forward a fist-sized pulp-fruit.

Meer turned it over in his hand. "Generous of you to share my own supplies with me."

To Meer's surprise, Treg laughed. "I wish the ones we grew tasted half as good as the ones Lial took from you. Try it, you'll see the difference. Dirt-grown and broth-grown are like night and day."

The pilot was right. The fruit was bland, the pulp mushy. Still, it went down easily.

"What did you mean back there, when you said you were sailing a food contract?" Meer asked.

Shrugging, Treg said, "Have to have a contract if you don't work basic and you expect to share the yield. That's the only way the community can bless or bar what you want to do. Mali's family and Loria have contracts to build boats. My family has one to run the coast for refugees."

"And you earn extra food for bringing me in?"

"Anyone can get a bonus for bringing anything useful into Epa-Daun. You'd be worth more if you were a woman, of course, but I can't expect every luck," Treg said, the grin returning. "You'd have gotten a bonus yourself if you'd managed to keep your boat under you."

Meer's expression soured. "I had every intention—"

"I'm sure. But we'll salvage it—the metal's worth the risk and trouble. Dorec goes wild thinking of that boat left at Edera as window-dressing. You have the right of first claim, if you want to be the one to do it. And if you don't, you might still collect a division for bringing it as far as you did."

Meer looked away. The end of the barrier island was in sight, and the sound of the surf was returning. Along the shoreline, he could see where the beach gave way to the rock of Kennabar. "You know I'm here for Kedar."

"Yes," he said.

"Then you know I'm not going to stay."

He made a clucking sound. "Nan Tirza doesn't pay me to tell people's fortunes," he said. "Just to find them and bring them in."

Meer looked back over his shoulder. "Nan Tirza?"

"She's wearing the red sash at the moment," Treg said, and

gestured toward the bow. "Last leg coming up. Mind you keep a grip, now. Winds are tricky here, and the water's very deep."

All along the headlands, white water crashed against black rock, sending plumes and spikes of water high into the air.

Treg kept the boat well out from the tumult, running along the edge of the mount's long afternoon shadow, but the water beneath them seemed to echo the power of it. More than once, a wave top sliced off by the boat's passage sprayed back and wet Meer to the skin, and the flexing and twisting of the vessel beneath him, the swaying of the mast above him, threatened to bring back the terror of the night before.

But he shrugged off the spray, fought the memories, and sat high, looking expectantly ahead, eager for the first glimpse of his destination and the comforting knowledge that his journey was at last half over.

That first glimpse was still eluding Meer when Treg called out to him, "You see? I promised we'd be in by sunset."

But moments later the headlands began to fall away, revealing a bright slice scooped out of the facade, a slice that quickly widened into a small valley. Looking back, Meer realized that they were rounding a promontory which had blocked the view north.

The valley was largely shaded from the sun by Kennabar, save for the upper half of the north rim, but Meer could still make out the mouth of the river and what appeared to be a few houses on the south side of it. The whole width of the valley could only have encompassed a fraction of Ana, and the river could not match at its mouth the size of Kawa where it flowed through Ana.

For a moment, Meer felt a twinge of embarrassment for Treg and his empty pride. Then he swept his gaze back toward the south rim of the valley, which rose from the river in a gentle curve. Though hardly lush, the slope was well painted with green. And dotting its face were clusters of dozens of structures, many showing broad splashes of bright red on their well-finished dark stone walls. He counted ten, thirty, fifty people moving among the clusters.

But that was not all. As the slope grew steeper, the structures gave way to regular patterns of clean-edged openings in the rock—entrances, by all appearance, to chambers and passage-ways. Some were glowing brightly enough to silhouette a human figure standing by them, as though the sun were piercing Kenna-bar and lighting the caves from within.

"You have tunneling nats!" Meer said, half in awe and half in accusation.

"I warned you we'd surprise you," Treg said, his pleasure at Meer's discomfort explanation enough for his silence on the water.

Meer crawled to the bow, as though a difference of half the length of the boat would allow him to see more clearly. "How many live here?" he asked, swallowing a knot of insecurity.

Treg thought a moment before answering. "Three hundred eleven when I left this morning. But Brinda's due to deliver Skett's baby at any time, so we could be one up or down from there by now. Up one, most like, since Brinda's had three, and her last came quickly."

Shunning the beach north of the sheer bluffs of the headlands, and likewise the sandy delta north of the beach, Treg sent the boat arrowing toward the mouth of the little river. Measured by Meer's impatience, it took an excruciatingly long time to reach the spot where three other boats were pulled up on the south bank.

That was as far as they could have gone, for the river was barricaded just above that point by a row of sharp-edged rocks so regular in size and spacing that Meer had no doubt they'd been placed there for just that purpose.

He climbed out of the boat on stiff legs and wandered away from it, letting Treg see to securing it while he looked around. Standing, he could see a substantial aquaculture dike a short distance upstream, four of its five compartments well-grown with greenery. Beyond the dike was a field of drying racks, many draped with harvest. And when he turned to the south and scanned up the slope, he could see clearly that the habitats extended all the way to the top of Kennabar.

Treg came up from behind and stood beside him. "I won't pretend we have everything we need, or that our backs don't ache at the end of the day. But I'm damn proud of these people, and I love every one of them."

Drawing a deep breath and letting it out slowly, Meer stripped off his improvised sun cowl and turned it back into an approximation of a blouse. As he did, he felt the hardness in the sleeve pocket, and it served as a goad and reminder. "Now what?"

"Introductions," Treg said, nodding. "Your arrival's been noticed."

Looking up toward the settlement, Meer saw a gathering of a dozen or more people moving down a well-trodden path toward them.

"What kind of reception should I be expecting?" he asked.

"Civil," Treg said. "By our standards."

They started up to meet the welcoming party.

Purposeful strides rapidly erased the distance between the new arrivals and the covey of exiles, their number now swollen to more than twenty. When only a few tens of feet separated them, Meer stopped and drew himself up, letting the others decide how close to approach. Treg continued on, though, and caught a familiar-looking youth up in a two-armed hug.

Quickly scanning faces in the dim light, trying to take the exiles' measure, Meer was taken aback to see another he recognized—the messenger, whose visit had thrown his life into turmoil. Meer stared at him, unable to check the sudden antipathy pouring out in his gaze. "So—you escaped," he said.

"So—you came," the messenger said, returning dislike in kind.

"It is him, then," said a woman standing beside the messenger. She was barely as tall as the messenger's shoulder, and as young in her face as Sachi, but she seemed somehow to be the focus of the group. Her black hair was bluntly cut at shoulder-length, and she wore baggy high-waisted trousers stained at the knees.

"Yes, Nan," said the messenger. "I would have recognized him sooner, but he wears his journey hard on his face."

The woman took a step toward Meer, her expression sober but burning with curiosity. "So you are Meer Faschen," she said. "There are many who thought you would never come— Storm among them," she added, indicating the messenger with a toss of her head. "I am Nan Tirza. I wear the red sash until the new year."

Meer took a breath and a step forward as well. "If you know who I am, then you know why I'm here."

"We all know," said Nan. "Kedar kept no secrets from us."

"Do you also *accept* why I'm here? Because I will need your assistance to do as Kedar asked. My boat was destroyed, and I will need a pilot willing to take me as far up Kawa as a boat with sails can go. I cannot pack a corpse on my back all the way to Ana from here."

"Such decisions will have to wait until all parties to them can be consulted," Nan Tirza said. "Tonight, I can offer you a guest's share of food and a place to rest. Tomorrow, we'll consider the other matters." She turned to Treg. "Will you take him up?"

Treg nodded. "Of course, Nan."

The assemblage parted, allowing Treg and Meer to continue up the path into the settlement. Storm was one of the last to step aside.

"*She* is your exarch?" Meer asked in an incredulous whisper. "That child?"

"The sash changes hands among the fertile women, their stake being greater than any," Treg said, and then his tone turned chilly. "But I wouldn't mistake her for your exarch, or call her that when anyone less understanding than I can hear you. Nor mistake her for a child, for that matter. Epa-Daun has never offered the luxury of prolonged innocence."

Clenching his teeth and bristling at the scolding, Meer followed Treg along a path which turned inland, parallel to the foot of the slope. As they passed between the houses, Meer found the eyes of everyone they passed turning to him, probing him as a curiosity. He did not have the energy to answer them back, and kept his own gaze fixed to Treg's heels as he led the way.

"There," Treg said at last, as they were nearing the limit of the settlement. He stopped and waggled a finger toward one small slant-walled, dome-roofed structure on the up side of the path. "That's Kedar's house."

Meer turned to him. "What is the point of this? I have no need to see the corpse. I only need a full belly and a place to lie down in the dark."

Shaking his head, Treg gave Meer's shoulder an impatient push. "Go on inside, before you make any more foolish noises."

"What, am I supposed to stay here?"

There was a shuffling sound behind Meer. He spun around to see a slender figure standing in the entryway, one hand raised against the wall to support his frailty.

"Ah," the man said. "I see you counted on a tidier epilogue. Forgive me, Meer. I seem to have endured longer than I expected."

"Kedar!" Meer fell back with a start, colliding with Treg.

The man in the entryway stepped into the dying light and smiled faintly, familiarly. His eyes showed no hint of his body's weakness.

"The bargain remains the same," said Kedar Nan. "Take me home to Ana, just as you planned. I promise to die before we reach the boundary. And until I do fall, I will carry my own corpse. What more can you ask, my old friend?"

9

Botad: The Sixth Bell

The awkwardness hung in the air for the long moment it took Meer to find his tongue again.

"Kedar, please," he said, stepping forward, his hands held out in supplication. "I am *not* unhappy to find you alive—but understand, it *is* a shock—"

"So your face told me."

Meer turned his back on Kedar to glare at Treg. "This one let me think that you were dead—they all did. And it's been so many days since you must have sent the messenger—it was an honest mistake, not a wish. I'm *glad* you still live."

Some minute contortion of Treg's expression conveyed his skepticism. But Kedar said from behind, "I am comforted to know that you can still say so."

Meer spun around to read Kedar's face for sarcasm, but found none.

"I was glad to learn that you, too, still claim breath from the air," Kedar continued. "And I am grateful that you found reason enough to accept my imposition. Will you accept my hospitality one last time?"

No words came. Meer stared at the entryway of Kedar's house as though it were the entrance to a trap.

"I see—you cannot quite go so far as to say you are *glad* to see me," Kedar said, a touch of sadness crossing his eyes.

Meer raised his hands over his head in a sudden violent gesture. "How can you?" Meer demanded. "After everything—all these years—what reason can there be to greet me this way, to make me a guest in your home? What can be in your mind?"

The older man's gentle smile did not quite drive the sadness away. "I have missed you, Meer—my friend. And I had hoped to talk with you again, in the way we once did."

"What is there for us to talk about?"

"All there ever was—the whole of life and existence."

Meer wrapped himself in his arms, his body stiff. "I will not talk about those days. I will not make apology for choices that were not mine."

"I did not expect that of you," Kedar said. "But surely, that does not limit us much. And I cannot believe that your curiosity has lost its voice."

"Curiosity is the friend of the young, who have everything to know and nothing to hide," said Meer slowly. "Silence is a better friend to some."

"No, no," Kedar said, shaking his head. "Silence is the friend of deception and ignorance. We can never let ourselves fear the answers so much that we refuse to ask the questions. And when others fear our curiosity, it is then we can be most sure that we do not yet know the truth."

Unmoved, Meer said, "You must know better than anyone how much the truth costs."

Kedar regarded him with a look of tender pity. "It seems you are as much a victim of Oran Anadon as any of us, old friend. But you see, we will have no trouble finding matters to speak of, even if we find none on which we can agree."

He came forward as he spoke, and laid his hand lightly on Meer's shoulder. "All beings must live a completed path. It is why I asked you to come, why I welcome you. Will you be my last guest in Epa-Daun, and allow me the comfort of your company as my circle closes?"

Swallowing, Meer drew and released a hard breath. "Put so, could I refuse and not despise myself?"

Pulling back his hand, Kedar retreated a step. "Forgive me— I have cornered you with my selfishness. It is enough that you came, and that you will take me home. If you will be more comfortable alone until then, Treg will show you to an empty round house."

Meer looked down, then sideways at Treg, and finally up at

Kedar again. "No. I will stay with you."

"If it does not feel like your choice, I would sooner you went with Treg."

Shaking his head, Meer said, "I cannot forget you are here." He shrugged. "Perhaps I will be through being surprised soon—and my curiosity will find its voice again." He tried a smile. "I may even be a little glad to see you then."

Kedar nodded acceptingly, and made no more of it. "I was intending to go to the river, to bathe. Will you come with me, or have you had enough of water?"

"You have a riverbank as well as a river, true?"

"Yes. We are not quite that poor here," Kedar said, his smile brightening. He looked past Meer to Treg. "Thank you. We will be all right now."

As the evening light quickly faded, Meer and Kedar started downslope.

The path Kedar steered them to wandered down through the settlement, which appeared to Meer to have grown up with no plan whatever to guide it. The placement of houses seemed completely haphazard. Their size, design, and spacing were apparently subject to whim. The foot-beaten paths which linked the settlement were maddeningly indirect—it was not possible to go straight to the river without trespassing through yards and detouring around clusters of buildings.

No spoke roads. No orderly circles. No neighbors over the wall—for that matter, no plot walls to create a tidy grid. Epa-Daun was as wild-growing as the green beard of Kawa, and as offensive to Meer's esthetic sense.

Most mystifying was the way the settlement hugged the rise of Kennabar, instead of the edge of Epa-Daun. The entire community could easily have fit in a fraction of the flatter land along the water, most of which had been inexplicably left empty. Meer could not imagine that the exiles were any less beholden to their river than Ana was to Kawa, and yet they seemed to have withdrawn from it as far as Kennabar allowed.

Madness.

Like Ana, the settlement had come alive at twilight. The paths were busier than when Meer had arrived, but he bore the curiosity of the exiles more readily now. Kedar nodded, smiled, and raised his hand to many, answered friendly greetings, but did not stop to talk.

The sounds of work—the beating of brushes, the knocking of stone, the wet cracking of a seed masher—floated on the air. A boy, no more than five, darted across the path ahead of them, laughing giddily.

Something wistful tugged at Meer's emotions as he matched Kedar's stiff-legged pace, something that made the foreign world, the moment, familiar. The memory ambushed Meer before he could name it and protect himself: After so many years, here he was, back in the streets with Kedar at twilight.

But so much more than time had been lost. Once they had raced the wind on light feet and with light hearts. Now they both walked in pain, like the stragglers in a festival run, lamed and lead-limbed, wavering.

"Look what we've become," he whispered.

If Kedar heard him, he gave no sign.

They went to the stretch of river below the diversion to the dikes and above the barrier of rocks. There were others there, several men, two women, the near-darkness making modest their casual nudity. One of the women put Meer in mind of Sachi, and his attention lingered on her while Kedar stripped off his manteau and waded into the water.

Then the woman looked his way, and the challenge in her posture invited him to attend elsewhere. Faintly embarrassed, Meer moved down to the very edge of the water and sat quietly on the bank near Kedar, knees tucked up to his chest. The water was a sheet of black glass which cut the bathers off at the waist and Kedar at the neck; when Kedar ducked his head under, he disappeared completely from sight.

The thought of joining them in the river was attractive. Meer's hard-beaten clothing was stiff from the sea spray, and foul, and his skin itched fiercely where it did not burn. But he could not bring himself to drop the shield the garments represented. He held himself apart, even at the price of his own comfort.

As he waited for Kedar, Meer listened as he could to the banter of the others, wondering how widely his arrival had been noted, wondering what was being said about him. But their chatter was easy and light, about a new liaison in the settlement, about someone's hopes to trade a round house for a hole house, about the stubbornness of someone else's child.

Still, their presence was inhibiting, his awareness of his own hunger discomfiting. He found himself wishing they would finish and be gone. Not long after, they complied, emerging from the water with talk about work to be done. As they were leaving, he risked one more glance in their direction, and found them still naked, carrying their clothing in hand. But the woman was already past, her back to him as she headed up to the houses.

"Her name is Val Maran," Kedar said from the water. "She was danera, in Pria Cluster. Storm brought her out three years ago. He is still the only man she honors."

Meer's head snapped around. "Brought her out? How do you mean that? Do you claim she came out by choice?"

"There are four hundred sixty people named in Epa-Daun's memorial, and I am the oldest of them," Kedar said. "How many have the arbiters banished since me? Enough to fill these houses?"

Frowning, Meer said, "Punishments of the ultimate degree are rare—if only because executions are not."

"The first part is welcome news, at least. I would not like to think we have missed more than those we found dead," Kedar said. "There are only a few true exiles here, Meer. One in three of the Dauns was born here. One in two came here by choice—a hard choice, but we try to help them once they've settled their mind. Many of them have helped us as well, with what they know and carry. We have never been stronger."

Meer stared. There were lights by the ponds now, yellow and flickering, and shadows moving on the berms. *The boundary is a filter, not a barrier—* "How do you feed so many?"

"On the generosity of Morada," Kedar said. "We take more than half our food from what she grows without our help. Out past the breakers, the current from the north carries along skimweed masses so thick the pilots call them islands—"

"What? The sea is alive?"

"More alive than the land, and greener. Boats go out every third day to harvest—they're out tonight, you missed them."

"They harvest at night?"

"Epa-Daun's day starts when the shadow of Kennabar frees us from our homes," Kedar said. "The boats will have hooked an island by now. They'll cut it up with an eye to the wind, and drag as much as they can back to shore—the longest and hardest part of the job. We eat plainly, but amply. What we grow from Anan stock adds some welcome variety, clothes us, and feeds the lamps."

Meer rose and looked seaward. "I suppose I am not surprised, in one way—from the first, the sea did not feel dead to me. But neither does it feel benevolent. I cannot say I understand why there should be such a bounty, or how you thought to look for it."

"Necessity drives harder than curiosity," Kedar said, emerging from the water with slow steps. "After a storm at sea, we would find fragments of strange plants on the beach—in time, six different types, none on Jiol's list of the seventy-four forms of minor blessing."

Kedar began to sluice the water from his body with his hands. "We were desperate for food then. So when two of the forms, the skimweed and the black cord, gave no offense to the stomach, we began to build boats in the hope of finding the source. Oh, they were pathetic things, those first boats. Morada teaches hard lessons. We buried our mistakes in her depths."

A new sound drifted across the river to them, from the direction of the lights. It was men singing, and the sound, if not the melody, was familiar to Meer's ear.

"What kind of song is that? Not a festival chant, or a blessing song, or a song to the apocryphals."

"No—none of those," said Kedar. "But it is a good song, all the same—say I, who devised it. I will gladly teach you your part, if you allow me."

"I do not sing outside of the temple, where other voices can hide me," Meer said.

"Ah. I could not bear to be without music." Kedar sighed, and crossed his arms to clasp his shoulders. "Do you miss the bells, Meer? Have you heard the silence yet?"

Meer looked across the water. "They made me hear it, just now."

"I have been hearing it as long as I have been here," Kedar said. "We can make the hanging drum, the ball pipe, and the five-tone flute. A corner-song sounds as sweet over the yards as it does over the rooftops of Ana. But there is not a bell anywhere in the valley. We have neither the means to wring copper and tin from the rock, nor the secrets and tools of the forger's art."

He turned away and looked toward the light. "I miss the bells almost more than I can say—the sweet calling of the blessing bells, like a woman whispering endearments—the power of the great bells of the arch— Do you know, when the wind blows hard down the valley, I still find myself listening for Eki, the watcher, and Kad, her herald. And I dearly wish I knew that I would hear them again."

Edging closer, Meer asked, "Kedar—what is killing you?"

Kedar waved a hand in the darkness. "My bowels bleed. Every joint has pain. Most days, my stomach will hold little. I have begun to waste. Which of the cancers has me, what organ will fail me first, hardly matters. My body knows what is coming." He caught Meer's elbow and tugged him away from the water. "Come—we must hurry back, or miss the news from Ana."

He did not think it necessary to explain, and Meer was forced to hasten his own steps to match Kedar's surprising pace back up the path.

As they neared Kedar's round house, Meer saw a flickering yellow-white glow from the entryway and at the vent hole of the dome. Then he heard a sudden peal of laughter—several voices, as though some gathering within had been convulsed by someone's moment of wit.

"What is this?" he demanded, catching Kedar's wrist and detaining him.

Kedar turned to Meer with a puzzled expression. "You know my house has always been open. Have you forgotten how it was? I have not changed. There are always a few who come for the listening, and stay to talk. Come, it has already started."

Confused and wary, Meer released Kedar, and reluctantly followed him inside. The light was an assault after the darkness, blinding him for a moment. But what he heard made him push forward past a body half-blocking the opening.

" . . . the trustee of power and water announces the following ring blocks will be serviced tonight: Block 2, Block 7, Block 8, Block 9, Blocks 16 through 18, Block 34, Block 40 . . ."

There was an intermittent crackle, a whistling buzz, which threatened to mask the words, but there was no mistaking the voice of Ana.

The voice was coming from a small object—it was not a receiver, so Meer did not know what to call it—resting atop a three-legged stool near the center of the single room. Beside the stool, and nearly as tall, was a twin-flamed lamp, burning so brightly Meer's eyes hurt to look at it, and adding its own faint sizzle to the noise.

Then he saw the trailing cable and the ragged-edged fragment of collector plate it led to—no larger than a platter, and propped against the legs of the stool, facing the lamp. This much was clear: Whatever the object, it functioned as a receiver, and drew its power from the light of the twin-flamed lamp.

" . . . the prefect of the honor school announces the selection of the following candidates from Wensha Cluster: Pai Thiatet, of the Halia. Jin Eirtet, of the Aythya . . ."

By degrees, Meer became aware that more than twenty people were crowded into the little house. They stood elbow to elbow against the wall, sat cross-legged on the floor, perched on stone seats and in the net hammock which Meer guessed to be Kedar's bed. The light from the lamp turned even smiling faces into harsh masks highlighted against black shadow.

Treg was part of the audience, and Storm, though Nan Tirza was not. They had made room for Kedar along the wall, near the hammock. He was still naked, and in the garish light his body was an obscenity, shrunken and frail. But others around the circle wore little more, with several, one a woman, bare to the waist.

" . . . may night bring each of us the peaceful rest of the hard-working, the honest, and the honorable. May the darkness restore the vigor of our hands and loins, that we may make the most of Ana's many blessings when the circle of the new day begins. These are the wishes of the exarch Oran-rami Anadon, Elect of the Councilors' Circle, and all the ministers and trustees of Ana's gracious joy. It is time for the city to sleep."

That was the end, but they did not treat it as such. They remained patiently silent for several minutes, as though expecting more. Then Kedar stepped forward, reduced the lamp's yield to a less hostile glow, and turned toward where Meer stood.

"The voice of Ana has been heard. The voice of Arania is still silent. So we mark the four thousand eight hundred sixteenth day of the vigil. Let there be an end to it soon."

There was a murmur of assent.

"Treg has called this salon, and presently I will turn its conduct over to his hands," he went on. "But I am happy to welcome so many—and one of you more than any. Before you begin, I greet my friend and guest, Meer Faschen of Ana, third intercessor for the common court of Banteng Cluster, serving the syndic of arbiters. He has come at my invitation, and under my protection. Meer Faschen, welcome to my house."

Meer felt as though the light were still at full brilliance and shining solely on him. He tried to forget the others and speak only to Kedar.

"It seems I am not yet finished being surprised," he said.

"How is it that the voice of Ana is heard in Epa-Daun? Is this trickery?"

"The air does not stop at Ana's boundary," said a man standing beside Storm. "Why do you think scout boats carry a receiver?"

Meer said, "My boat had no receiver."

"So Lial tells us. But you were coming to Edera, and you are not a scout. There was no reason to provide you with anything that would not be of use to you, but might be of use to us. I would guess a special boat was prepared for you. Did you have a light stick? A bronze anchor? A full locker of fuel?"

"No," Meer said, recalling his own suspicions. "None of those things."

"There is your proof, then."

"How do you know all this?"

"I was a scout in the east valley," said the man. "It is my boat which is sunk by the ruins of Edera. And it is that boat's receiver with which we keep the vigil."

"You see," said Treg, "we have many questions, but some answers as well. Stay and talk with us, and perhaps we can help each other." Treg gestured. "Make room for Kedar's guest, Gil."

To Meer's right, bodies shifted along the wall, opening a place for him. But the man displaced from the wall was Storm, who took up position behind Meer in the entryway, blocking the way to the outside.

Drawing himself up as best he could, Meer again looked to Kedar. "I am grateful for your hospitality and your protection," he said. "And I will stay a while, to listen. But I will need to sleep soon, to renew myself for the journey home."

He took the place offered him, wondering as he did when he had ever been confined with so many enemies, and whether Kedar's protection was enough.

But he was not the one attacked.

"I have called this salon as a court of conscience on the question of Kedar Nan's return to Ana," Treg said. "I am sorry to abuse my friend and our host this way—"

"Please, go on, I am fascinated," said Kedar.

"—but I must speak while my words can still reach him," Treg continued. "On principles of common morality, I submit that returning to Ana is an immoral act. On principles of personal integrity, I submit that it is a degrading and self-destructive act."

"Make what judgments you will, the choice is still his," said a woman half-hidden from Meer by the hammock.

"I'll state my purpose plainly. I mean to persuade him of the truth of both these propositions—and to see him declare his change of mind before our witness from Ana." Treg looked across the circle at Kedar. "And if I can't dissuade you, I mean to persuade as many as I can to do as I am resolved to do—namely, stand apart and raise no hand to help you."

"You would hold me here when it was my will to go?" Kedar asked, with eyebrow raised.

"I will not hold you. But I cannot bring myself to help you. Aiding an immoral act is equal to performing that act."

"I suspect the question of the morality of inaction looms before us," said Kedar. "But go on. I am listening."

Treg stepped forward, toward the center of the circle. "Kedar, I heard you speak to Meer of the completed path. I contend that you have already traveled a completed path, one which properly ends here, in Epa-Daun," he said. "I believe this wish to return is a surrender to weakness. I can find no wisdom, purpose, or justice in it."

"And you know that these are assertions, not arguments," Kedar said, settling back against the wall, one leg crossed over the other and his folded hands hooked on his raised knee. "Make your case for the first proposition."

Treg swept an arm in an arc that took in all those present. "There is no need for me to argue the dishonor and corruption of Ana. Everyone in this room can affirm that truth from their own memories. Should I catalog our experiences under Ana's power? Gil's—Storm's—your own? You argued here not twenty days ago that the measures of morality are harm and choice. Ana did us harm, and denied us choice. By your own standard, Ana stands convicted of its immorality."

Shaking his head, Kedar said, "I will not concede that evil acts make an evil city. Neither the virtues nor the transgressions of the part accrue to the whole. There are hundreds of thousands in Ana. How many of them bear the guilt for our injuries? A bare handful—a few tens of tens? My own list is short and specific. I bear no ill for the rest."

A head or two bobbed in agreement, but agreement was not universal.

"I judge those who act by what they do, and the rest by what they allow," said Storm. "If I void in a fresh drinking bucket, it surely holds more water than waste—but I still doubt you'll drink from it."

Several people laughed, and Kedar was among them. "Cleverly put, Storm—but analogy makes as poor an argument as assertion," he said. "There is much good and beauty in Ana as well. Is that not as powerful a contaminant, or do you choose to overlook it? The fact is that Ana is not so simple a thing as a drinking bucket, and you abuse fairness to make it so."

Kedar looked to Treg. "But I see the shape of your argument now, and it will not bear the weight. You may throw blame where you like, but I recognize guilt only where there is choice, which requires both knowledge and freedom. Most of Ana knew nothing of any of us—and most who did know had no power to choose. The argument fails. Continue with your second proposition."

"No," said Treg sharply. "I will not give up this point. Even if we excuse the masses, there is no excusing those who held the power—who still hold it." He pointed accusingly at Meer. "He could not have come without the help and knowledge of the councilors, if not of Oran himself. Is there any question of that? He attends their purposes, not yours."

Meer straightened. "I am here for no one but myself."

Anger blazed across Treg's face. "You serve under the shield of the syndic of arbiters. You carry the shield of the exarch with you. Do you deny it?"

"I do not. But—"

"You come here from the heart of the evil. Kedar, are not his masters and your list of the guilty one and the same? If you do what they wish—go with *him,* of all people—is that not as much as surrendering all our pride? Let him take you back to Ana, and you betray all our grievances against our enemy."

Kedar spread his hands. "I am going home to die, Treg. Or going home dead, as circumstance will tell. If there is surrender in that, it is not to Oran, but to time."

"But there is my outrage, and the mystery—how can you call that place your home?" Treg demanded. "They did not value you, and we do. They did not love you, and we do. They discarded you, but we embrace you. This is your home, and a better place by far."

Shaking his head, Kedar said, "The word means more than that to me. Home is where I came from, no matter where I might be—a house, a mother, sounds and sights and smells beyond forgetting. They need not all be good memories to bear the name. It's no different for you, for any of us. We are children of Ana. The difference is that you hate where you came from, and I do not. But it has the same hold on us both."

His mouth drawn tight with frustration, Treg turned his head away.

"Kedar—" Storm shook his head. "I'm not as easy with words as others here, and no match for you in a duel. But you cannot give away so much for so little. I would rather see *him* go home dead." His hand cut the air in Meer's direction. "But since he is under your protection, send him back with nothing but a message: We reject you. There is nothing in Ana we need, nothing in Ana we want. Let him report that you have found a better place."

"But there *is* something there that all of us need," said the bare-breasted woman.

"Not I," Treg said in quick denial.

"Being what?" asked the former scout at the same time.

"Kedar has already said it—our history." She looked at Storm. "Everyone who has known you keeps custody of a fragment of you. We hold a small piece of Ana, and someday she will need it. Ana holds a much larger piece of us. Someday we will want to claim it from her."

"I am not interested in claiming a heritage with murderers," Storm said. "I will give birth to myself, and choose my own kin."

Kedar sat forward on his perch. "That has never been the reason for Epa-Daun's existence. We have always looked and waited for change, and reunion. That is the meaning of the vigil."

"The vigil is not what we are," said Treg. "It is something we do."

"Do you think that anything has changed?" Storm demanded. "Do you think he has?" He turned on Meer. "Tell me—must women who cannot bear still give themselves to whatever man wants them?"

Meer was taken aback. "Everyone must earn their share, by whatever contribution they are best suited to make."

"And you have made the danera earn their share sweating under you, haven't you? And filled them with hope while you were filling them with your spark, to make them softer pillows." Storm's tone was caustic. "This is their idea of fairness—in reward for bearing five children, the dan are made privileged women. In punishment for bearing none, the danera are given to privileged men."

"What nonsense," Meer muttered, moving out from the wall.

"Do you deny it? They know how I found you."

"Your words are riddled with ignorance," Meer said. "No one in Ana chooses his share work. And Ana herself decides who to bless. If one of the danera was unhappy with her lot, she would find no shortage of company in the craft circles and the green rings. You learn the work from your teachers. Learning to be happy at it is a trick you teach yourself."

"Do you see?" Storm said, looking at Kedar expectantly. "He confesses their offenses as though proud of them. He's unworthy of your protection."

Kedar's expression was unreadable. "So much fuss over one old man," he said. "Your passion, and Treg's, honor me. But your conduct—that shames me. This is not why we come together—not to attack. We do this to ask and understand."

"I'm sorry, Kedar, if I've spoken with too much blood and not enough thought," said Treg. "But his lies must be challenged. Hard things must be said."

Meer stepped close to the lamp, within arm's reach of the pilot. "Say what you like," he said. "I am through listening. I did not come here to be questioned by you, or to defend Ana to you." He looked at Kedar. "I will find somewhere else to sleep. You can tell me in the morning what you have decided."

They did not stop him from leaving.

But he took with him the apprehension that he and Kedar both might die in Epa-Daun.

10

The Burning of Oran

I do not suppose that many Anans enjoyed the peaceful rest of the hard-working and the honorable that night. For any who did, the next morning surely swept away their tranquillity.

I had meant to be in the streets with the first faint light, so that I might run to Kedar's house before reporting for my work. I was anxious for my friends, and could not bear the thought of passing the whole day not knowing what had happened, or hearing what they knew.

But the morning song to which all of us, even Chane, had been trained to rise came late that day. I woke to Chane's hunger-crying, and found the windows already bright and Meli gone. She was sitting in the entry, beneath her blessing bell, looking out into the yard with Chane feeding at her breast.

"Why did you let me sleep?" I asked her.

"We haven't been called to the day."

I stared at the receiver, hanging on the inside wall near where Meli sat. "The sun must be full up by now."

"No one is in the streets."

I looked past her. Across the way, on the inner ring of our road, Nica was standing in *her* entryway, looking out at the day with uncertainty.

"Am I to stay here all morning? Something must be broken."

But Meli was not going to let me past her without an argument, so I went and readied myself, and then waited.

The full disk of the sun had cleared the roof of the next house by the time the morning call came. Restless with impatience, I started for the yard at the first crackle.

The voice of Ana called me back.

Most days, the call is a few phrases of the "Strong Hearts" corner-song, and a few ritual words of hearty encouragement known to and ignored by all. That morning, the song was "Witnesses to Glory," and the words an instruction to come to our receivers and listen.

And then Oran Anadon himself spoke to us.

I wish I could remember for you everything that he said, and the many different tones in which he said it. I had never heard Oran speak before, but I had assumed without thinking that he had a strong, but patient and reassuring voice—like Gowon had had, like Kedar when I met him.

Oran's voice had power, but it was the power of anger, and his words carried a tremble and cut with a shrill edge. He spoke for a long time, now with defiance, now with confidence, now with arrogance, now with contempt, now with a pleasure that approached glee. And it was clear almost from the first that something had happened overnight to change everything.

The message from Hoja den Krador—which Oran never acknowledged, only alluded to—was no longer to be cast as an annoying prank. That morning, it officially became a subversive act of conspiracy, a conspiracy which Oran declared threatened the peace and security of all of Ana. And he made quite clear where the blame was destined to fall, even to naming the first traitor.

That traitor was Lindor Savichen, who Oran described as the instructor of electrics at the honor school. "He has already confessed his role in the conspiracy, and taken his own life in shame," Oran told us.

Though I did not know Lindor, I was chilled, and afraid to hear Oran's next words—afraid more than ever for Kedar. But Oran was not yet ready to accuse anyone else. He settled for a thundering warning of swift and unflinching prosecution of the other conspirators, and a fervent promise to eradicate the subversive influence.

And then he told us that the councilors had met all night, and determined that the gravity of the crisis demanded emergency measures, the full cooperation of every citizen of Ana. In their name, not his, he began to recite a long list of temporary civil directives.

He closed the honor school, ordering the students to return to their home clusters and report to the hives for reassignment by the trustees.

He renewed the dusk-to-dawn curfew for that night, and said that the work day should be shortened accordingly.

He forbade public meetings of more than ten people, that being the ordinary size of a share circle.

He dispatched the surveyors, the ring men, the builders—every sweat circle whose work could be suspended without harm to the city—to report, with tools, to the captain of sentries for their cluster. They had been honored, he said, by being called on to serve as curfew monitors and guardians of the peace.

But Oran's last order was the most dismaying of all. "Despite the diligence of the syndic of public security, there remains a danger we cannot dismiss," Oran said. "Even without Savichen, the conspirators may attempt to use the voice of Ana to contact each other and to spread more lies and subversions through the city. This cannot be tolerated."

So we were sent to fetch our sharpest blades and snips, and told that on Oran's word, we were to measure up a hand's-width from the box and cut the feed cord to our receivers.

It did not stop there.

"When you have finished," Oran said, "go to the house beside yours, and see that your neighbor has done the same, and help them if they require it. Compliance must be perfect."

Meli was already moving toward the receiver, weaving snips in hand. I cried "No!" in a voice full of anguish, and lunged and grabbed her arms, pulling her back.

She must have thought I was stopping her from cutting off Oran's words too quickly, because she did not resist. But I was full of desperate rebellion. I meant not to allow Meli to destroy her receiver, or let anyone from outside try. We would lie, and say it had been done. I would find a way to make it look as though the cord had been cut. Somehow, we would defy the order.

But Oran took away even that choice. "The prefect of public information will send an alarm out after my words, a sound that you will hear plainly on the air," he told us. "That sound will be the sound of disobedience and disloyalty. Wherever you hear it, you will know that someone has not done their part.

"Find them. Help them. If any resist, report them for investigation as conspirators. Our enemies must be denied. Ana must endure. Your hands and your eyes must serve the hierarchy, so that this threat may be shattered, and this crisis may pass.

"Cut the cord now."

Those were his last words. A moment later, a shrill tone came from the box on the wall.

I was still holding Meli's wrists in a tight grip. "Let me go," she said, struggling to free herself. "I have to do it now."

I was near tears, pleading with her. "We have to be able to hear them. How will we hear them? Don't you see, Oran wants to hide this from us, just as Hoja den Krador said. If we submit to this, we'll only know what they want us to know—"

She was not listening. She could not hear me. With a strength I did not know she had, she wrenched herself from my grasp. I struck at her in desperation, but she slipped all the power of the blow, and ducked away. Ashamed, I recoiled from raising my hand against her again. I watched, helpless, as she reached up and cut the cable as though it were the thinnest weaving strand.

Then she turned toward me and fell back against the wall, panting, her eyes burning with accusation. "What is your madness?" she hissed at me. "Do you want them to come for me? Do you want Chane killed as a traitor's child?"

There was too much to explain. I said nothing, but could not stand her eyes. I stumbled out into the yard and stood there listening as the cry of the alarm was strangled house by house by house, until I could hardly be sure if I still heard it, or it was a memory.

I watched as the censors came along the road in twos and threes, knives in hand, eager in purpose, hunting down the last tardy offenders.

I wanted to pour all my fury out on them, but they had no notion of their folly.

For the rest of that day and for the rest of the days of the rebellion, every voice in Ana would be speaking of Arania, except one—the only one which mattered. In a bare few sunlit moments, that voice had been silenced, and by our own hands.

How strange it is that I have so rarely perceived the crucial turnings in my life for what they were.

Has it not been the same for you?

How often it seems that we face a decision of personal moment with our choice compromised, even foreordained, by past decisions we thought of no moment at all. We stumble toward a destiny, commit ourselves to a path, by small steps rather than large. Circumstances blind us—consequences bind us. We do not act, but react.

And out of that sorry parentage all glory and misery are born.

In that one morning, without the dimmest glimmer that I was doing so, I twice reworked my future. I cannot dignify either instant by claiming purpose or foreknowledge in my acts. Had I been so blessed, I would surely have satisfied myself with the first change—because the second undid all, condemning me to that which the first would have spared me.

Yes, I do not deny it—my own acts and omissions brought me here. But still, I remain in awe at how many stones can be toppled by so small a push.

When I left Meli, hard feelings were still circling. Each of us had committed a transgression the other found unforgivable. I thought her transgression by far the greater—enough to excuse, if not justify, my own. But she did not even see the harm she had done, which only deepened her resentment. She had brought me into her home, and I had repaid her with violence. I am sure that to her it was as simple—and incomprehensible—as that.

I did not try to explain myself. I did not stay and fight for peace between us. I waited only until the censors yielded the streets, and then left.

But I did not go into the center city that morning. I did not go to find Kedar. I did not go to the high bank.

Instead, I went to the retting barn.

A different life could have turned on no more than that.

If you find my action hard to understand, I can invent as many rationales as you require—even ones that reflect poorly on me, if you will find those more persuasive.

Why should I have gone to the high bank? Whatever had been said at the salon on the green ring no longer mattered. It was over. Those students who were not already gone soon would be. What use could I be to those making ready to leave?

And the memory of the sentries materializing from the darkness was still begging to be read as an omen. I had felt the danger, the darkness in them. Why return to the high bank, now that it was subject to the hierarchy's close scrutiny? Only the reckless would even have considered it.

What reason was there to find Kedar? He had lost control of the honor school, and Oran had preempted his authority over it. Surely it could not be long until Kedar lost title and status as well. A man who had served under him stood accused by the man he himself served. What immunity could he hope for?

The battle was already lost. Was it not inevitable that Kedar would be denounced as well? It would not be hard to find an offense to charge him with, or to invent one which would serve. And, if not—when all had quieted down, I would still be Kedar's friend. What need was there to call myself to Oran's attention?

I could have thought any of these things, and not been wrong— chosen any reason from the pragmatic to the ignoble.

The truth is I was too sick, too disheartened to do anything but what I did. In the span of one night, everything had come apart, and I was impotent to restore any part of it.

By the power of his words alone, Oran had destroyed one of the pillars of my life. In my helpless rage, I had damaged another. I went to shelter myself under the only one which remained intact, because I needed the reassurance of hard work and familiar routine.

And I did not enjoy even that much insight until much later, when many more stones had toppled.

All I knew that morning was that the sight of the retting barn and the sound of the thrashers already turning were both a comfort to me.

Any promise or expectation of normalcy was swept away the moment I arrived. I was pounced on by Kirl and Paja and assaulted with questions: Had I heard the strange announcements? Oran's pronouncements? Had I seen the apparition in the night sky? What did I think of it all? As others saw me, the ritual was repeated, until everyone had heard my answers.

It was not that they had any inkling I might know any more than they. A spinner who was even later to report than I was surrounded in just the same way. On the morning after the first night of mystery, interrogation was the proper form of greeting.

"Did you hear?" meant "Did it really happen?"

"What do you think?" meant "Does it make any more sense to you than to me?"

And the answers we wanted were "Yes" to the first and "No" to the second.

All across the cluster, it seemed, everyone's experience had been the same. I was startled by how little disagreement there was about what had been seen and heard. We were ready to believe it had been the same from one edge of Ana to the other.

But still, there was a great hunger to go one step further. It was not enough for it to be a common experience, perhaps because none of them wanted to deal with it alone. It had to become a shared experience—and endless talk was how that was accomplished.

As much talk as there was in the barn that morning, it was a marvel that any work was done, and I would not have wanted us judged on the quality of the fiber we turned out. The wheels were left to turn unattended while they consulted and argued in twos and threes and fours.

I could not escape hearing it, but for a long time I did not let myself be drawn in. I dirtied my hands in the broth scum, bloodied them on a broken screen, beaded my brow with honest sweat, and kept my thoughts to myself as long as they would keep.

They kept only until the circle turned to sorting out the *truth* of what all agreed they had seen and heard. It kept only until Tevin provided the push that pulled me back to this path.

It is difficult enough to distill any insight from ignorance. It is impossible for someone handicapped by arrogance. Tevin did not let that fact trouble him. In his own mind, his expertise on all subjects was unequaled.

Usually, the circle knew better than to either argue with or listen to him. But with so much uncertainty about, Tevin's insistence must have been appealing, and he was gradually persuading the barn to accept his version of the truth—which discounted not only everything Hoja den Krador had said, but the existence of the new apparition as well.

When I realized what was happening, I stopped my work to listen—with growing annoyance—as he pressed Kirl and Rown, two of the last doubters.

"There was nothing real in the sky," Tevin was saying, "only in your eyes. It was a false apparition. You know words are sent through the air to the receivers. The eyes are receivers of pictures, shapes, and colors—"

"If I walk toward what I see, eventually I will bruise my nose against it," Kirl said.

"*If* what you see is real," Tevin said. "But it need not be real for you to see it. Close your eyes, and you can still see lights and shapes and colors. Where are they? Nowhere but in your eyes. When you dream, the pictures seem as real as the waking world. Where are they? Nowhere but in your eyes."

Rown had his arms crossed, a frown on his face. "So you say that this man Savichen has devised a way to send pictures through the air into our eyes, just as the voice of Ana sends out words to our ears."

"Exactly," Tevin said. He exuded certainty, anticipated victory. "Think what mischief could be done if these conspirators are free to speak to the city whenever it pleases them to spread a lie. Think what confusion would result if we could be made to see things that are not real. How would we know what to believe? I am proud of the exarch and the Councilors' Circle. They have done exactly what must be done—moved swiftly and firmly to prevent chaos."

I suppose it did not matter much what they believed, or what blather Tevin spouted. They were spectators. Nothing was going to change because of what they thought to be so. But I had heard enough. Walking up to where the three stood, I invited myself into the center of their conversation.

"How do we know what to believe now, Tevin?" I demanded. "How do you know that was Oran who spoke this morning, and not another deception?"

"Paja said he knew his voice."

"And of course, no one could imitate such a well-known voice," I said, echoing his own grating whine back at him. "But even if it was Oran, trusting Tevin, how do you know that *Oran* told the truth?"

He looked at me with indignation. "I know what I know," he said. "The truth isn't some mystery that must be unraveled. The truth doesn't hide its face."

I think I laughed at him. "The truth, Tevin, is that you should hide your face in shame for being such a fool."

Before he could answer, I turned to the others. "The apparition is real. I know twenty people who saw it first three nights ago, and there must have been two hundred who saw it through a glass the next night. It appears as a new star to the eye, but holds itself fixed in place above the city. No one I know can say what the apparition is, but I promise you, it has more substance than Tevin's prattle."

Tevin grabbed my arm to twist me toward him, and thrust his face close to mine. "Liar," he said, his breath foul as his expression. "You invented this story. You had nothing worth saying since you got here—because you know nothing. You invented this, to spite me. There was no 'new star' before last night."

I did not need to defend myself. "No," said Kirl, putting a hand to Tevin's shoulder. "I remember—Meer asked me if I had heard any chatter about the night sky. That was a day ago at least."

"He asked me the same," said Rown. "I had nothing to tell him, and forgot the question until this moment. Let him go, Tevin."

Tevin released me and turned away, scowling, as Rown went on. "What more can you tell us? Wait, the others should hear."

Rown called to Garet, who called Paja and Bren up from the retting tanks. In a matter of moments, the entire circle had gathered around me, and I found myself appointed to lead my own salon, there in the middle of the raking floor. Even Tevin stayed. He hung back, glowering unhappily, but was too afraid of what he might miss to leave—that, or he hoped to catch me in some glaring error and reclaim his honor.

I did not tell them any of what I have told you. I said only that I had been coming home from visiting a woman north of the river, which they were ready to believe, and that I had happened on a loud gathering of students. I stopped, I told them, and the students shared their discovery, and allowed me a turn at the glass, and there was enough truth in that. And I made Weilin the expert—though I pretended not to know his name—so that they would not expect too much from me.

But I did not evade the question they most wanted me to address. Paja asked it, though it was in all their faces, for I had taken away the security Tevin had offered them. "If the apparition is not a deception," he asked, "and it is not a star, then what can it be?"

I had thought of almost nothing else since the night before, and I gave them the best of my thoughts.

"I think," I told them, "that if we had a way to cross the sky as we do to cross the land, we would find the sky has a ceiling just as the land has a horizon, though even farther away and harder to reach."

No one challenged that, though Garet's glassy eyes told me I had already lost him. But I went on with the rest.

"I think the apparition is another city," I said, "a city which sits on the ceiling of the sky, at the edge of the realm of the apocryphals. Its name is Arania, and Hoja den Krador is its exarch. Somehow they are bound to us, but the reason is lost with so much of our past.

"Three days ago, they lit a great fire to help us find them," I told them. "Last night, they spoke to us through the air, and waved festival flags in the auspicious colors, in the hope that we would remember. But Oran intends that we should never remember."

Those are still the best of my thoughts.

I did not mean for it to happen, but my words ended our work for the day, for they launched us into a dialogue as earnest and intense as any I had ever witnessed in Rida's house.

We had neither the means of proof nor disproof at hand, but that did not dampen the ferocity of debate in the slightest. Tevin thought me addled, Kirl declared me inspired—but no one thought tearing the bast from the shives more important than tearing each other's ideas into their component parts.

We were still on the raking floor, caucusing, when dan Sawai entered the barn. Though I did not know her well, I knew she was well-respected. Her appearance won even Tevin's silent attention.

"How can we help you, dan Sawai?" Kirl said as we rose in courtesy.

"By listening," she said with a faint smile, "and holding your tongues until I am done."

And then we learned that the students of the honor school had not scattered to their homes as Oran had directed.

Instead, they had crossed the river and gathered on the plaza of the arch in protest of Oran's directives—gathered in such numbers, said dan Sawai, that the sentries of the temple of the fountain had surrendered the plaza to them and retreated.

Emboldened, the students had marked all the entrances with the name *Plaza of Truth*. They vowed to occupy it night and day until the Councilors' Circle provided answers to their list of seventeen Fundamental Inquiries. At the time dan Sawai left them, a delegation was being selected to deliver the list to the high bank.

I was sure I would know at least some of the names of those chosen.

She picked two of us, Tevin and Garet, and asked them to carry the news to the craft houses on the thirty-fifth ring of the cluster.

"Leave your work and go to the plaza," dan Sawai told the rest. "Even if misguided, these are our sons—the best of our lines and our loins. They will need our help to survive their recklessness. Go to the plaza now and talk with them, before it is too late."

She spoke so carefully that I have never been able to decide whether she meant for us to stop the students, or to join them.

Respect did not equal obedience: Only Kirl and I were willing to risk doing as dan Sawai asked, and go at once. Others promised to come at the end of the day, but I did not count on their promises, thinking they would let the curfew keep them away.

I expected to find the plaza in the grip of chaos and fear. Instead, I found the same amiable disorder of the gather on the high bank, on a grander scale. Students were sitting on the fencewalls, milling on the plaza. Some seemed to have a purpose to occupy them, but most did not. They were waiting. Their presence was their purpose and their statement.

I felt no fear in them, no threat. No one challenged me as I walked onto the plaza. And nowhere was there a sentry to be seen.

The largest gathering of students was near the temple, on the river steps. I asked Kirl to make a circuit of the plaza and see what he could learn, and then started across it, scanning for faces I knew. Someone ran up and pressed a sheet of sugar paper into my hands, then ran off again.

On the paper were written, in a hasty hand, the seventeen Inquiries.

Reading them as I walked, I began to feel the fear for them.

The first inquiry asked: Why is there no truthful history of Ana?

The fifth: What are Oran Anadon's qualifications to lead the Councilors' Circle?

The eleventh: What is the true meaning of the star-apparition?

The last: Where is Prefect Nanchen, and why has he not spoken to us?

As I worried over the demands, someone caught me by the shoulder. I looked up into Lenn's eager face. "What is happening?"

"You came! Bless you—everyone who stands with us makes us stronger. Can you believe, there are more than a thousand here already. Everyone is down by the river—Chai, Jalos, even Weilin, poor creature—"

"Wait, wait—what happened to Weilin?"

Lenn's countenance darkened. "At his long house this morning—he refused to let anyone destroy the receiver. He was beaten, because people were afraid." He shook his head. "I am afraid he is hurt more than he will admit."

"Tell me where can I find him."

"In the shadow of the temple, I hope. When I left, Dejian was trying to coax him out of the sun. Come, I'll take you."

We joined the crowd at the river terrace just as the delegation of inquiry was setting off toward the Five-Ring Bridge.

I had expected the delegation to be long since gone. But I had not considered the difficulty of reaching consensus on any decision in a group of so many strong-minded. It was truly a small wonder they had managed a decision so important in something less than a full afternoon.

I would have argued against what they were about to do, but that argument had been fought and lost before our arrival. Or perhaps not completely lost—the delegation numbered seventeen, which might have had as much to do with safety as with symbolism. I waved them off with the others, and called good wishes to Kaixi and Chai, but not without wondering if I would see them again.

Lenn found Weilin sitting propped up on the second tier of the terrace, facing the river. The right side of his face was bruised purple-black, and his puffy-lipped smile showed a broken tooth. His left leg was stiff and straight, and he grimaced when I brushed against it. When he laughed or coughed, his eyes watered from the pain, making plain still more injuries were concealed by his garments.

With so much of the leadership away north of the river, Weilin was becoming a focal point for the north fringe of the gathering. I hovered near him until sunset approached, talking with him when he was not distracted by his many visitors, bringing him water from the river when he asked.

It was from him I learned that the curfew and patrols had prevented the grand salon, but that lights had burned through the night in the student long houses. Many students were still up when two junior instructors, each accompanied by a sentry, appeared at each long house before dawn to announce the school was closed.

"They ordered us to go at once, and waited for us to comply. Some did leave—more than half, in my long house. The rest wanted to hear the order from Kedar," said Weilin. "If we scattered, we would have become powerless. We had to know that Kedar would not need us. So we were still there, arguing, when Oran spoke to the city."

The instructors went white when Savichen's death was announced, Weilin said. "They were afraid, more afraid than I have ever seen two men. When I tried to save the receiver, it was the instructors who beat me. The sentry merely kept anyone from interfering."

Then he touched his own bruised face gingerly. "Docent Howin and Docent Chidori did this. Boli tells me Howin tore out the cable himself—and I was in his mentor group my first year in school. But I do not blame them. I think they felt they must prove their loyalty to the Circle, or end up like Lindor."

As dusk approached, I fretted at Weilin. "You should not spend the night on the ground," I told him.

"I have to stay," he said. "I have to let them see me."

I tried to kid him out of it. "Surely everyone who's drunk or passed water today has seen you by now."

"I did not mean the objectors." Weilin pointed across the river, at the high bank, and I turned to see the figures of twenty or more men scattered along its edge, looking across and down on the plaza. Many, but not all, showed the bright yellow of sentry blouses.

"We have their attention," he said. "We must make the most of it."

The failing light finally chased me from the terrace. I did not mean to stay on the plaza, and I did not want to be in the streets after the curfew began. Wishing Weilin a peaceful night, I set out for the half-west spoke road, scanning for Kirl as I went.

But finding anyone on the plaza had become far more difficult while I had lingered by Kawa. Beneath my notice, the plaza had continued to fill, until it was all nearly as congested as the riverfront. It was like a festival crowd, or a ten-bell calling. I could not go five paces without having to step around someone or stop to avoid a collision. If there had been a thousand people on the plaza when I arrived, there could easily have been five thousand as I was leaving.

And most of the new faces were neither young nor male. Older men in their labor garments, fresh-marked hostel girls clutching small pillows, house women with children in arms or in tow, dan escorted by young men with net bags of rind fruit—these were not students, but fathers and girlfriends and mothers, friends of the students, neighbors of the plaza.

It was obvious they had made their choice. They had come to stand with the students, and against the high bank. They had brought food, and shared it. They had brought lamps and precious fuel. They had brought paper, and sat making copy after copy of the Fundamental Inquiries by hand.

It had become something no one could have planned, and no one controlled.

I picked my way through the throng, marveling at what I was witnessing, becoming caught up, against my will, in the air of— what? confidence? determination? hubris?—I was feeling from them. I forgot about searching for Kirl. I looked into their faces instead of at them, and started to feel that leaving the plaza would be a betrayal.

That was when I saw Kedar.

He was crossing my path several strides in front of me, heading toward the temple. Only uncertainty stopped me from calling out his name. The cowl of his manteau was up and drawn forward, as though he meant to conceal his face, though probably not one in a hundred in that part of the plaza knew him by sight, not even those who had been writing his name. I caught only the briefest glimpse of him before he vanished again into the crowd.

I hurried after him, biting my tongue. Had it not been for his cowl, or had I seen him an hour earlier, I likely would not have found him. But he was taller than many, which helped me—and most on the plaza had bared their heads when the sun dipped below the houses, which helped me even more. I caught him near the center of the plaza, by the sigil of the argali, and placed myself in his way.

He looked at me with dark, tired eyes. "Have you seen my son Lenn?" was all he said.

"Your salon has been keeping near the river, west of the temple." I started to say more, but he nodded and turned away, toward Kawa.

I chased him again and fell in beside him, pushing people aside to stay with him. "Kedar, where have you been? Do you know that everyone is asking about you?"

He stopped and turned to look hard into my eyes. "Meer, go home," he said.

I told him he had more friends than he knew, if he would only call on them.

"It is not a good time to be my friend," he said bluntly, and pushed on, disappearing into the crowd.

I let him go. I do not know why.

After a time I turned away and headed once more toward the spoke road. It felt wrong, and there was little comfort in knowing I was doing what Kedar had asked.

Twilight was yielding to dusk as I reached the edge of the plaza. That part of the plaza was gripped by the rumor, which I caught in bits and pieces as it spread, that labor gangs were massing to drive the 'conspirators' from the plaza. Dozens of people were arranging themselves to barricade the entrance with their bodies. I could hear voices touched by worry and impatience shouting directions.

Then a murmur rose behind me, spreading, growing louder by the instant. People were clapping, jumping in place, pointing upward. I looked up. The sky had darkened enough that the new star had become visible, and it seemed to hang directly above the plaza.

What happened next is beyond faithful description. I cannot even think of it without getting chills.

But I will tell you what I heard, even though I cannot make you hear it: Without any plan or prompting, but with a single thought that merged thousands into one, the people on the plaza joined to raise their voices to the sky, as if to answer the greeting of Hoja den Krador.

It began as a wordless, toneless cry sounding in the throats of five thousand. Then, off to the east quarter, a handful of clear voices broke out in song, and the notion swept across the plaza in seconds. Gracefully, the cry transmuted into the nine-tone chant of the festival of the thirteenth bell, sung grand and happy and proud.

I had never heard such a sound before, nor have I ever since. I did not know pure voice alone had such power. The power was all around me, flowing up through me until I felt light, pouring out of me as song. If clear minds and hearts alone could have lifted us to the top of the sky, I would have seen those glories that night.

I do not know if Hoja den Krador could hear us, in his city on the ceiling of the sky.

But without doubt, Oran Anadon heard us, across the river on the high bank. Surely half of Ana heard us.

When the chant finally ended, I could not make myself leave.

I made the excuse to my conscience that it was too late, that I was safer on the plaza than in the streets—and then spent the second night of mystery helping stand watch over the half-west entrance to the Plaza of Truth.

We were restless and plagued by rumors. It seemed that every nightmare fear spoken aloud in question became, in the course of the night, a warning, an alarm, a certainty, and, in the end, a falsehood.

I heard these: Scout boats full of stickmen were on the river. The delegation of seventeen had been arrested. Sentries in disguise had brought poisoned food to the plaza—eat nothing you did not bring yourself! The sweat circles were massing outside the first green ring to drive us from the plaza—more people are needed at the gates! Oran's monitors were already on the plaza, slipping in by ones and twos. Do you know the woman next to you, the man beside her? Find people you know and sit back to back with them, for safety—

But when the sun rose over Ana, we were still there, and the plaza was still ours.

It was the brightest morning I can remember.

11

Ojawit: The Seventh Bell

With nothing that could be called a plan, no notion of where Nan Tirza might be found, and no appetite for asking further favors or inviting further confrontations, Meer found himself back at the river by Treg's boat.

He could hear bathers upstream from the rock barrier, but he could not see them, so he trusted they could not see him. Except for the bathers, he seemed to be alone. No one had followed him down the path from the settlement, or, for once, even seemed to take much notice of him as he passed.

For one wild moment, he contemplated dragging the boat out into the current, raising the sail, and fleeing Epa-Daun. It must have been the thought which brought him there, he realized, buried too deep for his conscience to find and reject it.

But in the end, it was a failure of confidence, not the exercise of conscience, which stopped him.

In the cold light of reason, Meer knew he had not watched Treg closely enough to practice his art, had not learned enough from the sea to master its challenge. And the memory of choking for air and sucking only bitter water, of clutching frantically for a life-grip in the blackness and catching only insubstantial foam, tempered any reckless impulse toward adventurism.

So with the laughter of the bathers and the quiet rush of the water in his ears, he curled up in the center sling of Treg's boat, and drifted on dreamless tides of sleep.

He was awakened by the weed boats coming in, or, more precisely, by the commotion which attended their return. It was still dark—he could not judge the hour. He sat up, still thick-headed, to see lights all across the river mouth, and to hear a shout pass up the hill that "two are in, cutters come down."

Across the river in front of him, the knife-shape of a sail picked up enough stray light from the lanterns to show Meer the first boat nosing along the shore while men and women waded into the river at its stern. Before long, there was a second boat along the opposite shore, and a pale light bobbing well out at sea that marked another coming in.

More help was coming, too, pouring down the paths in unhurried but purposeful answer to the call. Cutting tools and long hooked poles glinted in the exiles' hands, and chatter glittered on their voices. Meer watched, marveling, as they used the wide-spaced barrier rocks as a bridge, leaping from stone to stone by the light of a single lamp held high on the far shore. Not one of them fell.

Curiosity held him there for a time, until he had grasped the substance of the process. It took twenty hands or more to drag a single dark, tangled mass of skimweed partly ashore. Then the knives slashed, and the men with the hook poles lifted long sections clear of the ground and carried them away upstream toward the drying racks; forming a peculiar parade. The poles bowed under their loads, which—in the lamplight—looked like the sodden sea hair of some water spirit.

But as the third boat approached the mouth of the river, weariness tugged at Meer, and at last he clambered out of Treg's boat and quietly retreated. He followed the sound of the surf to the beach, avoiding both the paths and fringes of the settlement, then followed the beach until the sheer face of Kennabar rose up before him and walled off that escape.

There he made a bed for himself in the dry sand of the high beach, and stared up at the stars until their brightness hurt his eyes enough to fill them with tears.

The red-orange glow flooded the world and burned through Meer's inner haze. He sat up with a start, not knowing, for that one tremulous child-in-the-dark moment, where he was. But it was daylight splashing over him.

"Good morning," said a familiar voice.

Squinting, Meer craned his head in both directions. Kedar was perched nearby on a rock, resting his elbows on his knees, his chin on folded hands, as he gazed seaward and sunward. The cowl hood of his tan manteau hung unused down his back.

"When Nan did not know where you were, I feared you might have surrendered to some foolishness," he said. "The house is quiet now, if you want to come back. People have gone to their beds."

Meer began to brush the sand from his palms and forearms. "You must be ready to do the same. I am out of step with all of you."

"I do not do much more than nap these days, an hour here and there," Kedar said, straightening and shading his eyes with a hand. "My time is too precious to give half of it away."

Meer glanced out over the water, but could not find what had caught Kedar's attention. "Why do they work at night and sleep under the sun?"

"Have you asked the right question?"

"What do you mean?"

"Why do Anans labor in the sun, when they know that sun work burns the depths of the body, and brings the cancers and the mange?"

Meer groped for an answer and found none he would risk against Kedar's critique. "I cannot imagine Ana living upside-down like this," he said with a shake of the head. "The day begins with the sun."

"Death begins with it as well," said Kedar. "Children born in Epa-Daun do not receive the suite of first breath, to darken the skin and armor the lungs. We have no midwives keeping gardens, blending the essences of the minor blessings. When infirmity comes, we do not have even the feeble hope offered by a bed in the healing house. If we hide from the sun, it is only because we find life precious enough to prolong."

He twisted his head to the side and looked questioningly at Meer. "Perhaps Anans live in the sun because they find life less than precious. Or because some find the lives of others less precious than their own. Those are the only answers I can find."

Meer stood, walked to the edge of the water, and emptied his bladder. He came back to where Kedar was sitting. "What have you decided?" he asked bluntly.

"I have not changed my mind."

"Or theirs?"

Kedar flashed a small smile. "They are not usually like that. But they are struggling, too. No one has ever chosen to return to Ana before. It upsets many comfortable convictions. And that I am the one—that approaches the unthinkable. But it is important to think the unthinkable. Treg and I talked for a long time after the others had gone. I think progress was made. No, I am sure of it."

"Will they give us a pilot and a boat, then?"

"We will not need them," Kedar said, standing. "I mean to take a better way, through the mountains."

Meer gaped. "You mean for us to walk to Ana? That will take a festival month, at your best pace—if you last that long."

Kedar shook his head. "You will see. Storm makes this trip often. Trust me, Meer—I would not choose the harder way now."

Crossing his arms over his chest, Meer looked away down the beach, frowning unhappily.

"You are thinking of the weight of poor Kedar's corpse," said Kedar with a smile, "and the long empty places between here and home. I will amend my promise to you. I will not die *until* we reach Ana."

"How can you make any such promise?" Meer said angrily. "Death does not come by invitation. It respects no promises made in its name."

"Only I know how hard I must fight to hold on, or how easy it will be to let go," Kedar said, then smiled. "And if I reach the boundary alive, I will most certainly die at the hands of the sentries, yes? But I will risk that for a chance to hear the bells again."

Meer scuffed the sand with his toes, sending a plume of fine grit several feet up the beach. "I want to leave today."

"I expected so," said Kedar. "But it is not possible. I have many good-byes to say." He nodded toward the sea. "This is the first of them. I do not expect to see Morada again after today."

Turning, Meer looked toward the horizon. "What does that mean to you? I will be *glad* to say the same."

Stripping off his manteau, Kedar walked down to where the last gasping rush of a wave swirled around his feet. "Here is one edge of a circle," he said, spreading his arms wide, "a circle so great that I cannot even mark a line across it to the other side. Can you look on it and not wonder what it may encompass?"

Meer had followed to the edge of the dry sand. "It seems to me a realm not unlike the sky," he said finally. "Sea and sky both touch Ana, but they are not part of her, not a place for us. We belong in the place set between sea and sky."

Kneeling, Kedar cupped his hands and, in ritual succession, wet his face, his heart, and his groin with the brine. He lowered his head and mouthed a few words Meer could not hear. Then he struggled up and looked longingly out beyond the surf, even beyond the sun-flecked swells.

"Horizons, like limits to knowledge, are always with us," he said softly. "But there is something in me that cannot help wanting to see beyond them both."

He turned away, showing a bittersweet smile, and gathered up his garment. "Come," he said once he had slipped back into it. "There are things we can do to make ourselves ready while Daun sleeps."

They began at Kedar's round house, where he touched two fingers to his lips in a call for silence as he ducked inside. Following, Meer saw that the woman who had spoken up for Kedar in the salon was curled up in the hammock, asleep. The warm light from the crown hole overhead, diffused against the curve of the dome, flattered her face, half-hidden by hair, and the profile of her hip and buttock, which were not hidden at all.

Kedar was not occupied long enough for Meer's appreciative glance to become an intrusive stare. Gathering up an empty drawstring bag which hung on the far wall, he waved Meer back outside.

"I see you found better company in my absence," Meer said. "Perhaps you should thank me for losing patience with your friends."

Kedar pursed his lips, as though he were weighing a question of great import. "I do not think Dansi would have been inhibited by your presence," he said finally, and broke into a guilty smile. "She has been a joyful companion."

"No? Then I am the one who should be grateful. I do not think I would have borne well witnessing your mutual joy at close quarters."

Kedar's smile broadened, and he chuckled heartily. "If truth be told, you would not have needed to be at close quarters to witness it."

"Oh, braggart. Spare me."

"By no means," said Kedar. "I claim no credit for the magnitude of the disturbance. Dansi reaffirms my fond conviction that there are truly *seven* common arts. Though she is the master of more than one." He held up the bag, spreading its folds, and Meer saw for the first time that it was decorated with rich needlework, including the sigils of the Genet and the honor school. "The very best of them show us more kindness than we deserve. I have been blessed to know more than one such."

"She must be hard to leave," Meer said quietly.

"It is always hard to leave," said Kedar. He held his smile, but his eyes glittered wetly.

Kedar led Meer up a rising path which cut across the slope of Kennabar below the lowest rank of rock-holes. That was the closest Meer had been to the hole houses, and he fell behind a few steps at each as they passed it, peering curiously through the entryway. But there was little he could see, since there was little light within.

"These are not natural," Meer said as he paused before one.

Kedar had not broken stride, and his answer drifted back. "No, of course not."

Meer hurried to catch up. "How did you come by rock nats? Or have you already explained that, when you said Storm has made the trip to Ana often?"

"No—Storm is a fine thief when that is needed, but this was not his doing. Twelve turns back, three miners from Itaris came out together, our first from that trade," said Kedar, slowing as the path grew steeper. "Two are still with us—Izel was in the salon last night, though I do not think he spoke while you were there.

"They left Ana by tunneling out north from Itaris, concealing their escape with a collapse inside the lode rock. They took with them a great treasure in nats and work sleds, which they hid until we could help them retrieve them. With such tools and their experience of years underground, they have done wonderful things." He stopped at one opening and waited until Meer reached him. "Come and see."

Meer hung back. "I do not like the thought of being in a bubble of air under hundreds of feet of rock. There is something about it that offends good sense."

"Perhaps so," Kedar said, "but this bubble contains the supplies we need for our return to Ana. So I suggest you find some way to forgive the offense." He turned away and disappeared into the passageway.

Sweeping his gaze up the face of Kennabar to the top, Meer found himself rocking backwards in response to the sight. "Damn you," he said under his breath. Then, firming his shoulders and lowering his head, he followed Kedar inside.

There was a slight upward slope to the passage, and a breeze blowing at his back. Fifteen paces in, the passageway widened to a chamber three times the size of Kedar's house. What light there was came from the passage behind Meer and several openings spaced across the chamber's ceiling. The air was cool, the rock walls cooler still.

Kedar was already at one end of the chamber, browsing the waist-high bins of food which lined both sides of a narrow walkway, and dropping his selections into his bag.

"Is that for us both?"

"No," said Kedar, gesturing over his shoulder. "There are bags on the far wall and water bottles in the second bin. Pick yourself a bag, and a bottle for each of us."

Meer complied, stopping on the way to look up into one of the light holes. Far above, at the end of a shaft polished to a mirror gleam, was a patch of bright sky. Meer could hear the air rushing out the opening.

"Nats cut these?"

"Tunneling nats—in less than a day for each," said Kedar. "Five days for the chambering nats to open this space. It took us longer than that to haul out the tailings, even with miner's sleds."

"I did not realize what they were capable of."

"You still do not. Bring the bottles," he said, "and I will show you a little more."

The bags were plain, but otherwise much like Kedar's, with a drawstring of hemp cord and a body of coarse linen. The bottles were fewer in number, and familiar—wide-mouthed tin canisters like those he had had on the boat, perhaps even the same ones. The sight of them refreshed his hostility over the theft.

The bottles were empty, leading Meer to expect a trip to the river. But Kedar took one of the canisters from him and crossed to the wall opposite the entry passage, where three wooden-handled pegs pierced the wall. He held the canister's mouth up before the leftmost and turned the handle a quarter-circle. Instantly, a hard stream of water leaped out to rattle in the bottom of the tin.

"Kawa's staff! Water from the rock?" Meer moved forward and copied what Kedar had done, marveling at the force of the stream and the speed with which the tin grew heavy in his hands.

His tin full, Kedar caught a mouthful from the stream, letting what he missed splash on the floor and run toward the exit. Then he stanched the flow with a twist and a wooden squeak. "Not from the rock," he said. "From the river."

At that moment, Meer's tin began to overflow. He lunged for the handle, but turned it the wrong way, loosing a still larger stream that soaked the front of his blouse before he could correct his error.

"How?" he demanded when he was no longer distracted. "We must be seventy feet above the river."

"Closer to a hundred, I would think. We are nine hundred feet beneath it, as well."

"Damn you, don't tease me with pieces. Explain yourself."

"Have you tasted the river here? It is the same as the sea, bitter with chemicals, not fit for drinking." Kedar raised his arm and pointed at the rock ceiling. "Think of the cisterns under the houses of Ana. Five hundred feet above us, near the crown of Kennabar, is another chamber three times this size, filled with fresh water. Pipe-ducts the thickness of your thumb run down to every hole house and larder room."

"And the weight of the water feeds them." The wonder in his voice was undisguised. "By Kawa's staff."

Nodding, Kedar said, "These taps are for the people who live in the round houses. Everyone in the rock has their own."

"But how do you fill this cistern?" Meer protested. "How can it be both above and below its source?"

Even in the dim light, Kedar's smile was rich. He slowly dropped his arm until it was nearly horizontal, his fingers pointing toward the western wall. "We live in a walled valley. Epa-Daun enters it by falling nearly eight hundred feet from the high plateau, well west of here. Izel, Scot, and Briden cut a qanat through the rock to take our water from there, above the waterfall."

"How far?" Meer's voice was a whisper.

Kedar steepled his hands over his mouth. "The number eludes me. No, hold—the drop is one part in one thousand, and the fall over four hundred feet. So the run of the qanat must be well over a hundred thousand paces, yes?"

"Impossible," said Meer. "That's longer than the whole of Ana's boundary ring is around. Half again longer."

"It takes four days to walk up the valley to the great fall," said Kedar. "Not easy days, either, but worth it for the sight, I would add. No, I am sure of my figuring. The water in your tin has traveled the better part of half a million feet through the rock since it left the river."

The chamber was suddenly claustrophobically confining, and Meer fled it without explanation, slipping and nearly falling on the water-slick rock on the way. Kedar found him sitting beside the entrance, legs splayed wide to hold him on the slope as he stared down into the settlement, drawing deep breaths.

"So many secrets," he whispered as Kedar crouched beside him. "I am so weary of secrets. Everything keeps changing. Everything I know becomes a lie." He turned his head toward Kedar. "No one in Ana dreams of what you have done here."

Lips pursed, Kedar nodded slowly. "We have kept secrets when we must, from our enemies."

"Am I not the enemy?"

"You are not my enemy," said Kedar. "And it is a good thing for you to know that these people have reason for their pride. They do not have much—but they have used it well."

When both packs were filled with what Kedar pronounced sufficient provisions, the two men returned to his round house.

Inside, the air was still but dry, cooler than out in the sun but warmer than inside Kennabar. The shaft of light from the crown hole had crept nearly to the floor, and, once Meer's eyes adapted, the room seemed brighter than before. Dansi was still asleep in the hammock, though she had turned face-up.

In averting his eyes from her breasts, Meer noticed for the first time the hatchwork of short faint lines which marched at an angle down one side of the wall and across the floor. The lines were spotlit by the circle of light too perfectly for coincidence. As Kedar sat cross-legged, sorting through his possessions, Meer watched quizzically as the light beam continued its advance.

"A clock?" he said at last.

Kedar did not look up. "An unfinished project," he said, frowning. "I intended to calibrate it, with a pendulum, but something else always seemed to take precedence. It would have been tedious, which may explain why. A single surface is far simpler."

With a wordless murmur, Dansi stirred languidly in her sleep. This time, Meer did not look away.

"I have sat and watched her like this many times," said Kedar with affection.

Embarrassed, Meer dropped his gaze to the lines on the floor.

"No—go on, she would not mind," Kedar said. "But that is Dansi. The rules *are* different here, must be different—one woman for every five men, and only half of them fertile. It is always their choice, who and when and why. And you cannot judge one from the other.

"Gales has given away five babies to their fathers. Panna seems to bed every new arrival, as a welcome, but refuses most seconds. Loria and Ador bed only women, most often each other. And I have already told you of Val." He shook his head. "Newcomers are always confused, and often frustrated. The balance is fragile. It is hard for men to go without."

"Not only men," Dansi said sleepily. She peeked at them through slits, a smile tugging at her lips.

Chuckling, Kedar said, "Bright flower, your appetites spoil men for ordinary women."

"Kedar, you are such a slow learner," Dansi said, somehow flowing onto her back and then stretching provocatively, arms crossed above her head. "There *are* no ordinary women."

Kedar's hoot of laughter was strangled to a dry cough that went on and on, until both Dansi and Meer were looking at him with concern.

"You see, she can leave me wordless and breathless both," Kedar said after he regained his voice. Flush-faced and hoarse, he nevertheless managed a smile as he waggled a finger in Dansi's direction. "This woman has added five turns to my life, Meer—and taken them away again, too, I warrant."

It struck Meer as odd praise, but it seemed to please Dansi, who flung Kedar a kiss before closing her eyes.

"The balance is fragile, as I said," Kedar went on, picking up the thread of the earlier conversation, "and not all can maintain it. There was one Anan who came here, two, nearly three years ago—Damek was his name, out of Ammadi Cluster, or so he claimed.

"He bore no line mark, but he told a story to explain it that enough of us believed, about being wrongly accused of a petty theft, and leaving Ana in anger over it. I suspect now that he had been rightly convicted, and not of theft—and had fled to avoid the sterner punishment for some second offense."

"Even Panna shied from him," Dansi said, taking up the story. Her eyes were wide open now, but clouded. "But he did not want her—he took after Loria, and he pressed her no matter how she refused him. Her refusals challenged him, I suppose. He went to her house one morning and was as savage and hateful to Ador as words can be." She shuddered.

"That next day," Kedar said, "Damek caught Loria alone on the north beach, where she had gone to avoid him, and forced himself on her." He paused, staring off into a memory. "When we found him, the women cut him over and over, until the men dragged him to the river by his heels and drowned him."

Kedar paused again, frowning, his eyes still intent on sights only he could see. Meer could only wait mutely, chilled.

"Damek did not fight much when we pushed him under," Kedar said finally. "I think that our part in Loria's revenge was, by then, something of a mercy." Shaking his head, Kedar reached down before him, and held out a garment toward Meer. "Here. Your blouse is an abomination. This will serve you better until we are near to Ana."

It was a hooded waist-blouse of sun-bleached flaxcloth. Meer rolled the tatters of his scout blouse into a ball, with Oran's shield as the center, and forced it down into the tightly-packed drawstring bag. When he donned Kedar's gift, he discovered that it, too, bore the sigils of the Genet and the honor school as stitchings in colored thread.

He felt uncomfortable wearing it, but Dansi looked on approvingly.

"Yes," she said. "That suits you better."

The three talked for a time, of inconsequential things which drew their attention to neither the future nor the past. But as the air in the house grew steadily warmer, Kedar's head began to nod forward. Shortly after, he announced that he was going to nap.

Yielding her place without a word, Dansi helped Kedar into the hammock, then slipped in beside him, cradling him tenderly, their bodies molding against each other with the ease that comes only with familiarity. Meer was already edging toward the door when Dansi looked across to him. Her quick smile was soft and thankful, and stayed with Meer as he turned away and emerged into the dazzling afternoon sun.

The paths were deserted, though a few voices came faintly to his ear from somewhere up the face of Kennabar. Pulling the blouse's cowl forward until it shaded his eyes, Meer started down toward the river, his intention coalescing as he went.

If Kedar had begun his good-byes, there could not be much time left for Meer to satisfy any lingering curiosities. He had already learned a great deal which might have some value when he was back in Ana. But there were areas he had not yet explored, and he decided to avail himself of the freedom Kedar's nap afforded him to do so.

By Meer's count, at least one of the bigger boats was missing from the river landing, and he searched for it on the sea, wondering who else was up in the middle of the day, and why. When he spotted no sails, he decided perhaps someone had already gone to begin salvaging his sunken scout craft—a task which, it seemed to him, would be difficult enough by daylight, nigh impossible at night.

Carefully and unhurriedly, he looked over all the boats which were there, recording in memory any details of their construction he had missed up to that time. The right float of one of the twin-hulled boats had gone flaccid, and Meer found both the new split and evidence the bladder had been patched several times before. For a moment, he found himself grateful that he and Kedar were not returning by water.

Then the thought struck him that it would only be five minutes work with a knife, or even a sharp rock, to destroy all six boats beyond quick repair. The thought was oddly uncomfortable, but it would not go away, even when he left the landing and made his way cautiously across the rock bridge to the other side of the river.

He followed the bank upstream to the diversion dike and walked a complete circuit of the irrigated area on the enclosing dike, taking inventory of what was growing there. He counted only eleven crops, some planted in rows, some burgeoning in dense clusters, some rooted in soil, some in a mat of black sea grass which Meer guessed to be one of the inedible forms.

The farm was far too small to support three hundred people, but still surprisingly productive. A plethora of small water channels sliced across the enclosure, keeping all the roots wetted. A mound of excrement, apparently regularly mined, gave further testimony to the greenhands' thoroughness. On impulse, Meer added his contribution before continuing on.

It appeared to him that the drying field had begun as a part of the farm which had failed. The first few rows of racks were skeletons of thorn brush, cotton, and rosefruit. Farther on, they were supplanted by fence hoops of twisted supplejack—which must have come from elsewhere, since he had not seen it growing anywhere in the valley. All were draped heavily with the harvest of the night, turning the dead branches into a green garden.

Meer wandered down the narrow aisles, drawing in the sharp scent of the cuttings, examining the bubble-like bladders clustered on the skimweed stems. Many had already dried, burst, and split, but enough were intact to make him wonder if the boat-makers had found their inspiration in the very prize they pursued.

He had intended to turn back then, but spotted other diggings a hundred paces or so farther upstream. When he reached the spot, he found himself facing an expanse of low, circular mounds. Each varied from the next in size and height, but none was wider than his outstretched arms, or higher than his knee.

Walking among them, he started counting, then gave it up when the tally passed one hundred. On reaching the far limit of the field, he started back, still puzzled. He toed the hard face of one mound, circled another, climbed atop a third and peered around wonderingly, trying to find a reason for such modest constructions.

Suddenly he leaped off, seized by an apprehension.

He had never been told what the exiles, cut off from the reunion baths, did with their own dead.

When he looked around himself with new eyes, the answer was there. They sought reunion with Ana in the only way that they could, blanketed in her substance, sleeping in dark wombs of earth.

But it was a desperate, pathetic grasping, an empty and useless gesture. They would never be reabsorbed into her body, would never return the blessing to the source. They would wait here forever, lost to both worlds, the living and the dead.

And if Meer did not take Kedar to Ana, Kedar would join the others here.

The image was barely less obscene than the display along the river course, and grew more powerful the longer Meer lingered. Swallowing down the bitter taste that rose in his throat, he hastened to leave it behind.

The afternoon had fled while Meer carried out his explorations. By the time he was in sight of Kedar's house, the shadow of Kennabar extended across all but the fringes of the settlement, and there were stirrings of life on its paths again.

He found Kedar seated alone outside, his bulging drawstring bag beside him on the ground, waiting.

"It's time," he said simply.

Tight-lipped, Meer nodded agreement, and entered the house.

Dansi was gone. The hammock had been taken down, Kedar's other possessions taken away. The room was bare except for Meer's pack, resting near the entryway. The only sign that remained to mark Kedar's habitation was the pattern of lines across the wall and floor. Looking down, Meer fingered his cowled blouse, better understanding the bequest.

When he emerged, Kedar was on his feet, shouldering his bag. "We must go find Nan."

"Wait," said Meer, searching the ground.

A few steps away, he found a small red claystone. He caught it up with a sweep of his hand and went back inside, breaking the stone as he went. With quick, bold strokes, he chalked the sigil of the Genet large above the angled band of lines, then added what he could recall of the sigil of the honor school, so that the two blended into a single glyph.

As an afterthought, he circumscribed it with a sweeping circle.

When he stepped back to appraise his work, it did not greatly please him. But even so, it approached the limits of his skill, and Kedar was waiting. Dropping the nub of the claystone, Meer turned away.

Kedar was standing in the entryway, looking on wonderingly. But there was no explanation Meer could have made that the memorial did not make for itself.

"I'm ready now," was all he said.

12

Jineha: The Eighth Bell

Shouldering their bags, Meer and Kedar followed the sound of the five-tone flute down the slope toward the sea.

The sound led them to the east edge of the settlement, to where Nan Tirza sat at the edge of a large ring of stones with a tawny-haired girl just short of marking age. The flute was in the young girl's hands, and her fingers fluttered over the openings as it sang with her breath.

"You must let yourself hear Kennabar, and Morada, and Epa, and Taurin beneath you," Nan was saying, her back to the men as they approached. "They are always part of the music, the four corners of the song—play with them, not against them."

It was the young girl's anxious glance past Nan Tirza which betrayed Kedar and Meer. Her glance took in their bags, and her face fell.

"Rika, Nan does not praise you enough," said Kedar with a kind smile.

Nan made a noise of mock indignation. "Just who was it who told me a good teacher ought never praise too easily?"

"Love hears with different ears," Kedar said. "Rika, your playing is more beautiful every day. When your blood comes, you will be gladly welcomed to the circles."

His words did nothing to erase the girl's unhappiness. "But you will not be here to hear it," she said.

"I have already heard it, here," he said, and touched his heart. Then he held out his hand and she came to him, throwing one arm around his neck and burying her face against his blouse. He looked to the older woman. "Nan, I am ready to leave."

Her face creased with regret, Nan Tirza rose and came to join the embrace, resting her cheek against Kedar's shoulder, rubbing Rika's back with a slow, comforting touch. Then she stretched up to kiss Kedar's cheek, and said softly, "I will miss you."

That brought a cascade of tears to Rika's cheeks, and she clutched Kedar even more tightly as Nan stepped back, surrendering her claim. Uncomfortable, Meer looked away, shifting his weight from one foot to the other.

"We have no proper ceremony for this," Nan said, fretting. "Will you let me call everyone to gather, at least?"

"Please—no," Kedar said. "I need no more ceremony than this. How long can one say good-bye? Never long enough to prevent the leaving, only long enough to sharpen the grief."

She nodded. "As you wish, Kedar. You still mean to take the land route?"

"With your grant."

For reasons Meer could not understand, Nan looked at him thoughtfully before answering. "Kedar, I have no way to judge this, except that I have never been betrayed by trusting you. I will let your choice govern," she said, "and hope that you know better than I."

"Thank you," he said, and looked down his chin to Rika. "Can I ask one last thing from you, fond daughter?"

Eyes reddened and tears running freely, she looked up and nodded, not trusting her voice.

"Will you give me a kiss and your smile to take with me?"

She frowned, looking disappointed. "I would do anything for you--"

"Anything but let me go?" he said, slowly shaking his head. "Rika, I am not choosing to leave you—I am only choosing where to die. No day, no life, no blessing is forever. That is the way the world was made. But my spark endures in my children—in you. Because you live, I am not afraid to die. That is what you do for me, every day that you breathe, every day that you remember me. That is what your smile means to me."

And as he spoke, Rika slowly found a smile, one infused more with love than with sorrow.

"I will be your herald," she said brightly through her tears, "and

tell everyone that you have started home, so that they all can come
to send you off with smiles."

She threw both arms around his neck and kissed him quickly,
a woman's kiss, but shy and unsure. Then she broke away, flute
in hand, and ran up the path the two men had come down. Her
voice came back down the slope to them as she called out each
house as she passed it.

Kedar looked to Nan. "There will be bright days again, I
promise," he said in a near-whisper.

Reaching up and touching his cheek, she said, "I have never
doubted it. Blessed be, Kedar. May you find your way home an
easy one." She turned her eyes to Meer. "I envy you, that he chose
you for this. You do not know how honored you are."

Rika had performed her herald's task well. Before they had
gone even a hundred paces up the path, Kedar and Meer were
absorbed into the center of a swell of well-wishers.

Kedar slowed, but did not stop, carrying the gathering along
with him. Men waited for a chance to walk a few feet at Kedar's
elbow, to squeeze his hand or his shoulder and offer a few earnest
words. Women rushed forward or stepped in front to embrace him
and deliver kisses—some tearful, some wistful, some full of joy
remembered—and more earnest words.

Others, several children among them, trailed along a few steps
behind, content to be part of the retinue. Still other exiles walled
the edges of the path with their bodies, raising a hand or their
voice to Kedar as he passed.

Unhappy in the glare of Kedar's halo of attention, Meer yielded
his place to any who wanted it and the center to Kedar. Meer was,
at best, either invisible or an outright obstacle to those hoping to
draw close. He allowed himself to drop back with the stragglers,
and almost at once began to breathe more easily.

But even on the trailing fringe, Meer could still feel the warm
wind of emotion which swirled around Kedar, flowing in from
all sides—from outstretched hands, tender touches, smiles on
love-wistful faces, husky voices. The energy had almost as many
colors as there were people gathered. Their voices blended into
a drone of many timbres, from which Meer could extract more
feeling than words.

The feeling was the same one he saw on the faces: affection,
tempered as much by respect as with regret.

As they moved up the slope toward the foot of Kennabar, Treg appeared, and moved in on Kedar's right, drawing him close with an arm around the older man's shoulders. They bent their heads together as they walked, like two conspirators whispering in a crowd.

"Arbiter!" someone called just then, and Meer turned toward the voice.

It was the former scout, from the salon of the night before. He was standing off to one side with three men Meer did not know.

"Take this," the scout said, raising his arm and throwing a brown ball of cloth in Meer's direction. The ball unrolled en route to become a wrinkled expedition blouse, which Meer swept out of the air just before it settled to the ground. He looked up questioningly.

"Never been comfortable wearing that here," the man called. "But you may have use for it when you reach where it still commands respect."

It seemed to Meer as though the scout had shattered some taboo, for Meer himself began to draw attention as the procession thinned and continued up the face of Kennabar.

Next to speak to him was Treg, who stopped and waited on the path when he and Kedar were finished. Meer cringed as he drew near to the pilot, but Treg surprised him with gentle words.

"Safe journey, arbiter. Whatever your differences with Kedar, please—care for him as we would."

Stiffly, Meer said, "I will do all I can."

Treg stepped closer, but not in threat—in supplication. "He may have been a friend once to you, but he has been a father to many of us," he said. "Don't let them shame him. Don't let them steal his honor."

Meer swallowed. "I will do all I can."

The awkward moment ended when Treg scuffed a stone out of the packed ground with his heel and looked down the path toward the river. "I have work to do on my boat," he said, and backed away.

Then, as Meer lengthened his strides in pursuit of Kedar and his escorts, Dansi appeared from nowhere and hooked her arm in Meer's.

"Thank you for what you are doing for him," she said, tiptoeing to brush his cheek with her lips before she ran on ahead.

But by all appearances, she was alone in her gratitude. For others who had watched Kedar pass, the imminence and finality of his departure seemed to drive them not only to blame Meer, but to a desperate need to lash out at him while he was still in reach.

One such, a hook-nosed man half a head shorter than Meer, seized Meer's biceps in a painful grip and shook him, demanding to know by what right he was meddling in their lives.

Meer wrenched his arm free. "I came at his request," he snapped angrily, pointing up the trail.

"Is that how you measure fairness?" the hook-nosed man hissed at him. "Is that your morality, to do what you are told?"

His mouth working, Meer glowered at his accoster, then spun away and continued on, head lowered, jaw set.

"Such a brazen thief," another voice called after him. "You are stealing the jewel of this valley. Where is your shame?"

Meer steeled himself not to answer or look back. But the footsteps on the gravel behind him told him he had acquired his own retinue of hecklers, close on his heels. Their words burned his ears.

"—thief and coward both. Look at how he runs from honest questions—"

"—better that his mother had been barren than squander the blessing on his like—"

"—point to the high bank when you say 'at his request,' and put some truth to your words—"

"—she *was* barren, if this is all her womb yielded—"

He knew no way to stop them without fighting, or escape them without fleeing, or endure them. So it went on, a hundred strides, two hundred, five, until the insults and assaults had bruised his ears to deafness, and they let him go, bored at last by their game.

But that was neither the end of it, nor the worst of it.

Farther up Kennabar, as the path narrowed to a cut angling up the rock face, a light-skinned youth of no more than fourteen stepped out from an opening and placed himself in Meer's way. With chilling calmness, the youth warned that if Meer were a betrayer, he ought never sleep again.

"Because the first night you think you're safe, we'll come for you. We'll burst your eyes in your skull," he said, jabbing his thumbs toward Meer's face. "We'll tear the fingers from your hands. We'll grind your testicles between two rocks until they drop from your body. And we will sleep like babies when it's done."

Remembering Damek's fate, Meer could not persuade himself the threat was only bluster. Mustering as much threat in his own stance and voice as he could, he growled, "I am Kedar's guest, boy. Yield the path."

They locked eyes for a long moment, Meer's glare against the youth's glee. Finally, the youth took a small step back toward the rock, partly clearing the way.

But as Meer brushed roughly past, the youth whispered, "Remember—we can find you."

Higher yet, at a landing where the path switched back to head east, a slender, brush-haired woman of Meer's years or more was waiting. She walked calmly up to him and asked, "You are Faschen?"

"Yes," he said. There was something faraway familiar about her drawn, sculpted features which held him for a moment. His brow wrinkling, he paused in his steps to search his memory for her face.

In that moment, the woman leaned forward and spat a stringy globule of phlegm at Meer. It caught him wetly full across the cheek and the bridge of his nose, and he rocked back on his heels, as though she had struck him.

"That for Oran," she said, holding her head defiantly high. "Tell him Sela remembers. Tell him as long as we draw air, we will never forget."

He stared at her, recognition coming at last. "The first night— by the half-west entrance. You were with the students, on the plaza."

Bitterness contorted her features. "I am still there," she said. "The dreams take me back every day. The stars take me back every night." She shook her head despairingly. "Why has nothing been done? How can you suffer such a man?"

But she did not wait for an answer. Her message delivered, she fled from him as though he were something abhorrent. Mouth clamped shut and eyes averted, she vanished into the hollow places of Kennabar.

Sleeving the spittle away, Meer looked up the face of the mount. The way to the top had become a gauntlet, and the end was not yet in sight.

Head lowered, he hastened on, cursing Rika for her zeal.

Though the path climbed past a dozen more hole houses as it bent around a thrust of rock, to Meer's relief he encountered no one else until he reached the next switchback. To his even greater relief, it was Kedar he found there.

The older man was reclining against the rock, facing the valley, as though bathing in the cool air rolling down from above. His bag was at his feet, and Dansi sat on her heels beside him, holding his hand. Though his face was drawn and pale, Kedar wore a small happy smile.

"Listen," he said as Meer joined them.

Standing still, Meer searched the air for sound, suddenly aware of how quiet their surroundings had become. They had left all the sounds of the settlement below. His own breathing was louder than the wind, his heartbeat a drum in an empty temple.

"Do you hear? It is Rika, playing me up the mountain." Kedar pointed.

Meer cupped his ear and caught a few faint notes from the girl's flute, the melody rising and falling in a familiar line.

"A song of courting?"

"The argali. Yes."

"Is she truly your daughter?"

Nodding, Kedar said, "I am leaving six children—two who still draw breath, and four in the grave mounds. Rika was the first born, and has been the dearest to me as well."

Dansi and Kedar both noted Meer's quick curious glance toward Dansi.

"No," Dansi said. "I am danera—empty." She showed a feeble smile. "Kedar tells me it is of no consequence. But—"

"It is not the meaning of life, only the means of passing it," Kedar said, squeezing her hand.

"I will never wear the red sash."

"Nor will any man. That, too, is of no consequence," said Kedar, shaking his head. "It is hard enough to make good decisions for myself." He looked at Meer. "Nan Tirza is Rika's mother."

Meer frowned. "She must have been barely Rika's age when she took the blessing."

"If that. I see each in the other." Kedar let his head tip back against the rock and his eyes turn up to the sky. "Nan was the youngest of the survivors, blooded just once and bound for the hostel after the next festival—had Oran not intervened.

"We were still hiding along Kawa, feeding on the wild ring, and she was afraid. Afraid of dying, more afraid that without the rite she was dead inside. And words were not sufficient to reassure her." His eyes seemed to lose focus. "Those days seem like such a very long time ago."

"Rika had hoped to be blooded before you left us," Dansi said to Kedar. "She wanted your spark, as well."

"I know," Kedar said, looking down at her with a bittersweet smile. "I would sooner disappoint her this way than by refusing her." He listened for a moment, then pushed himself to a vertical stance. "She has stopped playing."

"How much farther?" Meer asked, looking up the path.

"Are you ready to go on?"

"More than ready. Are you?"

Kedar reached stiffly for his bag. "It will be easier after this."

But as the three continued upward, Kedar's promise stood as an incongruity, for once they passed one more row of empty hole houses and made the turn at yet another switchback, Kennabar became a sheer vertical wall. There, the path became narrow and steep enough to make any degree of haste dangerous. There was barely room for Dansi to stay at Kedar's side, holding his arm to help steady him.

Meer followed close behind, watching with alarm as Dansi's feet danced perilously near the edge. One misstep would take her—and probably Kedar as well—tumbling down the face of Kennabar, in a fall that would end with broken bodies on the slope far below them. If she slipped backwards instead, all three might finish their climb at the bottom instead of the top.

For his own part, Meer hugged the rock wall with his shoulder, pulling himself along by the handholds Kedar seemed to so easily find, testing the footing after each step before trusting his full weight to it. The valley was in full shadow, and the sky overhead was quickly blackening. He prayed that they would reach the top before night's full darkness fell.

Higher and higher they climbed, patient, measured step after impatient, measured step. By the time they reached the final switchback, Meer's own legs were rubbery, and his breath short.

But Kedar did not pause, following the path as it turned inside Kennabar itself. There it continued as a black tunnel up through the stone, lit only by circular window cuts looking out toward the river.

The curved floor of the tunnel forced them into a single file, Dansi in the lead. But because Meer could brace both hands against the sides of the passage, he felt more secure than he had on the cliff face—until he heard Storm's voice echoing hollowly down the passage toward him, offering a greeting to Dansi and Kedar.

They emerged onto the crown of Kennabar to find Val Maran waiting with Storm. The stiff breeze at the top blew words away, tore at hair and clothing, and seemed to want to push them toward the edge. Meer braced himself against it, and looked to Storm.

"Why are you here? Are you going with us?"

Kedar waved a hand and answered for them. "Storm and Val make their home here, at the top," he said, coughing.

Only then did Meer notice that Dansi was supporting much of Kedar's weight with an arm around his waist. Val was already moving to help share the burden.

"Will you come visit with us one last time?" she asked, preserving his dignity.

Kedar coughed again. "I think I would like to take some water and sit a bit before we go on."

Storm and Val's two-roomed house had been hollowed from the very top of Kennabar's northeast face. Each chamber had sky windows and sea windows both, though by the time the quintet descended the short entry passage, the only light within came from a smoky nut-oil lamp. Storm brought Kedar water, which he gulped noisily. When Val offered Kedar the use of their hammock while he rested, he considered for a moment, then accepted.

"Forgive me for delaying us again, Meer," Kedar said, "but I had not climbed Kennabar in longer than my bones remembered. Better that I lie down and allow them to forget again."

Then Val took his arm and disappeared with him into the other chamber, dropping a patch-quilt curtain across the opening behind them.

In the silence they left behind, Meer settled beneath the sea window, drinking from his own supplies rather than ask for hospitality Storm seemed in no mind to offer. The sound and air from the window helped make the room seem less closed.

Dansi stretched out on her back on the floor, just beyond fingertip reach. Storm sat on his haunches across the room from Meer, saying nothing, but burning Meer with his gaze.

"Kedar says you have taken several people out of Ana," Meer said finally, attempting conversation. "So you have made this trip more than once."

Storm made no sound or sign in response, as though Meer had not spoken.

"What are you thinking, Meer?" Dansi asked.

Meer shook his head and gestured toward the other chamber. "We haven't come a tenth part of the way—we've barely begun," he said, dropping his voice. "You saw what the climb took from him. What hope does he have of surviving a walk to Ana? Why are we doing this?"

"Because he needs to," Dansi said. "I thought that reason was enough."

"Enough for him," Meer said. "Is it enough for you, to let you see him like that without growing sick?"

Dansi sat up and turned toward Meer. The light and her expression added several years to her face.

"If he can bear his pain without flinching," she said slowly, "it would be an unkindness to show him I cannot bear mine, and add that to his burden."

The sounds that broke the long silence which followed came from beyond the curtain: the whisper of a garment settling to the floor, the creaking of knots, faint grunts, breathy exhalations, a throaty murmur. As Meer slowly realized what the sounds betokened, he sat suddenly upright, wearing his incredulity plainly on his face.

When he looked to Dansi, he found her eyes focused on the ceiling. Her contented smile shocked him.

"Dansi?" he hissed.

She turned to look at him wonderingly. "Is his pleasure as difficult for you as his pain?" she asked. "You don't know what this means for her. Everyone who hears of this will smile."

Meer's look to Storm carried her words as a challenge, demanding that he correct the error. Storm's gaze never wavered; his expression never changed. At long last he shook his head, so slowly that the motion cried for a different word.

"You should not be here," he said. "But that is the only thing wrong about what is happening. Give them the privacy of your silence."

So they sat in the room with the flickering lamp and listened, Dansi dreamy, Storm implacable, Meer discomfited and jangling, as Val said good-bye to Kedar in a way none of them would have thought she would choose.

After a time, it ended with Val's soft, almost shy cries of

blessing, once, and then once again, unmistakable in the silence.
Dansi's smile brightened on hearing the auspicious sounds, and
Storm dropped his gaze to his hands and nodded, satisfied.

"Perhaps seven," Dansi whispered to Meer, "if luck is with
her."

Before long, there were different sounds from beyond the curtain, including a gentle snoring and the scuff of feet on the floor,
and Val appeared once again, rejoining them.

"He is sleeping now," she said, letting the curtain fall closed
behind her. She brushed fingertips with Dansi as she passed, then
went to settle beside Storm, cuddling under his arm and resting her
head against his shoulder. Dansi came to sit beside her, clasping
hands with her and sharing a kiss.

The sight drove deep the loneliness which had been with Meer
since he had left Ana, or even longer. Leaving his bag by the
window, he fled the house, clambering up the entry passage to
the surface.

He went to sit alone by the seaward edge, above the surf,
hoping that Dansi would follow if only he stayed away long
enough. Waiting, he thought about what falling through the air
might feel like, and whether dying could be trusted to end pain.
But no one came to rescue him from his thoughts until Kedar was
stirring from his nap, and it was time to move on.

The night was half gone when Storm finally led Kedar and
Meer away from the house and the valley, west along the crown
of Kennabar.

Meer did not question Storm's company; he had surrendered all
hope of reading the mark of his hosts, and was content to settle
for any shadow of progress. And the signs were that Storm would
not be with them long; he carried an unlit lamp, but no water or
food of his own.

But when, after guiding them across no more than a thousand
feet of gently rising bare rock, Storm sparked the lamp, pulled
aside a flaxcloth concealment and began to lead them once more
below ground, Meer balked.

"What, are we stopping again? At this pace, we will never get
there."

Storm only laughed at the outburst.

"Ana is not as far away as it seems," Kedar said. "And this
is where we have been headed since we left Nan at the meeting
circle."

"This? Another hole in the ground?"

"Come," Kedar said. He seemed to be constraining his own amusement. "It is easier to show you."

The chamber below copied the delivery chamber of a chute mine, like those Meer had seen in the nineties north of the high bank, where a great outcrop of granite interrupted Ana's symmetry. On either side, amidst other tools and coils of fine spider cord, hung a pair of excavation sleds. At the far end of the chamber was a hole barely wider than Meer's shoulders—matching both the sleds' narrow dimensions and their bow-backed section.

"What do you mine here?" Meer asked.

"Time," Kedar said. "I told you how our water comes to us. Izel and his friends cut one further qanat for us before the nats were exhausted—a dry qanat that dwarfs every other space they opened for us. Briden died in the making of it. Had they not been dumped in the sea, the tailings would have raised the crown of Kennabar sixteen feet." Kedar pointed at the opening at the end of the chamber. "It does not look like much from here, I know."

Incredulity slowed Meer's understanding. "Where is the other end?"

"On Kawa's north plain, beyond the west slope of the barrier ridge—half-way to Ana."

"Impossible," Meer said, not wanting to believe.

Storm had hung the lamp from the ceiling and taken one of the sleds down from the wall. It was nearly his height, but he handled it with a familiar ease. "More than half the way," he said, carrying the sled toward the opening. "I can run from the exit chamber to the boundary of Ana in a night."

Meer pointed shakily at the opening. "You don't mean for us to go down that hole."

"I do," Kedar said. "I promised it to you—have you forgotten? It is easier going down the grade than up. And easier to ride a sled than to walk. We will put the highlands behind us by sunrise."

Staring, Meer shook his head in disbelief. "There is no air—there is no light—"

"There is air enough. Storm is the proof of that—he has made this trip more times than any. And the sleds have their own lamps, which draw on the inductors," Kedar said.

"But such a distance—how long will it take? What if Ana trembles while we are down there?"

"She has trembled many times since the two great qanats were cut. So far, she has preserved them," Kedar said. "I will trust her to leave them undisturbed a few more hours."

"I can't do this," Meer said, hugging himself.

Kedar smiled. "I have been waiting to do this since Izel returned from the first trip, glowing about a wonder it was to travel so far so quickly."

"The wonder pales," said Storm, who was positioning the sled in the opening of the chute. "I have been known to nap in the run."

"I would be disappointed if I did the same," said Kedar with a chuckle, turning toward him. "Is it ready?"

"When you are."

"I am ready now."

"Kedar!" Meer cried in protest.

Kedar looked back to Meer sympathetically. "Meer, I am sorry that I did not better prepare you. But I did not have Nan's grant until we started. And I do not have the luxury of alternatives."

Dumbstruck, Meer watched as Storm helped Kedar clamber into the chute and lie down on the sled, listened as he rattled off instructions.

"There's not much room to move, but if you mind your elbows, you can turn over without much trouble—some prefer riding face-down. Don't let the rock tempt your fingers, it burns on the way down. Tuck your bag behind your knees, so you'll be able to see past your feet. That's a good position to be in for the bump at the bottom."

"How much of a bump ought I expect?"

"A fair one. It's all sand at the bottom, but remember, these sleds were meant to go down and dig into whatever the nats had chewed loose. The only warning you'll have is the way the sound changes—I don't know how to describe it."

Kedar's tone was cheery. "That should be enough."

"Just be sure to send the sleds back. We only have two that can still make a loaded ascent. You've got no water ballast to dump, though, because these are coming back empty. Are you comfortable?"

"I am excited," said Kedar. "Good-bye, Storm."

"You are a crazy old man," Storm said. "I don't know why I love you."

Kedar reached a hand up above his head, and Storm clasped it tightly for a moment.

"Meer, I will look for you at the other end," called Kedar.

Bound by anger and helplessness, Meer said nothing.

Storm's body blocked any glimpse of what he was doing. But suddenly there was a sliding, whistling sound in the air, and when Storm turned away, Kedar was gone.

Meer rushed forward and knelt at the opening, staring as the sled bearing Kedar quickly fell away to a pale yellow light receding into what seemed an infinite distance. Abruptly seized by vertigo, Meer fell back against the wall of the chamber.

"The sled will be heavy for him," Storm said. "We will give him a cushion of time at the bottom."

Still fighting for control, Meer blew a noisy breath. "How did Briden die?"

Again Storm fixed Meer with his unblinking gaze. "He went down the hole during the cutting to free a jammed sled. The air was bad, or so Izel supposes. Briden's sled brought him back dead."

Meer stood on unsteady legs and retreated toward the entry passage.

"Where are you going?"

"Out," Meer said. "Anywhere but down that hole. Are you going to stop me?"

"Stop you? No. But I don't approve of allowing you to know about the dry qanat. So I would much rather you left that way"— he pointed toward the entry—"than this," he said, patting the mouth of the passage.

Meer's eyes narrowed in suspicion. "Why? What difference does it make?"

"Kedar is no longer part of our community. Which means you will no longer enjoy his protection here." Cocking his head toward Meer, Storm smiled an unfriendly smile.

After a long moment of consideration, Meer slowly sat down where he stood, at the opposite end of the chamber from Storm.

"Let me know when we have waited long enough," he said.

Disappointment registered in Storm's eyes.

The descent was an unending torment, the ultimate horror of a nightmare journey. Confined within the tiny dimensions of the open sled, with the whine of the inductors buzzing in his ears and the rock blurring by a foot from his face, Meer fought panic from the first second.

He could not judge distance, nor speed, nor time. He could see neither Kedar ahead of him nor the upper chamber behind him.

The latter had vanished in the first moments, when Storm took away or extinguished his lamp, leaving Meer alone.

Meer was a captive within a tiny bubble of light somewhere within a great, dark mass of stone. He was a dew-drop riding a fragile thread strung through Ana's body—if she stirred, even in sleep, the thread would surely snap. He was a freshly thrown clay vessel, falling in frozen time toward the floor. He was flotsam, borne along on the froth of a deluge descending unchecked through the qanat, and which would drown him when he reached the bottom.

He was in agony.

Down, ever down, the sled hurtled, carrying Meer deeper into the devouring abyss, with nothing to mark his progress but the subtle changes in the color of the rock enclosing him. Meer snatched his breath from air so cold it made his lungs ache. The arched ceiling flashing by dizzied, almost mesmerized him. He wanted so badly to reach out and make it stop that he had to close his eyes to stay his hands.

But that darkness was even more unbearable. It was a descent into the oblivion of sleep, the extinction of self, without promise of a return. It was a passage in misery, and it touched something primal—a memory for which there were no words, only the most exquisite flavors of frantic, helpless fear. It was death, or birth, or both.

It was forever.

Thought dissolved. Hope fled. Meer opened himself to his own deep reservoirs of pain and anger and fear, surrendering his body to them. From a safe, far remove, he listened with impersonal curiosity to the wordless, wretched screams that rattled up and down the shadowed tunnel.

Then there was a jolt which buckled his legs, and light that nearly blinded him. Reclaiming his body with an act of will, he polled his other senses. The world had stopped moving around him, and the screams had stopped as well. But a sound remained, which Meer fought to parse into words:

areyouallrightupwehavetogoupMeerlisten, can you hear me
"Are you all right?"

Meer clawed his way toward Kedar's face and voice, up toward fresh air and open space, until at last he burst forth from death into blessed life.

13

The Rising of Kawa

In the heady glee of that bright morning, I was no different than those around me. I thought it all but over. I thought the victory was all but won.

What did it matter that the delegation had been ignored, and still waited outside the keystone house for a chance to be heard? The students had shown their defiance and survived the display. They had called to their friends and families for support, and their calls had been answered. A full day had passed, and Oran had done nothing.

Was there anyone who had spent the night on the plaza who did not feel flush with triumph? You could see it in faces everywhere—I could feel it in my own.

The light of day had driven away the insecurity and replaced it with brazen confidence. Who could question what was obvious to all? The proof was all around us. The locus of power had shifted from the high bank to the low bank. How could Oran resist? He was helpless against the power of truth, and would surely fall.

They thought themselves invulnerable, because their cause was a just one, and reason would surely rule. But they were wrong in the first instant, and wrong in the last, and those errors would cost them their cause.

I do not say this to judge them, or place the blame on their shoulders for what followed. What anyone believed that morning neither bound nor freed Oran's hands, and cannot excuse what he did. Idealism is not a crime, nor is passion. And every runner who bears his mark to the festival line must believe for himself in that moment that victory is possible—for if not, then it is not.

But the people of the plaza had fixed themselves to a course from which there was no retreating. And what they believed— what we believed—shaped what we did, or did not do, and so set the pattern of the cast for Oran's play, each player placing his own stone in or out of the circle.

I picked up my stone, thinking the game was over.

Perhaps I should have stayed on the plaza, and bound my fate to theirs. But I could not have formed such a thought then. It was too dark for such a bright morning.

And as it was with me, so it was all around me. More left with the sunrise than stayed past it. Conscience chased thousands of us back to our homes and duties, to the smaller crises of our lives— though many promised to return that evening. The exodus began with the first pale streaks in the eastern sky, and did not end until the gathering had thinned to its essential core.

I do not think any of us considered how that sign would be read by the watchers on the high bank, or by their masters.

My crisis, you will have guessed, was Meli.

I knew I had let the breach between us stand by staying on the plaza. When I went to Meli's house and did not find her or Chane there, I knew that the breach had surely widened in my absence. I had abandoned her to face the night alone and afraid, compounding my transgression.

But, for whatever reason, she had not set my clothes outside the door. My striker still hung near the blessing bell. I retained, by however precarious an indulgence, the honor of her house.

That said to me she wanted a way to understand, a reason to forgive. That said she, too, wanted the breach closed. If not, she would not have given me a chance to return.

The breach was wide and deep. I had much to explain for, and words would not be sufficient to the task. But I saw a way to heal the breach, or thought I did. I would not try to explain. I would show her. Meli had to come to the plaza and see for herself. Then she would understand.

I knew the likely places Meli would go for comfort and companionship. But the time was not right, and I did not want to parade our private quarrel before the dan, her friends, or her mother. And there was the danger I might wash away my chance in a torrent of words.

So I did not look for her, or stay at the house to await her return. I changed to fresher garments, and left those which were covered with dust from the plaza where she would note them and know at least that I had returned. Then I reported to the retting barn.

Though I was late again, no one appeared to care. We bested our own young standard for indolence that day. Even our aedile joined us as we shared what stories we had of the wonder these happenings had become. Three of us had copies of the Seventeen Inquiries. All of us had opinions on them—some even measured and sturdy enough for Kedar's salon.

We were divided, to be sure, and Tevin made the minority equal in volume. But more voices were raised in support of the crusade than were raised against it, more defending the students' goals than attacking them. I heard the word 'sedition' used in praise as well as condemnation, the word 'revolt' spoken wistfully, even wishfully.

As I sat listening to the salon of the sweat hands, I felt such hopeful contentment that I wore a smile much of the day. In their words I found all the affirmation I could want for the optimism of the plaza.

I thought, if men such as these have taken these questions to heart, can argue them with such earnestness, then the world had already been recast. In one day and one night, the students of the plaza had managed to make change thinkable.

And by the principles of Kedar's salon, that which was thinkable was attainable, and that which was attainable was inevitable.

We would hear from Hoja den Krador again, and he from us. The crusade would triumph. And Meli would once more look at me with love.

I believed all those things without question. Do you think me a fool for that? I was twenty-two then. Is that not young enough to forgive me my illusions?

The aedile excused the circle from the barn a generous hour before sunset, and then left as quickly as any of us. I thought I knew why, and where he was headed. He was a graduate of the honor school, and the talk on the raking floor seemed to have awakened his allegiance.

I went home to find Meli.

She made that part easy. She was outside her house with Chane, sitting in the wall shadow and playing a game of hand and stone with him. When I swung myself over the flood wall, she glanced ever so quickly toward me, but went on with the game.

I joined them and watched, laughing when Chane laughed, but saying nothing, until Meli invited me into the game by holding her closed fists up to me. I chose the right, turning it palm-up. When she opened her fingers, a grainy red pebble lay there.

"I am glad to know I still have some luck with you," I said.

She showed a little smile and opened her other hand to reveal a second pebble, a near twin of the first. I had been away long enough, it seemed, to be welcomed back.

We left Chane to play and went inside for privacy. I made apologies for my loss of self and my absence, which she heard more generously than I would have dared hope. But it was no easy thing to persuade her there was any reason to go with me to the plaza. I did not know how Meli had passed her day, or what stories she had heard over the walls, but they had left her fearful.

"Something grand is happening there, something without pre-cedent," I said. "I want you to share in it. I want Chane to witness it, even if he will need us to help him remember."

Meli made every possible objection, but I was still glowing with certainty, still innocent of fear. That spoke most loudly, and she had no answer for it.

"We will be safe," I promised her. "And you will be glad you were there."

I carried Chane, and Meli walked beside me, her hand firm on my arm. Before long, it was clear that we were not the only residents of Liu Cluster headed for the plaza. I saw Isei and Jaun carrying deep baskets of jicama and sunchoke, and dan Sawai with her daughter, and Paja from the retting circle. No one walked alone. Our common destination drew us together in cheerful, loosely-bound groups.

There was a wagon partly blocking the first high crossroads, and five of Oran's monitors atop it. But they were men from Liu homes and long houses, as familiar in face to us as we must have been to them, and they offered no word or move to stop us.

Instead, they sat on the edge of the wagon, kicking their legs like children, or waving and calling out to us in friendly tones as we passed. One joked with Meli about her roundness, another cadged a sample from Isel's basket with a hopeful smile. I did not feel any threat from them.

We passed just one other wagon, at the tenth ring. It was positioned like the first, but its monitors paid us no attention at all. They were clustered on the side ring a few steps from the crossing, their backs to us and their voices raised in energetic debate about, it seemed to my ear, Inquiry Seven.

The streets only grew busier as we drew closer to the plaza. We were still two rings away when the crowd trying to funnel through the half-west gate reached such a density that our steps were slowed by the bodies in front of us. Had Meli not been with me, I would have gone to the top of the fencewalls to escape the congestion, as I saw many do.

If I had been one of them, I would have seen what no doubt would have been a remarkable sight—an almost unbroken sea of people filling the plaza from river to ringwall. Whatever the peak of the night before had been, it had already been doubled, if not trebled.

It was as if every person who had left that morning had brought another—friend, neighbor, kin—back with them that evening. But there was no more focus than the night before, and so the great numbers begat considerable noise and chaos.

Chane, looking out from atop my shoulders, had the best of it, and happily added his tiny voice to the din. But Meli, whose head barely reached my shoulders, had the worst of it. She was walled in by the other celebrants, and twice became separated from me as I pushed through the crowd toward the river.

Hardest of all for one with her shyness, she was faced with a seemingly endless succession of hands reaching out to touch her belly in the ritual token. She gamely endured it for a time, perhaps thinking that the throng was bound to thin as we got farther from the gate.

But just the reverse was true: As we moved toward the temple, the bodies seemed to press even closer in around us. When Meli found me for the second time, she pleaded for relief. Because I feared losing her consent, I gave up my intention of reaching the river and finding Weilin and the others from Kedar's salon, and made a path for us back toward the edge of the plaza.

Midway between the gates, we found a calmer vortex, where voices seemed quieter and most people had settled on the ground to wait—meaning Chane could be let down to wander without disappearing at once into a forest of legs. Someone made space for

Meli under the edge of a sun tarp, and I squeezed in beside her.

"You said I would understand, but I understand none of this," she said. "Why are they all here?"

So I gave her my copy of the Inquiries, and watched her as she read it. She handed it back with a troubled expression.

"What does any of that have to do with a woman's life?" she asked. "Will it explain why there've been no pit melons in Liu shares for six festivals, while Cor wagons deliver two to a house? Will it assure that the water runs long enough at night to fill my cistern?"

"No," I said. "This is about other things."

"Will it bring me curtain falls for my windows, to chase the dust from the air? Or a hammock for Chane—I've been waiting since he turned his first year. I will have two children soon—are both to sleep with me, one to a breast? These are the questions that matter."

"These questions matter, too," I said, waving the paper.

"Enough to take food out of mouths, and leave women without homes? Dan Marra told me of strikes in Kell and Agama, green hands leaving the fields."

"There are many rumors in the city. Few have any substance."

Meli shook her head, her eyes following Chane as he accosted a young man seated a short way from us. "Ana balances on the edge. There must be order if we are all to have a living share. Everyone must do their part. Everything must be as it is." She gestured toward the crowd. "How much disorder, how many discontented, will it take to bring disaster? Is anyone here asking that?"

She had attracted an audience from those seated around us, and her words would surely have sparked an earnest debate. But Meli had not spoken as in the salon, offering her opinions up for challenge. She had spoken her mind, and saw no reason to hear challenges. Rising with surprising grace, she went to reclaim Chane before he could make too great an annoyance of himself. When she came back with him cradled in her arms, she told me she wanted to go.

"We need to be home before curfew," she said.

Her words crushed me. My face showed everyone my dismay. How could she see those people, that moment, so differently? She had misapprehended everything. She had seen only the superficial, and missed or dismissed the substance. And now she meant to leave before the chant—mind, the first reason I had brought her there—could begin. The sky was darkening quickly in the east, but overhead, it was still a pale, dusty blue.

I could have screamed at her. I could have snatched Chane from her and disappeared into the throng. But I could not have changed her mind—not at that moment, or in that place. And I could not refuse her without undoing what healing had been done, and putting myself outside her life again.

I stood up. "Let me carry him," I said.

But there was no reason for me to hurry my steps, and I did not. I even turned us toward the south entrance, taking advantage of Meli's trust, the distraction of the crowd, and her ignorance of the plaza. We had almost reached the gate when the angle of the arch alerted her to my 'mistake.' When she questioned me, I cheerfully confessed to my stupidity, and allowed her to lead us back the way we had come.

That chicanery nearly kept us on the plaza long enough. We were just outside the gate on the spoke road when the cry went up and the chant began. I stopped and turned toward the sound.

"Listen," I said.

Meli clung to my arm. "What is it?"

"A call to the apparition. A glory song for the crusade." And even heard from outside the circle, the chant was glorious. A tenth of the city was on the plaza that evening, forty thousand or more, and their voices put fire into the air, made the walls sway and the streets tremble.

But the power which so enthralled me only frightened Meli. What was promise to me was threat to her. And when I joined the chant, softly singing the third part to Chane, she dug her fingers deep into my arm and did her best to drag me away from the plaza.

"Please," she begged, "we have to hurry. We can't defy the law."

I could have cried. She was deaf to it all. With no reason to linger, I turned away, and we started home, Meli setting a swift pace for us.

The monitors at the first crossroads let us pass; we were a man with child in arms and a woman in blessing, no danger to order and already bound in the direction they preferred. But as we passed, they turned away three young men headed for the plaza.

"Go back to your long house," the monitor captain said, rapping a stone-hard club gourd sharply against the edge of the wagon for emphasis. "Go home, off the streets. The exarch has called a curfew. Go on, do you want a beating?"

The chant was still going, still audible to all of us. "What about them?" asked one of the young men, pointing toward the plaza.

"They'll be dealt with. Don't make it your business. Be smart— go wet your staff instead. Don't volunteer for trouble."

Meli was urging me away, so I heard no more.

The monitors in Liu chided us gently, but waved us on. We reached Meli's house just as the last light was vanishing from the sky. She took Chane from me and disappeared inside, neither inviting nor forbidding me to follow.

I went to the roof instead. I sought the new apparition with my eyes, and found it in its expected place. When I cupped my ears toward the center of Ana, I thought I could still hear the singing, and took what comfort I could in that.

But the star seemed very much farther away than the plaza, and I found it hard to hold any hope that Hoja den Krador was looking down and listening, too.

Not a word was said about the Seventeen Inquiries, the crusade, or the plaza inside the Liu retting barn the next day. But it was not that we had lost interest.

We were each met at the entry by the cluster trustee for materials, who recorded our order of arrival—I was third that day, by good fortune. Then he gathered us to announce that our aedile had been relieved of his assignment for what was called "poor judgment."

"The blame for the disruption in the work of this barn is entirely his. None of you will be held to account for it," the trustee said. "I anticipate a swift return to normality under your new aedile, Tevin Liaschen."

He went on to tell us that new work rules had been set to help us in restoring productivity: no reading material allowed in the barn, no discussion of 'extrinsics,' no circle meetings except those called and witnessed by the aedile, no singing except of the "Joyful Labor" corner, no dismissal before sunset. All violations were to be reported to the aedile and referred to the Liu prefect of moral culture and other officials of the hive.

These were the things that were not said, but did not need to be: That the exarch had spies, probably many spies, on the plaza. That our aedile had been seen there last night, and the high bank considered that to be proof of disloyalty for anyone in the hierarchy, even those on the lowest rung. That everyone tied to the honor school was suspect, or a sweat laborer like Tevin would never have been raised to administrator.

And, of course, that Tevin would gladly and gleefully report any offenders, most especially Meer Faschen, and perhaps Kirl.

We bit our tongues, and signed obscenities behind Tevin's back so that we could think ourselves brave. But we did not speak of what had happened until we were in the streets, hurrying home before dark. I walked with Kirl, who despaired of dislodging the exarch from the high bank.

"They control the food and the share goods, and where the water flows. They control where we live and who works in the sun. They control appointment to the honor school. They control the sentries and the arbiters, who control where we can go and what we can say. They control the instruments of health and even the fate of our bodies when we die. Who can afford to offend them?"

"But they do not control the truth," I said, because I needed to believe it.

"I am not so sure of that," Kirl said.

When I reached Meli's house, the yard was filled with women: Fas, Meli's mother, the neighbors, the dan. The new baby had quickened during the day, and they had waited the ceremony for me.

Meli, her mother, and Fas went into the house alone for the ritual, about which I can tell you nothing. When they returned, I gave Meli the cut-weaving of her mark, though I had not found the time to adorn it as well as I had intended. But it seemed to please her and her mother both. Meli announced the names as Rurik, for a boy, or Machi, for a girl, and both names were thought well chosen for the Boroche line.

All this ceremony kept me from Fas. There was great comfort just in seeing her, but on seeing her, I was eager to talk to her of many of these matters. But her home was two clusters away, and the curfew was coming with the darkness. Fas was the first to leave, and I could not go with her, or leave for any reason, without offending the gathering.

Thus I saw nothing of Weilin or Kedar, Chai or Kaixi, nothing of the grand salon on the Plaza of Truth that night.

When the apparition made its appearance, I found means to slip away to the roof to listen for the chant. It is said that there were fifty thousand there on the fourth night of mystery, and that the sound they raised with their voices caused bells on the arch to ring. But the laughter of the women below masked it from me, if it was there to hear at all.

I am the wrong witness to tell the rest of this story.

The corpses that hang in the canyon—they are better witnesses than I. Kedar Nan was a better witness. Nan Tirza is another— I do not know how many more there may be who escaped the plaza and survived the years since, but any one of them would be a better witness than I, if only they dared awaken the memories.

I know what happened in the plaza of the temple of the arch on the fifth night of mystery. But I did not see more than the prelude, and Oran-rami Anadon says that what I did not see did not happen.

Of all the lies told by and for the exarch, that lie is the boldest and most intolerable.

The corpses of Kawa refute the lie, but no one sees them. The memories of the survivors refute the lie, but no one hears them. The hearts of the kin and children of the disappeared refute the lie, but those feelings are too dangerous to show. The consciences of the agents of Oran's vengeance will refute the lie, but that guilt is too searing to acknowledge.

So silence declares that there was never a night of mystery, never a night of terror. And time favors the silence over the corpses, the memories, the hearts, and the consciences all.

If we do nothing else, we must overturn that lie with the truth. That was all the students wanted. They did not know they would die for asking.

I am the wrong witness to tell the rest of this story. But since you question my honesty and my intentions, I will tell you what I can tell you, and you who know more than I can measure me as you will.

Through four days the same pattern had held: a few thousand in the plaza by day, tens of thousands by night. Did anyone guess the danger in that?

On the morning of the fifth day, Oran showed us where the danger lay.

When the first light gleamed on the arch, the exodus began as it had each morning the students had held the plaza. No one was impeded from leaving. No one saw any threat waiting outside on the spoke roads, was given any reason to turn back. The monitor wagons were even gone from the crossroads.

The threat they did not see was hiding in the ring roads, in empty workhouses, behind fencewalls, in the homes of friends of the exarch. During the night, the syndic of public security had quietly brought gangs of armed men into the center of the city. It seems they were mostly sweat hands of the Fourth and Fifth Hundreds, strangers to the plaza and the people on it. They carried gourd clubs and heavy sticks, some the tools of their trades— hammers and wedge knives and the spike-hooked grapples of vat hands.

What I know of this I know from a builder from Pria, who was one of them. I found him sitting in the ring road the morning after, tears running down his face, crying out to anyone who would listen.

"We were told that we would face an army of traitors. We were told they had sworn allegiance to Hoja den Krador and death to Oran Anadon," I heard him say as he wept. "We were told to believe nothing they said, that if we weakened or showed mercy, we would be destroyed and the city would fall to them. I swear, we did not know. You must believe I did not know."

And perhaps they did not. His anguish seemed real. But there were many who did know. The sweat hands were led by sentries and sentry captains—one to a gang of six or eight. Each gang had a place to go and task to do.

There must have been some signal for them all to act—I have heard there was a mirror flash from the high bank. However it was done, when the morning exodus was over, they moved as one.

They seized all four gates to the plaza and blocked them with wagons, so that no one could leave without being identified. They blocked every high crossroad out to the first green ring, so that no one who had left the plaza could return. They took control of the Five-Ring Bridges, upstream and downstream from the plaza, cutting the heart of the city in half.

And while it was happening, the delegation of seventeen, still keeping vigil outside the keystone house, was arrested and dragged away to a stockade on the high bank, though no word of this reached the plaza that day.

All this was accomplished so swiftly that there was no resistance. It took a bit longer to chase all the residents of the clusters which adjoined the plaza from their homes.

But when it was done, the plaza and people who remained on it were thoroughly isolated from the rest of Ana.

Only then, I am told, was the ultimatum delivered. Its content was the same as the announcement Tevin read to us in the retting barn at noon, the same as ten thousand across the city, on wagons and in workhouses, were proclaiming from identical hand-drafted orders:

"The plaza of the arch has been closed. No one may enter it. The curfew is hereby advanced from nightfall to sunset. Those persons unlawfully occupying the plaza are warned to observe the curfew and leave the plaza by sunset. Anyone who remains past that time shall forfeit the mercy of the city. By the order of the exarch, Oran-rami Anadon, servant of the people."

Even without knowing what had already happened that morning at the plaza, I heard Tevin's words as the coda to the crusade for truth. By nightfall, I thought, the plaza would be empty, and the grand saion would be over.

But I never dreamed it would end the way it did.

How much do I need to say of this? How much must I relive to satisfy you?

Tevin held us as long as he could, so that we would have no choice but to go straight to our homes. Even so, Kirl and I headed toward the plaza, determined to know how the last hours had played out, and to find and comfort friends. We did not know the circle had not yet closed, that thousands were still on the plaza, defiantly refusing to obey.

That night, the monitors on the spoke road showed Kirl and me no smiles. Pointing at the sky and repeating the new curfew, they firmly turned us away. We found a way past them, going down to the ring roads and taking to the fencewalls.

A few voices rose up from the yards to chide us, but we made our way as far as 6-in before we were challenged in earnest, chased back by three sentry stickmen. Kirl and I fled in different directions, and I did not see him again. I hid in the yard of a weavers' workhouse on seven, thinking that the city had gone crazy and wondering how I would get home.

I was still hiding when the chanting began. I listened to it in wonder and disbelief. The sound was brave, but thin and fragile, a bare echo of the grand voicing of other nights. But the realization the students were still there, had still not surrendered the plaza, drew me out of the shadows and onto the workhouse roof.

Such admiration as I felt hearing their song, I can hardly express. I thought of Weilin, who fought for the right to hear

Hoja den Krador's words. I thought of Kaixi and Chai, who carried the students' challenge to the door of their adversary. My heart was full as I raised my gaze to the apparition in the sky.

In that exact moment, just as I fixed its place, the new star blossomed with sudden violence into a flower of many-colored light, so brilliant that I had to look away or be blinded.

I heard cries and screaming from everywhere around me, and from the plaza, where the chant had died in their throats in an instant.

Then there was another sound mixed with the screaming, like the gurgling sound of the flooding of the streets, but deeper, angrier—

Damn you for taking me back there. Damn you!

Why am *I* telling this story? I was seven blocks away from the plaza, safe on the roof of an empty building, forgotten by the sentries who had chased me.

How can I know how it was to have understood what that sound meant? How can I pretend to know the horror of standing there on the plaza half-blind in the near-darkness and hearing that roaring wall of water come rushing down the river from the dam?

I listened to the terrified screams without the first glimmer of what was happening. But I know, yes, I know. The sluices of the dam had been thrown wide open, and the waters of the lake poured down the channel and swept across the plaza like a hand across a table covered with crumbs. It tumbled the students before it and beneath it, carrying them into Kawa's grasp and away.

And I have heard that eight of the seventeen were hurled from the top of the high bank as the deluge began.

I know too much of what happened. I wish that I knew less.

The sentries and their sweat-soldiers were waiting behind the walls and on the high roads to beat with clubs and fists any who tried to escape the plaza. And then, as the water receded, the gangs moved forward to finish the job.

The second flood which drenched the plaza was a red one.

No one who was caught was spared. Those who had been able to stand against the torrent, or had been pushed toward the houses and not the river—the half-drowned lying on the pavement—the lucky few who had found refuge in the temple itself—all were dragged out and broken by flailing clubs and sticks and hammers until their bodies held too little spark to feel pain.

And the lies began the moment the crusade was crushed. In the course of the night, the dead were carried away in secret, the blood washed away from the tiles, and the bold declarations of the students bleached from the matrix at the gates.

The voice of Ana was restored a day later, and admitted eight dead, three of them sentries. It said they had died in a skirmish between brave defenders of the exarchy and student seditionists armed with knives.

The dan counted more than eleven hundred missing.

It was said that the cisterns in Garet Cluster, downstream from the plaza, produced nothing but blood for three days.

I did not see that, though, so perhaps it did not happen.

14

Ixozacu: The Ninth Bell

The wild scramble to escape the qanat had left Meer lying in the open on pebbled earth, under Taurin's familiar star-specked night. His heart was a hammer in his chest, and his lungs greedily sucked down the sweet dry air blowing across his sweat-soaked body. But he had escaped the nightmare. He had endured.

There was little more than that for him to cling to. The long, precipitous ride had tested him and found him fragile. His whole being was tender with the memory of utter helplessness, and of his final, abject surrender to it. Terror had stolen his illusion of control, and confronted him with the prospect he might never regain its comfort.

A voice startled him. "I will need your help down below, when you are ready," it said.

Meer remembered then that he was not alone. Lifting himself to his elbows and craning his head, he found Kedar a crouching shadow outlined by a faint glow from the ground. A rush of shame came to Meer's lips as anger.

"Bastard. You knew. I curse your mother's sweat. You should have warned me."

Kedar shook his head slowly. "How could I have? What could I have said that would have prepared you? How could I have taught you so late to grasp the knife by the blade? It is not your way." Standing, Kedar became a frail silhouette. "I am sorry the passage was difficult for you."

A derisive laugh erupted from Meer. "Don't be gentle with my pride," he said, climbing unsteadily to his feet. "I am humiliated enough. Blinding your words will not blind my memory—or yours." Meer wrapped his arms around his shoulders and shivered from remembered cold. "I know what you are doing."

"You think I mean to harm you?"

"To punish me, at the least. Or destroy me, if that's what it will take to satisfy you. I do not believe your smiles anymore. You are not my friend."

Kedar took a long time to answer. "Then you should kill me now, I think, and remove the threat. I'm afraid I cannot promise not to fight, but I suspect the outcome is not in serious question."

"You mock me."

"Not for a moment."

"Do you think I won't protect myself?" Meer demanded.

"On the contrary—I have no reason to expect differently."

Meer drew himself up defensively. "Is that a rebuke? What are you trying to say?"

"I have said it plainly. Kill me, if you cannot trust me. You could easily make your way back to Ana alone from here." Kedar pointed into the night. "It is that way, as morning will confirm."

"You don't even deny it, then. You did call me out to destroy me. This is a death journey we're on."

"I will not argue what you believe or perceive," said Kedar.

Refusing to argue had been the ultimate sign of disrespect in the salons, and Meer did not take it gracefully. "Curse your mother's mark—I want the truth from you."

"You have already declared yourself unready to hear it."

"Don't treat me like a child in the temple. I have a right to an answer."

"But you do not want an answer. You want affirmation, and that I cannot give you, because you are wrong."

"I am not wrong," Meer declared. "I know what I know. I've been near to dying more times in these last days than in all my lifetime. You're losing everything, and you want to take everything from me as well."

"You see why I will not argue?" Kedar said, his voice rich with sadness. "Perception is more real than truth, and belief turns truths into lies. Look at me. How real am I? Hardly real at all now, even to you. I am the traitor who never existed, who fomented the revolution which never happened."

With such pain held up before it, Meer's indignation withered as though punctured. He turned his back to Kedar, hugged himself more tightly, and stared out into the darkness.

"Kedar—I disown my words," he said finally. "I am not whole. I feel as though I left some part of myself down there."

"Perhaps it will prove to be something you did not need," Kedar said. "Are you ready? We must send the sleds back, and I do not have the strength."

Meer turned back. "Ready to be done with it, but no more than that."

Kedar nodded. "It is enough."

None of what Meer saw going back down into the ground touched any memory.

The dark, steep entry descended thirty or more steps down, past where packed clay turned to rock. At the bottom was a long sand pit well marred by deep footprints and the track of the sled which rested near the middle of the chamber. The chamber was lit only by the sled's brightly glowing lamps.

A second sled hung from the wall of the chamber, opposite a worn sand rake made of bound thorn twigs.

Kedar explained before Meer could voice his puzzlement. "Your sled was still at the foot of the qanat, so it was easy to send back, and I have already done so. This one is the problem," Kedar said, fluttering his hand over the sled lying in the sand. "That sled behind you is kept here for Storm's use, so that he can bring back his trophies."

Meer peered back over his shoulder. "Are you not afraid that the scouts will find this?"

"If they should find the qanat, it hardly matters whether a sled is here. Ana has its own miners and sleds, after all. And an invasion of one is little threat."

"How can you be so casual?"

"We are a long way from Kawa, and the scouts do not come to this part of the valley, or even in this direction."

"But they could."

He nodded agreeably. "It seems a balanced risk."

"*I* know about it now—"

Kedar smiled. "That risk, too, we are willing to sustain."

"Do you think I won't tell them?"

"Will you?"

Meer met Kedar's questioning gaze, but had no answer. At last he said, "It is a bit late to wonder about my loyalty, after what you have shown me."

"If so, then equally late to declare it. Will you tell them?"

Dropping his gaze, Meer scuffed at the sand. "I do not know," he said. "What do you think of that?"

"There are worse answers you might have given."

"And you could trust me too much. I would tell them to protect myself. My loyalty is to Meer," he said. "Not to Oran. Not to the exiles."

"That is how I had gauged it," Kedar said calmly.

"Damn you, I mean to warn you fairly. I didn't ask to know any of this. The responsibility is on you, not on me—and if I were you, I would not trust me."

Kedar nodded. "That is one of the differences between us. But I accept the responsibility. And I will forgive you your flaws for a few more days, if you will forgive me mine."

It took both of them to carry Kedar's sled back to the qanat and place it in the passage. The sled seemed to grab the smooth rock and hang there, a hand's-breadth above the cushion of sand.

Kedar pointed out the ascent ring, and Meer started the empty sled scuttling up into the darkness, the traction nats sure-handedly grabbing at the rock with a whine like a wagon motor. Meer watched with a shiver as the ring of light quickly receded up the sloping tunnel.

"The return must take even longer," Meer said.

"Long enough." Kedar chuckled. "There is a sound pipe, only as wide as your thumb, cut between Storm's home and the qanat, six thousand feet from the top. He claims he can call a greeting to Val, so that she knows his mood. I have my doubts—but the sound of the sled itself is more than clear."

The chamber had quickly grown dark as the sled sped away, and Kedar stood and turned on the lamps of the remaining sled. "We must rake the sand back into the landing, for the next descent."

Meer took the rake down and began to work the splash of sand from their arrival back toward the foot of the qanat. "How is it that you bore the descent so well?"

"I have no secrets to tell you," Kedar said. "I was ready to make that journey, and you were not. If you had come to it willingly, you would not have been afraid."

"There must be more to it than that. The speed, the cold, the blackness above and below—how could you endure them?"

"Can you bear the truth?" asked Kedar. "I thought it glorious."

Shaking his head, Meer said, almost to himself, "I cannot see any kind of pleasure in it."

Kedar gave thought a breath before answering. "I found myself agreeably—focused."

"I do not understand."

"I have not explained enough for you to," Kedar said, and paused. "Perhaps it is different for you. But for me, all of the weight of living lies in what has passed and what is yet to come, while pleasure belongs to the present moment—"

"No, that is it exactly."

"Then perhaps you will understand—it has been damnably hard through most of my life to hold myself in the present. Most of the moments I have managed it have come in a lover's embrace, when the spark is strong and touch offers an escape from thought."

"Yes," Meer said. "It can do that."

"There is no mystery, then. The journey here offered me the same escape, the same meditation, much prolonged. And it was a blessing to have the weight of yesterdays and tomorrow lifted from me so fully for so long." Kedar waved his hand toward the sand at Meer's feet. "I think we have done enough here. Not much of the night is left, and it is still a long way to Ana."

They struck the lamps of the sled and made the climb back to the surface in darkness. At the top, Meer stood back and watched as Kedar spread a weighted square of loose-woven jute-cloth across the opening to the qanat.

"Is that enough to fool anyone?" Meer asked, his tone skeptical.

Kedar shrugged. "The eye is easily fooled, if the mind is inattentive."

Together, they started off across the star-lit valley toward the southwest. Kedar set the pace, a brisk walking gait. Meer walked abreast of Kedar, but far enough from him that it could not be said he walked beside him. The gap, the hour, and their fatigue all seemed to discourage talk. Only the faint sounds of their wrapped and sandaled footsteps on the ground, the rustling of loose-fitting clothing in the night breeze, marked their passage.

After a time, they stopped briefly to drink and pass water. When they started off again, Meer placed himself nearer to Kedar's elbow as they walked.

"Kedar—do not think me morbid—but there are things I want to ask you while I still can, if you are disposed to answer—"

"I will tell you what I can."

"Why are the corpses in the canyon?"

"Ah," said Kedar. He let a dozen steps slip by. "I was not there when it was done, but I know something of it. That was very early. Jarn was the one at the center of it—an older man, a weaver from Glede. His son was a student."

Kedar paused again. "You have to remember that there were more dead than living, and the living were the ones who were suffering. No one understood that it was over, that Oran had won. No one could imagine the city would accept what had happened to them. The survivors thought they would be able to return, in just a little while. And they were certain that someone would care enough to come for the dead."

"So they collected them?"

"As many as they could, from the water, and the banks, and the flats where the river had flooded, to save them for reunion. It was a horrible task, but it was something to do, and there was value in that which you may not comprehend."

"But no one ever came for the dead," said Meer. "And a way home never opened."

"No," said Kedar. "None ever did. And by the time I joined the exiles, the scout patrols were making clear that we were too close to Ana, and would have to move downriver or die. Jarn insisted that we take the bodies with us. He could only find a few who agreed."

"It must have been hard, being surrounded by so many reminders of death," Meer said, remembering.

Kedar nodded deeply. "There was no escaping it except by joining them. I remember two survivors who made no effort to eat, because death seemed more attractive. Everyone had known at least one of the dead. No one was untouched by the strain. Even so, the argument over the bodies divided us—nearly brought us to blows. And when we set out to go downriver, Jarn and his friends stayed behind.

"They were nearly as angry with us as with Oran. I suppose the anger fortified them. When we were gone, they dragged the bodies one by one to the river, and lashed them together with clothing and sticks to make death rafts," Kedar said, and paused. "I think Jarn only meant then to overrule us with action. We were to wake up to find the bodies still with us.

"But it was almost as though Kawa wanted the bodies back. Once the rafts passed the junction with the south river, they were caught in the current, and swept past us in the night. In the rough water of the pass, one raft was pulled under, another was torn apart, and the only woman in Jarn's party drowned—a new casualty."

"The others must have reached the lake," said Meer.

"Yes. And started all over again to retrieve what bodies they could."

"There would have been no way to come back up the river, though."

"No, none, even now," said Kedar. "We did not know what was happening until two of Jarn's party came back to us. They said Jarn had become a madman, that he and the others were staking the corpses to the rock with stone hammers and wooden spikes. They begged us to stop him, and six of us went to try.

"But they had been a long time finding us, and it was a hard climb to the place they told us—made harder because none of us knew the land. When we reached the end of the river pass, we saw what you saw. It was already done." Kedar shook his head. "Jarn was no madman. He simply did not want us to ever look away from what had happened. What they did with the corpses was as much a reproach to us as to Oran and Ana."

"What became of them?"

"Jarn is there still—"

"What!"

"He hangs from the rocks with the other victims of the plaza," Kedar said. "Some think he must have fallen in an accident. Some think he threw himself down the cliff when the work was done. From what I heard of him, I favor the latter."

"And the others that were with him?"

Halting, Kedar turned toward Meer. "We never saw their trace or crossed their path again." He shrugged and smiled faintly. "Perhaps they went in search of their apocryphals. I hope they found them."

Meer was quietly thoughtful. "You have not quite answered the question I meant to ask," he said at last. "Why are the corpses still there after all these years? Were they left there to frighten the scouts and protect Epa-Daun, then? Or was it that no one could be found to undo Jarn's work with him watching."

"The first has been a hope—the last has been the reality. But neither is truly the answer to your question," Kedar said, frowning and wrinkling his brow. "Yes, we have made a burial ground for our own in Epa-Daun. But the victims of Oran Anadon do not belong there."

"No?"

"They belong to Ana," said Kedar. "The students of the plaza are waiting on the rocks for their brothers and mothers to come and reclaim them. When they do—if they ever do—then we will know that Ana has come to terms with its crimes."

They had not gone much farther when morning began to lift the sky. The air seemed to brighten, and the fine detail of the ground under their feet started to become distinct—the scattering of pebbles, the subtle grades of color, the tiny rivulets and larger gullies testifying that rain did sometimes fall on the dust-dry land.

When Kedar stopped to look back the way they had come, Meer followed his example. There were clouds both high and low over the horizon, and the sun was rising into a band of pale green sky sandwiched between bold yellow streaks and a sullen red-black mass. Across the green band floated wraiths of threaded black, like wisps of smudge from a lamp flame.

"Do you need to rest, or sleep?" Meer asked, studying Kedar.

Shaking his head, Kedar said, "I want to watch the sun come up."

Meer looked back toward the east. "It's a strange sky today."

"It often is, over Morada. This one will become a storm, I think."

Sucking his lips between his teeth, Meer dropped his focus to the valley and the gently rising span of rock which dammed it. "You need not worry about my loyalties," he said. "I am lost. I could no more find the way back to the qanat than build one."

To Meer's surprise, Kedar insisted on pointing the way. "Draw a line from the highest point north of the river, down through the white thrust—there, below and a little to the left. The entry lies on that line—from which your eyes will tell you we have wandered."

"I will not need the knowledge," Meer protested over the end of Kedar's explanation.

"I would not want you forced into protecting us through ignorance," Kedar said. "Now you still retain the choice."

Meer frowned and shook his head, then turned away, feeling and showing no gratitude for that consideration.

The disk of the sun broke clear of the low clouds, chasing the green tint from the eastern sky and flooding the valley with light. Kedar closed his eyes for a moment and tipped his head back, as though bathing his face in the glow. Then he slowly pulled the hood of his manteau up over his head and turned away.

"We can go on now," he said, "for a while at least."

"I remember," Meer said as they walked, "the time in Rida's salon when Rothe declared the origin heresy, and they argued half the night whether the apocryphals were real."

"I remember."

"And afterwards you and I talked—"

"You were indignant about the whole discussion, and wanted to know if I believed in the apocryphals," Kedar said. "And I told you I did not, had not for many years. You tried to convince me that our relationships with Ana and our apocryphal give shape and meaning to our lives."

"Yes. But you said that you preferred to be the one who gave meaning to your life." As he spoke, Kedar turned his foot in a gully and stumbled, and Meer reached out and caught an arm to steady him.

"Thank you. Yes—I remember."

"Am I imagining that something has changed?" asked Meer. "I think you hold your mark more highly now than I do mine. And when you spoke of the apocryphals back there—I suspect I was the only skeptic."

Kedar bobbed his head slowly. "Perhaps so."

"Have we changed places, then? I am surprised."

With a sigh, Kedar said, "To believe a myth is as easy a thing as breathing the air. But holding one's breath for a lifetime—that is difficult." He turned his head toward Meer and smiled ruefully. "No doubt you think I have surrendered my judgment to death fear. But there is more to the world than what we see. Surely we both know that."

"There is more to the world than what we know," Meer amended. "And we can imagine things beyond our sight. But does that make our imaginings part of the world that is real? If

imagining the unknown made it real, I would have found exiles
in Edera."

Kedar frowned. "You have become so cold, my friend. If there
is no promise of transformation, then what is the reason for our
struggle? Are we to be in pain always?"

"No," Meer said. "Only for thirty or forty turns round the circle.
Then we are free."

"You pillow me with all the comfort of a rock."

Meer shrugged helplessly and looked away. "I simply cannot
believe the promise. The mark is only ink under the skin. The
spark and the blessing reside in the body alone—have you not
proven that in Epa-Daun? The apocryphals are stories for children,
to answer the unanswerable."

"What answer would you give them, then? What made us, do
you think?"

"What made the world?" said Meer, throwing his hands wide.
"What made Taurin, and the apparitions of the night? What made
the water and the stone? They are all the same question, and all
equally unanswerable."

"Ah. Then you have nothing for the children—or the heart."

Meer shook his head. "Why must we pretend to knowledge we
do not have?"

"Perhaps they need to have some vision of their place in the
order of things."

It was Meer's turn to ponder his words. "Then I would tell them
we are the eyes of the creation, by which it may behold itself—
but that we can expect no courtesy for our service."

Grunting, Kedar said, "That is something, at least. But you have
still left them alone in the world."

"Why deceive them with any other notion? Why have them
looking to the temples or the night for comfort? Rothe was right.
The apocryphals are an invention, an empty tradition—a habit of
speech without substance or meaning. We *are* alone."

A fit of hard, wet coughing postponed Kedar's reply. "What
place do you give to Hoja den Krador, then, and the apparition
of the plaza? What are they?"

"Gone," said Meer bluntly. "Which is proof enough that whatever they were, they were not apocryphals, and had none to
protect them. I cannot believe we are any different, or any more
generously blessed."

"Perhaps not." Kedar coughed again, and spat thickly on the

ground. "But I caution you: There are no meaningless traditions, Meer—even if our myths are newer than this world."

As the sun rose higher and the bare ground drank in its rays, the air grew ever warmer around them, until it began to shimmer and toss with Taurin's exhalation. The heat slowed both their tongues and Kedar's steps, and Meer began to wish for a swirling sea in which to bathe his feet and head. But Kedar pushed on deeper into morning than Meer expected of him, until they were both slick-skinned with sweat and wobble-legged with fatigue.

Finally, Kedar stopped and let his bag fall heavily from his hands. He stood teetering, peering into the distance toward the city, his expression at once cross and sorrowful.

"I cannot see it," he said, his voice a husky rasp. "And I cannot go another step. Tell me, can you see it, Meer? Can you see Ana, or even the gleam of the arch?"

"No," said Meer, standing round-shouldered and limp-armed, panting. "Not even a horizon it might lie beyond. Just dust haze and air mirrors."

Kedar dropped gracelessly to a cross-legged seat. "I hoped to see it before I closed my eyes again."

"It seems we are not Storm's equal," Meer said. Kneeling, he burrowed in his bag for a tartfruit, hungrily tore the skin open, and took a wide-mouthed bite that left juice trickling down his chin. "The end of the day may be kinder to you. The night will surely be kinder to us both."

Nodding wordlessly, Kedar dragged his bag closer to him and drank long from his water bottle, then dropped his hood to his shoulders and combed his sodden silver hair back with his fingers.

"I was the last Genet in Epa-Daun," he said wistfully.

Meer was not too weary to hear that with wary alarm. But he adopted silence as a strategy, busying himself with his meal, and Kedar did not pursue the thought, at least not aloud.

Still, Kedar's words revived an apprehension which had never fully vanished since it had first appeared: that Kedar still had more to ask of him. The apprehension had hung over every step and nearly every word since they had come through the qanat. Meer's conviction that Kedar meant to punish him had only changed shape, not vanished.

And the longer Kedar waited, the weaker he became, the more Meer feared the imposition and obligation to come—not because he doubted his ability to resist and reject it, but that he dreaded the prospect of saying good-bye with a lie or a denial.

My life belongs to me, he thought fiercely. *I will not give it up to take up yours.*

"It is a curious thing," Kedar said then, staring out into the distance, "that I am so poorly disposed toward pain." He spoke as though to himself, to Taurin, with Meer only a coincident witness. "It seems that what wisdom I have was paid for in pain. And yet I cannot help but think there should be a more joyful road to follow."

Then he turned suddenly to Meer and fixed him with an earnestly intrusive gaze. "Have you been happy, Meer?" he asked gently. "What kind of dreams do you dream?"

Taken aback, Meer swallowed and tried to draw the curtain Kedar had thrown open. "What does a man need?" he said in answer, his voice hoarser than he would have liked. "I have found a comfortable place."

Kedar nodded, apparently satisfied, and turned back to gazing toward Ana. "Greater ambitions than that are not often rewarded," he said. "I would like to have been able to content myself with comfort."

The words prickled both conscience and pride, but Meer clung to his determination, and said nothing that might encourage Kedar to say more. He watched as Kedar burrowed in his pack and found a sugar stalk, which he broke off and chewed slowly—the first food he had taken since they had stopped.

"You know that everything in my house was destroyed—everything that could be burned, burned?" Kedar asked in a fragile voice.

"Yes," said Meer. "I saw the wagons there, the day they emptied the archives. The sentries threw it down from the windows, and raked and shoveled it like dirt."

"Oran had me taken to witness the burning," Kedar said, his voice barely audible, his words slurring. "I wept for every one of the dead, Meer. But I confess I wept and raged longest over the archives. I think that has been the hardest part—knowing that all the questions are still unanswered, all our work was destroyed. It seems somehow a worse betrayal of the students than their murders—the killing of their very thoughts."

A long sigh dropped Kedar's shoulders, and his head bowed. "Fatigue owns my tongue. Forgive me." He stretched full-length on the ground, turned his face from the sun, and pillowed his head on his arm. "I will sleep now," he murmured.

Meer closed his own eyes in relief.

But despite his fatigue, the hard bed and the blanketing heat conspired to guarantee Meer's rest would be fitful and dream-plagued, and his escape from Kedar's voice imperfect.

When his accumulated discomforts finally drove Meer to his feet and wakefulness, the afternoon sun hung only three times its own diameter above the western horizon. The dust haze had reddened its disk and stolen the harsh edge from its heat.

Kedar was still stretched out prone, though his bag was now his pillow, and he had turned his face to the east, away from the sun. A cough convulsed his body, but did not seem to wake him. Meer left Kedar undisturbed and walked a large circle around their resting site, stretching and trying to work out the aches in his shoulders, right hip, and right knee, the tightness in his back.

When he returned to the center of the circle he had traced, Meer stripped off his clammy blouse and let the air scrub his skin to a fresh dryness. Then he dug into his bag and retrieved the blouse the exile scout had given him. But he hesitated before donning it, shaking out the wrinkles, fingering a small snag hole in one sleeve.

"Go ahead," Kedar said. "You should be wearing that the rest of the way, for safety."

Meer glanced up in time to watch Kedar struggle to a sitting position, and sent him a resentful glower. "What do you expect from me?"

A hint of puzzlement touched Kedar's eyes. "Only what you have already done, and will do."

Meer's expression called Kedar a liar. "Haven't you played out this game long enough? What aren't you telling me?"

Kedar shook his head, his brow wrinkling. "I do not understand your question."

In sudden frustration, Meer snatched up a palm-sized rock and threw it as far as he could out onto the plain. The exertion woke fire in his aching shoulder, and he turned away and retreated a few steps while he massaged his tender muscles and emotions.

When he returned, he did not look at Kedar. His lips pressed into a tight line, he sat on his haunches as he extracted the shield of the exarch from the shoulder pocket of his own tattered blouse and purposefully moved it to the same pocket of the blouse he wore.

"Whenever you're ready to go on," he said.

"Will you explain your anger first?"

Meer ducked his head and hid his eyes behind his hand for a moment as the rush of resentment and indignation flooded out of the hidden places. He fought against them, but when his body had absorbed all it could as corded tension and clenched teeth, he sprang to his feet and paced off the excess.

"Meer—"

"Damn you, how can I raise my voice to you? You know the debt I owe you. Do you think I am that shameless, that I can forget that much? I have no right to complain."

"If you think you need permission to be angry—"

"You'll give me more reasons to despise myself?"

"What is it you want, Meer?"

Turning toward Kedar, Meer raised his chin from his chest, and blew out his breath in noisy puffs as he met Kedar's questioning gaze.

"It's not much," he said, his voice rich with bitter sarcasm. "I only want to know what hasn't been said. I only want to hear what purpose gave you the right to abduct me from my life. Just tell me why the hell I'm here, so both of us will know."

With a sad-eyed frown, Kedar shook his head. "It was not by right that I asked you to come, Meer. It was from need."

"Then why the test of honor?"

"I was afraid you would not come," he said simply. "And I was not ready to face *this* journey alone."

Meer edged closer, but his expression remained hard. "Anyone could have made this trip with you. Anyone. Even Rika."

"Perhaps so," Kedar said. "But you were the one I wanted, Meer."

Meer averted his eyes and hugged himself. "Then what I don't know is why."

"That is the whole reason," Kedar said, then added, "Beyond the fact that you are such a cheerful, light-hearted companion."

The laughter started deep in Meer's belly, but quickly bubbled up his throat and broke out into the air. Stepping forward, he offered his hand, and Kedar grasped it to help himself to his feet.

"Damn high bank honor boy," Meer said, shaking his head. "I never did understand more than about half of what you said. And nothing has changed."

Still clinging firmly to Meer's hand, Kedar bobbed his head

approvingly. "Nothing that matters. Nothing that need make any difference to us. See, you have the first piece of it after all."

Awkwardness prolonged the moment, but an echo of old intimacy illuminated their wry and self-conscious smiles.

"We had better get started," Meer said finally, "before we're reduced to tripping over our feet in the dark again."

They gathered their few articles, and Kedar allowed Meer to take custody of both bags. As a mutual courtesy, neither took note of the gleam of tears the day's last light betrayed in the other's eyes.

Turning their backs to the gathering night, they continued on together toward Ana.

15

Xehaniv: The Tenth Bell

To Kedar's keen disappointment, darkness conquered the land before Ana presented herself to their eyes.

But they walked on, talking of small things, safe things, mining the years they had lost for humor and anecdote. Kedar related his adventures discovering he could both float and swim in Epa's gentle current, and his trials trying to persuade others to learn as well. The difficulty vanished "in a hand of days," he said, once he seeded the rumor that his idle paddling was the secret of his potency.

"After that, I was never alone in the water," he said, his face lighting up at the memory. "And the women started to come to the banks to watch us, the way they come to their rooftops in Ana when the men run the streets.

"There was no magic in it when I began. I only wanted to break down the fear they still carried—they would not even build near the water, as you saw. But there was magic enough in it when we were done."

In turn, Meer told of meeting Huyana when her mother came before him as a witness. He took delight in relating the absurdly complex three-cornered complaint which brought them there—featuring a woman who moaned too loudly, another who took offense, mysterious slanderous graffiti, a hail of stones over a fencewall, a peacemaking dan battered, and a climactic rooftop shouting match of exceptional vulgarity.

"The longer it went on, the funnier I found it, but I seemed to be alone," Meer said. "I was hurting myself not to laugh, and here they were, earnestly arguing whether this one called that one a gourd-fucker and a flat-back, and whether 'sewn-lips' was an insult or a fair description. But then I saw that Huyana was having as much trouble controlling herself as I was. That's how I knew I would like her. Her eyes and her smile got me through that hearing.

"So I went by her hostel that evening, and we hooted like crazy people over it all, out walking together. And she invited me to night with her—but what would you guess? Huyana was so vocal herself that everyone in her hostel already knew what they called her 'singing voice.' I couldn't finish—but neither could she. We spent ourselves laughing, instead." He smiled to himself, seeing her. "It was a good beginning."

But Kedar's cough returned with the darkness, and soon became a nearly constant thing, sometimes deep and violent enough to rack his body and halt him in his steps. He seemed easily winded, and they had to stop frequently so Kedar could renew himself.

And one time, while they paused, Kedar asked about Fas.

Crouching, Meer swirled his fingertips in the dust by his feet. "She has been gone for eleven turns now," he said. "And I have missed her."

Kedar nodded. "How did she die?"

"Hard," Meer said, a catch in his voice. "I do not want to think about it."

Capping his water tin, Kedar nodded again. "I understand. I have found myself thinking about Lenn of late, though the thoughts come uninvited."

His face suddenly stabbed with guilt, Meer stood and retreated a few steps into the night. "She was *imoda,* but not dan," he said, his back to Kedar. "She still bled, and her house felt empty to her when Novi went to the hostel and Meli set me out."

"She wanted a change child."

Meer closed his eyes and nodded. "Dan Tria counseled her against it, but she would not be turned. As *imoda,* she had her choice, and lay with a Sika, from Banteng, and took the spark. For two quarters she carried the blessing well."

Turning, Meer looked at Kedar with pain in his eyes. "But the child never quickened. At the third quarter, dan Tria declared it dead inside her, and the midwife tried to deliver Fas of it. But the labor she brought on, or her tools, or the stillborn itself tore Fas inside."

He dropped into a crouch again, resting his chin on folded hands. "She died before they could find me." Slowly, he shook his head. "I never knew a body held so much blood."

"Perhaps you should be glad you were slow to her side," Kedar said. "I have been witness to enough death. There is nothing to recommend it."

"Perhaps not," Meer said, his voice now husky. "But I wish I had thanked her, the last time I saw her. I wish I had known to say good-bye."

The newly somber mood stayed with them as they went on, cutting them off from their comfortable tale-telling. With every step carrying them closer to Ana, time was slipping away. In a another day, half a day, half a night perhaps, they would be at the boundary.

To his surprise, Meer found he could not look on that prospect with either joy or relief. Not a word had been said about what they would do when they reached Ana, as though Kedar was prepared to simply surrender to events. But the end of Kedar's path was shadowed by ominous portents, and more and more Meer began to think that Treg had been right, that Kedar's attempt at repatriation was a ghastly mistake.

Meer made one earnest attempt to coax Kedar to consider turning back, but Kedar brushed him off. "You think me a stronger swimmer than I am, to suppose I can make way against the current of my whole life."

"Kedar—please—don't give yourself into Oran's hands."

"I have trusted myself to yours," Kedar said. "Oran cannot touch me where I am going. I do not fear him."

"What good is there in this for anyone?" Meer's voice was sharp with anguish.

Kedar reached out and touched Meer's arm. "Please—let it be enough that I can see it, so I need not carry the weight of your doubt as well. Let it be enough that I know my heart."

But Meer could not. "Do you think that they will receive you as a changeling, returning alive after so many years? There is as much fear as awe in those mothers' tales. And they will want to test the magic the apocryphals gave you."

"No," Kedar said. "I am not counting on myth or deception."

"Then how can you not be afraid? I am afraid for you. What do you know? What have you not told me?"

Kedar shook his head. "Only those things you have not asked to know—or have asked not to know. Whatever happens will be right, Meer. If you cannot see it, you will have to trust my sight."

They went on through the night, walking and resting, walking and resting. Once, then once again, Meer thought he could smell the city on the breeze, a faint complex of scents tagged to the living—warm bodies, fragrant foods, the very breath of Ana. It played rich against the dusty emptiness of the world outside.

But he said nothing of it to Kedar. He had found no peace in Kedar's words, no trust in his vision. Their journey could only end badly, and the knowledge that the end was pressing close placed a burden on Meer from which there was no escaping: the burden of choice.

He had thought that the hard part was over. The truth was it had not yet begun.

How should it end between them? The choice was now his. Kedar had given him a second chance to say good-bye. But, so far, Meer had stubbornly resisted its opportunities.

It was not that he could not imagine a better ending, but that he could imagine many worse ones. He had carried the weight of their last parting for fifteen years, and found ways to make it part of him, to make it comfortable enough to forget—the way a fat man forgets that his step was lighter when his belly was flat and his legs only carried the weight of one.

To reopen old questions and rewrite old history threatened that comfort. He knew how to sustain the old pain, and carry the familiar weight. In separate ways, each shielded him. The pain was an alarm which warned him against looking deeper, the guilt he admitted to a buffer against questions he would not examine.

The return of Kedar to his life rocked those compromises. But Meer had responded by stubbornly refusing any reconsideration of the past. All he had wanted was to satisfy his two masters, Oran and Kedar, and then return unchanged to the quiet corner that was his life.

But as the end rose up before him like a wall, he came to know that that would not be possible. He would not be able to escape the knowledge that he had chosen silence—that he had endorsed that which, until then, he had only accepted by repeating to himself that he was helpless to change it.

And in the end, though the battle was a bitter one, the old fear was overturned by the newer. Meer was forced to recant the vow he had made, and Kedar had accepted, when they were reunited in Epa-Daun. He had to ask, even at the risk of his own tranquillity, the questions which would soon be unaskable.

The cistern might be poisoned, but his thirst was too great. He had to drink, whatever the cost.

"Kedar—" he said. "I want to know everything you know. What happened on the high bank, in the days of the crusade? And what happened to Hoja den Krador?"

"That will take some time to tell," Kedar said.

Meer caught him by the arm and stopped him. "Then let neither of us take one more step toward Ana until I have heard it all."

Frowning, Kedar said, "Some of what I can tell you Oran would kill you for knowing."

"Then I am already at risk, just from having been with you. He will *think* you have told me, so you may as well do so."

"Ah, but you did not believe I was alive," Kedar said. "Does he? A corpse cannot betray many secrets, after all."

Meer stared. "Is that why you deceived me? To protect me? Even though you thought I would go to him?"

"You had the right to choose this burden, or refuse it."

Frowning, Meer raked his hair with his fingers. "But you *are* alive, and when we reach the boundary, he will know."

Kedar nodded, and said, "Which is why I promised you I would die before then." He smiled sadly. "I can only return as a corpse, or all of my friends outside are in danger, not only you. If I am not already gone when we find the boundary, you must help me die."

Numb shock took over Meer's face, and he took a step backwards. "Is that how we're to complete our path? Is *that* the vision I'm asked to trust? You brought me here to force me to kill you, or be killed myself—yes, I sacrificed you once to save myself. I won't shame myself further by denying it. But I will not let you take your retribution this way, by making me do it again—"

"No," Kedar said sharply, then was interrupted by his own cough. "Listen, and for once accept what I say." The force of his words stole his breath, obliging him to stop once more. "If we come to that necessity, it will be right for both of us," he said in a softer voice. "Understand, please—you would be doing me a kindness. I have learned enough lessons from pain."

Fighting off nausea, Meer wrapped his arms around his shoulders and hugged himself. "How can you ask such a thing?"

"I have not asked it, yet. I hope I will not need to. So let us put it aside for now." Kedar turned as though to resume the trek.

"Wait—" Meer said, dropping his arms to his side.

"What is it?"

"I have not changed my mind. I still want to hear what you know. Oran be cursed—keep nothing from me."

Kedar studied Meer's face. "Very well," he said at last. "Let us pick a place to sit, and I will tell you what I can."

It was a conversation that wanted privacy. A few dozen steps to the south, they found a dry cut-bank draw deep enough that it might conceal them, and perhaps even help stop their voices from carrying across the flat land.

"You know more of this than perhaps you realize. How much more of it you may have guessed, I do not know," said Kedar, sitting on his heels, his back against one side of the water scar. "But it began for us much as it began for you, only three days earlier—for Hoja den Krador spoke to the high bank first—"

"Did he come to you? Did you see him?"

"No. Oh, no." Kedar shook his head. "All we ever knew of him was his voice, and his words. The same is true of the woman who spoke to us—"

"A woman too!"

"—whose name was Denar Nchode. I can tell you nothing about the form of their bodies—only the form of their thoughts."

"How did they speak to you, then?"

"Much as they did to you," said Kedar. "You did not study the eight technologies, but you can understand this: There are five modalities of speech-by-air. The first is for the voice of Ana, the second for the library boxes of the clerks, the third so the cluster hives and the sentry posts may speak with the upper hierarchy, the fourth by which the syndic directs the scouts, and a fifth used only for testing and instruction.

"The modalities are the same in principle: The differences lie in the receivers. Some can hear, some can speak as well—some can write in symbol, some can remember what they have heard.

The receivers of the Voice are the simplest—they can only hear, and only the first modality. Some very few devices, the omnons, embrace all the possibilities.

"These last are in the custody of the curator of electrics, and kept in his archive room—I must explain that, yes? There is more to the school than what you have seen. The curator of each of the eight technologies has archive space below the high bank, safe away from the light—"

"Below—like the hole houses in Epa-Daun?" Meer asked, leaning forward.

Kedar nodded. "And for the same reason—to shelter something precious from the wilding rays. The archive rooms are where the nat templates of each craft are maintained, and the master library of stocks and samples kept—as complete as can be had, and carefully tended. You see, the curator and his apprentices must test and inventory the archive almost constantly—neglect has deprived Ana of too many tools already.

"This is why Lindor Savichen was the first man of Ana to hear Hoja den Krador.

"Lindor had gone down to the archive. When he entered, he heard a paging call on an omnon, in the fifth modality. Thinking an apprentice had borrowed from the archive without permission, Lindor demanded an explanation. He did not believe the explanation that came—but he ran to find me, even so."

"Then you were the second to hear?"

"Yes," Kedar said. "But while Lindor searched for me, he sent word to the circle house and the keystone house. So it was not long before Oran Anadon, seven from his circle, and two other curators had joined us in the archive of electrics."

Kedar shook his head. "There will be no surprises for you in what we heard: a man and a woman speaking in Ana's own language, with odd accents and slurs and a few unfamiliar words, but a message clear enough—a wish to meet, to talk, to exchange gifts, to share histories.

"But they spoke as if we should have known them, as though they thought themselves our brothers, and you know there is no place for that in the truth we learn from our mothers' lips. We Anans are alone at the center of the world—created by the apocryphals, endowed with their aspects, but imperfect, impermanent, dependent on the spark of Kawa and the blessing of Ana to preserve our fragile claim on life."

"But you did not believe that then."

"No. I did not," said Kedar. "And that is why I was one of the two people in that room who had any grasp of what Hoja den Krador's words might mean."

"Two! Who was the other? Lindor?"

"No. The other—the other, Meer, was Oran Anadon." Kedar shook his head. "I do not know what he knew, what prepared him. But I will swear to you that what I remember in his eyes is not the lost fear of the unknown, but something else—the cold dismay of a man who recognizes an enemy."

"How could that be?"

"I still do not know," said Kedar. "In all the following days, Oran never admitted to any thought beyond suspicion of trickery—later, treachery. But from the first, he guarded what Lindor had discovered as though far more was at stake."

"What do you mean?"

"No one who was not in Lindor's archive when Oran arrived was allowed to enter, or ever learn what happened there. And we were nearly made prisoners by the responsibility with which Oran charged us—to argue the meaning, and decide how we should answer.

"I think he did that only to occupy us—he had already decided his course. But we did not know that then."

Kedar was showing signs of fatigue. He propped his head on his hand, temple to palm, and closed his eyes as though searching his thoughts.

"You should eat something," Meer said. "You took so little when we stopped last morning, and nothing when we started this night."

Kedar raised his hand in what looked like a gesture of acknowledgment, but did not reach for his bag. "The others—the others were bewildered," he said. "They wanted to believe the students had tricked Lindor. I had to tell them that was wrong. I had to tell them that the world was larger than they knew. And they were hungry enough for an answer that they listened, even though I was the youngest of them, and newest to the circle house.

"They listened while I shredded the grand myth and offered them the origin heresy in its place. Even Oran listened—oh, he listened most carefully. And I was so caught by the moment—blessed Ana, here was the proof of the heresy, and a chance to answer all our questions!—I was so lost in my own excitement that I did not realize I had set myself against Oran." Kedar shook his head. "I should have been more clever. I should have listened to Oran's silence."

That thought seemed to catch Kedar in a sorrowful reverie, from which Meer had to prod him to return. "What did you tell them?"

Kedar straightened his back. "I said that Hoja den Krador and Denar Nchode were surely our kin in flesh and spirit, brother and sister of the same mother—by whatever name they might call her, Ana or Arania. I promised that the only mistake we could make would be to refuse their invitation, that what we learned from them would make us stronger.

"But Oran ordered us to the circle house, to consider the question. He allowed Lindor to stay—to listen for other messages, and determine their source. But Hoja den Krador had already told us the source. He told us where to look for him in the sky."

"What was the apparition? *Was* it the city of his people?"

"No. Oh, no. Not a city," Kedar said, looking surprised. "There is nothing which can hold a city in the sky." He turned his face to the stars. "But I am sure that it was a made thing, all the same."

"I do not understand."

Kedar slowly lowered his gaze. "One day I was sitting atop Kennebar, looking out on Morada, wondering about what I could not see. I thought, if somewhere there was another shore, another Epa-Daun, another people, how would I ever know, so long as our boats are too frail to venture any farther than the currents which bear the skimweed?

"And then I thought, if in that very moment I should see a sail, far out on the horizon where no bladder boat dares go, I would know that it must be a great sail, on a great ship, to be seen at such a distance.

"Even if no other man but me could see that sail, even if it vanished from my sight in the next moment, even if that boat had been bound for my shore, only to founder in sight of it, I would know something of its makers by what they dared. And I would never again look to the horizon again without knowing that somewhere beyond it, there was a people which dared so boldly and built so grandly." He cocked his head. "Do you remember the committee on technologies, and their fancy of a boat of the air?"

"Yes," said Meer. "I remember."

"Then you will remember their great triumph, the spinstick with the wooden blade like the prop of the scout boats, which they could make climb to twice a man's height for a heartbeat or two—"

Meer leaped to his feet. "What do you mean to say?"

"No more than you said on the beach in Epa-Daun—that the sky is a realm akin to the sea. We stand on its shore looking out at the horizon, and cannot know what lies beyond it." Kedar paused and steepled his hands before his mouth. "But for a moment, in the nights of mystery, you and I looked up and glimpsed the sail of a great boat—a boat of the air, in which Hoja and Denar had journeyed from somewhere beyond our horizons."

Meer stared, but could not speak. In another moment, he was crying.

Kedar drank the last of his water and some of Meer's as well, then took the time to suck another sugar stalk. When he continued with the story, he told it sparely, in broader strokes, as though he were being hurried by someone's impatience.

"We argued for two days, eating in the circle house, sleeping in the keystone house. Oran missed much of it. At times he spelled Lindor in the archive room so that he could join us. I do not know where he was the rest of the time. Perhaps he wanted us to think he would truly let us decide.

"Or perhaps it was that we were harmless so long as we were so badly divided. The curators were with me, but the councilors— to listen to them, I could hardly believe they had all come through the honor school. Such narrow vision—such timidity—such rigidity. Even so, I thought I had won three of them when Oran finally allowed a vote.

"I was wrong, but it did not matter. The curators were sent out, and Oran brought with him the proxies of the other six councilors, those who had not been sequestered with us. My proposal failed. Oran's passed. Only one councilor stood with me—Jiu Vachen, the prefect of invention."

Kedar's voice turned bitter. "And so Oran went to the archive of electrics with Lindor and gave the Aranians our considered answer: He ordered them to leave, and leave us alone.

"But he did not stop there. Oran told Lindor to gather and disable every fifth-modality receiver; when that was done, the archive was to be sealed until the apparition was gone.

"That would have been the end of it, but for the students."

"The gathering on the lawn," Meer guessed. "Now I see why the sentries chased us."

"You were part of that?" Kedar chuckled tiredly. "Yes—you deserved to see Oran's face when he heard that his tidy secret was becoming common gossip in the streets. You gave the dissenters new hope, and reopened the question—this time before the full circle of councilors.

"But the problem was the same as before: too much fear, of both Oran and the unknown. And though there was great confusion at first, the outcome promised to be the same as before. They talked of 'controlling the situation' and 'suppressing harmful rumors.' They were not interested in confronting the truth.

"So Lindor bravely tried to force them.

"The curators had been closed out, but Lindor had spoken with me and knew the prospect. He did not ask my approval or even hint at his intent—I do not know what I would have told him had I known. But sometime that day, he found a way and the privacy to answer Hoja and Denar himself.

"I do not know what he said to them, only the results. I think he must have told them of the war on the high bank—and I think it was he who invited them to take their message to the entire city."

"And for that, Oran had him executed."

"No," said Kedar sadly. "That much of Oran's pronouncement was true. Because after Hoja den Krador's address to the city, *I* was the one Oran suspected. *I* had invited the meddling of the Aranians. *I* was informing and directing the students." He paused. "Lindor confessed to protect me, taking it all on himself. And then he cut his belly open and killed himself, there in front of them, in the councilors' meeting house, to defy their right to judge him."

"Sweet blessing—" Meer breathed.

Kedar fell silent for a time, almost as though he were reluctant to continue. "Lindor shocked them, and that weakened Oran's hold on them, and strengthened me. The occupation of the plaza strengthened me. For a day, two days, I spoke with the moral authority of his martyrdom. I found myself leading an army of conscience, and the councilors had to listen. I was a friend to unknown powers, and they had to respect me.

"But it was not enough," he said sadly. "It was never enough. Because while I deceived myself that the struggle could be won with words, Oran made preparations to destroy my army of innocents and chase my friends from the sky.

"I failed them, Meer." His voice was hollow, fragile. "I failed them all—Lindor, Hoja den Krador, Lenn, all the thousands of the plaza. They were looking for someone to follow, and I led them to their deaths. They tried to help me, and I turned their sacrifices to dust."

Meer could only stare wordlessly and listen.

"I had always believed that ideas were all-powerful, that words were the best weapons. But Oran taught me a lesson about power, Meer. The morning of the drowning, he asked me again to turn against the demonstrators, to renounce the heresy. My answer should have shamed him, shriveled him. I was angry, I was eloquent. I said that he was blind and stubborn, and had betrayed the people, and a hundred other truths.

"Oran listened quietly, his face as blank and emotionless as a wall. Nothing I said touched him. And when I was done, he had me arrested. Not one councilor spoke against it. And Oran had the sentries keep me there long enough for me to hear the vote that followed—when he asked for unlimited authority to move against 'the agents of conspiracy.' Not one councilor dissented."

Kedar stared down at his hands, which were shaking. "The rest," he said in quiet anguish, "I think you know."

Swallowing hard, Meer looked away into the night. "It was not your fault," he said finally. "You did everything you could."

"No," said Kedar. "I could have killed Oran. Or I could have surrendered to what he wanted, and asked the students to leave the plaza."

Quietly but firmly, Meer said, "I do not think they would have believed those were your words, or your wishes."

Kedar lifted his eyes to Meer. "Perhaps not. But still, I could have killed him, if I had realized how ruthless he would be—and that we would have to be equally ruthless to defeat him."

"It doesn't matter," Meer said, shaking his head. "You did not ask Lindor or the students to risk themselves. They did so by their own choice, for their own reasons. Their deaths are Oran's responsibility, not yours."

"I know," Kedar said. "But guilt does not always track the footsteps of responsibility, does it? And it is hard not to wish for a second chance."

Meer let the question hang unanswered in the air.

A short time later, Kedar tried to stand. But his knees buckled beneath him, and he slid back down the side of the draw. "My legs are numb with cold," Kedar said. "I am shamed by my weakness."

"Eat something," urged Meer. "Let me peel a tartfruit for you."

"I do not need food. My stomach is too tender," Kedar said. "I just need to close my eyes. Will you wait with me?"

Meer swallowed and nodded. "I will wait."

"Meer—"

Dozing himself, Meer sat upright with a start. Kedar was standing in the draw, supporting himself with a hand and looking starward.

"What is it?"

"Does anyone in Ana remember when the night burned?"

"No one who does remember speaks of it," Meer said. "Kedar— Hoja's boat of the air—how was it destroyed?"

Kedar shook his head slowly. "I do not know," he said finally. "I wonder now if the exarch has an archive, too, and in it tools and secrets of his own."

Meer felt his way to his feet. "Are you ready to go on?"

"No," Kedar said, turning his face once more to the sky. "Meer, is there any reason to hope? Is the truth ever spoken? Has the blood bleached away from hands as well as from the stones? How many are left who were in the plaza? How many are left who know why they were there?"

Those were dangerous questions, and Meer answered cautiously. "Not as many as a year ago."

Kedar sighed. "When the last of us has forgotten or been silenced, Oran and the butchers will have won."

Meer's skin crawled—the moment had come. Now he would hear it at last, the reason for everything that had happened, from the message Storm had brought him to the secrets Kedar had shared. With unwavering conviction, he was certain he knew what Kedar was about to ask of him, why he was called out from Ana. It would end in a lie or a refusal, after all. But he could not help but try to deflect it.

"There is Epa-Daun," said Meer. "The boundary does not stop the sound of voices talking."

"How many did you count at the vigil?" asked Kedar. "Those who were there care greatly. But far more do not." He shook his head unhappily. "They will never go back to Ana. It has become unthinkable. They have become too comfortable. Without me, they will give up the vigil within a year."

Meer took a tentative step toward Kedar. "What do you expect of me?"

But Kedar's next words ignored his question. "But *they* will not forget," he said, jabbing a finger skyward. "I had hoped to last long enough to see it—to bear witness, and to be witness, when the kin of Hoja den Krador return. But it makes no difference that I will miss it. They *will* return, to punish Ana for Oran's crimes."

Only then did Meer realize that the imposition he had been dreading was not to come. Kedar had nothing more to ask of him. His debt was already satisfied.

As though reading his relief, Kedar moved close and said, "Meer—I do not blame you for what you could not change. I thank you, instead, for what you did change. I wanted to die, beside my son. I am glad that I lived."

They clasped hands in the darkness, a strong, warm connection which was both affirmation and reunion. Silent tears wet Meer's face.

And Kedar said softly, "Meer, my friend—you have been living afraid. Forgive yourself, and move on."

It was Kedar who insisted they resume their journey, even though clambering out of the draw was a struggle, and even on level ground he needed the support of Meer's right arm.

For there was no longer anything to impel Meer toward Ana, and every reason to defer the next step. He would gladly, even gratefully, have waited in the draw while Kedar slept. Or talked their time away until water and food were both gone, and their bodies gave them a reason to move on. Or followed the watercourse to or even away from the river, simply to be on a path which might still have surprises.

But Kedar still had a reason to continue. "This is the festival day of Xehaniv, and they will ring ten bells at sunrise," he said. "I want to be close enough to hear them."

"You still count the days on the temple calendar?" Meer asked, astonished.

"Part of me has never left Ana."

So on they went. It seemed that Kedar's body was fueled by defiance, and the pace he struck respected neither pain nor fatigue.

But the price was that walking became Kedar's whole focus, and conscience constrained Meer from breaking that focus with talk. He had found other questions, but he held them. His emotions had been unbound, but he contained them. For Kedar was weakening, and he needed Meer to be strong.

So Meer lent Kedar the strength of an arm to cling to—later a shoulder and the support of an arm, until Meer was carrying much of Kedar's slight weight. And all that time he held his tongue, though he knew that Kedar would never be stronger than at that moment, and the questions might go forever unasked, the words unsaid.

Because none of that mattered. In the course of a thousand steps across the night landscape, Meer's life became greatly simplified. All that mattered now was beating the dawn to the five hundredth ring of Ana.

When Kedar's knees and ankles would no longer support him, Meer tied the two bags together by their draws, so he could drape them from his neck, then took Kedar on his back, as a man carries a child, a father his son. He went on until his body was sweat-drenched and panting, his arms and shoulders screaming with fatigue, his own legs threatening to buckle.

"Just a few minutes," he told Kedar as he gently let him down. "Let me take some water, a few bites of food. Then we can go on."

But Kedar lay on his side and curled his body into a ball. "It is all right. Rest," he said. "I will sleep now."

Meer sat close enough to hear the reassurance of Kedar's slow breaths, and kept himself company with new thoughts.

And when he was sure Kedar was sleeping, he gave voice to the thoughts he had been containing, whispering in the soft air:

"In all these years, Kedar, I have had no better friend than you. My solitude has been my defense. I have allowed no other man to draw close. I hid myself, and from myself.

"But now—now you have abducted me from my life. How do I go back to what I was?" He closed his eyes and swallowed. "And how do I say thank you—or good-bye?"

Meer was awakened by rain on the back of his neck. He sat sharply upright and looked around him at a gray dawn blanketed by low, fast-moving clouds. But the dawn was not so gray that it hid the smooth rise of the boundary mound, so close that he could hardly believe he had not sensed it when they stopped. Nor was the rain so heavy as to blur the square shapes of houses and ringwalls twenty or thirty blocks farther in, along the outermost finished ring.

They had made it. Ana was spread out before them.

"Kedar," he said, turning to where Kedar lay, just beyond arm's reach, his back to Meer.

"Kedar," he said with a touch of urgency, crawling across to shake Kedar's shoulder.

The skin under the fabric was slack and cool to Meer's touch, like another garment.

Meer jerked back his hand and stared. "No—sweet blessing—Kedar—"

The raindrops fattened and slapped into the dust all around him.

With exaggerated slowness, Kedar rolled from his side to his back. His arm dragged limply across his hip as he turned, then dropped numbly to the fast-muddying ground at his side. His eyes were closed, his face as gray as the sky.

Not Kedar, Meer's eyes tried to tell him.

He grabbed Kedar's hand, and touch told him the same.

Not Kedar.

Kedar's body—

Kedar's husk—

Kedar's corpse.

Through the rain, Meer heard the bells of the arch ringing, calling the blessed to the festival.

He gathered Kedar up in his arms and held him, rocking and weeping, as the skies opened and the rain poured down.

16

The Judgment
of Kedar Nan

The day after the drowning, Ana became a city of whispers and masks.

The whispers were how the word of what had happened in the night spread. There were survivors, but not many, and they were hiding. There were witnesses, but not many, and we were afraid. The sticks and hammers, blood and screams, had limned the first lesson of the plaza with perfect clarity—those who challenged Oran Anadon could expect neither justice nor mercy from the forces he controlled.

The masks were how we protected ourselves. There was anger, but anger was an admission of knowledge we were not meant to have. There was fear, but fear was a confession of complicity. There was grief, but grief was a revelation of questionable loyalties. It did not feel safe to show them to anyone who did not have an equal stake in secrecy.

This was true even before the voice of Ana was restored, and Oran once more set us on each other—which did not take long, and was not a proud time.

We still had criers that morning, but they did not have much to say: the curfew still in force, the plaza still closed, work hard and be alert for suspicious behavior. The only real news was that the repair of the Voice's receivers would begin at once, and

normal announcements were to resume that night—anyone whose
receiver had not been restored by dusk was to go to a neighbor's
whose had.

That was how I knew beyond question that the terrible light
in the night meant we would not hear again from Hoja den
Krador.

As I walked to the retting barn, it seemed I saw toolmen everywhere, hurrying along the spoke roads and ring roads, gripping a
bundle of splices in one hand and a joining vise in the other.

When I reached the barn, I found the same kit waiting for
me.

It turned out that, under orders to have the whole city ready
to hear from Oran Anadon by nightfall, the toolmen were only
attending to every fifth house on their first pass. Kirl and I were
just two among the many drawn from other crafts to fill the gaps
the toolmen were leaving. I was given two blocks to work, with
more than eighty plots on each side of the ring road—more than
three hundred houses for me alone.

How opportune, you must be thinking, for me to spread the
news of what I had witnessed. I had only to be like the toolmen,
repairing the truth in every fifth house, and then letting it spread
over the walls.

Just a whisper: "Do you know what happened on the plaza?
Listen, and pass it on—"

But I swear to you, there was no time for ten or twenty or fifty
such conversations. The repair work had likely been divided by
how many joining tools were available, and they were not common—but that did not mean Tevin would not hold me responsible
for completing it all.

Even though it took little more time to repair the cables than
it had taken to disable them, I had to step quickly. I had no wish
to call attention to myself, or to give Tevin a reason to single
me out.

Is that hard to understand? Don't you remember how it was
when a sibling stirred your mother to fury, and you strove to be
so perfectly behaved that you became invisible—lest you become
the next object of her wrath?

That was my state on the day after the night of drowning.

I think that was the state of most who knew any part of the truth.
And it seemed that most knew at least enough to be afraid.

I saw it on the faces, house after house. The masks were
not perfect yet. They were suspicious of me, afraid of *me*. I

represented the power of Oran to them. I was an intruder, and I would leave another intruder behind: the Voice. Even those who knew me seemed uncomfortable with my presence. Even those who claimed to welcome me held themselves back from me.

If they had wanted, they could have asked: "What do you know? What do you hear?"

But no matter who spoke first, the other would have suspected a trick. Even if I had had the luxury of time, few would have been willing to listen. The horrors of the night and the whispers that were their echoes had set the tenor. Ana was already profoundly in the grip of terror, as though we could see what lay ahead.

Three hundred houses. By dusk, my hands ached. The strains of the "Fertile Blessings" corner-song, played all day as a test to help us, ran maddeningly through my head. But I did not go home hoarse from talking. That whole day, it seemed I barely spoke at all.

Meli's house had not been touched yet, so she and I heard Oran's invitation to fratricide at a neighbor's, in the company of a houseful of others from all the surrounding homes.

Our hostess—I have forgotten her name now—was determinedly cheerful, telling every new arrival how glad she was that the city was returning to normal. But few of us, if any, could match either her enthusiasm or her self-deception. I saw tired eyes, eyes that had cried, tight smiles, resigned smiles, many masks. I heard little except idle talk about innocent subjects.

We understood we were waiting to be told what to believe. There was no reason to publicly voice thoughts we might shortly regret having said.

I looked at them and wondered how much each of them knew.

Meli had heard the full story from me, once I managed to make my way home past the patrols, through the confusion. I was still shaking from my escape as we huddled in the darkness of her house.

I wondered what part of it had she shared, with which of her friends. I wondered how they were looking at me.

I wondered that even more after Oran was finished speaking to us.

I did not expect to hear a message of healing and forgiveness. But neither did I expect what I heard.

Oran did not put the boldest lies in his own mouth. It was the voice of Ana who told us that crisis had ended peacefully.

Most of the 'disruptive elements' had given up their 'misguided demonstrations' and renounced their 'treasonous heresies.' There had been a 'brief scuffle' with a small number of 'irrational intransigents.'

A few masks slipped. One man turned his head away in disgust. A woman hid her face in her hands. There were a few mutters, a cluck, and a shake of the head.

There would have been more, but I suppose that resignation numbs the senses—the sense of outrage most of all.

Or perhaps they were just waiting for the rest.

Oran thanked the people for their loyalty and cooperation during the crisis. "The greatest danger is now past," he said. "Ana is safe, for the moment. But all of the guilty have not yet surrendered. The conspiracy spread more widely through the city than we first dared believe, and we were betrayed by some of our most trusted brothers.

"The body of Ana must be purged of every last remnant of this threat, so that we are never placed in such peril again. Therefore, I must call on you once more. I ask you to open your eyes and your ears and your memories, and assist the syndic of security in your cluster. Bring him word of any official of the hierarchy that you have reason to suspect of disloyalty."

By 'any official,' he explained, he meant any with the responsibility of supervision or administration—from trustee, syndic, and prefect down to the aedile in the smallest craft house and the lowest clerk in the hives. He did not say "any who came to their post through the honor school, because I do not trust them," but he might as well have, since every appointment he named was held for such.

Then he told us how we would know the people being sought: those who spoke against authority, who sympathized with the demonstrators, who changed their habits and companions, who refused to work, or encouraged others to do the same, who possessed seditious literature, or forced it on others, who was a member of an unauthorized circle. By the last he meant the salons—which of course had been neither authorized nor forbidden.

When I heard that, I did not dare let myself wonder who knew, and how they were looking at me now—lest my own mask slip and fear show on *my* face.

"All these are signs we must heed," Oran said, "if we are to secure our safety. Do not confront those you suspect. The syndic of security will investigate, and those who cannot explain their actions will receive justice before a court of those they betrayed. Some of you may be called to serve for a time on this court of the commons. I know that you will show the same steadfast loyalty with which you honored me while the peace of our city was so gravely threatened."

Then he yielded the air to a woman who read the names of those already being sought by the syndic of public security. They were to surrender themselves by dusk of the next day, or face a further charge on the offense of flight from justice.

I closed my eyes, lowered my head, held my breath, as I listened. But I knew only one name announced, and it was not mine—it was Tevin's predecessor as aedile of our retting barn. I was heartened to learn that he was not yet in their hands, even though the reason might be that Kawa had swept him away.

Still, Meli and I went home like so many must have that night— trying to measure our own vulnerability, and wondering if anyone would come for us.

"No one will help him," Meli said to me when we were alone. "No one will turn in their friends—the friends of the people who were murdered."

"They will," I told her. "They will fight to be first. They will fall over themselves with eagerness."

She would not believe me. But that next morning, there were lines at the hives as soon as dawn freed the city from the curfew.

Do you see how easy Oran made it for them, how he divided us, how he isolated those he had marked as his enemies?

By pretending that the rebellion of the plaza had been limited to the honor school and its alumni, women were made safe from accusation—and were therefore freed to accuse.

As for the men of the circles, the sun workers and craftsmen, they were the heroes of the plaza. They had stood arm in arm with the sentries, and bought a presumption of loyalty for their entire class. Excused from suspicion, the sweat circles could look at those who had once held power over them and return fear for fear, abuse for abuse.

There were many grudges settled that way.

To be sure, the sentries had proven their allegiance as the sweat circles had, by spilling blood for Oran. Their reward was the freedom to revel in their power. They did the exarch's work—who would question them? Perhaps a few senior captains, those who had balked and shown softness in the first days of the occupation, the first nights of the curfew—perhaps a few of them quietly disappeared. But after the drowning, the sentries ruled Ana for Oran. No one would risk accusing them except Oran himself.

You might hope to hear that those Oran had singled out for sacrifice at least conducted themselves with honor. But some fell as low as any in those awful days, turning on each other in a desperate attempt to buy safety for themselves at the price of betraying a brother.

Oran's conspirators were a fiction, until we created them, and delivered them to him. We listened to his lie, knowing it was a lie, and then transformed it into the truth.

I wish that Meli had been right. But, to our shame, Oran had all the help he needed.

I do not know how many disappeared in the purge. But no one ever came for me.

That was how I knew Kedar had protected me.

Tevin would have denounced me for the sport of it, and perhaps he tried. But Oran did not want me. Meli and I did not need to fear.

We were afraid, all the same.

I do not know how many disappeared in the purge—thousands, at the least. There was a court of the commons in every cluster, and some heard thirty, even fifty cases.

The court for Banteng Cluster heard twenty-four, in eleven days. That I do know. I sat at the left end of the panel for all of them, for I was one of those called to serve with steadfast loyalty.

I will say this but once: I did not invite that appointment, or welcome it. Perhaps others did, thinking that it meant opportunity in the new order. It did not appear that way to me. Or to Tevin, who delivered the notice himself.

"I could think of no one more fitting to offer them," he told me, making no attempt to disguise his glee. "I spoke so well of you that I almost believed my own words." He leaned closer, until I could smell his rank breath. "This will teach you how wrong you were. They were fools and traitors—and you should not have defended them. You should thank me for doing this, Meer. Now you have a chance to atone for your own foolishness."

Do you see? It was an appointment that no one could refuse, but some could avoid being offered. But I did not even have that choice.

It does not matter now. I could not make Meli understand, so I doubt that you do. I have said I did not want this—but I could not refuse it. There was no reason that would have sufficed to excuse me. If I had not served on the common court, they would have dragged me before one.

Tevin understood, even if Meli did not.

Perhaps you would be more forgiving if I pretended a different motive. I could say I thought I might help the accused receive a fairer trial, a more just sentence. I could tell you I hoped I could be the secret ally of the innocent. I might even win your sympathy.

The truth is that everyone knew the courts of the commons would be an empty show—an arena for airing charges and pronouncing sentences, not for the determination of the truth.

At least, I knew. I cannot say how well it is known now.

Perhaps I did have a choice. I will not argue too strongly. But I could not have changed anything, and I wanted to survive.

In every way, the courts were every bit the sham I was expecting.

Accusations were considered their own proof. The accused were held to be guilty from the moment of their arrest. The trials—call them hearings, if you find that less offensive—were conducted in secret, with no witnesses except the participants and a court monitor assigned by the Councilors' Circle. The outcome was always foreordained.

How could that be? Better to ask how could it be otherwise.

In theory, the judges had all seven degrees of punishment available to us: shame marks, reduction in share, removal of the line mark, beatings, directed suicide, execution, and exile. But before each case was heard, the court monitors gave us "guidelines" on sentencing—guidelines in which there was no latitude. If the accused confessed, a given sentence was specified. If they offered a defense, a harsher sentence was usually called for.

Oh, yes, they could deny their guilt. They could even request an arbiter to make a defense for them. But the arbiters were selected by the syndic, not the accused—and had to submit their arguments to the syndic for censorship before presenting them to the court. The presentation of a defense did not greatly lengthen a hearing, I confess—or alter the result.

You see why it did not matter who served in the courts. We were symbols, mouthpieces. The sentries watched the accused. The monitors watched the judges.

But even so, Oran took steps to ease our conscience, so that we would not feel any need to defend ourselves, or otherwise spoil the pretense. Every court was made up of a panel of three judges, and every vote was announced as 'a ruling of the majority.' No one of us had to think that we were responsible; one vote was not enough to pass sentence. We could hide in the majority, or even pretend to dissent.

What's more, we were—or were meant to be—looking out from the panel at strangers. Oran had already used classism to divide us—he was not above letting cluster boundaries divide us as well. No judge served in the court of his home cluster—we were all sent elsewhere. And scattered, so that the three judges on a given court came from three different parts of the city.

That is how it was that I was sent from Liu to the court of the commons for Banteng Cluster, where Rida kept her home and Kedar his archives—Banteng, which had been my second home.

As to why—I would not be surprised if Tevin had a hand in that turn, as well. No doubt it would have amused him.

One after another, they were brought before us in ritual sup-plication.

We sentenced a cold chemist who had stolen vat milk for the students to a beating by the stickmen. A clerk found with a copy of the Seventeen Inquiries was ordered branded with a shame mark for twenty days, and reassigned to sun work in the Fifth Hundred. A senior trustee of food shares who failed to prevent the "looting" of his warehouse earned sixty days of shame marks, sixty days on half-share, and a beating of sixty blows.

Those were some who did not deny their crimes. Others made it harder.

I remember a prefect of physical culture, whose workhouse faced the plaza. He was accused of allowing students to drink from his cistern and shelter themselves from the sun under his roof. Defending himself, he protested that he was driven by compassion, that there could be no crime in kindness.

We listened, our masks in place, and then told him he would be allowed to kill himself. The compassion we offered was a promise of reunion.

They brought the custodian of the temple of the arch, a round-faced engineer, before us. The charges were that he had conspired with the radical leadership, and cooperated in the unlawful seizure of the plaza. His defense was a denial, and he screamed it at us, in terror and fury. The sentries had to keep him bound to restrain him. Even then, he spat at them and tried to bite them as he writhed to free himself.

He had done nothing wrong, he pleaded with us, nothing at all. The students had taken the temple by surprise and sheer numbers. It was an open structure—he had no way to close it to them. He had stayed on his post in the temple out of duty, not out of sympathy. He did not care about the politics of the high bank, only about doing his job.

The custodian's defense ended with his tears. He began to tell us he had two new sons, but that had been forbidden by the censors. The sentries silenced him by cuffing him until blood ran from his ears and he bowed his head, chin to chest, in surrender.

I cannot speak for the other judges, but I knew that there had been no plot such as the charges described. I knew enough to believe him. He was one of the innocents.

But we had guidelines to follow, and a monitor to satisfy. We sentenced the custodian of the temple to execution by staking in the sentries' killing yard, three days from that day.

That was considered a small mercy. The condemned are usually given seven days to look forward to their suffering.

A joke? Perhaps a bitter one. Do not think that this was easy for me, not ever when the sentence was for death. The others I could shrug off, whatever the injustice of the charge or the sentence— they would survive.

But those who received the higher degrees of punishment—

Of the first nineteen offenders, six were condemned to die, four of them by their own hand. Each time, I cursed Tevin, and I cursed Oran. I cursed the monitor and the sentries and the men who sat to my right allowing it to happen. I cursed myself.

But I held my tongue, and held up my mask.

And when I went home each night, I let it all pour out on Meli. She was the only one I could tell.

But I was the only one she could blame. Her feelings had turned, you see—and I was still on the wrong side. She set me out on the eighth day.

The next morning, for the first time, the sentries brought in someone I knew.

Lenn.

Though any joy in the discovery was destroyed by the circumstances, it was still a shock to see Lenn alive. All of the others from the salon had been staying near the temple, right on the river. There was no good reason to think any had escaped drowning.

But seeing Lenn, I remembered Kedar coming to the plaza. I thought then that he must have known what was in the offing, and had tried to warn his son—or perhaps even to trick him into leaving before the sentries closed the plaza.

I could only guess and wonder. There was never a chance to ask.

The specification of charges against Lenn was a long one: promulgating lies harmful to the community, rioting and conspiracy to riot, theft and conspiracy to steal public property, unlawful demonstration, unlawful publication, a dozen more. It was not only the salons; Oran had declared everything the students had done forbidden.

Listening as the judge at my elbow read the specification, I realized that if these were truly crimes, I could justly be charged with at least half of them.

I realized, too, Lenn could easily denounce me at any moment. All he need say was, "Yes, I did all those things—but you should know that he was with us"—and raise his hand to point at me.

It would not have saved him, but I am certain the monitor would have listened with interest.

Lenn was no more than sixteen, and facing his death—though perhaps he did not know that. But Lenn did not denounce me. In fact, he said nothing at all in court, neither confessing nor offering a defense. Through the whole proceeding, he stood mute, looking directly at me, looking right through the mask.

I could not look through his.

I could not tell his thoughts, so I colored them with mine. And what I saw then in his eyes was contempt.

His eyes paralyzed my hands. His face was so young, but there was no innocence left in it. When the time came to pass my voting card to the center, I could not do it. The lead judge finally snatched a card from in front of me—I did not even see which one. If I had been sitting in the center of the panel and had to speak, I would have been as mute as Lenn.

He blinked once as he heard the sentence, but kept his head high as they led him away to die.

The sentence was execution by staking in the killing yard, to begin that same day at sun-zenith. I did not understand why so quickly—not until the next trial.

As they were taking Lenn out, two other sentries brought Kedar in, and the monitor came forward with his next report.

I cannot tell you how I felt when I saw Kedar enter. I have turned away from that memory for so long that it has lost all depth, and faded into the distance. Was I numb with shock? Did my skin grow hot with shame? Did I rise from my chair, speak his name?

I do not know. Lenn's trial had seemed to take forever. Kedar's flew by in a haze. The remnant of the memory is like a nightmare all but lost to first light.

Have you not found that there are moments in each of our lives when we look at the draw of the tiles and know without question the shape of the game, and that however we play, we will lose? Moments when we clearly see our part in things, and know the limits of our power to effect change—because no one of us controls the game?

It is like a waking dream, with a dream's peculiar qualities of wonder and inevitability.

I think that is how I felt when I saw Kedar. I think that is how Kedar felt when I saw him.

His eyes were hollow, his face wan. His shoulders were rounded, and his mouth drawn in a tight line. I saw a flicker of recognition when he looked at me, but nothing more. He looked battered, defeated.

I could do no more to save him than to save Lenn, or the custodian of the temple, or the prefect. Kedar's expression told me that he knew that.

I had not expected to see Kedar in the Banteng court. I thought that they would deal with him on the high bank, that Oran would find some special torment or end for an enemy of such high status. But Kedar was not treated any differently than the others who had come before us. Oran and the councilors did not come to gloat over Kedar's humbling; the charges against him, though many, gave him no special credit. His title and posts were not even named. He was Kedar Nanchen, a criminal of the rebellion, and nothing more.

Only once did I see in him any of the quiet passion by which I knew him: when the lead judge asked for his plea.

"I do not plead," Kedar said, his voice clear and his shoulders firmed. "A child pleads for forgiveness. I do not want forgiveness for my acts. I proclaim my guilt. I only wish I had done more, so that I might have prevented the acts for which Oran Anadon can never be forgiven."

They allowed that, and would have allowed more—perhaps to prove to him the uselessness of words. But Kedar had no more to say. I suppose he had already grasped that lesson.

He was sentenced to the quick death, under the sticks of the sentries—but given the full seven days for reflection.

That was when I understood Lenn's sentence. Oran wanted Kedar in the holding cell, looking out at his son in the killing yard, watching him slowly die.

They wanted to break him, to grind his heart and spirit into pulp and dust.

Of all the cruelties Oran has fathered, is any worse than this, to force a man to witness the torture of his own child?

There was nothing I could do. But I forgot that truth. Through the rest of the day, it was forced away by another thought: I could not leave Kedar to the fate Oran had chosen for him.

A man who acts helpless, is helpless. But a man who dares sometimes finds luck favors him. And a man who lies boldly is sometimes believed.

I could not take Kedar from the sentry compound by force. I had no weapon, no army of allies. But I did have at least a semblance of authority. I had a title. If the autonomy of a judge of the court of the commons was limited, that did not diminish the power of the court and its rulings. And the sentries were not party to the machinations of Oran's monitors. They brought accused men into court, heard them sentenced, held them prisoner, enforced their punishments. The courts were a sham—but they were still feared, because they had power, power that flowed down to them from Oran and the councilors.

I usurped a tiny measure of that power to win Kedar's freedom.

When night had settled, I went to the sentry compound and presented myself, with title, arrogance, and my best approximation of a stentorian voice. I thought that by then any special visitors Kedar might have had would be gone, that the sentries who had worked prisoner escort that day would have gone home or given way to others.

I told them the court had reviewed the day's trials and discovered an error, and I sent them to bring Kedar—asking for him by number, not by name, lest I be the reason they remembered his celebrity. I said that he should be bound and gagged, as for transport. And before they could wonder, I offered the excuse I had devised:

"In his confession, this criminal defamed the exarch. For this further crime, his sentence has been advanced from the sixth to the seventh degree."

I showed them an order I had written myself, on the back of a page bearing our monitor's mark and sign—part of a sentencing report, which I had taken from the panel that afternoon. The order said that sentence was to be carried out at once, and the monitor's few words above his mark seemed to fit the context.

It was a frail tissue of a lie, which they could have blown away with a breath. But they did not. I came to them in the name of the court, with a document of the court, instructing that a punishment be increased, and they accepted it all. The captain of the compound had Kedar brought, and called out two sentries to take him to the boundary.

Had Kedar been denounced to the city by Oran, had his trial and imprisonment been marked by special handling and precautions, they would surely have questioned my order before obeying. But Oran had chosen not to make public that a councilor of the ruling circle, a prefect of the honor school, had turned against him. Kedar was not to be honored in death by such attention.

That, more than anything, accounts for the success of my lie.

They bundled Kedar into the back platform of a three-wheeled hand-bike. One of the sentries mounted the front seat, and the other ran alongside as they started out toward the half-east spoke road. I went with them, trailing behind where Kedar could see me, hoping that with eyes alone I could make him understand I meant to save him.

If the sentries had been careless with him, Kedar and I together might have overpowered them. If there had been friends of the rebellion to call on, a very few could have stopped us and freed Kedar as we made our way to the boundary. But neither option presented itself. We reached the boundary by midnight.

The sentries removed the bonds from Kedar's ankles and dragged him to the top of the mound wall. They freed his hands, then threw him down the embankment into the borrow trench. The sentry who had run pronounced the exile.

"By the order of the exarchy and for the good of the people, you are exiled forever in life from the body and the community of Ana. So long as you stand, you stand outside. Do not attempt to return, on pain of death. May your suffering illuminate your offenses against those who were once your people."

I counted on Kedar to grasp the opportunity I had brought him. I counted on him to accept the exile and run off into the night, so that we could report his sentence fulfilled. I expected him to run off and come back when we were gone, to reenter the city. I would have helped hide him. There was more work than ever to do.

But as the order of exile was recited, Kedar picked himself up and tore the gag from his mouth, then started back up the embankment to where we stood, raging and demanding that we take him back. The sentries knocked him to his hands and knees and kicked him down the slope, and he came back again, this time begging.

"Take me back. Take me back to my son," he pleaded. "He needs me. I can help him through the pain. I can help him die strong. Please—he needs me, Meer."

But as many times as he climbed the mound, the sentries drove him back. They beat him until he finally surrendered, until he turned away, bloody, to stagger off into the night and the void.

No one ever questioned me about that night, or the exile of Kedar Nanchen.

I do not say that no one knew. Surely, they did.

But it was a curious circumstance I presented to them. So far as anyone could see, my offense was excessive zeal. Any other interpretation endangered the captain of the holding compound, and the sentries who had done my bidding, and even the court monitor whose name I had appropriated.

And what harm had been done? The honor of the exarch had been defended. The court of the commons had shown its loyalty. The offender had received the ultimate punishment he had so clearly earned.

So the lie became the truth. Kedar Nanchen's sentence was officially changed to exile, for so long as those records were kept—which was only a dozen more days, until the last of the courts completed its work. Then all records of the courts of the commons were destroyed, to protect those who had served in them, and to mark an end to the strife, so that it might disappear from Ana's sight and thoughts.

The plaza reopened seventeen days after the drowning, in time for the festival of Botad. I walked it from one edge to the other, and found no mark of what had happened there, though I swore I could still hear them.

Not long after, I first heard the rumors that a dark apocryphal had been the cause of what people called only 'the trouble.' That lie Oran spread over the walls, not through the air. It took root as a myth sturdy enough to shadow what was left of the truth.

The city was hungry for order and the ordinary. They shaped both from whatever they could find. And so did I.

When the work of the courts was done, there were many vacancies in the hierarchy of the city. I was offered one, as a reward for my service—a post as arbiter in Banteng, hearing common disputes, one step above the dan.

Kedar was gone. Meli was gone. I did not wish to return to the barn with Tevin as its master.

I took the path that was open to me. I accepted the offer I was made.

Judge me as you will.

17

Ana-imoda:
The Eleventh Bell

The warm rain fell hard and steady for nearly half the morning, washing the dust into a landscape of brown puddles and rivulets which betrayed every undulation of the ground.

His clothing soaked and his hair glued into black points by the downpour, Meer clung to the hand of the corpse which rested beside him and struggled to come to grips with the realization that it was over. There were no more questions to ask, or answer. There were no more claims upon him.

All he needed to do was wait where he was. The rain might delay it, but eventually a boundary patrol would appear, making its slow way from the north gate to the river along Ana's periphery. The scouts could not fail to see him. Oran's shield would protect him. They would take custody of Kedar's body, and he would be free to go home.

But to what?

Oran had been satisfied. Kedar had been satisfied. By the end of the day, he could be back in the workhouse, back in Sachi's arms—perhaps even Huyana's.

So why was that thought so unsatisfying?

All beings must live a completed path—

Shivering with a chill he attributed to being wet to the skin, Meer looked down at Kedar. Kedar blankly faced the sky, his head tipped just enough that the corner of his right eye had become a well for raindrops.

"We both should be done now, then, right?" Meer asked the corpse. "Is that why I feel so empty, because everything is finished?"

He did not need to hear an answer. He knew that everything was not finished. There were other reasons for the emptiness.

All beings must live a completed path. Kedar's words had been annoyingly persistent in Meer's mind. And they invited dangerous questions.

Meer reached out and brushed the water from Kedar's eye, then pulled Kedar's hood across his face to shield it. "Where does my path end, if not here?" he whispered.

Drawing back, Meer stood and wandered a few steps away. With his arms folded over his chest, he peered intently into the curtain of rain. All he had to do was wait. Somewhere out there were the scouts—probably sitting out the storm under a hastily erected sun canopy.

It did not feel finished.

Where did Oran Anadon's path end?

"Damn you, Kedar," he said to the hissing rain.

He allowed himself to think of the young dead on the plaza, and those who died at the zenith of the sky. Were *those* completed paths? Had their lives ended in anything but tragic waste? The survivors still in Epa-Daun, the corpses on the rocks—were these completed paths? It was nonsense wisdom, a delusion of meaning and purpose and order in the world—a myth from Kedar's personal culture, as pernicious as the notion of the apocryphals and their aspects.

When had Meer shown the hidden strength reputed to the Genet? It was Kedar who embodied the aspect of the Genet—no wonder he believed in their reality. Kedar had endured the destruction of his life's work, the death of his friends, the execution of his son, exile from his loved ones and beloved Ana, and even his own death with more grace and resilience than Meer could hope to measure in himself.

And yet, absurdly, Kedar had thought himself a failure.

As the rain began to slacken, Meer turned back and looked down on Kedar's body. "I know the work is unfinished," he said. "But if you could not bring it to completion, how can I? Perhaps they are still looking for someone to follow. But I am not the one—and you knew it. That can be the only reason you asked so little of me. You would have wanted more if you had thought me equal to it."

He shook his head. "I have spent a lifetime regretting that I was not as good a man as you."

Squatting on his heels, Meer swirled his fingertips in a pock-marked puddle, making smoky trails of silt in its depths. "You see, you were right, Kedar," he whispered. "I *have* been living afraid."

The wind had picked up, and was beginning to tear small blue rents in the canopy of clouds. Meer stood and scanned along the boundary for any sign of a patrol. Soon—they would be along soon.

But still, it did not feel finished.

Meer returned to Kedar's side and sat down in the puddle which had spread under the corpse. Overhead, the wind blew the clouds into tatters, and chased the tatters toward the hills. Sunlight exploded onto the city spread out before him. Before long, the ground began to steam, giving the rain back to the air as a shimmering veil of haze.

Tugging back the cape, Meer wistfully studied Kedar's face. He thought of Rida, still displaying the totem of her honored, and of Lenn, dying alone in the killing yard. He remembered the sound of Rika's flute carrying up the face of Kennabar, the faces of Nan Tirza and Dansi as they let Kedar go.

He closed his eyes and let himself see the macabre forms of Jarn the weaver and the victims of the plaza, still in pain after nearly sixteen years. Was Jalos among them, or Chai, or Weilin Red-Eyes? Meer had not dared ask Kedar, for fear that the answer was yes.

They all deserved something more. They all deserved a better ending than this.

"How?" he asked Kedar. "How do we stop him from winning? What is there that can still be done? How can I make it right now, for any of you? It is too late. Even you gave up the fight, Kedar—you were hiding, too—"

The accusations which tumbled out embarrassed Meer into silence. He sat watching the gloss of water disappear from the ground around him, and waiting for a glimpse of motion north-round along the boundary.

Soon. It would be over soon, and he would need never think of any of it again.

But he continued to mull the problem he had set himself, and as he did, the kernel of his reflections became a seed of rebellion. *Is that all that your exile meant?* he thought, looking at Kedar's death-slack features. *Is remembering all that matters, waiting all that honor requires?*

It has become unthinkable, Kedar had said. But perhaps he had spoken more truly of himself than of the colony of exiles. He had endured his trials, but at what cost? Perhaps at the cost of his willingness to chance failure.

How could he ask the survivors to risk their lives again, when they all had already lost so much—for which, however wrongly, he felt responsible?

Or perhaps it was even simpler than that, and more personal. Perhaps Kedar had found he could not bear to see those he loved endanger themselves for a cause which became more remote with every passing day. He had coaxed them back into the water, but no farther.

Better to put his energies to transforming the myth of Edera into the reality of Epa-Daun. And how liberating it must have been to shift the responsibility for retribution to the kin of Hoja den Krador.

Self-deception, in the service of his peace of mind? Meer held the thought gingerly. It was just possible.

They will never go back, Kedar had said. He had spoken with the utter conviction of the heart, with a certainty that could only come from empathy with them.

They will never go back. But *he* had. Why?

Because the prospect of death had sparked a reappraisal. And because the questions for which so many died still demanded to be answered.

Meer stood and again scanned for patrols, this time with appre-hension. *If there is any chance, any way, and I do not try—I will never have peace. If Oran is not taken down, neither the living nor the dead will ever have justice.*

Why had Kedar come back to Ana? Whatever the reason, per-haps it had been enough to show the exiles that it was possible—to make the unthinkable thinkable again.

And suddenly Meer saw his path clearly. He had come a full turn around the circle, to the same juncture, the same decision point—except that this time, he would decide his future by passing sentence on Oran Anadon. In a moment of breathtaking clarity, Meer saw what he must do to become the man he had spent a lifetime regretting he was not—what he must do, not to satisfy Kedar's expectations, but to honor his memory, and to satisfy his own conscience.

"You were wrong, Kedar—remembering is not enough," Meer said tersely, as he began to strip off his blouse. "This we must do for ourselves. But you can rest now. You gave enough, for long enough. It is time for me to pay the price of conscience."

Meer's wet garments clung to him as though resisting his intent. Removing Kedar's was far harder, a trying, clumsy, distasteful business, made more so by haste. But dressing Kedar's corpse in the expedition blouse, float belt, and high-waists was the worst by far. Kedar's limbs were leaden and uncooperative, and the garments ended up even more sodden and muddy than they had been when Meer began.

But finally it was done, and perhaps the dishevelment suited the tableau Meer meant to create.

The warm sun felt deceptively good on Meer's naked skin, but he could not stay exposed. He scrubbed the stain of Kedar's death-void out of the manteau with the last of the drinking water, then slipped the garment over his head and let it drop. It was clammy and heavy, and something inside him squirmed, wondering if it were unlucky to wear another man's death cloak.

But at the same time, there was something that felt powerfully right about the exchange, as though by trading clothing, he and Kedar had traded worlds. As the hot breeze leached the moisture from the fabric of the manteau, Meer fingered the threads of Dansi's handiwork in colored thread.

"Perhaps I do not deserve to wear these marks," he said to Kedar. "But I will wear them anyway, and we will see."

Hoisting Kedar under the arms, Meer shouldered him like a warehouseman shoulders a grain sack. Then he swept up both drawstring bags with his free hand and started toward the boundary, only a few hundred steps away.

The borrow trench was knee-deep in brown water, and the slope of the barrier mound was slick with the slime mud the rain had made of Ana's fine dust. But Meer struggled his way to the top, clinging to a precarious balance, dropping the bags so that he could secure his grip on Kedar's corpse.

A swivel of his head and a quick scan told Meer he was still alone. Gently, he lowered Kedar to the ground and laid him out face-up on the inner slope, as though he were looking toward the center of Ana. Then Meer hurried to retrieve the bags, one of which had rolled into the water and was bobbing gently on its surface.

The bags reclaimed, Meer returned to where Kedar lay and knelt beside him. "Kedar, I cannot look after both your body and our cause," Meer said, digging in his bag for his torn and balled-up expedition blouse. "Please forgive me if I neglect the dead in favor of the living."

His fingers found the hardness at the center of the roll of tan cloth and worked to free it. "I am afraid this would burn you if you still claimed breath," Meer said, and laid the bronze disk of the shield of the exarch at the base of Kedar's throat, framed by the vee of the blouse's neck-hole.

Then Meer took his finger and marked in the fast-thickening glaze of mud beside Kedar.

This is Meer Faschen, he wrote in compact glyphs, *honored of Rida Valtera, a woman of Hebei. Take him to her house, that he might be properly remembered, and be granted reunion.*

"This is the most I can do here," Meer said, sitting back on his heels. What would the patrol do when they found the body? The sentries had logged his departure—would they accept this as his return? There was the shield, and the Genet mark, and a superficial resemblance to persuade them.

If the scouts' report did not find its way at once to Oran, they would likely be more concerned about who had left the corpse there than whose it was. And Hebei was much closer than the high bank—surely they would do the easy thing, and take Kedar home to Rida.

It was a cord woven from fragile hopes. But even if the report did reach the high bank, how much interest would Oran have in a corpse? Kedar had shown Meer the way. The best escape from the threat of Oran's power was to already be dead.

And even if the deception utterly failed, what did it matter? Kedar was safe—Oran could not touch him. And Meer was irrevocably committed, whether Oran thought him a corpse or an outlaw.

"Good-bye, Kedar," Meer whispered, and leaned forward to kiss the corpse's grime-smeared cheek. "I cannot stay any longer."

Then he scrambled over the top of the mound wall, splashed through the water in the trench, and ran back the way he had come.

●　　●　　●

Speed mattered more than the deep footprints his long strides left in the sucking silt surface of the desert valley. It was important that no one follow him, but more important that no one catch him.

A chaos of footprints and ground marks showed where the men had stopped, where Kedar had died. Meer did not pause or even slow his pace. He had no way to erase the sign they had left since the rain had started. But beyond that point, the rain itself had helped the blowing dust obscure their night passage. The only trail was the new one his feet were marking in flight.

The air was so thick with moisture that his chest ached, and the sweat clung to his skin. Meer began to let himself drift southward toward Kawa as he ran. He did not look back until he reached the cut-bank draw.

There he paused only long enough to make sure that no pursuit was yet in sight. Then he scrambled down the sloping side of the draw and plunged into the knee-deep water he had counted on finding coursing through it.

Crossing to the other bank, Meer picked his way southward for fifty, seventy, a hundred steps, taking care to leave a generous sampling of hand- and footprints above the water, working his way nearly to the top of the draw. From there he pushed off, leaping backwards into the stream.

Standing with the water swirling around his legs, Meer quickly sorted the contents of the two drawstring bags. One canister, the waist-blouse, and the remaining thick-skinned wet fruits went into Kedar's bag.

The rest went into what had been Meer's bag, which he released into the current. Floating high on the air trapped in the empty water tin, the bag bumped along with the flow in a promising way. Meer hoped it would go a long distance before running aground, and help pull the scouts in that direction.

Then he turned north, away from the river, and started up the draw as quickly as his legs could manage against the depth and flow of the water. As Meer drove himself, he held one image in his mind: of the plaza of the temple of the arch once more filled with joy, and voices raised to celebrate not a brief moment of power, but final victory.

He thought he saw a way to make it real, if he could only make it back to Epa-Daun, and they would only listen.

●　　●　　●

By the time the water running through the draw had been reduced to a trickle too feeble to erase Meer's footprints in the stream bed, the sun had crossed the zenith, and the open land all around Meer was fast returning to a parched, hard-baked desert.

There was no point in going farther in the draw if it could no longer conceal him. His destination did not lie to the north. So Meer paused to weigh the risks of waiting against the risks of starting east across the valley.

There was still no sign of pursuit. Perhaps the patrols had not even found Kedar yet. Perhaps they had taken his misdirection and were looking for Meer to the south, along the river. If he waited in the draw until darkness could hide him, the ground heading east would be hard and dry enough to conceal his passage.

But the longer he waited, the more scouts could be scattered to search for him. The longer he waited, the greater the likelihood his simple deception would fall apart. The longer he waited, the more ways and time they had to find him. He was still not that far from Ana's boundary.

He would not wait.

With cupped hands, he drank as much as he could from the trickling stream. But he only filled his water tin a third full. The sun would be over his shoulder, not in his face, for the rest of the day. The weight of a full tin would only slow him down.

Then he climbed out of the draw, took a sighting on the highest point of the eastern massif, and headed off at a brisk trot to find the doorway through darkness.

Night, not fatigue, ended Meer's search. Though he had pushed himself as hard as his body would stand, dusk found him still well short of the gentle rise of the massif along which the entrance to the qanat lay.

But when he stopped, the weariness in his legs and lungs dragged him to the ground. He did not fight sleep. There was little chance he could find the entrance by starlight, and he had come far enough that he no longer imagined the breath of his pursuers on the back of his neck.

Meer passed the night undisturbed, except by wild dreams that vanished from his memory when he opened his eyes. Shortly after daybreak, wandering south along the edge of the slope, he found himself on the line Kedar had traced for him, from the highest point down through the outcrop of white rock. He turned back toward Ana and found the entrance within a hundred strides.

The entry was slick from the rain, the chamber below pitch-black and humid. The sand squished underfoot as Meer felt his way along the wall to where the sled hung. His senses jangled, reminding him that the danger was no longer behind him, but now lay in front of him.

He would have to be ready for Storm at the top. He would have to be ready to fight.

It did not take Meer long to get the sled ready. But when it was resting in the tunnel with its dim lamps glowing, waiting for him to clamber aboard, he hesitated.

He tried to tell himself that it was only because, looking up into the unyielding blackness of the qanat, he had caught an image from last night's dreams. The image was of a horrible collision in the tunnel—of whistling upward through the darkness, only to see the light of another sled hurtling down at him—of watching helplessly as it grew brighter and brighter, the two sleds racing toward the same point—

But there was more than that in his thoughts. For in that moment, all the doubts had come rushing back. He assayed himself, and did not find the strength, or the wisdom, or the centered sense of purpose he had always found in Kedar. How could he lead them where Kedar could not?

Because I can be a bridge—

What can I teach them?

That they are as strong as they dare to be—

What can I do?

The answer pressed forward to his lips, and he whispered, "You can try. At least you can try."

Ducking his head, he crawled into the opening, twisted onto his back, and settled his body into the sled. His right hand found the controller, and his left tucked the loose folds of the manteau beneath him. Then he closed his eyes and listened to his own breathing, until it was calm and regular. This time, he was ready. This time he would not be afraid.

Opening his eyes, Meer craned his head to look upward. There was nothing but darkness above him. But somewhere beyond the darkness, there was light. He had to believe that to begin. So long as he believed that, he would be strong enough.

He squeezed the release, and the sled began to rise.

In subjective time, the ascent passed quickly, for Meer had much to occupy him. The changing pitch of the nat crawlers finally alerted him that the sled had begun to slow, calling him back from his thoughts. When he twisted his head to peer up the shaft, he saw the glowing circle of the upper chamber above him and growing larger.

The sled finally stopped less than half its own length from the opening. Reaching above his head to grab the lip of the shaft, Meer pulled himself out gracelessly. The fabric of the manteau snagged twice on the sled before he was clear, and he ended up barking an elbow and landing on his knees on the floor.

"So," said a familiar voice. "You came back."

Meer looked up to see Storm standing at the other end of the chamber, blocking the way to the surface. Picking himself up, Meer tugged his garment into place. "Yes. And not to be stopped by you. I want to talk to Nan Tirza."

"You presume a lot—not least by wearing his clothing." Storm took a small step forward. "I don't like that. I don't like that at all."

"I am not the enemy, Storm," said Meer. "But don't make yourself mine. This is too important for me to let you stop me here. If I have to fight you to get out of this room, then come on, and let's have at. But don't count on winning. I didn't come back here to lose."

Storm cocked his head. "Why *did* you come back?"

"Because it will take all of us to bring down Oran Anadon."

Shaking his head, Storm said, "He is your problem. No one here cares. We have chosen to look forward, not back."

"I hope to show you that you're wrong—and why you're wrong," said Meer. "If you're not too frightened I might succeed, then take me to Nan Tirza." He took a step forward himself. "If you are, then let's end this chatter. Come try to take me, and I'll find her myself when I'm finished with you."

Storm grunted derisively. "You are bold with words for a man who is no fighter."

"I will be whatever I need to be, to see this done."

Blinking, Storm studied Meer for a long moment. "I do not trust you. I do not think any of them should."

"I have not asked for your trust, yet. I want a hearing."

"You will have that, at least," said Storm. "I will insist on it, so I can kill you in free conscience." But he turned and let Meer follow him to the surface.

There had been more than warning of his approach; there must have been anticipation as well, to judge by the surprise he found there. Waiting in the near-blinding sunlight were Treg, Nan Tirza, Dansi, and more, ten or twelve exiles in all, forming a large circle around him.

But who had they expected to see? They did not react in any way Meer could detect to the sight of him. They could well have heard the exchange below ground—had that dissipated the surprise? Was this the disappointment of people who had responded to Storm's alarm with hope that Kedar was returning?

He squinted at their faces and caught a nervous smile flashed by Dansi, a sideways glance by Nan Tirza at someone else in the circle. But he did not see disappointment, or surprise, or confusion. He was the one confused. They seemed to be just— waiting.

Meer swallowed and blinked back sun tears. "This time I've come by my own free choice," he said, "to try to finish what Kedar started."

A man stepped forward, his deep-lined face at once familiar and unfamiliar. "I told them you would be back. Storm did not believe me."

Meer stared disbelievingly. "Boli?"

A generous smile brightened the man's face. "They asked me to hide myself before, because they did not know you, because they did not want you to know. There are only seventeen of us left from the plaza, and me the only one from Rida's salon."

Meer could not find his voice. But Boli came to Meer and embraced him, a fierce, heart-rich embrace that battered at Meer's surprise until he could answer in kind.

"The only one until now," he said, stepping back and holding Meer by the shoulders. "I did not get to say this on your first arrival, so I insisted on being the first to say it now. Welcome to Epa-Daun, Meer Fas. Welcome to the city of exiles."

That made several of those watching break their silence with grunts or mutters of disapproval.

"Boli forgets that many of us do not consider ourselves exiles," Treg said by way of explanation.

"But you are," Meer said, turning away from Boli to face Treg. "Whether by force or by choice makes no difference. You are separated from your own history, from the traditions that shaped you. You have stolen little pieces of the whole and brought them here to sustain you. But you delude yourself if you pretend that Ana is not part of you, and you part of it."

Before Treg could respond, Meer turned next to Nan Tirza.

"Will you call a circle of the whole, and allow me to take the center? Because of what I must ask of you, there is much I must tell you."

There was a curious sparkle in her eyes as she studied him— part amusement, perhaps, and part fascination. "I will announce it for tonight, at shadow dusk," she said finally. "I cannot order anyone to take part, of course. But I will come, and listen to what you have to say."

They met from when the shadow of Kennabar first touched the meeting circle until darkness denied them each other's faces, and then again the next night, and the next.

In all, it took six days for Meer to present his apologia. Each evening he talked himself hoarse, then disappeared into the round house they had given him to sleep. He walked, took his meals, and went to the river by day, keeping himself apart so that he could not hear what they were thinking.

For the most part, they did not question him while he held the center, but he was harder on himself than any questioner could be. He made himself naked before them, pressing honesty to the point of pain, so that no one would have cause for any thought of deceit.

But it was also a welcome unburdening, a housecleaning of memories he had hidden away or hidden from, and for that reason liberating as well as ravaging. He would have gone on for that reason alone, so long as there was even one witness to his confessions.

There were many more than one. They sat and stood two deep around the circle of stones the first night, and four deep by the last. Nan Tirza, wearing the red sash, was there for every word, as was Dansi, and Treg, and many others whose names he did not know. Beginning with the third night, Rika sat quietly beside Nan. Meer recognized some faces from the salon in Kedar's round house, and honored their collective departure for the vigil as the signal of the end of the gathering.

Storm came and went unpredictably, and always stood off a few paces from the last row, as though by doing so he did not need to count himself part of it. Meer did not see Val Maran, or Lial, or the pale youth who had threatened him on the trail. But Sela, the woman who had spat in his face, found a place in the front on four different nights, and at times he found himself speaking as though to her alone.

When there was no more to say, Meer signaled at last that he would yield the center. "Judge me as you will," he said, fatigue and relief pushing him almost beyond caring. All the secrets were told—he was free of them forever.

"I do not think we have come here to judge you, Meer," said Nan Tirza.

"Some have," he said, scanning the circle slowly. "Perhaps many have. Storm has told me himself that he does not think any of you should trust me. Perhaps he has said the same in your hearing. Storm, do you want the center now, to make an argument against me?"

Storm waved off the offer. "Your own words are enough. No man who willingly serves the exarch of Ana deserves my trust."

"Kedar served the exarch willingly," said Meer. "Did you forget that, or forgive him for it? Or perhaps you held him suspect, as you do me." Meer looked about the circle. "You know that Kedar honored me with his trust. But perhaps you should question Kedar's judgment. I did, as I have told you. Clearly, one of these men, Storm or Kedar, is wrong. You will have to decide which, each of you for yourself."

Boli used the shoulder of the man beside him to help himself to his feet. "For what it is worth," he said to the circle, "in every matter of which I have knowledge, Meer Fas spoke truthfully." He turned toward Meer. "I do not know what plan you have, only the intent you declared when you returned. But if there is a place for me in it, you have my hand, and my pledge."

Meer smiled gratefully. "Thank you, Boli." He pivoted to face Nan. "The truth is that I dared hope to win you all. But if even twenty of you, knowing my flaws and failings now as well as I know them, or you know your own—if even twenty of you are willing to say that it is time for Oran's lies to end, that it is time for justice for those who *cannot* win it for themselves—"

Stopping himself, he looked around at their faces. "I would rather have a hundred, make no mistake. But if even twenty will commit with me, I promise you that we have a chance to take Oran from the high bank, and take the city back from him."

"A fine chance to be tricked into capture," Storm called. "A better chance to die, I'd guess. Of course you'd rather have a hundred—that would make a fine trophy for you, wouldn't it?"

Meer turned on Storm with dagger eyes. "You heard the wrong question. I am not asking anyone to volunteer to die. We are all assured of that, whether we hide in the shadows or challenge the sun. I am asking how you want to live until that day comes. And I, for one, have had enough of shadows and silence. If we fail and I fall, so be it. But if I fall and we succeed, then by Kawa's staff I will have died better than I lived these years since the drowning."

"Is it for you, then, that we are to do this," Storm asked archly, "so you can wash your conscience in more blood?"

"Enough, Storm," spoke a woman. Heads turned, and Meer saw that it was Sela, rising from her seat. "You have made your heart ugly with hate, as I have mine. But you have gone so far that you cannot hear what you will not hear."

She then looked at Meer. "Storm is my brother, you see, and has carried his own quarrel of conscience. He was not on the plaza when it was closed because he was too young." She stepped into the circle and approached where Meer stood. "I owe you apology for my conduct on the crown trail—if you will accept it."

Dumbstruck by a rush of gratitude and wonder, Meer could do no more than nod.

"Then count me as the third of your twenty," she said, and looked expectantly out at the encircling faces.

In the startled hush that followed, one by one others rose and made their way forward to be counted, offering Meer their name, their hand, and their promise, until Meer, who had stood alone in the center for so long, was surrounded.

Then Nan Tirza rose, unknotted the sash at her hip, and carried it across to a tall woman standing half-way around the inner circle. "There is no wisdom or insight in the sash, Lisha," Nan told the startled woman. "Look for them in yourself."

Backing away, Nan then joined the group at the center, saying nothing to Meer except with her eyes.

But Boli turned proudly to Meer. "These are the seventeen I spoke of," he said, "the last witnesses to the drowning." He craned his head, eyes darting from face to face. "Who else will stand with us?" he called.

Treg had been standing with arms crossed and head lowered, a frown on his face. Now he muttered something that made those around him laugh, startled. Meer looked that way as Treg edged forward to the circle of stones.

"I would not want to see a fine debacle canceled for lack of a quorum," he said with a wry grin, triggering a ripple of laughter. "And I have grown bored with sailing, and where will I find a challenge even less in my favor? Count me as your nineteenth fool, Meer."

"And count me as twenty, which makes it done," Rika said, bouncing to her feet, her face full of defiance in anticipation of an objection. But Nan held her hand out in invitation, and Rika ran to her.

"Hardly done," Nan said to Meer, "but ready at least to begin."

"No," said Meer. "No, we must have someone else. Is Izel in the circle? Is Scot?"

"Here," said a voice.

Meer turned toward the sound and peered into the darkness to see who had spoken. "I am Izel," said a short, thick-armed man standing in the back row. "What do you want from me?"

"We must have one more tunnel," Meer said. "Two hundred feet long, or little more."

"Where?"

"Under the high bank of Ana."

Izel laced his fingers and hid his mouth behind them, palms out and elbows high, and said nothing.

"I know what I am asking," Meer said. "I know that Briden died in making the dry qanat to the valley, the passage Kedar must have asked for. And I know it is unfair to place this burden on you. But Oran has left us few options, and the best plan I have cannot succeed without you."

The entire gathering, two hundred or more, was startlingly quiet as they waited for Izel's response. The breeze blowing across them made more noise than their voices.

Izel lowered his hands. "We would need fresh nats."

"We will get them," Meer said.

Izel frowned. "I swore after Briden died that I would never work the rock again, that I would spend the rest of my life in the light," he said, and Meer's hopes began to plummet. "We finished that cut for him, not for Kedar."

Meer swallowed down a lump of disappointment, and started to nod.

"But I know why Kedar wanted the qanat," Izel continued, looking down at his hands as he flexed them. "He meant to keep the way back open. He told us as much, and that was our reason when we started the work." He looked up at Meer. "You are the first to want to use it as Briden thought it would be used. So we will go with you to Ana and do what you need done, lest we make his death pointless, too."

A cheer ripped through the circle, and Izel and Meer both found themselves descended on by a tumult of back-clapping well-wishers and surrounded by gleeful, daring-to-hope faces.

"Are we allowed to know what we've volunteered for now?" Treg called to Meer over the throng. "Or are you to be the only one in the light? How does it begin?"

Meer laughed giddily. "It begins as it ended," he called back. "So first, one of you must teach me to swim."

18

Kawa-rami:
The Twelfth Bell

By the time they were ready to move, Meer had his hundred, and a dozen more. Even so, the first step depended on what he had to do alone.

Four went into the city in the first wave: Meer, Izel, Scot, and a young man named Poli, who had come out of Ana on his own within the last year. Izel and Scot were to go into the north city, into Hiku and Itar, into the mines themselves if necessary, and acquire a tunneling kit, or discover what it would take to do so. Poli's role was as messenger and scout.

But Meer had taken on himself the burden of finding them friends within Ana. Storm had refused the conspirators the help of his own small network of contacts.

"They care about getting people out of Ana, not bringing them in," Storm said. "They would come out themselves but for that. I won't endanger their chance to leave by letting you draw them into this."

But if Storm had meant to strike a blow to their plans, he was disappointed, for Meer had not been counting on that help.

"I do not want to rely on people who have so little love for Ana," said Meer. "We need those who have a stake in staying, and therefore a stake in change. And ten will not be enough. We need hiding places for a hundred, and ten thousand to fill the plaza. If we cannot find that many who care, the most we will achieve is to change the name of the man we all despise."

"Do you know where to find them?" Nan Tirza wanted to know.

"I know who does," was his answer.

When what Boli called 'the edge of the wedge' was ready to leave Epa-Daun, Storm relented on one part of his vow, though in purely self-serving terms.

"I will take you into Ana," he told the foursome. "I need that road to stay open. What Meer did with Kedar was bad enough. I can't let your clumsy stupidity call any more attention to the boundary between the rock and the river. And I want to warn *my* friends in Ana to be careful until this is over."

By Storm's insistence, Meer and Poli went first. If there were no problems, he would return and bring the miners in at another point, by another route.

Carrying nothing that would betray their origin, the trio crept into Ana under the stars. There were no obvious signs of increased vigilance at the boundary, but Storm was quick to discourage overconfidence:

"Any night, the syndic could bring five hundred sentries out here and post them a hundred feet apart, on the inside of the mound wall. No one could get past them without being heard, and you'd never know they were there until it was too late. And if I were the captain, I might wait until a night I might get thirty prisoners, instead of three."

But they continued into the city unchallenged. When they reached the construction in the mid-four hundreds, Storm left them, disappearing into the night on his own mission.

"Have you considered that he might betray us?" Poli asked when they were alone.

"Enough to limit what he knows about my plans."

"Does he know enough of you to guess at them? Sela is still safe in Epa-Daun. If he gives us away now, only you and I are lost—and he will not mourn you for long. Perhaps you should have brought Sela as your messenger."

"I thought of it, when he said he would guide us," said Meer. "I would rather think that he is helping us all that he can allow himself. He cannot admit it, but it is as important to him as to anyone that we succeed."

• • •

No one was in the yard of Sachi's hostel, and the lights were out in all but one sleeping room. There, behind a yellow entry drape, the flickering glow of a nut-oil lamp accompanied murmured sounds of lovemaking.

Poli continued past that doorway to the last sleeping room on the west side of the structure. Its doorway, too, was draped, but he heard no sound from inside. Reaching up, Poli gently jangled the ceramic wind bells hanging in the doorway.

"Sachi," he said softly.

There was a rustling within, and in a few moments the drape was pulled back at one edge to reveal a woman's face. She peered at Poli curiously.

"I do not know you," she said. "And I have lain with enough strangers. Come back and talk to me in the light."

Poli's hand shot out and caught Sachi's wrist before she could retreat. "Wait. I have a message from a friend, a traveler, who wants to see you again."

Her eyes opened wide in surprise, then narrowed. "Meer?" she whispered.

He nodded. "Will you receive him?"

"Yes—"

Poli motioned, and Meer stepped out around the northwest corner of the building and crossed the few feet to Sachi's doorway. She heard his soft footsteps and came out to meet him, wearing only wonder on her face.

"They gave your house to someone else," she said. "I was sure that you—"

Meer touched his fingers to her lips, stilling them, then took her hand and held it firmly.

"Let's walk," said Poli.

Voices had a way of carrying in the quiet of the night, and true privacy was hard to find on the streets. But Sachi knew a place to take them, a house one ring out with a collapsed roof, empty and awaiting a building circle. They settled close together on the rubble within the shell of walls and kept their voices low.

"Twenty-two days," she said. "I took you for dead. There is a woman in your house now, with two children. Jiu Tenachen is arbiter."

"Those things do not matter. Nothing can be the same now. There will be more change, if I have my way."

"What has happened? Have you been outside all this time?"

"I found friends outside," Meer said, "and my conscience. Sachi, what do you know of the night the sky burned, and the drowning of the plaza?"

He could feel her sudden discomfort. "That was before I was blooded."

"What do you remember?"

"I know this—it is not safe to speak of such things," she blurted. "I asked our neighbor Wesa what had happened, because my mother said she did not know. Wesa beat me for asking, and my mother allowed it. And when Wesa left, my mother beat me again, and told me never to speak of that night, or to listen if others did." She hugged herself. "Letha was not a cruel mother—that was the only time she ever hurt me."

Meer reached out and touched her, coaxed a hand free to clasp in his own. "Then it's time that you knew what Wesa and your mother feared, that made them act so. It is time you knew the reason for your pain."

He had carefully planned what he would tell her, and it came tumbling readily out of him, spare and powerful, simpler than the truth but honest enough not to betray it. He made her feel the tragedy of the innocents, made her see their sun-shriveled corpses, still waiting for both justice and reunion. He made her touch the horror of the witnesses, the anguish of the survivors, both still crying to break the silence.

"So if I am thought dead, so much the better," Meer said. "I am here in the name of the dead—for my friend Kedar-rami Nanchen, and the thousand ghosts of Kawa. We want to reclaim for the living what Oran has stolen from them—lives without fear, memories without guilt, the freedom to grieve, but most of all, the truth about who we are."

Sachi had become uncomfortable again. "And there is something you need from me to do that? What use can the dead make of what I have?"

"I cannot be seen in Banteng by day," said Meer. "And there are others coming who will need clothing to let them pass without question, and food and safe places to rest for a few days."

"Did Huyana refuse you her help, then? Surely she could better meet all *those* needs than I can."

"I have not gone to Huyana," Meer said.

"Why not?"

"She is happy with her lot. I do not know what she would risk for change. And because of a promise I made, that this would not touch her house."

"A self-serving promise, since you share two unmarked daughters who might be culled if Huyana were condemned."

Meer was taken aback. "That is true," he said quietly. "But it was not in my thoughts, because I do not mean to fail."

"Even so—you see that I have less to lose and more to gain than she," said Sachi. "This is a revelation, Meer. I did not think you would ever admit to knowing that there was more I wanted."

"I have been changed," Meer said. "I do not yet know all the ways."

"I favor this one," she said. "And I will shelter you, Meer, as I can. How many others?"

"Three now, and twenty soon."

Sachi shook her head. "I cannot repeat your story twenty times, or count on others to hear it from me as I heard it from you. You must give me something simpler for them—a promise to put against the cost. Tell me what use the truth will be to them, what change will mean."

Poli spoke up. "In Ep—in Edera, anyone may have a home, man, woman, or child. You need not take the spark to have that right. There are no blessing bells—all women stand equal."

An eager hope filled her eyes. "Meer, could I go there? Would you take me?"

"If that is what you want, when we are done," Meer said. "If the changes here do not give you reason to stay."

"Any of us? Any who help you?"

Meer nodded. "You would be welcomed."

She drew a long breath and lifted her eyes to the sky above the ruined wall. "Do you know how the danera hate the sound of the bells, when Ana trembles and they are ringing from every doorway, saying 'Come fill me again'?" she whispered. "Do you know how it is to hear that on every side and know that you can never join the song? Oh, to never again hear the taunts of the bells, or a woman screaming to shut them out—" She looked back to Poli. "For that promise, I am sure the danera will hide you."

When they returned to the hostel, Sachi collected enough stone bread and leaf cake from the common room to make a breakfast, then left the two men in her sleeping room. She returned a short time later with another woman in tow. The new arrival was sleep-tousled but alert-eyed, a span shorter than Sachi and perhaps three or four turns older.

"Poli, this is Daila," Sachi said. "I have told her enough to satisfy her—she does not want to know more. But you can go with her, and stay in her room."

Poli looked questioningly at Meer. "There's no more we can do tonight," Meer said. "And we will get little enough sleep tomorrow. Come back when they call the morning."

Nodding, Poli followed Daila outside. When they were alone, Meer and Sachi fell wordlessly into a fierce hug which had less to do with passion than with relief.

"I missed you," he whispered.

She did not try to speak, for she was crying.

They nestled together on Sachi's well-compressed bedding mat, ignoring the hardness of the floor beneath it. Meer caressed her cheek, kissed her eyes, and tried to open himself to the old intimacy and its enclosing halo of peace.

But his mind was restless, and what he felt seemed more like a memory than a renewal, their bodies somehow awkward together even in quiet embrace. It was him, he thought. He could not let go of his focus, even though her closeness was a distraction. What did she sense in him? How did she read his mark? The hours to sunrise might be the last quiet ones they would have until it was over.

"You warned me that nothing can stay the same," she whispered then, "so I will not count on only the changes I might want. But I am glad that you chose to trust me. That gives me something I need. And I will do everything I can to help."

Then Sachi kissed him with a familiar intensity. "You have found a stronger spark," she said at his ear. "It has burned the weakness out of you. Share it with me, please, before too much change takes you away."

He thought at first he was too weary, but she showed him he was wrong. And for that short time, at least, he found a simpler and more joyful focus.

When daylight came, Meer sent Poli out into the morning foot traffic to do a first walking survey of the security around the plaza and the high bank, while Sachi slipped out to begin her recruitment of the other danera. Meer stayed behind in Sachi's room, protected from discovery only by silence and the etiquette of the hostel, which respected a drawn curtain as though it were a barred door.

He tried to sleep, but it was impossible. Lying on his back on the mattress, Meer listened to the voices and sounds as the other residents of the hostel stirred: the teasing and laughter over events of the last evening, a quarrel over meal duties, frank critiques of a particular minor official's shortcomings by three women who found little about which to disagree. With his impatience and anxiety both stretching the empty time, Meer felt like a prisoner.

But there were too many people in Banteng who knew his face, and too many questions he did not want to answer. It was not easy to surrender responsibility to anyone else when he felt it so keenly himself, but there was no other way. He had to trust Poli to be his eyes, and Sachi his voice, and somehow wait out the endless day.

When Sachi returned, toward sun-zenith, she brought him washing water and a night pot. "I have places for five now, but there are too many freshly-blooded women here," she said. "I am going with Daila to the hostel on twenty-four which is nearly all danera, and where Daila has friends."

"Poli has been gone longer than I expected—"

"If he is not back when we return, you can tell me where he went, and I will try to find him. And I think tonight I should introduce you as a new lover, so you will be free at least to walk in the yard." She kissed him quickly and was gone.

Not long after, Poli ducked in past the curtain. Passing voices kept him mute at first, but he signaled success with fist-and-finger. When the women lingered near the doorway, Poli shrugged and curled up for a nap, annoying Meer with the ease and speed with which he drifted off.

But later, in mid-afternoon, there was blood-singing, four or five women gathering in a room across the breezeway to dance and sweat and sing up their blessings. Their strong young voices more than covered the whispers as Meer questioned Poli about what he had seen, and, having heard the answers, spelled out the plans for that night.

At sunset, Poli and Meer were in the streets with the young runners and the craftsmen leaving their workhouses. Meer kept his head hooded and lowered, though Poli argued that at such an hour that only made others more curious, not less.

"I tell you, half those we pass are taking note," he insisted.

"Let them," Meer muttered. "Let them think I am a sick old shell going off in shame to steal some vigor from a young man's staff. It does not matter. I do not want to be stopped by someone who thinks I am dead, and will make gossip of seeing me."

They separated at the half-west spoke road, Poli turning toward the center city, Meer continuing on toward Kell. "Bring dan Amra as quickly as she will come," Meer urged.

"I do not know why she will come at all," said Poli, shaking his head.

"Just tell her as I said: that he whose name is silence is worthy still, and now *she* must do something for him. She will come."

Dusk was heavy on the sky and the streets of Kell quiet by the time Poli and dan Amra appeared in the ring road where dan Ula had her home. Meer rose from the wall where he had been waiting and approached, dropping his hood as he did.

She did not startle at the sight of him. "So—Meer Faschen. It was said that you took the runner's dementia, and were found face-down in the road, far out near the boundary," she said. "But you do not look nearly dead. Are you a changeling, then, or a servant of a dark apocryphal? You appear to my eyes to be only a man."

"So I am. It is Kedar Nan who is dead, and I who am now the exile," Meer said.

Her eyebrows flashed. "Whose part is the better in that exchange?"

"Mine," said Meer, "because I have come back to Ana with a chance to achieve what the first crusade could not." He looked to Poli, standing two steps behind dan Amra's shoulder. "You can go on with the rest, then."

Poli nodded and began retreating. "If they are there to be found, I will have them in their beds by dawn."

As Poli turned and ran off, Meer's gaze swept back to dan Amra. "You obliged me to come a long way, and I am chilled with sweat," she said before he could speak. "Did you mean to offer me any shelter from the night wind?"

He inclined his head. "This way—dan Ula is home now."

Though she showed dan Amra the courtesies of their common station, it was plain that dan Ula did not welcome their intrusion.

"Do you think I do not know who you are?" she demanded of Meer in a voice strong enough to carry to the street. And when he tried to caution her, she became belligerent. "I am not interested in any conversations where I must worry who might hear," she said, even more loudly. "I have nothing to hide, and I am not fond of watching my words."

Meer met her challenge directly. "Dan Ula, I am glad to hear that you will not try to hide your knowledge of these matters." He puffed out a breath, and plunged on. "I have been outside of the city. I found Kedar Nanchen in Edera, and spent two days with him before he died."

Their silence gave him permission, if not invitation, to go on. "I have brought back his knowledge and taken up his cause. I mean to carry the crusade for truth to a better ending, in Kedar's name and the names of the drowned. Seventeen who survived that night on the plaza are still alive in Edera. They are coming back to Ana as well. We mean to hold the exarch to account for his acts."

"At least you are speaking more plainly than the last time you came to me," said dan Ula.

"Will you do the same?" he asked. "What have you heard from Hebei?"

Covering her mouth with her fingertips, dan Ula looked past Meer to the wall behind him. "What would you expect me to hear? Hebei is a long distance away."

"Rida Valtera. Has there been any gossip? Surely you made inquiries after I was here."

Dan Ula cradled her face in her hands. "I do not like to dwell on sad news of friends."

"What? What news?"

"She has taken a deep madness, they say. Not many days ago, she presented a body at Hebei-Giyan for reunion. She declared it to be her husband, and called him by a name no one knew."

A grin spread across Meer's face. "There is no madness in that."

"Except it is well known to all her neighbors that she had opened neither her legs nor her house to anyone for many turns," said dan Ula.

"Kedar had been outside for a long time—"

"—And the custodian of the temple reported that the body she brought to him no longer had a face, or hands, or staff."

Meer spun away, squeezing his eyes shut against the pain of the vision dan Ula had sprung on him, clenching his fists in empty threat. So the deception had failed. Meer had misread the cue— his own 'death' meant only that Oran wanted the city closed to him. The sentries *had* delivered Kedar to Rida, but not before

Oran had indulged himself with one last amusement.

"He should not expect any mercy," Meer whispered, silent tears glittering in his eyes. "I want his blood on my own hands."

Dan Ula went on, "They say that when the captain of sentries can learn the body's true name, Rida will be called for a hearing on his murder. Was that the news you wondered after? Was there more you meant to tell me?"

Meer turned back, his expression a sharp caution against dan Ula's barbs. "Kedar escaped Oran long before the knives touched him. He died as easily as a man can, by his own will and in my company. See that Rida knows—"

"You claim the right to order me?" dan Ula bristled.

"You called her a friend. Why would you let a friend believe the lie that the knives carved on Kedar's corpse?"

Closing her eyes, dan Ula shook her head.

"Then tell her, too, that I grieve him," Meer said. His voice had softened, but his fists were still clenched at his side. "And that I will revenge him."

"Meer—you have said what *you* intend. What are you asking of us?" dan Amra asked.

Blinking, he turned toward her. "You are right, dan Amra. That is what is important now.

"Dan Amra, dan Ula—I came to you because, as much as one exists, the dan are the memory of Ana. You are her everyday conscience, and your tongues speak her true voice. Your power is the counterpoint to the power of the high bank, and its equal. Your weight on the rope, whichever end you choose, can settle which way the players fall.

"We do not need your help to take the high bank. But we will need your help to keep it. This cannot be a few old men settling an old grievance, and nothing more. All that will mean is a new exarch, and a small lesson for him about excess, and the killing yard for us, because we do not have the numbers to stand forever against the sentries.

"If there is to be any lasting good, the circle of councilors must hear you when we speak. There must be so many voices raised that you take the sticks from the sentries' hands. The people must claim the power for themselves."

"And what is my part in that?" asked dan Amra.

"Awaken their memories," said Meer. "Help the unspoken become spoken-with-anger, boldly, as it never was. And when the time comes, lead them back to the plaza without fear."

"And invite more death?" demanded dan Ula. "You are sun-addled, or stupid with bitweed."

"We will take and hold the dam. There will be no more drown-ings."

"You have already said you cannot stand against the sentries," dan Ula said, flipping her hand in dismissal. "No. Go away. I do not care a whit for the struggles of hierarchy. It is always the same—contests and conquests and control. It makes no difference to me who stands at the top, who is on the ground when your street fight is over. One is no better than the other, and no worse."

Meer appealed to dan Amra with his eyes, but she slowly shook her head. "Our power is not a power that makes and unmakes an exarch. Our power is a soft power, diffuse, made of little pieces. Our power is what we know, and who will listen, not who we lead."

"It comes to more than that," Meer said. "You have never tested it. You do not know what you can do."

"You do not understand," said dan Amra. "We have taken for ourselves what best suits our purposes, and left the rest to you. We have influence, yes, but we preserve it respecting the line drawn between the dan's world and the exarchy. If we challenge that division, or choose a champion, we will mark ourselves a threat. I am sorry, Meer—dan Ula is right. We cannot do what you want. We cannot be the captains of your army."

There was little talk as Meer escorted dan Amra back to Banteng. Meer was caught up in a war against despair, trying to recast the throw of stones into a winning play, and dan Amra respected that struggle with silence.

Only twice did she intrude into his consciousness. The first time was as they crossed into Banteng from Arontar.

"Meer," she said, "these seventeen who survived, who are coming home after all these years—are any of an age that they might have line-kin still in Ana?"

It took Meer a moment to refocus his thoughts. "Some," he said. "One was only a girl. Most are no older than I am."

"Tell me their names, and what you can of where they once lived."

"Why?"

"Why did you give dan Ula a message for Rida?"

Mouth puckering, Meer considered her offer for a dozen strides down the now-empty road. "Nan Tirza, of Deiran—she is the youngest of them. Boli Tirachen, I think last from Fanja—"

Dan Amra listened carefully, and repeated the names back without an error when Meer was finished. She said nothing more then, but the promise in her request was enough to lift his gloom for a time.

But well before they reached her house, his thoughts had reduced him to disheartenment once more. Even if dan Amra somehow found as many as a hundred mothers and siblings and children of the survivors, it would not be enough to secure their gains. Even if each of the hundred could marshal ten more, honored mates and trusted friends and strong young sons, it would not be enough to paralyze the circle of councilors with fear, or stay the orders of the syndic of security.

It was necessary this time that the people would rise up in numbers which dwarfed any memory of the first crusade—to not only fill the plaza, but spill over to the streets and rooftops which surrounded it, and between them raise such a noise that even a man of Oran's temper would tremble at the thought of making himself their enemy.

The dan could bring such numbers to the fight—but he had misjudged them.

That was when dan Amra caught his arm to stop his feet. Looking up, he realized that he had nearly walked on past her house without noticing.

"Thank you for coming to listen, dan Amra," he said through a frown, turning to her.

"What will you do?"

"Whatever can be done, with the opportunities we can make," he said. "Neither the memories nor the witnesses can live forever. If it does not happen soon, it will happen too late, or not at all."

She looked up toward her house, toward the window where a proxy child stood looking down on them. "Meer—how had you thought to tell us when we were needed, and the plaza secure?"

The question startled him, but reawakened a comatose hope. "As Hoja den Krador spoke to us. We mean to deny Oran the use of the Voice, and to claim it for ourselves."

She worried her lower lip with her teeth as she turned back to him. "No," she said, shaking her head. "There would be too much confusion, too much suspicion. You forget we have trained ourselves to doubt what we hear from the little boxes. You cannot undo that in an instant and replace it with trust."

"I know that," he said sharply. "That was why I needed you, to prepare them, to make it possible for them to believe—to make a model to them of your own trust." He shrugged. "But we will do what we can. There is no other choice now."

Reaching out, she touched his lips, then pulled him closer, until they stood as close as lovers. "Listen," she whispered, "and I will give you another way. The power of the dan is in what we know, and in who we choose to tell. I am going to tell you one of the vowed secrets of the *imoda*."

He listened as her words guided him into the temple of the arch, beneath the altar platform, and to the foundation of the arch itself. "There is a small chamber there—the womb of Ana—where the water of Kawa flows in and touches bare soil. This is where the chosen *rami* are sent on festival mornings, one man for each bell that must be rung that day. This is the entry to the arch itself.

"When you need the people to come, climb the ladder to the crown, and make Anadan-Kawadon alone to ring," she said. "I will put out the word in whispers, and try to make that a sign no one will mistake or ignore. Do what I have said, and I will know you have won your victory—and we will come and help you preserve it."

Sachi and Poli were both waiting for Meer when he reached the hostel. In the first moment, by the yellow light of a nut-oil lamp, they all measured the excitement in the others' faces, and the words that followed were almost unneeded.

"Did you find them? Did Storm keep his promise?"

Poli grinned broadly. "Izel and Scot are in, and safe at the other hostel. And more—Izel insisted on going by the Itaris mines before coming back, since we were so close. Nothing has been changed since they left—everything in the same places, and as carelessly kept and watched."

"Does he think they can get a tunneling suite, then?"

Poli's grin broadened. "We already have it, controller and all."

"No!"

"He walked in, and walked out with it under his arm, and we scampered. It was no harder than that, for him. He has it with him in the hostel, and wants to know when we start—says the city smells foul to him, and he can't wait to be done and leave."

Meer punched the air with both fists. "Bless his staff."

"Will the dan help us?"

"In their way, at the time they think right," Meer said. "Sachi, what luck did you have?"

"I have found places for twenty—and a dozen women who will hold you to your promised reward." She pointed into a corner, and Meer saw a bundle of clothing he had not noted until then. "Six waist-shirts and duskies from three different houses, four wrap-skirts, two manteaus, and I am promised more tomorrow."

Meer bounced forward to hug her with the same ferocity with which he had punched the air, then looked to Poli.

"Is it time, then?" asked Poli.

"You know your legs better than I. You've been on them a long time already today."

The grin turned cocky. "I am too young to be tired. And there's enough night left to get me well clear of Ana."

"Carrying all of that?" Meer asked, jerking his head toward the garments.

"I'll make a back burden of it. It won't slow me."

"Are you sure?"

Poli's expression turned serious. "Is there any reason to wait?"

"No," said Meer. "Tell them to come in. The core circles first, in two nights, as we planned, but we will want the others, too, right on their heels. Tell them we are ready for them. Tell them we're ready to begin."

The grin returned. "That's a glad message to carry," he said. "It will shorten the way."

19

Anadan-Kawadon: The Thirteenth Bell

Was my plan for taking the high bank truly as fragile as some say? I have heard it disparaged as a notion conceived under Eki. But surely none of us thought so then. When those who were to risk themselves finished arguing their concerns with me, what was left was still very much what I had envisioned.

They believed we would succeed. Perhaps they believed because they needed to believe—I was no different from them in that. Perhaps they believed because I believed—I encouraged them in that. What doubts I had, I chewed into grit and swallowed. You cannot make a man bold by feeding him timidity. Or run to triumph on legs bound by hesitation.

I knew that if I was wrong, we would die. I did not think I was wrong. But I did not *know*. I could not know, unless we tried.

There was no mystery in what it would take to defeat Oran. It was necessary to deny him his instruments of power—which meant it was necessary to correctly identify them. And then it was necessary to reach him while he was still powerless.

There is no more to a revolution than that.

But how many times had others tried? How many others had tested him? Surely some had, in all the time he had been master of the high bank. And each unsuccessful attempt would have strengthened him by showing him his own weaknesses. Without doubt, Oran was far more practiced at protecting himself than we were at such attacks.

I had never challenged a man like Oran Anadon. I had never fought a champion—not in Fas's house, where Eral ruled, not in the streets, not in my circles. I had always coveted the second place, not the first.

But perhaps Oran had never fought a man like me—like the man he made me. He shaped me carelessly. He only saw what I was, not what I might become. Kedar was a better teacher—but I learned from Oran, just the same.

This is how I saw his instruments of power: The security of the keystone house. The modalities of speech-through-air. The allegiance of the sentries. His influence over the circle of councilors. And perhaps the secrets of the exarch's archive—which, if it existed, I thought likely to be the most important of them all.

I believed it did exist, for whatever power Oran had turned against Hoja den Krador could have come from nowhere else.

But that belief did not dictate our strategy. Necessity did.

By everything we knew, Oran rarely if ever left the keystone house, and never the high bank. Even before the crusade, he only appeared in public on rare high festival days, to speak to a crowd on the plaza from a platform on the high bank, and signal the start of the run by dropping the blood scarf of the *imoda*.

And of course, after the trouble, even those appearances ended. We heard his name often, and his voice when there was good news. But he hid himself away, out of reach.

So we would have to go to him—no easy business. There were stickmen outside both gates of the keystone house, and sentries in the yard. There might be still others inside, but even if not, it was safe to presume the house contingent had the means to signal for more—and the hive of the Arbor of Steadfast Prosperity, with its complement of twenty sentries, was very close by.

And while we dealt with such obstacles, Oran would be free to retreat into his archive, which, if it existed, was certain to have its own protections. We knew the archive of electrics had locking doors which only their curators could open—that was the least we could expect.

We argued these problems, right here in this circle, until there was no one left who could argue.

We had to have another way in.

That was what Izel and Scot could give us. That was the idea which turned me back at the boundary after Kedar died—to come in from below, in a tunnel cut up into the high bank from the bottom, from below the surface of the river.

It seemed the perfect use of all the tools at hand. The night and the river would hide us. The water would mask the sounds of the nats at work. The tunnel would clean itself as it was cut, the tailings washed away on the current.

If there *was* an archive under the keystone house, we would find it first—and if it was deserted, or we could win control, whatever protected it would protect us, too, until we were ready to move on. A well-timed feint outside the house could keep Oran from fleeing, or even drive him into our hands.

I had seen it all as a single vision, with all the tensions, all the prospects. I believed in the plan. I knew, with a frightening certainty, that we would get in.

But it would not be easy.

It took two nights to bring in the rest of the twenty, eight each night. The twenty of us would lead what we called the five work circles: one each for the dam, the ministry of information, the temple of the arch, the tunnel, and the feint against the gates.

If disaster had struck—the boundary closed as Storm thought it could be, or the qanat discovered—we would try to do it all alone. But we wanted more hands for every target, and while we finished our scouting and adjusted our plans to what we had learned, Storm brought twenty more exiles from Epa-Daun.

We hid them everywhere, but knew we could not hide them forever. My worst fear was that dan Amra's whispers would move too quickly, and reach the wrong ears. The first night we were ready, my sixth in Ana, the second crusade began.

We started after the evening announcements, with the streets at their quietest and the sky at full darkness. The eighteenth ring bridge-dam was our first target, not only to secure the safety of the plaza, but because we needed the use of the scout dock below it.

The dam was not guarded by sentries. We had only to surprise two gatemen and the engineer of turbines in their control shacks at opposite ends of the bridge, and that was easily and quietly done. The dam fell to us quickly and quietly. The dock was deserted, and we took it at the same time.

But we had to hold the dam through the night, and so that circle had ten men assigned to it—all of them among the seventeen survivors of the plaza. No one would fight harder, I thought, if—

more likely, when—we were discovered.

Three of the exiles took the clothes and the places of the gatemen and the engineer, while the other seven arrayed themselves as though they were a work crew repairing the upper face of the bridge. I shivered to see them carrying tools of the kind that had been used against their friends by the sweat gangs—and the looks on their faces and tone of their voices made me pity anyone unwise or unlucky enough to contest their claim to the dam.

It was Copin's turn next: As the strongest swimmer, his job was to take one end of a double spidersilk line all the way from the dock to the spot beneath the Five-Ring Bridge which Izel had picked for the cut. The line itself had three jobs: as an anchor for the miners against Kawa's current, as a signal cord, and as a safety line for the rest of us when it came time to follow Copin downstream.

The tunnel circle was the largest of all five groups—there were sixteen of us, counting the miners. Most would not be needed until the cut went through, and so were still back at the hostels when Copin entered the water.

But for those who were there, that was a hard moment— waiting, pressed against the bank or hiding in the boats, watching Copin's line play out from the coils and disappear into the dark, churning water. It seemed an eternity before the clicker on the signal cord, muffled with a pad of fabric, told us the line secure, and Copin ready for the miners.

Here is where the plan was the most fragile. Even I must confess it.

Everything depended on Izel and Scot being able to do their work water-blind, on a slippery rock face swept by a constant, clutching current, catching lungfuls of air in the dark and then ducking below once more. They were irreplaceable, and the task we had set them was the hardest that any of us faced. But they had never balked or backed away from their promise, and I had found myself admiring them.

In the last hours before sunset, though, Izel had begun to worry me. He complained to me again and again that he could not guarantee the cut if he could not prepare the surface. As he went over his notes and set up the controller, he voiced a litany of sour-mouthed projections of disaster—the river scouring the nats right off the rock and carrying them off, or a set-up error that would make the tunnel useless or bring it up under the feet of the sentries at the gate.

None of those dangers was any surprise. None of them had been overlooked. I did not know what to think. Was it just Izel's own anxiety breaking through as the pressure mounted? He had every right to be frightened. Or was he trying to prepare me for something? Because everything did depend on the miners, my own anxiety pushed me to wonder if he would willfully sabotage us—for any reason.

As the day faded, I kept Izel away from the others as much as I could, gave him empty words of reassurance—he knew the craft, after all, and he had to do it, not I—and said nothing to anyone else. But when Izel and Scot waded into Kawa with the nat controller in hand, I still did not know what to think.

Everything not only depended on the cut, but was tied to the timing of it.

Scot had told us the cut would take no less than half the night, more if there was no archive room under the house, and we had planned around that expectation. When Copin came back from the Five-Ring Bridge, we took a time mark off the sky, and I sent runners out across the dam to the north city where Treg and the feint circle waited, and down the twenty-fourth ring to the hostel.

That time mark told the rest of our circle when to come to the river, and the temple circle when to go to the plaza. It sent the Voice circle hurrying east on their pilgrimage to the high bank by way of the Twenty-Ring Bridge. Boli and another honor candidate led that group of six. They were to take down as much of the air net as they could before the cut was finished, if it could be done quietly, without arousing a general alarm.

Taking much the same route as Boli's circle, three more runners headed out to the spots along the northeast boundary where Storm was to bring in the rest of the exiles. I expected as many as sixty—whatever number had managed to come down the qanat in the slack time of the last six days. Rika would be among them, and Seba. If they were not met at the boundary, they were to turn back. If they were met, they would reach the center of the city as reinforcements when night began drifting toward morning.

All these movements were spun together into a single binding that we meant to draw tight around Oran.

We had scarcely begun when it came apart in our hands.

• • •

Waiting had made me restless and edgy, so I had left the dock for a little while. Walking helped. Getting away from the water helped, too. The longer I sat there, the stronger the impulse grew to put myself in the river and go downstream to check on the miners' progress.

My edginess was my own fault. Despite the clicker on the signal line, I'd failed to ask Izel and Scot to teach some of us the miner's code and make periodic progress reports. All we had were a few simple, pre-arranged signals.

Even so, as we waited with no word, it was easy to think that something had gone wrong—they had been heard, or seen, or their catch lines had come loose, or the nat suite had failed, or—

Imagination and idleness bear many ugly children.

I finally weakened enough to send Poli down along the west spoke road to the Five-Ring Bridge. But all he saw of interest was a pair of sentries crossing the plaza on a night patrol. There was no sign of any activity under the bridge or on either bank. Which was how it should be—unless they had dropped the controller to the bottom, or drowned, or—

That was when I made myself leave the dock, before my anxiety infected everyone else, or pushed me to some even more foolish step.

I went up to the dam and said a word or two to everyone, encouraging those who needed it, trying to lance the tension for others. Then I looked out toward the dock, curious to see how obvious our presence was. I saw Poli scrambling up the stairs from the dock to the spoke road, and then running up the road toward the dam as though something was chasing him.

When I realized that, I started running, too.

We met at the south end of the dam, by the gatemen's shack. "They're in!" he said, in a hoarse half-whisper.

His words were a slap. "What?"

"They're in—we just got the signal on the line."

I was sure he had to be wrong, and he must have seen that in my face. "I know, I know," he said, throwing his hands up. "We asked for a repeat. Same thing came back—three clicks, two, three. Everyone heard it that time. They're in."

I didn't need to look at the sky. "Damn it all, it's too early—something's wrong. Or if it isn't, it's going to be. Nobody's here, and Boli's people haven't had enough time—sweet breath, and Treg's going to be late—"

"I can find him," Poli said.

"There's no time." I turned back to find the whole work crew had come up behind me to listen. One after another, I pointed at five of them. "Go with Poli to the dock. You just changed circles."

They gaped at me, until I grabbed one by the blouse and shoved him toward the road. I think that what froze them was the unexpected boon: Remember that all five were survivors. And they now had the chance to go into the tunnel after Oran.

If they were happy, I was not. I had kept survivors off the tunnel circle, saying I needed younger, stronger bodies for that. But the true, unspoken reason was that I wanted Oran alive long enough to answer my questions, or at least hear them. I did not think the seventeen had that same interest.

Of the last two on the bridge, I sent one back to the hostel as a messenger. By then the other man was wearing a look of dismay, equally likely to be from being left to defend the bridge alone, or from being left out.

"Send the first man who gets here from the hostel out to find Treg," I told him. "The next five are to follow us. The rest are yours. Don't let me down."

His look did not change.

We had meant to be under the bridge before the nats broke through, ready to climb the walls while they were still hot. We had meant to burst through on the heels of the blast of heat and bubble of steaming gases that would have erupted when the floor or the wall melted away. We had meant to take control while any witnesses were still confused, frightened, or fleeing.

Instead, we had announced ourselves, then done nothing. All I really can remember of my thoughts as I left the bridge-dam was a gut terror that it had already come apart, that I was going to be too late.

I didn't go to the dock and swim down the guide line. I ran up the west spoke road half-way to the Five-Ring Bridge, until I could see to my satisfaction that the bridge was deserted. Then I swerved, stumbled down the bank in full stride, and threw myself headlong into the river.

I had no business doing it. I had had exactly fifteen days of practice at Kedar's sport. My plan had been to hold the guide line and let the current take me; I had coached the others to save their strength and do the same.

I forgot all of that—which is why I was the first to reach Izel, Scot, and the new tunnel into the high bank.

But I wasn't the first one inside.

When he saw me, Scot lunged for me gleefully, sending water flying. "Meer—it's just like you said—only bigger—"

"How do you know?" I demanded.

"We thought someone had better go in," Izel said. "In case we were the only ones who could."

"It's huge, Meer," said Copin, "and empty as a girl's belly— not a sound, and barely enough light to see your feet. The air's dry—smells like, I don't know, burned dust. It sucked the water right off us."

The first of the others reached us then; it was Poli, and he was startled to see me when he wiped the water from his eyes. I ignored him.

"I don't know *what* you found," I said to Izel. Another head bobbed up beside us. "But I can't fuck with a limp staff. Show me."

They had sized and sloped the entry for climbing, so we had little trouble getting in, except that the rock was still warm enough to move us along quickly. The nats had come up somewhere in the middle of the archive, at the boundary between a floor and a wall. The cut opened a way into both a room and a narrow passage I wanted to call a breezeway, only the air was dead still.

Dead still and dead silent. The only sounds I heard were our breathing and the dripping of water from our bodies onto the floor. Both sounds were not only dismayingly loud, but echoed in an emptiness where a whisper was a shout.

The light came from a bead that ran down the center of the ceiling—pale and yellow as a wick set just above extinction, but steady, without a hint of flicker. When my eyes adjusted to it, I saw that the walls were made of the same material as the floor— not raw rock, but a matrix, like in the old houses.

"Could you open spaces like this?" I asked Izel, peeking into the room we'd damaged.

"Square-corner chambering? No, never. Not with any suite I know." He craned his head and scanned the passage. "But I begin to think there are things I don't know."

The buzz of the others speaking their own wonder was growing. "Let's scout this place, and quickly," I said. "Light feet and still tongues—hand signals only. No one goes into a room alone. Make sure someone else has you in sight, always. If I wave you in or pull you back, I want everyone to know it in two breaths. Stay on this level, but look for a way to the top. We're fifty feet under the high bank, and I don't want to stay here."

There were ten of us inside by then, and we slowly spread ourselves to the limits of the labyrinth. An early discovery was that there were outlines of doorways spaced along the walls, as though the builders had marked where they meant to put them, but never gotten around to doing so. There were small sigils marked within the outlines; I thought that the one closest to the tunnel resembled the mark of the Gaur.

Then someone reached up and touched a sigil, and we learned that the builders had finished their work after all. The wall split in the center of the doorway, and then either half—I had the clear perception that they did not *move* so much as *contracted* to either side. I jumped back the first time I saw it. Then I looked around and saw the open-eyed fright on the faces near me. Jeng seemed close to bolting.

"Curtain nats," I said as loudly as I dared. "A suite that wilded on the outside."

It was only a guess, but it helped keep us moving. Even so, I did not see much eagerness to open doors and see what surprises they concealed. The strangeness of everything made most of us timid explorers.

But there were no surprises, at least none to fear. When we drew together again, we had found nothing but more empty passages and closed doors. The rooms that had been entered were as empty as the passages, and as alike as a string of shells along a ring road.

Tabar said what we all had been thinking. "Meer, this place has not been used for a long time."

"Maybe Oran can't keep up with so many women anymore," someone said, and a few laughed. The keystone house has twelve rooms, and the common joke was that the exarch kept women in eleven of them—for what other use could a man have for so much space?

But Poli looked at me with shaken eyes. "Meer—why all this? It looks like a place for people to live—like a great hive, or long house. Not an archive. The run of it must span the whole fifth ring, the whole high bank."

I had been thinking of the hole houses of Kennabar myself when he spoke, but I do not know what put the words I spoke into my mind. "Maybe this is the seed from which Ana grew."

I said it quietly, but it snapped heads around in my direction. "But we will need more time to know—time we don't have now," I said. "We must not let this become a trap. We can't let ourselves be stopped here. The way to the top must be behind some door no one opened, or in some form no one recognized. One of us has to find it."

"Why can't Izel just make us a shortcut?" asked Premm, pointing at the ceiling. He was one of the five I had taken from the dam.

"No," Izel told him, with a shake of his head. "We used the full suite to get in, for speed."

Premm drew back, scowling. "Whose stupid decision—"

"Mine," I said, laying a hand on Premm's arm. "But it doesn't matter. Don't you understand? This hive was not always empty. We need to find out how those who lived here left here, and follow them."

Our number swelled to fifteen while we were still searching, the late arrivals from the hostel emerging breathless and fresh from the river to join us.

They found us short of patience and edging toward panic. We had gone over the hive well enough by then to have mapped it: two hundred forty rooms in eight ranks of thirty, opening onto five long passages. But the passages led nowhere but to other rooms or other passages.

"Maybe this is a killing yard," Poli said to me. "Maybe this *was* a trap."

That idea had been gaining supporters as their trust in me and their confidence in themselves flagged. "We ought to leave while we still can," said one man, and there was a murmur of agreement. "While there's still time to call back the other circles."

I was on the verge of losing them, and the threat pushed me into anger. "Go, then," I said, shoving him toward the tunnel. "We've risked everything and gained nothing—what better time to quit?"

"But we're stuck, Meer," Scot said. His voice was calm, but his eyes were pleading. "You have no better idea what to do than we do. There isn't any way out of here except the way we came in."

I flew into a rage at him. "You're talking nonsense—coward words. These people were no smarter than we are. There's something different about how they thought, that's all. They had different tools, not different needs."

Then I turned on the others. "Stop thinking like a pack of shame-cheeked thieves sneaking into a stranger's house. By your mother's birth sweat, try thinking like you belong here. Maybe the way out doesn't lead up. Maybe it goes deeper down, or sideways. But there has to be a way out, because there had to be a way in. And if we're too dense to find it, then by Kawa's staff we deserve to die here."

That shocked them into an uncomfortable silence. They were looking at me as though I'd become a demon. I caught their looks and started to walk away in disgust.

Someone touched my arm and said, "Meer—"

I jerked away and spun around. "What?"

It was Adura, one of the men from the dam—a survivor, though not a student. I hardly knew him. He was part of the second twenty, and a man who listened more than he spoke. But he did not flinch from me.

"Maybe—I wonder if their ladders are like their doors," Adura said. "Maybe they don't exist until you need them, so looking isn't enough. Maybe we have to search with our hands."

I stared at him, all the dark thoughts squeezed out of me. "Let's try."

Adura was right. We had been looking in the wrong places, and for the wrong sign.

The right place was in the rooms, not the passages. The right sign was a glyph at head-height in a dimly-lit back corner. The glyph meant nothing to any of us—until Premm touched one, and the corner melted away to reveal a ladder shaft.

A shout went up, and everyone came running. It was hard to hold them back when they saw. All the discontent washed away in a breath.

We divided up among five rooms, five shafts, and started climbing.

The next level was a twin to the first: the same plan, and just as dark and quiet.

The third level had a different plan, with the ladder shafts opening onto wide passageways. We tried several doors, but none would open for us. There was still no sign of anyone else in the hive.

But the fourth level, where the shafts ended, had bright light, and warmth, and music.

We followed the music. It led us to Oran Anadon.

I was not sure it was him at first. He was sitting in an open room, his back to us as we approached, looking out what I wanted to call a window. But the window was the size of a huge wall, and the view through it kept changing. What I saw distracted me from the man in the chair: white water tumbling down through broken rock, mist rising from a cliff face carpeted in dark green, and something moving among the trees that was not a man—

As I stood there, Jeng rushed by me, dragged Oran from his chair and threw him against the window wall. The way his head snapped sideways and his body crumpled, I thought the blow would kill him. But he shook himself and started to rise. Jeng's knife came out. I jumped forward and pinned Jeng's arms to stop him, but he fought me.

"No!" I shouted in his ear. "Not this way!"

Premm edged forward, circling the kneeling man. "Meer's right—we can do better than a quick death. We've waited so long. Let's not hurry." Then Premm's leg flashed out in a kick that raked Oran's face and snapped his head back. Blood ran from his temple and below his eye.

"This isn't what we're here for!" I shouted at Premm.

"It's why I'm here," he said. But Poli came forward and dragged Premm away. I threw Jeng back toward the door and the others.

That was when Oran looked up and saw me.

There was no fear in his face, and that chilled me.

"Yes," he said, struggling to his feet. "Yes, do not be hasty. Let me show you what it means to be my friend."

"That can never happen," I said.

"Perhaps you should wait to hear what you are refusing before being so final."

"I only want to hear why you did it—why you made the students your enemy, fifteen years ago. Tell me why Hoja den Krador had to be destroyed. Tell me what secret was so damned important that two thousand people had to die."

"Yes—yes, I can help you understand all of that." He edged stiffly forward, and caught the back of the chair with his hand. "Display off," he said. The music stopped, and the window-view faded to white. "You were very clever to get this far. You will have to tell me how you did it."

"He's stalling," someone said, just as the same suspicion came to me.

"Damn it—all the noise we made—there must be other people nearby," I said, never looking away from Oran. "Premm, Copin, Jeng—pick yourself partners and go run a sweep, heads down and mouths shut. Find out where we stand, and get back here fast. The rest of you—stay alert. I don't want anyone crawling up my back—and we don't want him getting away."

Oran's expression never changed. "I can tell you where you stand. You stand at a decision point, Meer Faschen—you and all of your friends," he said.

"That decision was made before we started."

"Then you are not as clever as you think you are. Not nearly so."

"You threw away so many lives. You threw away everything we could have learned from Arania—"

"Display select," he said, and the wall behind him filled with glyphs. I could feel the others startle.

"Meer—what other tricks can he play just by speaking?" said Poli. "We should silence him, at least until we can get him out of here."

"But I thought you had questions," said Oran smoothly. "Archive title: Arania. Begin scan."

He must have thought the sentries were coming. He must have thought that anything we learned would die with us in minutes. He dazzled our eyes with sights, not half of which I understood— plains covered with trees, machines flying through the air over cities which themselves were built up to the sky, fires burning in the rock of mountains, four-legged apocryphals loping through tall grass—and all in some other world.

"You see that there is little Hoja den Krador could have taught us of Arania," Oran said, as the barrage of pictures began to draw in the men behind me. "If you have questions, here is where the answers begin. If learning the truth is what you care about, then learn to trust your eyes. Everything is here—more than you could see in a lifetime. This is what being my friend means. These are the secrets the exarch protects."

I think he had almost succeeded in making us forget him when Jeng returned.

"Everything's quiet for the moment," he said, coming up beside me. "We could only find two other people—both claiming to be councilors, and neither of them any trouble to us. Both of them are looking pretty scared, in fact, and one's being very helpful.

We've found the passage to the house—it's locked, and Jeng and Scot are watching it. And our new friend bent to persuasion and is taking Copin and the others on a tour—"

Oran had heard enough. "Light off," he said, and the entire level was plunged into darkness. "Display off. Archive wipe—"

I was the closest to him, but I could not see him. I had been looking into the bright display, and my eyes were dazzled. All I could think was that he would be heading for the entryway, and I lunged blindly toward where I thought he might be.

I collided with Jeng, who had the same idea, and we both missed. But the next man behind us did not. I heard grunts and a cry, and bodies hitting the floor hard.

"Light on," I said.

I did not really expect the hive to obey me, but in an instant, the room was bathed in light. I saw Oran lying on the floor, pinned there by the weight of Ral, a Boroche, and a larger man even than me. Poli sat on his heels nearby, panting, a smear of his or Oran's blood across his blouse.

Oran stirred and made a noise. "Let's get him out of here," I said. "And Ral—don't let him say a word."

I was afraid to let him speak anywhere, not knowing what powers he could call on, what more he could control with a word. But I was more afraid that Jeng and the others would silence him too finally, too soon. I had them stop in the corridor and put him down, away from anything I could recognize as animate or electric.

"Why?" I asked him. My voice broke. "You said you could make me understand."

He looked up at me without shame or fear. "Children need rules," he said, his voice thin. "And most people are children their whole lives. They cannot be trusted to know what is best for them. They cannot be trusted to know what is dangerous. They know— only what they want. But they cannot be given everything.

"That has been the meaning of the exarchy, ever since the beginning. The man who chose me, and gave me this trust— the man who chose him—back to the founding. We have held the secrets safe. We have given direction, and kept order.

"I am not an aberration," he said. "I am a necessity."

"That's not enough of an answer for the dead," I said angrily.

"The dead do not ask questions, or demand answers," Oran said. "They know their place. If you knew yours, you would give yourself up, so that Ana might be preserved."

His words stunned me, and infuriated the others. I had to place myself between Oran and Jeng once more, and he and I nearly came to blows as we shouted at each other. Oran watched it all with curious calm.

"You see," he said. "Nothing changes. Nothing will change. The circle turns and returns to its start. Your mistake was made at the beginning. If you give them their pleasures, they will forget their duties. You will see."

I was still with my back to Oran, watching the others. "Meer," he said. When I turned, I saw in his face that he knew we were going to kill him, that I would not or could not protect him much longer. And as I looked at him, his mouth tightened, and his eyes went cold and angry.

"Do not trouble yourself looking for Chane," he said.

I stared, my throat dry.

"I was not amused by your—trading places with—Kedar Nan. You betrayed me, Meer Faschen. An exarch cannot allow—such behavior."

"What are you saying?"

"Your impersonation—was imperfect. I decided I must help you perfect it. Your son Chane—he went to the killing yard in Brader, eleven days ago."

His words broke me. I wanted to kill him, but I could not move. I only stared, his smugness searing me. There was no hint of defeat on his face. He was savoring my pain, his own power.

"Here," said someone, and pressed a knife into my hand. "You take the first piece of him."

I threw the knife down. "No!"

"If you don't I will," said Jeng. "He's drawn enough breaths."

I was shaking my head and backing down the corridor. "No— don't touch him," I warned them. "Don't kill him yet. Not until he knows. Not until there are more to witness. We made a promise."

"Where are you going?" Poli demanded.

I didn't answer, and I couldn't stay. I ran back the way we had come, skittered down the ladder shaft, and slid out the tunnel to the river, seeing Chane staked in the sun every breath of the way. The water shocked me from it for a moment. Then the current grabbed me, and I struck out toward the low bank and the plaza.

I came ashore just downstream from the temple, which we already held, though I did not know it then. I am sure someone greeted me or questioned me, but I cannot remember them. I do not remember going beneath the altar, or finding the meditation room. I do not remember climbing the passage up into the arch, all five hundred steps to the crown.

I only remember sitting down to straddle the bell lever, my legs braced against one side of the little chamber and my back against the other. I remember how cold the metal was in my hands and the great weight I felt against it when I started to pull. And I remember how the power rushed through me when Anadan-Kawadon tolled, how every hammer-strike made the lever vibrate in my hands and my body lift.

I remember how my arms worked as I made it ring louder and louder. I wanted it heard to the boundary and beyond, every strike aimed at Oran's heart. I rang it for Chane. I rang it for Kedar. I rang it for Lenn. I rang it for every man and woman who had died, though they were beyond counting. I meant it to sound to the top of the sky, and to the depths of Ana's heart, so that wherever Kedar was, he would hear.

I rang the great bell until I was deafened by it, until I was blind with tears. I did not stop until someone came up into the arch after me and took my hands from the lever, and took me into their arms.

It was Nan Tirza. She held my hands and pulled me away, saying, "It's enough, Meer. It's enough. Come down now. Come down and see what we've done." I could hardly hear the words, but I let her lead me back out of the arch, and onto the plaza.

I did not expect daylight. I could not imagine when the night had passed.

"Look," she said. "Look."

The plaza was a sea of people, and so was the edge of the high bank, and so were the bridges that joined them. We climbed up together onto the temple roof to look out on the throng, and it grew larger when we did, back to the first rings and the roofs of the houses.

"It's just as you said it should be," Nan whispered to me. "Do you see? They've come back."

Then a sound swept across the plaza, and thousands of arms were raised, pointing across the river. When I saw what they were pointing at, my throat closed, and my whispered "Thank you—" became a croak.

For the crowd on the edge of the high bank had parted, and a handful of men had come forward into the gap. I could recognize Treg, and Poli, and the man they held between them. They brought Oran to the edge and showed him the plaza, overflowing with people, made him look out and see what had come of his power.

Then Treg shouted something that the people on the high bank responded to with a cheer.

"Yes," I said, even though I could not hear Treg. "Now is the time. This is where his path ends."

Nan squeezed my hand. For a moment, everything seemed to stop, as though to help us all remember every detail.

The crowd roared as Oran fell, and danced and sang its joy when he was gone.

There are many stories from that night, and in some I am hardly named. I like those stories best—how Boli masked the two alarms that came from the archive with false calls that confused the sentries—how Treg and his circle made their feint a real assault, thinking we were in trouble below, and took the keystone house.

One man died in that fight, Gan Keichen—there is a hero, if you must have one. I am no hero. I am at best a lucky man.

I came back to Epa-Daun to keep a promise to a friend, who will be staying with you. She has not asked for praise, but we needed what she did as much as what any did. And I will miss her. Please treat her well, and make her welcome.

Change is coming. Change is already here. There will be a new city begun within a year, I suspect, somewhere below Ana, or on the new river. Epa-Daun will change, too. More people will be coming, and they will be different—you may not like everything they bring.

And more of you will come to Ana, if only to remind yourself, and show your children. They should hear the bells at festival, and come to sing in the temple of the arch when they are old enough. Do not deny them that. It is part of who we are.

I am going back to be with Nan and Rika, and to continue the work of the new salons in the great hive. It has taken all these days to make even a beginning in the exarch's archive. Oran cast away the knowledge of Arania as he tried his escape; all that remains of it are our few memories from that night. But there is far, far more that he had no chance to destroy.

Though what we understand changes every day, this much we know: We *are* the children of the apocryphals.

But the apocryphals were not animals, only men and women who bore their marks as tokens in a scheme of mating. They came to Taurin in a ship that crossed the sea of night, a sea that dwarfs not only Morada but imagination.

That ship is still above us, still keeping the logs and archives of the people it once carried. We cannot reach it, though we can still speak to it. Oran Anadon used it to destroy the ship of Hoja den Krador. Our ship's name is *Quirin,* which means traitor's stone. *Our* ship.

The name tells us that the apocryphals left Arania in defiance. They came here to change a world, and build themselves a paradise. We do not know all that they did, all that they intended. But they expected it to be easy. The planet would be remade for them. They would remake themselves, with a suite taken at birth. And Ana would be built for them by the nats, and copy the familiar way they had lived while journeying, while waiting for Taurin to be made ready.

All this was two thousand one hundred fifteen turns ago. That is the true year of the people of Ana.

We know this, too: that Ana nearly died in her first days.

The great hive was the first habitation, made for those who were guiding the changes to the air, directing the building of the city, beginning the greening of the land. When the first hundred rings were complete, the others came down. I do not know their number, but it is recorded that it took twenty trips of *Quirin*'s three skyboats to deliver them all.

They had been a seed without water, or soil, or light. It must have brought them great happiness to have come to their journey's end, and to receive the blessings of Ana, the spark of Kawa.

It is a measure of their joy that by those names we remember the first children born to Taurin: the first girl, who her mother called Ana, or beginning, and the first boy, who his mother called Kawa, or celebrated one.

But they were not ready for Taurin, or Taurin for them. We do not know if it was impatience or imperfection which betrayed them, but in the second year, a great dying began. The sun mange appeared, and other cancers which ravaged the body in secret, out of sight. Anans of every age began to fall, but most of all those who relished the light and the heat of the day. Women began to bring forth dead and diseased issue. Others found they could not take the spark.

In the fourth year, one of every five Anans died. A city which had been growing found itself facing collapse, and a people which had been living a dream found themselves enduring a nightmare.

There is some confusion in what we have found so far. I do not know everything they did to try to save themselves. Surely they searched for answers everywhere, in the eight technologies, in the common arts, in the marks they wore and the powers they represented, in the substance and spark of Taurin itself.

But some chosen few must have been returned to the protection of the great hive, or perhaps had never left it. If so, it is easy to see how grief and fear became rebellion, and rebellion took as its focus the abandonment of Ana, and a return to the security of *Quirin*. The experiment had become costly, the easy way brutally hard.

They would have gladly surrendered their claim to Ana. But that choice was taken from them. The praking of the colony, a man called Atar den Valin, ordered *Quirin* emptied, and its three skyboats grounded atop the splinter mount which lies south and west of Ana. There they were destroyed in fire.

Thus it was that Ana, too, became a city of exiles.

As the drowning of the plaza shaped the present, so did that moment shape the past. We have been created by what we lost, and by what that loss called from us.

Ana was to be completed in a thousand years, but it stands unfinished after twice that span of time.

The children of the apocryphals were to live a gentle life on the labor of the nats. But the tools to create and maintain them are on *Quirin,* and exhaustion and wilding have taken away much of what we once had. We have had to survive on our own sweat and fire.

We were expected to enjoy the liberty that comes with self-sufficiency, but instead we have known the control that comes with scarcity.

The transformation of Taurin was meant to encompass its whole surface, and to end with a richness of forms and beauty we can hardly imagine. But that treasure is still waiting in the vats on the ship. Our animals are there, waiting. We were meant to have them with us. We were not meant to be alone here.

Like Ana, Taurin remains unfinished.

It is hard to hear all this, I know, and harder to understand. We have found so much so quickly, and every revelation recasts the world.

I have even found some sympathy for Oran Anadon, now that I know what he feared: the vengeance for not only lies, but broken promises—an accounting for the suffering of not fifty years, but a hundred generations. Knowing what he knew, how could he have seen Hoja den Krador's promise, and our curiosity, as anything but the gravest threat?

But this is to be the end of the epoch of fear, and silence. The truth is unfolding before us now, and we will not look away.

The corpses of Oran's victims are coming down from the rocks, and will be returned to Ana soon—I saw the work beginning as I came here. They will have what they have waited for.

We have climbed the splinter mount now, and seen the skeletons of the skyboats. And we have seen the light of our own apparition in the night sky, and know its nature—though I cannot guess how long it will take us to climb back to that height.

But I have promised Kedar's memory this: that if the people of Arania do not come to Taurin again before we are ready, we will go to meet them in their own sky. That is the vision to which I have committed my days, though I doubt I will live to see it. But we will have new sons and daughters, and their eyes will see farther than ours.

Some call this the rebirth of Ana. If that is truly so, I note that the child we sparked was born under the thirteenth bell, as Ana trembled.

There is no more auspicious beginning.